A SHADOW ON THE DOOR

DI ROB MARSHALL
BOOK FOUR

ED JAMES

For Fiona

OTHER BOOKS BY ED JAMES

DI ROB MARSHALL SCOTTISH BORDERS MYSTERIES

Ed's first new police procedural series in six years, focusing on DI Rob Marshall, a criminal profiler turned detective. London-based, an old case brings him back home to the Scottish Borders and the dark past he fled as a teenager.

1. THE TURNING OF OUR BONES
2. WHERE THE BODIES LIE
3. A LONELY PLACE OF DYING
4. A SHADOW ON THE DOOR

Also available is FALSE START, a prequel novella starring DS Rakesh Siyal, is available to buy on Amazon or for **free** to subscribers of Ed's newsletter – sign up at https://geni.us/EJLCFS

POLICE SCOTLAND

Precinct novels featuring detectives covering Edinburgh and its surrounding counties, and further across Scotland: Scott Cullen, a rookie eager to climb the career ladder; Craig Hunter, an ex-squaddie struggling with PTSD; Brian Bain, the centre of his own universe and bane of everyone else's. Previously published as SCOTT CULLEN MYSTERIES, CRAIG HUNTER POLICE THRILLERS and CULLEN & BAIN SERIES.

1. DEAD IN THE WATER
2. GHOST IN THE MACHINE
3. DEVIL IN THE DETAIL
4. FIRE IN THE BLOOD

5. STAB IN THE DARK
6. COPS & ROBBERS
7. LIARS & THIEVES
8. COWBOYS & INDIANS
9. THE MISSING
10. THE HUNTED
11. HEROES & VILLAINS
12. THE BLACK ISLE
13. THE COLD TRUTH
14. THE DEAD END

DS VICKY DODDS SERIES

Gritty crime novels set in Dundee and Tayside, featuring a DS juggling being a cop and a single mother.

1. BLOOD & GUTS
2. TOOTH & CLAW
3. FLESH & BLOOD
4. SKIN & BONE
5. GUILT TRIP

DI SIMON FENCHURCH SERIES

Set in East London, will Fenchurch ever find what happened to his daughter, missing for the last ten years?

1. THE HOPE THAT KILLS
2. WORTH KILLING FOR
3. WHAT DOESN'T KILL YOU
4. IN FOR THE KILL
5. KILL WITH KINDNESS
6. KILL THE MESSENGER

Other Books

Other crime novels, with Lost Cause set in Scotland and Senseless set in southern England, and the other three set in Seattle, Washington.

- LOST CAUSE
- SENSELESS
- TELL ME LIES
- GONE IN SECONDS
- BEFORE SHE WAKES

CHAPTER ONE
HISLOP

All businessmen desired an empire.

And Gary Hislop was certainly building his.

The low sun cut along Union Street and spread early morning light across his little corner of Kelso, making his new shop sign glow. A special moment every morning, lasting mere seconds until the sun was lost behind the taller buildings opposite. He took a satisfied breath and turned to face the shop.

Roxburgh Street Hardware.

Cream background, dark grey text. Sophisticated. Unlike the kebab shop over the road. But like that, he was spreading a chain across southern Scotland. Brick by brick, step by step, a small shop in the arse end of Galashiels was growing into a decent-sized network spanning Selkirkshire, Berwickshire and Roxburghshire, the three old Borders counties people still talked about. Soon to add more, even to Peebleshire.

That homely feel you got from the quaint naming system he'd devised. Instead of some corporate name like BuildCo or TradeX, Somewhere Street Hardware represented the fabric of the community, a shop that was central to a town's high street just by virtue of its name. Registering trademarks for every town over five thousand in Lowland Scotland meant he'd captured them too. And it meant he also got genuine customers in, like old Ian there.

Shuffling out of the shop, left leg dragging slightly. Scraggy-arsed trackies and tattered old Scotland Grand Slam rugby shirt. 'Morning, Gary.' Ian took a long look at the proud display in front of the shop. 'Bit late in the air for those snow things, isn't it?'

Hislop grinned at him. 'Salt pipes, not snow things.'

Ian picked one up to inspect it. 'What's so good about them?'

Hislop took one and grabbed it at the base. 'Much easier to shake, right? And easier to store than a sack of salt.'

Ian looked convinced. 'Decent price too.'

'For now.' Hislop shot him a wink. 'Special offers like this create a time limit, which creates a demand where there was none before.'

Spoken out loud like that, it sounded like a drug business model. Mainly because it was one.

Ian laughed. 'I'll be back before Friday to pick some up, then.'

Hislop tipped his imaginary cap and tucked his thumbs into his apron. 'Thanks again, Ian.'

The old sod toddled away, carrying a fancy Roxburgh Street Hardware bag. Poor bugger woke up at five every morning, unable to sleep. Meant he was in the shop every day at opening to buy some random crap for his latest project, both inside and out.

Another good customer was the lad inside at the till, buying supplies for what Hislop took to be a card school run out of a farm. Probably high stakes, sucking in the local farmers seeking cheap thrills – or expensive ones.

Or maybe Hislop was just too cynical.

A car drove past, slowing to allow the couple inside to peer at his store. Remembering the name and the special offers tastefully advertised in the window – as cheap as the middle aisles in Lidl and Aldi, but available all year round.

Aye, Hislop was building a solid chain here. And a chain had opportunities for him. Supply networks, for one. And more stores meant increased footfall, so any watching eyes would tally up the money going through his books with visible activity in the shops.

And he was able to tap into all the fears stoked by the various paranoid conspiracy theories about the UK's descent into a cashless society. A five-percent discount for cash courted both those nutjobs and the tighter ones who didn't want to pay the card companies.

So all that extra cash flowing through the business allowed him to inject ill-gotten money into his books and launder it like a dry cleaner. And, of course, he was paying tax, much more than he should do, which meant he was investing in legitimate opportunities.

Actually... He scratched his chin. A dry cleaner would be a good avenue to explore... Definitely one to take up with Callum.

His phone chirruped a notification.

Hislop brushed his apron aside to fish it out of his pocket. The apron was a nice touch – made him look like an old-fashioned businessman. Trustworthy. Genuine. Real.

Not an important text message or an email, just a calendar reminder that the Melrose RFC 1998 Old Boys Reunion was at half past seven tonight.

It'd been in the diary for so bloody long and now it was here. A night to remember, surely. Or one to forget.

His mobile rang in his hands. He glanced at the caller, then put the phone to his ear. 'Morning, Callum.'

'And good morning to you, Mr Hislop.'

Hislop laughed. 'Just call me Gary. It makes me feel less like a mafioso.'

Over the road, a gang of kids ambled up the street. Jackets off, ties hanging loose, hair all perfectly ruffled. Less than an hour until school started.

Hislop turned away from them. 'How can I help you, Mr Hume?'

'Just calling to inform you that the screws are back in stock at Scott Street Hardware.'

The Galashiels store and the western end of his empire, soon to expand further out to Peebles and Moffat. Sold more screws every day than either his giant orange rival or the newer one with the word *screw* in its name.

'Excellent stuff, Cal. Way we're selling them, we should think about getting another order in tout suite.'

'I shall arrange that forthwith.'

A car pulled up and a friendly face got out.

'Let me know if you need any more stock sent over from here. Better go.' Hislop killed the call and pocketed his phone, then thrust out a hand. 'Good morning, sir.'

Allan Field took the hand and squeezed it. Big guy, bigger grip. Military. 'Morning, Gary.' He scratched at his neck. 'Just, eh, wondering if you've got the merchandise in stock?'

Hislop did a quick check up and down the street. Very quiet, just a tall schoolgirl with headphones on powering along the pavement. 'We have it, aye. I think. Come on in.' He stepped inside the store and walked up to the counter.

Catherine was behind the till. Long nails in a violent green colour with a spreading pattern – must've taken *hours* to get them done. Looking like they were going to scratch her phone's screen as she tapped a message to someone. She looked up through a flurry of fake lashes. Heavy make-up turning her eyes into almonds. Tattoos everywhere, spreading up from the sleeve covering her left arm to her neck – there was plenty of virgin territory on her other arm, but she seemed happy to keep it over to the left side. 'What's up?' Always seemed on edge, like she was up to something she shouldn't be. Then again, the amount of time she spent on TikTok or Instagram on Hislop's dime...

'Mr Field here would like some—' Hislop laughed. 'Sorry, Allan, what was it?'

Field smirked, but his attention was crawling all over Catherine. 'Need a few things, love.' He passed over a hand-written note.

Catherine was ringing it all up, frowning.

Field held out a wad of cash with a shaking hand. 'Here you go.'

Catherine smiled. 'I'll just check it's all in stock?'

'It's okay.' Hislop held up a hand to silence her, then focused on Field. 'I'll get one of the lads to deliver it this afternoon.'

'Sounds good to me.' Field handed over a hundred quid.

Hislop watched as Catherine rang it up on the till, then handed back his change.

Clockwork.

Field dipped his head then walked off into the dull morning. The sun was already lost behind the buildings.

Catherine was frowning. 'But we've got hammers and screws in stock?'

'He's after specific ones, though.' Hislop didn't make eye contact with her. Kept his focus on the flats above the kebab shop opposite. Had to be careful they weren't being watched from up there. Actually... He should pay them a visit – hand out some flyers with a discount voucher. Get the measure of the tenants and see if they were cops in there. 'Man like Mr Field is after specialist tools. You don't need to worry about it. I'll call the supplier. There's a van drops stuff off every day. It'll be with us by four o'clock. Wee Tich will deliver.'

'So it's like a pharmacy?'

'Just like a pharmacy.' Too much like one, just didn't need a prescription for what would be wrapped around the merchandise. 'Can't have local builders running out of stuff, eh?' He stepped outside to make a call to Tich, but a worry nibbled at his earlobes.

How much did she know about the operation?

Maybe he was wrong to look at the flats above the kebab shop – maybe the surveillance was in here.

Aye, he needed to have a think about her.

No matter how much you dug into someone's history, there could always be hidden stuff.

The phone was still ringing.

A schoolkid swerved on his bike, slaloming up and down from the pavement at speed. Ploughed into the display outside the store. Sending the tubes of snow salt into the road.

'You wee bastard!' Hislop stepped onto the cobbles and shook his fists in the air.

Not that it achieved anything.

The kid looked around then stood on his pedals, flicked his middle finger, and bombed away.

Aye, he'd get what was coming to him.

Hislop heard the roar of an engine behind him.

Way too loud.

And way too late.

Something swept his legs from under him, drove into his

right hip and tipped him up in the air. Seemed to take forever to swing up and down. He landed on the heavy cobbles with a sickening crunch.

Pain roared up and down his whole body.

The car shot off up the street.

Hislop got a good look at the licence plate.

And recognised it.

CHAPTER TWO
MARSHALL

Staying in someone else's flat – someone you loved – was like a tightrope walk across the Grand Canyon.

On the one hand, DI Rob Marshall got to see Kirsten Weir as she wanted to live. Nothing was hidden. The pots stacked up in the sink. The dishwasher not emptied or refilled. The three half-empty bottles of wine on the counter.

On the other, Marshall appreciated her honesty. She wasn't hiding shite away in cupboards or forcing a fake impression on him.

No, he got to see it all. The chaos.

Her day job was gruelling hours scraping the finest traces from the grimmest crime scenes. That would force someone in one of two directions – germaphobia or, well, germaphilia.

And she embraced both. One offset the other to give a strange balance.

Marshall sipped at his weak coffee and checked his watch – he really should be on his way. He didn't necessarily need to have *the chat*, but to prepare the ground for it. It'd been too long and it was getting to be a concern.

The kitchen area was empty and quiet, despite the chaos. Not even a radio playing. He liked quiet at this time of day. The other half of the room had a sofa, an armchair and a monstrous TV. The bay window looked along Gorgie Road in both directions, though the windows blocked out the worst of western Edinburgh's early morning commuter noise. Buses fought with taxis and cars in the race to get into the city centre or out to the business parks near the airport. The pandemic had supposedly changed everyone's working habits to be much more at home, but Marshall didn't see much evidence of it here.

Kirsten stormed into the kitchen in a flurry of activity, trailing her perfume and shower gel scent. Her hair was darkened from still being wet, hiding the blonde streaks that were the result of a recent hen weekend in Majorca. The tan still lingered, despite it being April. She nudged him out of the way and poured her own coffee from the filter jug. 'Sorry.'

'Sorry?'

'For the coffee being crap today. I need to get some more beans. Thought that would be enough.' She raised her eyebrows as she drank it. 'Or someone needs to stop drinking so much of it.'

'Not just you that says that. My doctor too.' Marshall opened the dishwasher and found the last free space in the top for his cup. He made a point of putting the tablet in, then turned to face her. 'Listen, we really need to have that chat.'

She sighed as she started filling the bottom of the dishwasher from the gunk in the sink. 'Chat, eh? The worst four-letter word beginning with C and ending with T. So much menace in one syllable.'

'It's nothing like that. Just... We've been meaning to have it for ages and... Well. We haven't.'

'You never shut up, Rob. We chat all the time.'

'I'm serious.'

'So am I. I love how expressive you are, but if we're at the point where we have to schedule time to talk... That's... That means you've got issues, Rob.'

'I know I've got issues. But I'm open and honest about them. And we really do need to talk.'

'Not now, Rob. I'm really pressed for time. This place is a shit tip because I'm so busy. I've got to head down to Gala now because your bunch of idiots in the Borders MIT are moving in today. It's going to be bedlam and I know I won't get away until *midnight.*'

Not the words of someone keen on having a serious discussion about their future. She'd been cooling off recently and Marshall didn't know why. It wasn't like he could get any worse.

'So you don't want to have the chat?'

'I do.' She sighed again, then slotted the encrusted plates into the wrong shelf. 'It's just... I'm so busy and my head's full of noise... Do you want any breakfast?'

Not that there was anything to eat it off...

He smiled instead of voicing his thoughts. 'I thought you were pressed for time?'

She slammed the door and pressed start on the machine. 'I am, it's just... I'm trying to be polite.'

The dishwasher started hissing and clattering. The sink was still half full of dirty pans.

'Thanks for the offer, but I'm meeting a friend for a coffee before court. I'll grab something then.'

'Oh? Anyone I know?'

'Rakesh.'

'Oh, Shunty? Say hi from me.' Kirsten walked over to adjust his tie. 'You look good enough to eat.'

'I just hope the judge doesn't want to.'

She smiled. 'How are you feeling about the case?'

Marshall felt that tightening deep in his gut. He couldn't look at her. His mouth felt dry. 'Not great, but I've got my big boy trousers on.'

'Come on, then.' She grabbed his hand and led him outside into the corridor. 'Oh, hi, Todd.'

Her dickhead neighbour was resting against his door jamb like he'd been waiting. Centre-parted curtains hung down to his jawline – an ancient haircut that hadn't become hip again, even now when half the kids sported ridiculous mullets. 'How's my favourite neighbour?'

'I'm okay, Todd.' Kirsten slammed the door behind Marshall and locked up. 'Got to rush, so I'll catch you later.'

'Oh, I can't wait for that.' Todd looked at Marshall with a sneer, but didn't say anything, then he slunk back inside his flat.

Marshall followed Kirsten down the spiral staircase, through the fug of cat pee and student deodorant, then out into the busy street. 'He doesn't get any less creepy, does he?'

'Nor any less over-friendly.' Kirsten leaned over and gave him a big kiss. 'I'll see you later. If I can get away, maybe we'll have that big, ominous chat tonight?' She got into her car and the radio din bled out onto the street.

Marshall walked down the road towards his car. He *really* hadn't missed living in a city. Weird how nine months back in the Borders had reacclimatised him to the quietness of rural living. Even the honk of a shop door opening set his teeth on edge. He longed for the distant bleating and mooing.

He stopped by his new car and hoped it played ball today. The Beast, Kirsten called it. A hulking four-by-four that was practical for a Borders winter, but was totally out of keeping with city driving. And more temperamental than a certain DCI...

Kirsten drove past, singing along to the radio, and waved at him.

Marshall put his car into gear and tried the ignition.

Nothing.

Great. He eased the clutch in, then tickled the key in the lock until it finally roared into life.

Great car, when it got going, but the previous driver had absolutely melted it. And the salesman had seen Marshall coming a mile off.

Crap!

He'd forgotten to ask Kirsten.

He got out his mobile and texted her while the engine ran:

> It's Thea's birthday tonight. I'd love you to come with me, but understand if the whole Auntie Kirsteeeeen thing doesn't work for you x

He added a wink emoji and smiled at his own joke about how his mother couldn't accept how Kirsten wanted her own name to be pronounced.

But he didn't add a second message about how his niece had asked specifically for Kirsten to be there.

Or mention the chat about their future. And whether they really had one or were just deluding themselves.

CHAPTER THREE
MARSHALL

Sod it.

Marshall thought he'd be able to steer the Beast into the space on George IV Bridge. Whoever George IV was. Was he the one who went mad? Or the regent from Blackadder? All that time spent focusing on criminal psychology and nowhere near enough on British history.

A honk came from behind, met with a raised finger from Marshall.

There, he managed to get in. The engine died before he twisted the key. Bloody hell, this car was a lemon. And the kind you couldn't make lemonade out of.

He slid the 'On Police Business' sign onto the dashboard, then got out into the spitting rain blown around by the howling wind.

This bloody city...

He tucked his collar up and charged on.

One thing about growing up in the Borders when he did, years before they reopened the train line, was the only way for a bored teenager to get into Edinburgh was the bus. Ninety minutes and it wasn't cheap either, so he hadn't bothered much. Other things on his mind. And he hadn't really missed much. The city was pretty enough, but the cold austerity always butted up against him.

And he'd fled to Durham, which had an honest earthiness in amongst its own opulence – and the locals weren't that different from nearby Newcastle, not that you'd ever call them Geordies to their faces.

Aye. Edinburgh remained a mystery to him.

His phone rang out with the ringtone he'd assigned to his sister. 'Morning, Jen. What's up?'

'Rob, I was just on my way out the door for my shift, already late, when a delivery driver blocks the drive. Dropping off a box of wine for you.'

Marshall's blood chilled. Another one. Shite. 'Okay, sorry about that.'

'Don't you have enough wine in the flat?'

Marshall didn't mention who it likely came from. 'Just leave it and I'll sort it out later.'

'It's nice stuff, so I could take a couple—'

'No. It's a mistaken order. Don't touch it, please.'

'O-kay. See you later, dickhead.' And she was gone.

Marshall raced inside the café. The rain had already soaked him through to his shirt. First time he'd worn this new suit jacket too.

DS Rakesh Siyal was sitting at the back, facing away from the door and the windows.

Schoolboy error.

Marshall sneaked up on the big bugger and prodded him on the neck.

Siyal barely reacted. 'Morning, Rob.'

Marshall had expected him to jump out of his skin, maybe

even twisting as he stood. Having to step back, waiting for the punch.

But Siyal just sat there. 'Ordered you a pour-over Colombian with oat milk.'

'Okay, cheers.' Marshall took the seat opposite. Behind Siyal, he could see the High Court, but he tried not to think about it. About why he was here. He brushed his hand through his damp hair. 'Word of advice. If you sit in a pub or café, face the door so you can see who's coming in.'

Siyal focused on the table, like a wee bastard being interviewed. 'Right. But I saw you coming using the reflection in the glass of that picture.' He pointed at a chintzy etching of Greyfriars Bobby. 'I'm not daft, Rob. I knew you'd prefer the power seat.'

'The power seat.' Marshall laughed. But Siyal didn't join in. 'You okay there, Rakesh?'

'Aye... It's just...' Siyal sat back and let out a deep sigh. Finally made eye contact. 'Getting hassle from the landlord in Gala. Won't let me rent that flat out to Jim McIntyre's mate.'

'I thought you could sublet it?'

'Haven't been there a year yet. So I'm having to pay that plus I'm not getting rental income from my own flat because I live in it. Rent *and* mortgage. Double damn. And interest rates are going up every month.'

'Aren't you on a variable rate?'

Siyal nodded. 'Ten-year fixed. Comes up in 2030.'

Marshall laughed. 'So why are you worried, then?'

The waiter put Marshall's coffee down in front of him.

'Thanks.' He waited, sipping his coffee, then sat back. 'Because it's your first day in a new job?'

'Exactly.' Siyal finished his coffee and had the look of a man who wanted to order another. 'A detective sergeant in Professional Standards and Ethics.' He shook his head. 'Answer me straight, Rob – am I up to it?'

'Not for me to say, really. If I were you, I'd cling to the fact that DCI Pringle supported your application. Not me or DI Elliot, but Jim's two ranks above you. Shows you're good at managing up the way. That's a core competency for the Complaints. You'll probably be working directly for a superintendent.'

Siyal waved at the waiter and pointed at his cup. 'I don't feel like things are on the same basis as when I applied for the job, though.'

'Wait, what? Why? You caught a bent cop who not only covered up an abduction and rape, but was directly involved in both. *You* did that, Rakesh. Your persistence. Your determination.'

'Aye, but...' Siyal took his fresh cup. Marshall could remember a time when he didn't touch anything caffeinated, now he was like a junkie itching for a fix. 'Heard on Friday that there's a new boss.'

'Oh.'

'Aye, some big shot from down south. Milne or something.'

'Never heard of him.'

'Not London, so I doubt you'd know him. But... New broom, right? He'll want his own team and, of course, I'm the last one in.'

'Aye, but you're in there, Rakesh. Perfect start.' Marshall smiled. 'Especially after your last one.'

Siyal frowned, like he hadn't considered that.

Some people had bad first days, but Siyal's catastrophic one had lived long in legend, at least down in the Borders.

Marshall took a long drink of his coffee. Nowhere near hot enough, but much stronger than what he'd brewed at Kirsten's. 'Remember that policing isn't stable. Things change all the time. Think about the nine months we worked together. Or the fifteen months you'd been in that team. How many new cops joined in that time? Me. Big Jim McIntyre. Ash Paton. And they came in after you. And Jolene's just been promoted, plus your replacement is starting today.' Marshall dipped a spoon into his cup. 'The police service is like a spoon in a coffee cup... when you pull it out there's that gaping hole where it used to be.' He winked at Siyal. 'No, as soon as it's gone, the coffee closes in. Same in policing... as soon as you're not there, it is like you never were. And if you want a team that doesn't change every five minutes, go into uniform.' He let the word sit there. 'But that's not your strength, is it? You've already shown you're great at sniffing out dodgy cops. Just keep doing what you do best and you'll thrive.'

'If you honestly—'

'There thee are, O wise gentlemen of the parish!' DCI Jim Pringle strolled in, rain smearing his face and flattening his quiff. His suit seemed to hang off his shoulders, which had lost a lot of their muscle tone. His fly was hanging open and the end of his pink tie hung out. He sat between them at the end of the table. 'Are you talking about me? Deny it! I'll believe you. Thousands wouldn't!'

Marshall leaned in to whisper, 'Your fly's down, sir.'

'Aye.' Pringle clicked his fingers in the air and attracted the waiter's attention. 'Can I get a tea to go. Make it like Guinness – black and comes in pints.' He laughed. Nobody joined in. Didn't seem to deter him any. 'Chop, chop, my kind sir!' He watched the waiter go, then shifted his gaze between Marshall and Siyal. 'So. I spotted you both outside.' He grabbed Siyal's hand. 'Congratulations are well in order, eh? Sorry. Can't quite remember your name.'

Marshall laughed, even though the joke hadn't landed. Assuming there was one.

Pringle scowled at him, menace flashing across his lips. 'I'm serious.' He was still clicking his fingers. 'What is it?'

'It's Rakesh.'

'Ah, yes! Shunty! The man who left us all in the lurch like that.' Spoken with venom on his voice and a snarl on his lips.

Siyal frowned. Then it deepened – the anger seemed genuine. 'Sorry, sir. But you're the one who proposed me applying for this role.'

'Oh yes, of course I did. But you're too good for the Rat Pack. Rat-a-tat-tat. You lousy, stinking rat.'

Siyal checked his watch. 'Sorry, sir, but I'm running late to be sufficiently early, so I don't want to leave a bad impression.' He got to his feet. 'Catch you both later.' He marched over to the counter and tapped his mobile off the card reader, then shuffled off out of the room with his takeaway coffee.

Pringle watched him go. 'Did I ever tell you the story of where he got his name?'

Marshall nodded. 'Heard it a few times, aye.'

'Last January. The roads were icy. He chased an escaped—'

'I've heard this, sir.'

Pringle slammed a fist off the table. 'Don't be like that with *me*.'

Marshall wanted to put it down to nerves over the case finally hitting court. But Pringle was dangerously close to getting a smack in the chops. Or more likely, a stern word in his ear.

'Wait. What? Oh. Right. Court. Court.' Pringle sat back as the waiter put the cup down in front of him. 'Come on, then. I've got to go to court.' He grabbed his tea and walked off.

Marshall strolled up to the counter and paid for them both, worried about his boss's state of mind.

CHAPTER FOUR
ELLIOT

DI Andrea Elliot had her car door open, listening to the rain thudding down and the Melrose bypass rumbling over her head. Nirvana played on the radio, one of their songs she didn't know and certainly didn't like, but she couldn't be bothered to find something else to listen to. She had to have music on, regardless of the time of day. Stopped the noise inside her head.

At least she thought it was Nirvana.

No sign of him, so she texted:

> You're late

She switched the channels through boring talking and more boring classical, then found one playing Simply Red, so it was back to Nirvana.

A couple hurried through the rain, two little spaniels at their feet, all of them soaked and miserable, then disappeared off towards the football and rugby stadium.

Raindrops bounced into the Tweed a few metres away on

the pebbly riverbank. She'd got really badly sunburnt down here once. Must've been fifteen, horsing around with her pals during the summer holidays... Then the redness didn't fade after they ran home. Whoops – a lesson she'd learned a ton of times since. Apply the factor ginger suntan lotion before you go out, not that the colour had been seen on her head in twenty-five years.

A car swooshed into the car park, rocking as it crossed the potholes and pulled up next to her.

DCI Ryan Gashkori opened his door and didn't get out. He looked exhausted, just staring into space, his fatigue probably the equivalent of four pints of strong ale.

Thing with the clowns in the drugs squad was they always overcompensated with their motors, but in the opposite direction from the fella with the wee fella. No, they went for the worst banger possible, so they threw all shade away from them. Elliot had never heard of the manufacturer and had no idea if it was Polish, Chinese or Swahili.

Gashkori knew how to read the writing on the wall, so he got out and walked over to sit in her passenger seat. 'Morning, Andrea.'

'Morning, Ryan. Feels like we're doing a drug deal.'

Gashkori laughed. A bit too loud. 'Aye, it does. Kind of apt, I guess. We're speaking to someone who does just that.' He looked around the car park. Not even nine and he needed to shave again. 'Where is he?'

'Not here.'

'I can see that.' Gashkori chuckled. 'Shame for me to drive all this way, just to be stiffed by your guy.'

'One, Edinburgh to Gala isn't exactly far. Two, he's not my guy. Sure, the information came from a source I've been running, but he's not mine.'

'Noted. But you should be mindful of the fact I hate being let down.'

'Give the boy time.' Elliot held out her phone. 'He's not responded to my text.'

'And you still haven't told me who "he" is. Hence me bothering my brown arse to get down here.'

'Are you allowed to say "brown" these days?'

'I am. You're not.'

'Doesn't seem fair.'

'Whole load of words you can use, as a woman, which I can't.'

'Right, guess so.'

'And I've heard all the bad ones, Andi, so I'm joining my Pakistani brothers and Indian cousins in taking matters into my own hands. "Brown" is totally fine these days.'

Elliot got out her mobile and held up a photo – an old surveillance job she'd kept back from Gashkori's mob. 'Blake Innes is who we're meeting. Friend of Gary Hislop's from his rugby club.'

Gashkori inspected the photo. 'This'll be the same rugby club where he sources all the intel you pass on to us?'

'Same one. Not sure what he's getting out of half of what he sends on, but he thinks he's got stuff on me. He doesn't.'

'You're a braver woman than me, Andi. Fighting fire there.'

'You're not a brave woman, Ryan. You're a cowardly man. And a brown one at that.'

Gashkori laughed. 'Aye, keep telling yourself that.' He tapped at the clock above the radio. 'Shouldn't he be here now?'

She tapped the display. 'Supposed to be here half an hour ago.'

Gashkori swung around to glare at her. 'You told me to meet at nine!'

'Aye, I did.'

'You're a sneaky cow.'

'Aye, true. And even you aren't allowed to call a woman a cow in this day and age.'

He rolled his eyes. 'Is the woke term a Karen?'

'No, that's even worse. Has hints of racism to it as well.'

'Yeah, I guess so.' Gashkori blew air up his face. 'Seriously, though? What are you playing at?'

'Nothing. I've got my reasons.'

'Sure you do, aye.' Gashkori stroked his stubble. 'You got his home address too?'

CHAPTER FIVE

ELLIOT

The main drag in Gattonside ran parallel to the Tweed, lined with posh houses and a couple of fancy restaurants. Couldn't quite see Melrose over the river from here.

Elliot pulled off onto a street winding up into the hills and parked opposite Blake Innes's address.

That dozy sod Gashkori was nowhere to be seen. Not even five miles from where they met and he'd got lost.

A few curtain twitchers on the street, but nobody important. Nobody on their radar.

Some kind of bird of prey hovered above them. Elliot had no idea what it was but had a better idea of what it wasn't. Probably a kite or a buzzard.

No, there he was. Gashkori's crappy old Mazda rolling along the street. He pulled up and it sounded like a gunshot went off.

There was undercover subtlety and then there was drawing attention to yourself like this.

Elliot got out of her car with a deep sigh, then waited until Gashkori did likewise. 'Ryan, we need to have a word about that motor of yours.'

'What's wrong with it?'

'Absolutely nothing that wouldn't be solved by parking it in Langlee and leaving the keys in the ignition.'

He smiled at the joke, but she knew it was worthy of a bigger laugh. 'Langlee's the council estate down here, right?'

'Right, aye.' *Keep up, dickhead.* 'Where most of Hislop's merchandise ends up. From the Gala shop, anyway.'

He nodded for a few seconds, then her phone rang.

DC Jim McIntyre calling...

Aye, that wasn't going to be a load of tedious nonsense, was it?

She bounced it to voicemail and walked up to the house door, then knocked. One of those doorbell cameras tinkled away. Nobody seemed to notice it. No disembodied voices asking questions.

Decent enough place. Stone built, two floors. Semi-detached, but it'd cost more than a whole house where she lived.

Gashkori smirked. 'Not like you to bounce a call, Andi.'

'When the patron saint of paperclip procurement calls, you don't pick up. Swear, some cops get over-promoted, but some... Some can't technically be demoted because he's at the bottom of the ladder, but he's two levels above where he should be...'

'Who is?'

'Oh, I don't name names, Ryan. You know that.'

'Sure.' Gashkori rolled his eyes. 'What's he calling about?'

'Probably about the new lad starting today. Going to sit

24

between us. Old DS has been off for three weeks. I tell you, Ryan, you need to keep a really close eye on who's not taking their annual leave.'

He scowled at her. 'Come on. That's basic stuff.'

'Aye, but we can't be everywhere, can we? But it didn't happen on my watch. In case I need to remind you, someone carved out my guts last summer.'

He shut his eyes. 'Shame they stopped there, eh?'

Elliot laughed.

Her mobile rang again.

DC Jim McIntyre calling...

'Bugger off.' She bounced it again. Maybe this time he'd take a hint and leave a voicemail. She knocked on the door again. 'This isn't looking too good, is it?'

Gashkori rasped a hand across his chin. 'I'll take a look around the back.' He scuttled off to the side, crunching over immaculate pebbles.

Lights inside triggered when Elliot looked in the front room. Proper bachelor pad – two brown leather sofas, massive telly mounted on the wall with no visible cables. Sod all else. No music playing. Nobody talking. No nothing.

Just Gashkori crunching back to the front. 'No sign around the back. Place looks empty. Kitchen's clear.'

Sod this for a game of soldiers...

Elliot walked over to the small hedge separating the houses – sure enough, a telly blared out of next door, some inane chit-chat midmorning talk show. She hopped over and walked up the path to the door. Nice when you knock and someone actually bother themselves to answer.

When did that go out of fashion?

A tall woman peered out, a good few inches taller than Elliot herself. Severe bun, jeans and a blouse. 'Can I help?'

'Looking for Mr Innes.'

'Haven't seen him today. Sorry.' She made to shut the door.

'Police.' She showed her warrant card. 'DI Andrea Elliot. This is DCI Gashkori. We need to speak to Mr Innes as a matter of urgency.'

'That's the thing. Blake left last night. Suitcases in the back of his car. If I had to guess, I'd say he was going on holiday.'

Elliot saw her disappointment reflected in Gashkori's eyes. Another one...

He smiled at the neighbour. 'Any chance you've got a spare key?'

'I do. Water his plants when he's away.' She reached inside, then hopped over the hedge with more grace than Elliot had managed. 'The key's a wee bit bent, so...' She opened the door and stepped to the side. 'I'll wait outside.'

'Sure thing.' Elliot stepped into the hall. A banister-free staircase climbed upstairs. One door led into the living room, but she didn't get any more from being in it than from peering in through the window.

Another to a kitchen. Innes was a neat freak – everything precisely organised. Nothing out on the counters, except for a kettle, cold and empty. No toaster, let alone any crumbs.

Gashkori nudged open the bathroom door and his eyebrows rose. 'Smells like my girlfriend's mother's place. Nobody's crapped or peed in there today, that's for sure.'

Elliot went back to the hall and climbed up the stairs. Had a flash of vertigo as she climbed – who lived in a house without banisters?

Still, she was upstairs. Three doors.

One was a master bathroom with a dry tub and sink.

Another was a spare room with a minimalist desk and

computer setup. Office chair that was barely even there – she had no idea how you'd begin to sit on it. Like something from *Star Trek*. And not the old stuff with Kirk or Picard, but the new one where everyone cried all the time.

No loft hatches.

If Innes was still here, the only choice was the final door.

And if he was still alive...

She took her time opening it. Sure enough, a master bedroom. Bed was made, all neat like a hotel – the white bedspread freshly ironed.

En-suite as dry as the other bathrooms, just a robe hanging from the back of the door. Towel was soft but felt freshly laundered.

Gashkori opened the pine wardrobe. 'A few empty hangers, no luggage.' He stared at Elliot. 'Andi, it looks like he's flitted.'

She didn't see any other explanation. 'Shite.'

'Aye. Shite.' Gashkori walked over to the window and peered out. The Eildons climbed up above Melrose. 'Let me get this straight – someone's warned him off meeting us and he's flitted. Meaning someone's leaked.'

'Bit of an assumption there, Ryan.'

Gashkori glared at her with fierce eyes. 'You got any other explanation?'

It felt like she'd been stabbed in the guts again. 'Nope.'

He looked away. 'Not blaming you, Andi, but this isn't the first contact of Hislop's who's cut and run just before we had a wee chat with them, right?'

'Right. But the other two haven't been found yet.'

'Just means we've got another three corpses to search for.' Gashkori punched the wall. 'If it was just Innes, then we could put it down to coincidence. But it's happened so many times now—'

'—that it's not co-inkydink.'

He rolled his eyes at her. 'Come on, Andi. You're better than that.'

'I'm not and you know it.'

He laughed. 'True.'

'But you agree it's not a coincidence?'

'Right. Someone's probably leaking stuff.'

'Aye. Someone on your team or mine is leaking straight to Hislop. Then he's arranging for them to disappear.'

'Hislop...' Gashkori looked like he was going to punch the wall for real this time. 'That whole act... "Oh, officer, I'm just an honest businessman who hears stuff at the rugby club..." It *is* just an act. Right?'

'Right. Of course it is. Trouble is, he's getting better at covering his arse. And at the same time, he's expanding his empire out from Gala. Shop opened in Kelso last month. One in Hawick next week. Peebles and Moffat too.'

'Pal of mine said Hislop's been to see a shop in Broughty Ferry.'

'*Dundee?*' Elliot could see it. A national chain meant a solid distribution network. Money laundering on a grander scale. And they hadn't been able to pin anything directly on him. 'We've got to stop him.'

Gashkori nodded.

'Sadly, this is becoming a standard procedure.' Elliot got out her phone and called McIntyre. Barely two rings. 'Jim, it's Andi. Need you to action yet another BOLO, this time for one Blake David Innes. Description's in the case file.'

'On it, ma'am.' Sounded like the daft sod scribbled something down. 'Listen, I tried call—'

'Bit busy just now, Constable.' Rank always put them in their place.

Almost always. Some didn't recognise they even had a place. 'The reason you've got two missed calls from me is—'

'Jim, it can wait.'

'No, it can't.'

'*Excuse* me?'

'Hear me out. One of your system alerts has gone off. Because you didn't answer it, it got routed to me. There's been a serious vehicular assault on Gary Hislop.'

CHAPTER SIX

MARSHALL

First time Marshall had been in this courtroom.

Edinburgh's High Court.

Not the oak-panelled grandeur you'd see on a TV show about the higher courts in London, but more a lecture theatre in a provincial university. Big TV screens everywhere. The lawyers' table sat perpendicular to the judge's raised bench, though any woodwork was hidden behind an IKEA-style partition.

Marshall's own seat was comfortable, though – fifteen minutes sitting and he hadn't fidgeted once. Usually his leg would be jigging, but it was his mind that wouldn't stay still – he couldn't dampen down the thoughts whirring around inside his skull, so he just let them come out and float free.

About how he should've been here years ago. And not as a police officer. Same case, though, just a different suspect.

The right suspect this time.

Back then, Marshall had prepared himself, sat with his lawyer and a pair of detectives for a few sessions to make sure his story stood up. Tell the truth, the whole truth and nothing but it.

Trouble was, he hadn't known the truth, just his surface view of it.

They had the wrong suspect. But they had the right one now and he hadn't died on remand.

'Could do with a coffee.' Pringle's leg was jigging like Marshall's. His empty cup sat at his feet. 'Think we've got time to—'

The side door opened and a bulky court officer stepped through, followed by Graham Thorburn. Head low, with a cheeky grin on his face like some actor or rock star getting unwitting attention at a sporting event – "Aye, it's me".

Today's main attraction.

Serial abductor, serial rapist, serial killer.

Marshall hadn't seen him in months, but he'd aged years. His dark hair was threaded with silver more befitting his age and his skin was pallid. And those eyes...

Once Marshall had taken them as enthusiastic, encouraging and kind, but now he saw cold lumps of coal.

Just like they'd planned to back then, Marshall was going to take the stand to give his evidence and survive a cross-examination. He'd done tens if not hundreds of them in his career, but none where the case related to his own girlfriend's death.

All those years had passed and Marshall wasn't the same man, but it still stung.

The slimy shit's defence lawyer would try to tear him apart.

How he had a personal stake in the crime.

How Thorburn was his stepfather, the only father figure in his life, save for his paternal grandfather.

How Thorburn helped raise Marshall and his twin sister.

How Thorburn was a university lecturer who guided the careers of countless professionals, including Marshall himself.

How Thorburn was an innocent man.

How Marshall blamed Thorburn for what happened.

Marshall knew it all. All the tricks they'd use. But it didn't make it any easier to contemplate going through it. Still, he owed it to Anna to endure anything. Owed it to all of Graham Thorburn's other victims.

Marshall spotted Anna's mother a few rows in front. She stood and turned to face them, arms folded, focusing on Marshall. Watching his reaction. She'd put some flesh on those bones since he'd last seen her, and looked like she'd managed some sleep now she had answers to her daughter's fate. Still, the lingering question of whether Thorburn was going to face justice for what he did was hanging heavy on her.

Nice to be on nodding terms with her again, at least. And not be the wrong target of her righteous fury.

The back door opened and the judge shuffled in to stand at his bench.

Pringle nudged Marshall in the arm. 'There was a snooker player called Thorburn, wasn't there?'

Marshall did his best to ignore him. All of his focus was on Thorburn. Standing there, head bowed. Stoic.

Another nudge. 'I understand if you don't want to go through the pain of a trial, Rob.'

'Thank you, sir, but I do want to.'

And shut up!

'—do you plead?'

Thorburn took his time looking up. Licked his lips. Scanned around the room, drilling his gaze into Marshall, then Mrs Kelso.

'Was it Cliff? Cliff Thorburn? Canadian, wasn't he?'

Marshall dug Pringle in the ribs and hissed, 'Shhh!'

Thorburn turned and faced the judge again. 'My legal defender has advised me to plead not guilty.'

A groan swept around the court.

Anna's mother was still on her feet, arms now outstretched.

Marshall felt everything clench. In a few months, he'd be standing in that dock, being torn apart.

For absolutely no reason. Just a complete waste of time. Thorburn had done all of those things and faced a cast-iron prosecution. He just wanted to twist the knife he'd already plunged into people who'd already been to hell and back.

Thorburn stared right at Marshall. 'And that advice notwithstanding, I shall be entering a plea of guilty.'

CHAPTER SEVEN

MARSHALL

The court officer let out a deep sigh. The same guy who'd shown Thorburn into the dock. Early thirties but his hair was thinning, and he had a thick beard to compensate. 'Shouldn't really let you do this, to be honest. He should be on his way back to HMP Heart of Midlothian and we won't see him again until sentencing. But...' Another sigh, releasing every ounce of weariness. Marshall only had to deal with this infernal place – or others like it – periodically, but this poor sod had to be here day in, day out. 'Seeing as how he asked to speak to you, Robert, we're making—'

'It's Rob.'

'Right. Not a Bob or a Robbie?'

Marshall motioned towards the door. 'He calls me Robert. Only ever Robert. I hate it.'

The officer chuckled, then hoiked up his trousers. 'Every-one's different, eh? I'm a Robert but everyone calls us Neil. Nelly or Nelson.'

'Middle name?'

'Nope. Don't have one.'

O-kay...

Marshall nodded at the door. 'So, we can speak to him?'

'Sure thing, aye.' Robert or Neil or Nelly stepped aside and let them in. 'Just don't leave any signs that you've kicked the shite out of him.'

Pringle laughed. 'I've brought a rubber hose with me!' He barged into the room and took the seat nearest the door.

Marshall took his time following him, pacing the room like a lion. He hated having his back to the door, but there was no choice here – Thorburn had chosen a seat first.

Marshall took his time sitting. Didn't say anything. Made eye contact and held it, then looked away, trying to show boredom despite his heart hammering away in his chest. That sour taste in his mouth.

Thorburn stared hard at him with those icy blue eyes, flinching as he looked him up and down. He covered it over with a wide smile, but Marshall spotted it. A weak point, maybe. 'You're looking well, Robert.'

'I feel well. Been able to sleep for the first time in years.'

'Right. That's good to hear.'

Marshall stared right into those cold lumps of coal. 'Have to say, Graham, you look like shit.'

'Charming.' Thorburn sniffed. 'After all I've done for you?'

'After what, precisely?'

'Raising you. Helping your mother through her darkest moments. Dealing with you and your sister.' Thorburn left a pause but nobody filled it. Pringle whistled something quietly. 'Would it ease things for you if I told you I was dying of cancer?'

Marshall scanned every line on his face, looking for any signs he wasn't telling the truth. He didn't see anything, but Thorburn was a master liar. 'Bullshit.'

35

Thorburn laughed. 'Of course it is. But I just wanted you to wonder.'

'You're *sick*.'

'That's true. It's why I've pleaded guilty. Or is it pled? I can never remember.' Thorburn drummed his fingers on the table. 'I hate this. The whole thing. Being in prison, even on remand. I can feel my brain rotting with every passing hour.'

'That's good to hear.'

Thorburn laughed. Too loud and too hard. 'But I mean it, Robert. You are looking well. Last time I saw you, you seemed so heavy. Not as fat as you used to be, but weighed down by the world.'

'Aren't you surprised?'

'Why should I be?'

'I know what happened to Anna all those years ago. What you did to her. I was walking around under a raincloud constantly. That... mystery, I suppose, was a weight on my shoulders, dragging me down every day.'

'You know, the Romans used to make those they found guilty and charged with crucifixion carry their own cross on their back. The story in the bible was backed up by other sources. They actually did that. It's a vicious way to kill someone. Driving stakes into their hands and leaving them to die. Fear is how they ruled such a big empire.'

'That what you're planning? Drive the stakes into my hands?'

'No, Robert. You've suffered enough.'

'The weight's lifted. I mean, I still miss her. Every single day. And maybe we'd have split up a week later, but maybe not. Either way, I'd still rather she was alive to live that life. But you made sure that wasn't going to happen. That's the cross I've borne. You did that to me. And to others. Like her mother. Her father. And other victims too.' Marshall left another pause.

Pringle was licking his lips now, metronomically every couple of seconds. 'Graham, the next best thing to her still being with us is knowing what happened to her back then. And I'm taking great comfort from the knowledge that the animal who did that to her is going to face justice for what he did. I could give you credit for sparing us all the pain of a trial. Myself, Anna's mother, all the families of your other victims since. But I won't thank you. Never.'

'I did that for you, Robert. I thought it was better to spare you more stress.'

'Okay.' Marshall looked up at the ceiling. A dark patch was spreading across the paintwork. He looked back down. 'We're done here.' He got to his feet.

'Wait.' Thorburn held up a hand. 'Don't go.'

Marshall hadn't stood as part of his police officer's technique. At least, not consciously. He was genuinely going. He stayed standing, didn't walk any closer to the door, didn't acquiesce to Thorburn's request. 'I've had enough. You asked to speak to us and we have, but you're just toying with me.'

'Robert. Over the last nine months, I've faced up to the fact that I'm going to die in prison. In so many ways, I'm already a dead man. But I've decided that I wanted to give you and all those others that closure.'

'Not all.'

Thorburn barked out a confused laugh. 'What?'

'Not all of your victims. The ones we know about, sure. And the ones who you killed. But you don't want to talk about the other victims, do you? The ones we don't know anything about.'

Thorburn said nothing.

'Why is that?'

Thorburn looked away.

'We've got you for the crimes you committed over a long

period. There are big gaps in time, so we suspect there are more. Many, many more. A man like you, with that lust for power and control? Of course there are more. You might not have killed them, but you did something to them. And you won't talk about them.'

Thorburn looked at him. 'No, I won't.'

'Why not?'

'Because I don't have to.'

'That might be true. You don't *have* to. But what it butts up against is you saying you're pleading guilty to these crimes for *our* benefit. Myself, Anna's mother, the other victims whose loved ones died as a result of what you did. Why not do the same for your other victims?'

'I haven't killed anyone else, Robert.'

Marshall gripped his chair back. 'I'm just supposed to believe that?'

'I hope so. It's the truth.'

'But there are other victims, right? People you didn't kill. Did you just abduct them?'

'Some. Others I just... you know.'

'Raped?'

'Robert, I'll never talk about my other victims. It's in nobody's interests for me to do that. And I know I'm never getting out of prison, so there's *nothing* you can do to sweeten the deal for me.'

'This isn't a victimless crime. If you abduct someone, repeatedly rape them for a week and then let them go, that leaves a mark on them. Psychologically, if not physically.'

Thorburn was drumming his fingers again. 'And your point is?'

'Don't those people deserve closure for those attacks?'

'It's not as simple as that.'

'Nothing is...' Marshall wasn't going to get embroiled in a

philosophical debate. 'Anna killed herself. Is that the only reason you're talking? This is just about death? Not the abduction and trauma of the others? Do you see what your actions do to people? They have an effect! Just because she killed herself when she escaped... Others would've killed themselves too, maybe days or weeks or months or years later. What about *them*?'

'Robert, you're shouting.'

'Of course I'm shouting.'

'Sit down.'

Maybe Marshall could get something out of him. He looked at Pringle but got nothing. Whatever was happening, it was on him. He took his chair again. 'I'm sitting. I'm trying to remain calm.'

'Robert, listen to me. With all the notoriety of my recent arrest, the victims themselves would know it was me, should they still be alive. And yet they didn't come forward. There's your answer, Robert – not everyone needs you riding in on a white horse to save them. I knew who would tell and who wouldn't, so I didn't waste my efforts on those I knew would stay silent, and obviously I have profiled them perfectly.'

He was trying to sneak out of it. Tease Marshall with a promise he wasn't going to follow through on.

Marshall gripped the table and took a deep breath. His heart sped up, each beat that bit heavier. 'Here's an idea. You talk to me, Graham. You give me names and places. And I'll look into it and see what crimes I can match them to. I'll tell them who did it, that you've faced justice and will be serving however many life sentences. No press, no TV. Unless they choose it.'

Thorburn sat back and stared up above Marshall's head. His throat had a sharp nick over his Adam's apple. Looked sore. He locked eyes with Marshall. 'I think—'

'Cabbages.'

Marshall jerked around to look at Pringle.

'You're sitting there, talking about *cabbages*.' Pringle jabbed a finger in the air at Thorburn. 'Cabbages! Cabbages! Cabbages! Talking about fucking cabbages!'

Marshall grabbed him by the arm.

Pringle shook free. He was up and rounding the table towards Thorburn. 'Cabbages! How can you talk about—'

Marshall locked an arm around his throat and hauled Pringle away from Thorburn. 'Come on!' He got him outside into the corridor.

'Cabbages!'

No sign of the court officer.

Marshall stared hard at Pringle. 'What the hell are you playing at?'

'Cabbages!'

'Cabbages? What the fuck are you talking about?'

'Don't you see? Cabbages!' Pringle slumped back against the wall and slid down. By the time his arse touched his heels, he started crying. Thick drops hit the carpet between his shoes.

Marshall only noticed now that he had mismatched socks.

And his fly was still down.

Marshall was stuck. Caught between getting justice for unnamed victims and with sorting out his boss in some kind of mental health crisis.

Sod it.

'Stay here.' He prodded a finger into Pringle's arm, then went back into the room. 'I'm sorry about that.'

'I'm not.' Thorburn was on his feet, staring at the ground. 'I was about to make a huge mistake there, Robert. You're wrong – nothing good can come from me naming them. They've all moved on with their lives or made their decisions. I won't haul them back.'

'Graham. Please.'

'Oh, if you say *please* then of course...' He shook his head. 'The answer is still no.'

'I'm begging you.'

'While I appreciate the sentiment, Robert, the answer has to remain a solid no.'

Marshall knew him. When he made up his mind like that, that was it. Over and done with. 'Okay. Well, this is the last time you'll ever see me, Graham. Goodbye.'

He stormed out of the room with no idea whether Thorburn said anything or made any attempt at clawing him back.

In the corridor, the court officer was helping Pringle up. He noticed Marshall – considering the people he dealt with on a daily basis, this had spooked him.

Join the club.

Marshall held out a hand to Pringle. 'I'll take him home.'

'No, no. I'm fine!'

Marshall grabbed his shoulders. 'No way. Whatever's going on, you're not fit for work.'

'I am!'

'You just shouted "cabbages" at an interviewee! I was close to getting him to open up about additional victims and you—'

'He's going away for decades, Robert. It doesn't matter.'

'It does to me. It does to those victims. It does to their families! I'm not looking to add to the statistics or put years onto his sentence. I want justice for those victims. I want them to get closure on what happened to them. To prove that justice hasn't failed them.'

'Robert, I know what's going on. You need closure for what happened to you. This Messiah complex of yours is going to kill you.'

'I'm sick to death of biblical references. It's important we prove to the victims of crimes that they get solved.'

'That's not what's—'

'Come on.' Marshall gripped his sleeve and walked him along the corridor. 'I'm taking you home. Where is your car?'

'My car?' Pringle searched his pockets. 'I can't remember.'

'You *can't* remember?'

'No, I...'

'How did you get here?'

'When?'

'This morning.'

Pringle gave up searching his pockets with an orange flash of a train ticket. 'I don't know.'

Marshall took the ticket – Tweedbank to Waverley, stamped that morning. Explained a few things. But raised yet more questions.

Pringle was charging along the corridor. 'Where are we, Rob?'

'We're going home, sir. Where is home?'

'I'm... I'm staying with my brother in Kelso.'

'Okay. Well, Kelso it is. I'll talk to your boss. Everything's going to be okay.'

CHAPTER EIGHT
ELLIOT

At least the rain had stopped.

Kelso glowed in the post-shower sunshine, the market square cobbles shining. An old man tripped on one and turned to glare at it.

Elliot reached up to tug down the sun visor, then took a right and headed along Roxburgh Street, back out towards Floors Castle. One entrance was in the town, but the main way in was a few miles out. Decent café there, mind. No, a really good one.

The road was blocked off, with a muscular uniform directing traffic anywhere but up Roxburgh Street, his beefy arms windmilling around. He held out a hand to stop her.

A flash of her warrant card got her past and she pulled up behind a long row of squad cars and a couple of pool bangers she'd been lucky enough to avoid by virtue of being first in.

Hopefully the move to Gala would mean some of them got replaced, but with Pringle in charge...

She tried his number again, but it just rang out. There was

managing upwards and there was having Ronald McDonald as your boss...

She got out and walked towards the big lump manning the outer locus. Took her a few seconds to recognise him as she signed in. 'PC Warner, isn't it?'

'Sure is, ma'am.' Irish accent. Wide grin, almost as wide as his stance – no pushing him over. 'Liam.' His forehead creased. 'C'mere, do you mind telling us why you're here?'

She frowned back at him. 'Me?'

'Yeah. You lot are the MIT, right? Why are detectives here?'

'When someone gets run over, you don't expect detectives to turn up?'

'That's the thing. I expect it, sure enough. But *we* didn't call you out. I checked with our sarge.'

'Nope. But don't worry your pretty little head about it, Constable. All will become clear in time.' She patted his arm and walked past, then stopped. 'I gather the victim was the shop's owner?'

'That's right. Gary Hislop, I think.' He waved off in the direction of Berwick. 'He's in A&E at Borders General.' Which was in the opposite direction from where he was pointing.

'Do they think he'll pull through?'

'Paramedics were a bit... noncommittal. And if you're asking, it looked like he had a second kneecap halfway up his thigh and his head was like a burst tomato.'

She patted his arm again. 'Keep fighting the good fight, soldier.' She walked over to the store along cobbles seared with tyre marks like a steak on a barbecue.

Roxburgh Street Hardware.

Shared the same look as the original shop in Galashiels, the same design and layout, the same arrangement of cheap tat in the window. The big difference here was someone had smashed the hell out of the curated display of crap out front.

Despite it now being rainy season in these parts, several pipes of snow salt were scattered across the road. Some shovels and other work tools lay in the gutter. The displays were mounted on a bench, but the wood on the right side was only good for a fire now.

She checked the cobbles in front of the store but saw only a thin smear of blood. The rain must've spread and washed it away.

An attack like that was easily survivable, especially as the whole town was a 20 zone, but Elliot knew from bitter experience how the problems started when the blood didn't get out.

Internal bleeding would kill you before you noticed.

The shop sat opposite the kebab shop and the wee lane leading around to that lovely ice cream place and a nice pub that was less nice when she was in uniform years ago. A few people were giving statements to officers she knew. Half her team, half Marshall's.

But they were all Indians with no chiefs.

Christ, she better not let Gashkori hear her say something like that...

DC Ash Paton came free. Cropped dark hair, suit tight over the frame of a feminine man or a masculine woman. For a time, Elliot hadn't been sure which pronouns applied and, short of asking that question, it was hard to know these days. Not that she could complain, her own Sam was definitely a "they". And out here in the real world, misgendering someone was stepping in a huge pile of shite.

Paton had a huge smile for Elliot. 'Ma'am.'

'Ash.' Elliot returned the grin. 'Not seeing any of our sergeants.'

'Well, no. Jolene called to say she's on her way and Shu— Sorry, ma'am. DS Siyal left a couple of weeks ago so—'

'I know that. His replacement's supposed to be here today.'

'Nobody told me that.'

'Sorry.' Elliot clenched her jaw. That was basic stuff and she'd blundered. 'That's on me and I can only apologise.' She gave her a smile. 'Are you getting anything?'

'Nope. Well, nothing much. Everyone saw a car racing up the street, but nobody agrees on the make or model.'

'CCTV?'

'On it.' Ash flipped open her notebook and scribbled something down.

At least she wasn't the only one who'd made a basic error.

Elliot pointed at the kebab shop. 'Has anyone been in there or to any of the flats?'

'Not sure.'

'Okay. That's not on you, Ash. It's why the Good Lord created sergeants.' She smiled then stepped away. 'Better make a few calls.'

'Hairdryer treatment, eh?' Ash winked then walked off with a long stride.

Elliot could certainly shout, but her roar didn't sound like a hairdryer at full blast. Or burn as hard. Still, she needed to keep an eye on that one – she was going places. She spotted Big Jim McIntyre clocking her and avoided him by putting her phone to her ear.

'We're sorry but the caller is—'

She snapped it away and stabbed the end call button before the voicemail started recording.

Then she tried someone else.

'Hey, boss.' DS Jolene Archer sounded out of breath. And driving.

'Sergeant, thanks for taking my call. I've just turned up at the crime scene and I can see your team, but not you.'

'Sorry! I'm running late. Wee Joe's been a nightmare this morning.'

'Aye, aye. How far away are you?'

But she'd gone. The joys of all the mobile reception black spots around here. Still. Not that Elliot put it past her using that to her advantage. Shoogling airplane mode to simulate a dropped call.

She tried Jolene again but it just rang and rang, so she tried Marshall instead.

'We're sorry but the—'

Bloody hell.

Okay, so she was the only senior officer here – she needed to establish an investigation strategy. And quick.

Back to basics.

A motor vehicle collision where the driver left the scene.

Hit and run.

Felt like an attempted murder, given the target, but proving it was intentional and not just recklessness followed by attempting to flee liability was a nightmare.

Still, her experience taught her it was better to think the worst and overreact than to assume it was a minor bump gone wrong and underreact.

That happening to someone under observation felt like it meant something.

Two teams had Hislop on their radar – her lot and the Gashkori drugs cavalcade up in Edinburgh. She found it hard to shake the feeling that nobody could be arsed to do their bloody jobs and just arrest the bastard. She'd given them enough, hadn't she?

When she got into Pringle's position, she'd sort them all out.

She walked over to the shop and started taking in the damage.

Up close it seemed less bad – the shopfront was intact.

She had to decide if it was an attempt on Hislop rather

than just a random accident. It felt like he had been targeted, but had needed to keep an eye on some random boy racer zooming around the corner to batter into him...

Hard to put any credence on that, but... It could've happened. And that was the fucking problem – Marshall would want to look at all the possibilities, assign probabilities and avoid... what was it?

Oh aye, investigative tunnel vision.

If it was an accident, then no amount of murder squad detectives could put Gary Hislop back together again. Needed specialists – and bloody hell, Marshall had two years under his belt in that world. Serious Collisions or something stupid like that.

Focus.

Two cops were inside the shop, speaking to a sole staff member standing behind the till like the place was still open. Pretty lassie, but all dolled up like it was Saturday night and not Tuesday morning. Lashes big enough to achieve lift-off when she flapped them, like she was doing to that Geordie uniform lad. Stish, everyone called him.

'Boss?'

Elliot swung around.

A big lump strolled down the street from the direction of the town square. Slightly shorter than her, but immaculately dressed. Navy suit, crisp shirt, red tie. Dark hair slicked to the side. The slight popcorn edge of cauliflower ears. 'Take it you're DI Elliot?'

'That's me.'

'DS Struan Liddell reporting for duty.'

Cheeky bastard.

Elliot tapped her watch. 'What time do you call this?'

'Sorry, I—'

'First day on the job, I expect you waiting for me at the station before I'm there.'

'I was.'

'Eh? You were sitting in the station and all these detectives piled out, heading towards a crime scene and you didn't think to follow?'

'Didn't see anyone.'

'There was nobody in Gala?'

'Gala? I was in Melrose.'

Clown!

Absolutely bloody clown!

Elliot stepped closer to him so nobody else heard the rest of the exchange. 'Sergeant. You were *told* to head to Gala, not Melrose.'

'Nope.' He fished a printout from his pocket. 'The email's here.'

She looked at it and there it was in black and white.

Shite...

Trouble with the standard interview process was there were no questions about whether someone was an arse-coverer.

DS Struan Liddell had played his hand way too soon.

'Anyway.' He grinned at her. 'I'll try not to hold it against you.' A crafty wink, blink and you'd miss it. 'Okay, here I am now, how can I entertain you? I mean, how can I help?'

Elliot swallowed down her anger. 'Here's the SparkNotes on this case. Hislop is an upstanding member of the local community in the Borders. Heavily involved in the local rugby club. Sponsors the kids' league. Even set up a Borders Down's Syndrome team. Loads of great stuff.'

'Sensing there's a monstrous *but* here?'

'He's a drug dealer. Well. A supplier.'

'How big?'

'Seven figures per annum is the estimate. All laundered by means we haven't managed to nail down yet. Looking to multiply that by a factor of ten this year.'

'And he's not been arrested because?'

'Because he's very careful. Very, very careful. The way he launders the money is so clever we don't even know half of it.'

'How can you be sure it's happening?'

'Oh, it's happening.' She clapped him on the shoulder. 'But it's great you're here, Struan. I need someone to make sure we're covering all the bases.' She waved up above street level. 'Those flats over the road would be perfect for surveillance of the shop. Need to know if the occupier is a nosy sod, or if drugs have a sneaky obbo in there.'

'Peachy.' Struan frowned. 'Surveillance? Drugs have this place under surveillance?'

She stepped closer. 'Not sure. This is the third in a chain of shops. He's expanding massively in the next few months. Don't know how familiar you are with their MO, but keeping secrets from us seems to be a large part of it.'

Struan nodded along. 'Perfect for money laundering.' He looked around. 'Okay, if you introduce me to the team, I'll smash a few heads together while you pull together a strategy.'

'Start with finding nearby CCTV, aye?'

CHAPTER NINE
MARSHALL

Marshall drove fast, following the long wall stretching around Floors Castle, then broke off and headed towards the high school, passing a wooded area on the left. A pair of lads wandered out of the entrance, maybe fourteen years old and looking like they should be in class at this time. Both of them couldn't have dentist's appointments. And woodside dentistry wasn't exactly a thing in these parts anymore.

Three squad cars blasted past, but Marshall had no idea where they were headed.

Pringle banged his fist off the dashboard. 'Cabbages...'

Back to that again...

Great.

'Where's your brother's, then?'

Pringle looked over at Marshall like he was surprised to both be in a car and have someone else with him. He blinked hard a few times. 'Down by the garden centre.'

Marshall knew Kelso well enough to know not just the

garden centre but the fancy houses leading up to it. 'Mayfield Lane, right?'

'Right.'

'How near?'

'To what?'

'To the garden centre.'

'Three houses away.'

'Got it.'

They were going the wrong way, so Marshall weaved right at the roundabout and ploughed down the road past Lidl. 'How long have you been staying with your brother?'

'Not long. A few months, I think.'

'You think?'

'A few months, aye.' Pringle glared at him with his old focus. 'I'm not stupid.'

'Nobody's saying you are, sir.'

'I know what you're up to, Rob. You're after Thorburn's extra victims for selfish reasons.'

'I'm looking for justice. That's all.'

'Hmmm.'

Marshall had to stop for traffic backed up behind a delivery lorry. The taxi driver in front was leaning out and shouting, not that the two lads delivering a sofa gave a shit.

'Oh yeah, baby!' Pringle smacked the dashboard again, but more affectionately. And no mention of cabbages. 'John must've driven me.'

'John?'

'My brother. John. He must've driven me to Tweedbank for the train this morning. That's how I got into Edinburgh.'

'Older?'

'My wee brother.'

Once again, Marshall wondered what the hell was going on inside that head. How could he forget?

'Kelso, Kelso, Kelso...' Pringle chuckled. 'Pretty ironic, eh?'

The lorry up ahead was moving now, stranding the lads with the sofa.

'What's ironic, sir?'

'I'm living in Kelso now and I was on the way to a case about the death of an Anna Kelso.'

Marshall felt a stab in his gut at the mention of the name.

'Shit, Rob. Sorry. She was your girlfriend when you were a boy. How crass of me.'

Marshall got past the lorry and sped up, hitting thirty in the town's twenty – the sooner he got there, the sooner Pringle would shut up.

'Toponymics.'

Marshall slowed as he neared the vets. 'What's that?'

'Kelso. It's a toponymic surname. Named after a place.' Pringle waved his hand around the area as it blurred past. 'Yours is an occupational one. I looked it up for you. Literally means "horse servant". *Mare* meaning horse and *ska*-something or other. Germanic or Frankish. Something like that. Literally. Lover of horses. And not like that bloke down by Hawick who we arrested in—'

'What type of surname is Pringle, then?'

'I always assumed it was some kind of patronymic, like Johnson or Macbeth. But no! It's actually both a toponymic and an occupational one. It was originally a corruption of "Pilgrim", hence the occupation. But it comes from Hoppringle, a place near Stow. The "Hop" got lost to the annals of time. My name is one of the most popular in the Borders. And wider too, I suppose.'

Marshall pulled up outside the house, though whether his brother lived there was anyone's guess. And hard to determine if it was the third from the garden centre. A nice enough place, walking distance of anywhere you needed to go in Kelso. One of those Borders towns that hadn't been too badly corrupted by the modern age and the subsequent collapse of the high street – the gaping holes in Gala and Hawick weren't to be found here. 'This it?'

'John started looking into our ancestry after our dad died. Didn't get very far, but I picked it up recently. Found a few loose strands I could tug on. Being a detective, you're always trying to solve mysteries. Determination and stubbornness have led me down some interesting paths. I'm not eighteenth in line for the throne or anything like that, but there are a few interesting inheritances in there.'

The present was a fog, but his mind seemed so caught up in the past.

'Sir. Is this your home?' Marshall pointed at the house.

Pringle stared at it like he'd never seen it before in his life. 'I do believe so.' He opened the door and got out.

Marshall followed him and raced up the path. 'Are you going to be okay?'

'It's not like anybody cares about me, is it?'

'I've just driven you back from Edinburgh, sir. I care. Can I get you a cup of tea? Some food?'

'I'm fine, Rob. Seriously. Just need a little lie down. It's just the stress of the day. I thought I was fine with it, but apparently I overestimated my own resolve.'

'You have done that.' Marshall watched him try to get the key in the lock like a drunk at half three in the morning. The seventh attempt was successful and he went into the giant house. Slammed the door in Marshall's face.

No time for that cup of tea or even the pee he needed.

Marshall took out his phone as he walked back to the car.

A ton of missed calls from Elliot.

Despite him being in court all morning.

She was like a dog with a bone at times. And like a good

owner, he knew when to restrict attention to train away negative behaviours.

A text flashed up from Pringle's boss:

> Rob – in a meeting but got the gist of your vm.
> The situation is under control. Is Jim okay?

> Sorry to interrupt, ma'am, but I did feel it was urgent. I've just dropped DCI Pringle at his brother's in Kelso now. Let me know if you want me to stay and keep an eye on him.

> I'll give him a call in a few minutes. This is my situation to seal with, not yours. Thanks Rob – it's been noted.

Another text flashed up:

> *deal, not seal!

Marshall didn't feel like he could just leave Pringle there, but he didn't see any other options.

Still nothing from Kirsten about his message. It wasn't feeling right. Not in the slightest.

His mobile rang.

Elliot calling...

Well, he really could make her wait...

Sod it. He answered it. 'Marshall.'

'Robbie! Finally.' She was out of breath. 'Where the hell are you?'

'Long story. What's up?'

'Someone tried to kill Gary Hislop.'

CHAPTER TEN
MARSHALL

That certainly explained why there were all those squad cars hurtling around Kelso.

Marshall walked up to Roxburgh Street, usually a busy street with local people scurrying between local shops, but now the whole place was blocked off.

A crime scene, but no tent.

He spotted a good twenty cops, including most of their team and over half the Borders uniform contingent, but no forensics officers.

DS Jolene Archer was in the middle of the maelstrom, talking to her three DCs. Smiling, but with that hard look in her eyes. 'Okay, check back in after half an hour.' She strode over to Marshall, checking her blonde ponytail was still in place. 'Rob... Thought you were in court today?'

'Nope. Long story.' He covered his sigh with a smile and thrust out his hand. 'Congratulations on your first day as a full DS.'

'Thanks for pushing me through the promotion board, sir.'

'You're a good cop, Jolene. It was easy.' Marshall clapped his hands together. 'Okay, what's going on here?'

'Well... I'm warning you now – Elliot's on the warpath. Stressed as hell and lashing out worse than ever.'

'How's that possible?'

She laughed. 'When she's backed into a corner, all she can do is turn around and fight.'

Took Marshall a second for the joke to click.

'What are you pair giggling at?' Elliot looked like she'd swallowed a wasp byke with all the little critters still alive inside, now stinging away.

'Morning, Andrea.' Marshall smiled at her. 'Are you thinking this was an attempt on Gary Hislop?'

'I'm still playing catch-up myself, Robbie, and blah blah investigative tunnel vision, but it looks that way, aye.' Elliot pointed at the shop. 'First thing this morning, Hislop was outside on a call and someone drove a car into him. We've had all sorts of makes and models, ranging from a Mini up to a BMW 7-series. Try as we might, we haven't narrowed that down any. Forensics will get paint samples from that lot.' She pointed at the smashed-up planks of wood that would've been a display first thing in the morning. 'Local uniform are investigating, along with my lot. And yours.' She scratched her neck as she looked at Jolene. 'Hopefully we can get enough CCTV to piece together a timeline.'

Jolene took the hint and nodded. 'I'll see where we're at with that. A few cashpoints around the corner and some street cameras. If we can pin down any speeding cars, we've got our attacker.'

'Thanks.' Marshall watched her go, then pointed at a drying patch of blood on the cobbles. 'I was expecting his body to be lying there, under a tent.'

'Nope. Still alive.'

'You mentioned about forensics, but—'

'Aye. Kirsten's been called out but I've no idea where she is.'

Marshall resisted the temptation to call her, instead focusing on Elliot. 'How long have you been here?'

'Hour and a half, give or take?' She pointed over at a pair of uniforms interviewing a schoolboy resting on a bike. 'Soon as the responding PCs searched Hislop's name, an alert klaxon went off in Edinburgh and Jim McIntyre got the call.'

'Why not you?'

Elliot tapped her nose. 'Secret.'

Marshall felt they'd made so much progress recently, but sometimes she'd remind him of how annoying she could be. And nakedly ambitious. 'You're going to play it like that?'

'Always. Robbie, this is potentially an attempted murder on a known drug dealer, so we need to treat this like it's actually one.' Elliot looked around the area at the assembled cops. 'Struggling with a lack of staff. And a presence of some.'

'Go on?'

She sighed. 'Had to wait for ages for the new Shunty to show up.'

'Struan Liddell, right?'

'Right. Hasn't give it the whole Borders boy returning home nonsense I got from you last summer, but I doubt many senior officers in Glasgow will be missing him. First day, and the clown turned up late.'

Marshall just had to smile through it. 'How late?'

'Hours. It's almost lunchtime... Giving me some crap about Pringle not telling him to go to Gala nick this morning.'

Marshall tried to stop his eyebrow rising.

'What's up, Robbie? Are you having a stroke there?'

'No, it's just... Pringle...' Marshall's sigh was louder than hers. A sharp rasp like sandpaper on wood. 'He's not so much misplaced his marbles as gone absolutely batshit crazy.'

'He's always been weird. Worked with him since I started. Always been in each other's orbits. And he's always been a lot further out than any other cop.'

'No, I know, but this is the worst I've seen him, though. We were interviewing Graham Thorburn.' Marshall felt everything clench and tighten. 'I was leading and was close to getting him to name some of his other victims... Then Pringle shouted "cabbages". Sure, one you can recover from, but he kept on about it. Cabbages, cabbages, cabbages. Had to grab him and get him out of there.'

Saying it out loud made Marshall doubt whether it'd actually happened.

But it had.

'Jesus.' Elliot shook her head, her forehead tight. '*Cabbages?*'

'I know. What the hell's that about?'

'Never mentioned them. Not even a cabbage schmabbage.' She held his gaze for a few long seconds. 'Where is he?'

'Dropped him at his brother's not far from here.'

'He's got a brother?'

'Aye, kept that quiet, didn't he? But he's... finally lost it.'

'So we're flying without adult supervision?'

Marshall shrugged. 'I called "she who cannot be named" and it's all in hand.'

'Meanwhile, we've got a major case and no senior investigating officer.'

'Andrea, you're the one with fire in your belly and more ambition than a new MP. Happy for you to be SIO until we hear otherwise.'

'Okay. Thanks.' She let out a deep breath, like she'd

expected a battle over it and hadn't got one. 'Need to put our heads together, then.'

'What's your gut telling you?'

'My gut? Well, it's always shouting "don't get stabbed in me again, please". But otherwise... I guess the elephant in the room is that Hislop's under surveillance for drugs. If it's nothing to do with that, then we've got someone with a grudge against him.'

'We've got a whole county with a grudge against him, not to mention a few cities. Edinburgh, Glasgow, Newcastle.' Marshall motioned around the vicinity. 'How tight is the surveillance?'

'The harbour at Eyemouth is one of the few places we've got eyes on. He owns a fishmonger there. That's how he's getting *some* product into the country. Two boats meet out in international waters, stuff a few cod full of coke and smack, bingo.'

'But him specifically? Any surveillance there?'

'Nope. Tried, failed. Ran two months of it and all we saw was the inner workings of a busy hardware store owner. The funding got pulled three months ago. He either hasn't done anything or he has a sixth sense to know when he is being watched. High hied yins didn't want to spook him and make him flee.'

'That likely?'

'It wouldn't be a surprise if he did.' She laughed. 'What I'm thinking, Robbie, is along the lines of it being a deliberate murder attempt.'

She was reaching there. Still, the likelihood of someone accidentally running him over was on the low side.

'Just a sec.' Marshall wandered back down the street towards the square. 'Bingo.'

'Eh? What are you playing at?'

'I worked Serious Collisions for two years in the Met. I know a thing or two.' Marshall pointed to a spot maybe a hundred and fifty feet from the shop. 'Acceleration marks. If you factor in a decent acceleration of about fifteen miles an hour per second, then—'

'How can you have miles per hour *per second*?'

'Rate of acceleration. How much the speed increases per second. At that rate, in four seconds the car would've travelled about a hundred and fifty feet but would've been doing about sixty miles an hour. Combine that with the spread of debris on the street and, of course, the presence of skid marks at the start but none at the end... Aye, looks intentional to me.'

'You think it's attempted murder?'

'Take a yes from me for once.'

She didn't seem to, given the depth of her frown. 'So, a rival? Someone inside his firm?'

Marshall raised a shoulder. 'Either is possible.'

'Aye, tell me about it. This case has been leakier than a colander made of paper.'

Marshall scanned the area again, focusing on the faces of his and her teams. 'You *honestly* think there's someone leaking to Hislop?'

'I do. You know he's been feeding me stuff, Robbie, but what I've been getting... It's... not what he's giving me... But...' Her lips twisted up. 'This might sound daft but, assuming I'm reading the tea leaves right, he knows things only someone on the case could know.'

'What kind of things?'

'Hard to describe. Look, I get stuff like "a boy in the rugby club was asking about something or someone". We spend a few weeks trying to put a name to said "boy in the rugby club". We spend another few weeks teeing up a chat with said boy in the rugby club. Said boy in the rugby club doesn't turn up to the arranged meeting. Said boy in the rugby club gets the fuck out of Dodge. Said boy from the rugby club is never heard from again.'

Marshall played it all through and it sounded like a definite ploy. 'My speciality is in psychological profiling of serial abductors and killers, so I don't have much experience of organised crime. But I can see the logic in what you're saying. He's giving you some information that's watermarked like a banknote. He can trace what he's hearing from you back to who's leaking from his side.'

'Right, exactly.' She tugged at her fringe, tucking it behind her right ear. 'I mean, with anything like this, it could all just be a coincidence, right?'

'It could. Of course it could. But... Also, not. We need to look into whether this is connected to the leaks.'

'Wait, in what way?'

'If someone's heard word they're going to get disappeared, maybe they decided to take out the top dog.'

She nodded. 'Got it. But we need to just investigate and then draw conclusions from the evidence.'

CHAPTER ELEVEN
ELLIOT

E lliot struggled not to raise her eyebrows.

Marshall was down in a plank position, looking under a nearby car. Sure enough, he could hold himself down there for a good while, but it was performative. He kicked back up and scuttled over to chat to a local uniform.

Elliot left him to it. Let the bloody clown show some competence for once.

One thing scratched at the back of her brain, though. He'd backed off too easily, letting her get her arms around the case. Starting to think this was a hospital pass and he knew it.

But whatever. Thing with hospital passes was you were going to get mullered by someone tackling from behind. She was an expert at leaning into that challenge, minimising the injury and winning the foul. Avoiding hospital too.

Well, mostly.

Still, enough of this shite – she really needed to show them she actually was boss.

Like, right now.

She knew she was giving off chaotic energy, so she took her

time walking into the shop, inspecting the various flavours of paint. Not flavours... Brands? Colours? Aye, brands and colours. They had one of those colour-mixing things, which turned hundreds of tins into millions of colours. The shop seemed to have pretty much anything you'd want, despite its size.

And that dining room needed a good repainting – only so many times crayon could be cleaned off without it taking the paint with it.

Elliot's phone rang.

DCI Ryan Gashkori calling...

Bugger that. She pocketed it and let it ring out.

Struan Liddell looked around from speaking to the staff member by the till. He gestured at the lassie she'd seen from outside. 'Boss, this is Catherine Sutherland.'

She was all fingernails and eyelashes. 'Cath.' She held out a hand to Elliot. 'Nice to meet you.'

'DI Andrea Elliot.' She gripped it tight and got a slight scratch from those nails – sharper than the metal ones they sold. 'That's not a local accent, is it?'

'Ah come fi' Aberdeen, aye.' Overly stressed, like everything she'd said up to that moment was her best attempt to disguise it.

'Got you. What brings you down here?'

'Work.'

Struan took charge of the chat by passing between them, filling the space with a blast of his aftershave. 'Cath just told me she didn't see much of the incident.'

Cath pointed at the till. 'I was serving a customer.' Back to her best attempt of a Borders accent.

'You know who it was?'

'Not on first-name terms, sorry.'

'What about last names?'

'That too.'

Struan smiled. 'Cath's going to take us through the CCTV.'

Elliot snorted. That was Jolene's team's job. She needed to sit down with this clown and spell out how she expected him to operate. 'Why hasn't she already?'

Cath held up her hands like they were pointing a gun at her. 'Mr Hislop's the only one who had the PIN.'

'It's ready now, though?'

'Aye, aye. Just took a while to get in. Sorry.'

'No worries. Please, play it from just before the accident – I want to see what we can of it.'

The video was already playing on the screen behind the counter. The machine was so new it had that fresh-laptop smell, a slightly metallic pine.

Crystal-clear image of the shop from the inside, smooth framerate, just in black and white. Couldn't have everything, could you, but it was an absolute dream to work with.

Struan stroked her arm. 'Cath, you don't have to watch this.'

Cath stood close to him, her gaze focused on the monitor. Too close? Maybe.

Onscreen, Hislop was standing outside, phone to his head. Only downside was he was in the doorway and the window displays obscured the rest of the street.

'You got that call?'

Struan shook his head. 'Asked the team to get the caller logs through.'

'Good, good.'

Hislop scowled at a kid passing on a bike.

Elliot hit pause and glanced at Struan. 'Can we track down the laddie?'

'On it, boss.' Struan jotted it down, but with a grimace.

'Most schools will solve that riddle in seconds. If the wee bugger is in as much trouble in school as out of it, they'd be happy to dob him in shite with us.'

'But?'

'Not sure it'll give us anything, boss.'

Then Hislop was gone, lost to a blur of movement.

Cath had some skill with the jog wheel, running it backwards then smoothly easing through the frames.

First frame, a car flashed into the right of the image.

Then it was inches away from Hislop.

Next, he was flying up and away.

'My God.' Cath walked away from the screen, covering her mouth.

Struan looked up at her, but didn't say anything, instead whispering, 'Told her she didn't have to watch...'

Elliot took over the controls and jogged it on.

The next frame showed the car in full detail.

Struan pointed at the screen. 'BMW 520. And unless I'm very much mistaken, that's the M5 model, which came out three years after the vanilla model. Off the top of my head, I'd say we're looking at a J-reg through to a P.'

'That's like early nineties?'

'Aye. 1991 to 1996, to be precise.'

'So a pretty old car?'

'Aye, but it's a classic. No electronics in that bad boy. One of the last ones that's entirely mechanical and electrical. Cars nowadays are just computers on wheels – once a part goes, you have to buy a new one. That baby, you can keep it running so long as you don't let rust set in.'

'Sounds like you know your cars.'

'Mostly, aye. Bit of a nightmare as a kid, if you listen to my parents. Took me to Edinburgh Zoo once, but I spent an hour in the car park and couldn't be arsed with the animals inside.' He smiled like it was something to be proud of. 'Did a stint on the serious accidents team down at Gartcosh.'

Elliot struggled to not roll her eyes at him. 'You and Marshall have something in common.'

'Marshall?'

'The other DI. Listen, did Pringle actually brief you?'

'A bit, aye. Where is he?'

'Off sick.'

'That's a shame.'

Elliot didn't want to tell him too much more. She wound the video on and it took two more frames before Hislop's shoes appeared on the right of the screen, sliding down to crunch onto the cobbles.

Right where that patch of blood had been.

Meanwhile, the car's front-left bonnet hit the display and it swerved off back onto the road.

The next few frames had stacks of snow salt pipes and spades flying everywhere.

A man ran over to check Hislop.

Struan circled him. 'We've spoken to him. Allan Field. Bought something from here just before.'

'Good.' Elliot patted the monitor. 'I want this video combed frame by frame for any details. Okay?'

'Sure thing.'

'And run through today's customers. I want to know everyone in here during the morning.'

'On it. Tall order, but we'll do our best.'

'After that, go through the last fortnight, assuming it goes back that far. I want everyone spoken to. No matter how daft that seems, I want to know everyone who's speaking to Hislop. And anyone who's in here or outside daily. If someone's staking out this place, so they know Hislop's patterns of movement.'

'Of course. Smart thinking, boss.'

'You'll get used to it, Struan.' Elliot wanted to give him a nickname, but the key to making one stick was to wait for the right one. Something like 'Shunty' didn't come along on everyone's first day. 'Dr Donkey' took her months. Now she used 'Robbie', but it made him cringe just the same. And she loved it.

'Just so we're on the same page, is there a reason—'

Her mobile blasted out the Scissor Sisters.

Unknown caller...

Perfect timing, but if it was some timewaster... 'Better take this. Get to the bottom of the CCTV, okay? And the phone records!' She got a nod and walked outside. 'Hello?'

'Good morning.' Pin-sharp voice. Fruity, but posh Scottish. Local enough. 'Am I talking to Andrea Elliot?'

'You are. Who's this?'

'Ah, my name's unimportant but to fashion a degree of trust between us, I shall of course give you it. It's Callum. Callum Hume.'

Meant absolutely diddly squat to her. 'Okay, Callum Hume. Afraid I'm a bit tied up just now, so if you could call back when —'

'It's about Gary Hislop.'

'Oh?'

'I work for Mr Hislop, helping him establish a network of stores across Scotland.'

Well, you're a stupid prick.

You weren't on our radar, but now you are.

'I gather you're investigating a vehicular assault on him this morning, correct?'

'You should know we can't divulge details of an active investigation that may or may not exist.'

'Ah, of course. Of course. Listen, the reason for the call is I'm in hospital with Gary just now. He's adamant he speaks to you before his surgery.'

CHAPTER TWELVE

MARSHALL

Marshall's phone buzzed with a text message. He got up from looking under cars and checked the display:

ELLIOT

Can you speak to Cath Sutherland? Woman in the shop. Something not clicking there for me. Thanks.

Marshall had to laugh – he could see her over the other side of the square getting into her car but she couldn't be bothered coming over to speak to him. If that was a portent of what she'd be like to work for if she ever got Pringle's job...

Maybe he'd been a bit hasty in letting her act up – reporting to Elliot felt more than a bit weird...

The only other message was from Pringle's boss:

Meeting over so I'll just call Jim. Not sure DI Elliot is a good fit as SIO, but please operate on that basis for now and keep me posted. Thanks again.

Okay. Well, that was odd. Usually people at that level were very guarded about what they let slip. Still, she was at least on the same page as Marshall.

Office politics was the number two reason Marshall had been going to leave the police a year ago. Now he'd relented but was back in that whole world again.

He walked over to the shop and caught the attention of Struan Liddell.

A snappy dresser, which was always a red flag to Marshall – subconsciously, cops like that were projecting a clean image, but beneath the surface was usually some inner turmoil they were trying to cover over.

That, or Marshall was just being a judgmental twat.

He offered a hand. 'DI Rob Marshall.'

He got a fist to bump instead. 'Good to finally meet you, chief.'

'That implies that my reputation precedes me?'

'Doesn't everyone's?'

'Fair enough.' Marshall gave him a smile. 'Does yours?'

'Hope so. You could use a detective of my calibre here, mate.' Struan's forehead creased. 'Just wanted to say I've been following your case with great interest. Must've been pretty difficult to go through all that.'

'All what?'

'You know. What you went through.'

'Difficult for some.' Marshall smiled at him again. Even with Thorburn's sudden change of heart, he was nowhere near the point where he felt like he was out the other side, despite what his brain told him. He waved off at a car driving away. 'Do you know where DI Elliot went?'

'Said she's Acting DCI Elliot.' A conspiratorial flash of eyebrow. 'And no, she didn't tell me anything. Just asked me to focus on the CCTV. Very kindly.'

'Did she. Well, DI Elliot asked me to have a word with Catherine Sutherland. Which you seem to have been doing.'

'Just teeing her up for you, boss. Goes by Cath. She was working when the accident happened.' He stepped in close. 'Between us, I think she's a bit shaken up by it.'

Marshall stepped back. 'Have you got anything useful out of her?'

'The CCTV system? DI Elliot's asked me to focus on that.' Struan raised a hand. 'Sorry, Acting DCI Elliot has.'

Marshall pointed at Jolene. 'Make sure you check with DS Archer so you're not both doing it.'

'On it, boss.'

'And aside from the CCTV? What else have you got out of her?'

'Well, that's it. She got a bit upset when we played the video.'

'Okay.' Marshall needed to have a word with her, didn't he? 'Thanks. Can you liaise with forensics and get their system transferred onto ours?'

'Already on it.' Struan stood there, smiling, then took Marshall's silence as the instruction it was and buggered off.

Marshall entered the shop slowly. 'Hello?'

A woman was perched on the edge of a stool at the back. Arms folded across her chest, obscuring most of the letters of "Roxburgh Street Hardware" on her apron. Tight jeans, low-cut top. Long green nails with an elaborate design like the Brazil flag. She looked up at him through a flurry of eyelashes, then down and up again. She got up and wasn't that much shorter than him, then held out a hand. 'Hi, I'm Cath.'

'DI Rob Marshall.' He took her hand and shook it. She seemed familiar somehow, but he couldn't place it. 'I'm sorry to hear that you witnessed the incident earlier.'

She exhaled slowly. 'Aye...' She tilted her head to the side. 'Takes a lot to shake me, you know?'

'I'm glad to hear it. You from Aberdeen?'

'Aye.' The Doric version of the word was almost as protracted as the local Borders one. 'From Portlethen.'

'Just down the coast, right?'

'Right. Aye.'

'What brings you down to Kelso, then?'

'I'd say the promise of fame and fortune, but I've got family nearby so I thought I'd sponge off them for a bit.' She laughed. 'What happened to Gary has put us right on edge. Mind if I have a fag?'

'Outside, sure.'

She stepped out into the morning light and walked up to a female uniform on her phone, probably messing about on Instagram as she took a smoke break. 'Here, mind if I crash a fag?'

'Oh, aye, sure.' She flipped open the lid.

Cath took one and smiled at Marshall. 'You want one?'

'I don't smoke. Sorry.'

'Good on you. I quit a few months ago, but seeing that happen to Gary... If ever there was a day to restart...' She sighed. Gave him the up and down again. 'Truth is, I got into a bit of a situation back home and I didn't know where to go, so I moved to Gala.'

Marshall had the measure of the woman. A drifter who'd probably left school with not many qualifications, but whose brain was as sharp as anyone with a PhD, just so happened that her expertise was in a different domain. 'You been working here long?'

'Few months, aye. Started in the Gala shop. Didn't think I'd last long, like.'

'Any reason?'

'Oh, just one of *those* jobs. I'm a hairdresser, by trade, but I just needed something a bit more low-key to tide me over. Thing is, Gary seemed to think I was good and suggested I move over here to this shop when he opened up. Bit of a bugger driving here, but... It's the prospects, right? Gary said I can show the ropes to the new laddie and lassie and was suggesting I could manage this place once he's happy it's running like clockwork.' A flutter of lashes. 'Thing is, I learnt at a very young age to never trust what people tell you. Especially from men. Always go by their actions.'

'In what way?'

'That situation back home... Let's just say... Nah, let's not.' She laughed again. 'You're local, right?'

'Melrose, born and bred.'

'Ooh, fancy.'

'Not that fancy. And you wouldn't want to have lived my life, believe me.'

'Something happen to you, big guy?'

Marshall smiled at her. 'Long story.'

'I've got time.' She gripped his arm lightly. 'If you want to get a drink to chat it through?'

Oh shite.

Just in the door and she was hitting on him.

The anxiety fluttered around his stomach, rose up his chest and made his heart skip a beat.

He clocked movement outside – Kirsten watching them. Then she came inside the shop. 'Need you lot out of here, thanks.'

Cath frowned. 'Thought we were going to be able to reopen today, quine?'

'You can do whatever you like, *quine*, but only after we're done. Right now, we need to scour this place for evidence.'

'But I've got to work.'

'Not my business, I'm afraid. Need to take that up with the owner.' Kirsten pointed out onto the street. 'I wasn't asking, I was telling. On you go.'

'Come on.' Marshall led Cath outside and then over to the opposite pavement, far enough away from any of his colleagues. The rain started spitting again. He tried to make eye contact with Kirsten again, but she didn't notice. What was she up to? Storming in like that and ordering them around. Not his immediate priority, so he shifted his focus back to the flash of lashes and puff of smoke.

He cleared his throat. 'Sorry about that. How about you recount your story to me?'

'I already told Struan.'

'Struan?'

'DS Liddell, I think?'

'You know him?'

'No, but I like him. Seems like a good guy. And you. Both of you. I like the cut of your jib, DI Marshall.'

Marshall cleared his throat again. 'Okay. Can you tell me what you saw during the incident?'

'Not much. I was with a customer, ringing up his order. Supposed to get Tich to deliver it later... Should I?'

'Should you what?'

'Get Tich to deliver it. With what's happened to Gary...'

'Listen, this place is a crime scene just now, but we'll all be gone within the hour. It's up to your firm's management to do what they want with the business. Stay open, shut. That's all up to Mr Hislop's business partners.'

'I think he's the sole owner.'

'But he must have a deputy?'

'Right. Callum. He's the one who had the CCTV code.' A curl flashed across her lips. Soon replaced by a smile. 'Okay, I'll have a chat with him.'

'My colleague felt you had more to say than you originally let on. Is there something else on your mind, something you held back on to start?'

She tugged at her hair. 'Not really.'

'Sure about that?'

'Look, I should have rushed to check on Gary.'

'But?'

'I called 999 instead. I thought he was *dead*. Feel so fucking guilty about it. Then I heard him moaning, but I couldn't go out and face him.'

'You did the right thing calling an ambulance. He needed professional help.'

'Thing is, just before the ambulance showed up I swear I heard him say "I'll kill him for this".'

'You know who?'

She shook her head. 'Nope.'

Marshall nodded at her. 'I need your honest answer to this. Have you ever seen any drugs here?'

'*Drugs?*'

'Have you?'

'No. I haven't seen any drugs here or in Gala. If I did, I would've quit...'

'That's very noble of you.'

'I'm serious. Found out my ex was into... stuff.' She ran a fingertip down her long fingernail. 'You think Gary's selling drugs?'

'It's possible, aye. Any help you could furnish us with would be greatly appreciated.'

'Thing is, I don't know his entire operation. But...'

'Go on?'

'I can't.'

'Please. It could be pertinent to what's happened here.'

'It's just... there are a lot of speciality orders.'

'What does that mean?'

'People come in and pay cash. For deliveries. Couple of people working in vans deliver stuff. Tich and Sharon.'

'That's quite interesting.'

'That's the business model. I think he's into that cashless society conspiracy theory. You know, how they can monitor us? Way he described it to me is the stock isn't in a warehouse like Amazon but it's distributed across the shops, kind of like Argos but even more so. That way, he can shift stuff from Gala to here pretty quickly if it's needed.'

Marshall appreciated the honesty, but there wasn't enough to rule things in or out, including her complicity.

Struan wandered over and lurked nearby. 'Hi, boss, just need a second?'

'Sure.' Marshall stepped away from Cath. 'Can you leave the keys to lock up and a contact number for whoever's in charge when we're done?'

'Oh, okay.' Cath walked back into the shop and started writing a note.

Marshall looked at Struan. 'You okay there?'

'Sure. I was just speaking with, uh, Sally is it? The CSI. Said they're going to get the CCTV onto our servers.'

'Right. I need you and Jolene to co-ordinate efforts on that. Don't want any duplication.' Marshall leaned in close to Struan. 'Before that, can you get Cath here to recount her story in detail? Names, faces, all of that. To cross-check against the video. Also, it sounds like she was organising a home delivery. If this is drugs, we need to drill into that. Okay?'

'Peachy. You honestly think this is drugs?'

'That's a discussion for another time.' Marshall left him to it. He tried to piece together his thoughts, but this case needed shoe leather work more than anything. Track down that car, investigate it, reconstruct everything.

Kirsten was staring at the pile of smashed wood outside the shop. 'Someone looked interested in you.'

Marshall felt himself blush. 'Eh?'

'The lassie over there.' She didn't even glance in the direction of Cath. 'Flirting, much?'

'Aye, she was. A lot.'

'Had her hand on your arm.'

'Like I said, she was flirting. A ton.'

'You didn't fend her off?'

'I'm a cop, Kirsten. If a witness is coming onto you, you don't shut them down. You get them to spill.'

'Mm. Sounds a bit dodgy to me.'

'Sounds cold, but you've got to use whatever you can.'

'Mm.'

'Come on, you don't think I was flirting back?'

'No, just...' She swallowed hard. 'Nothing. I'm being stupid.'

'No you're not.'

'I am. Of course I am.'

'Kirsten, you're one of the smartest people I know, and I've been on a PhD course.'

'Okay, you silver-tongued devil. Seeing her coming onto you like that...' She swept her hair back. 'You did nothing wrong, Rob, but it just struck me... I actually would've been jealous if you'd responded to her. Made me realise there's such a thing as turf and that she was standing on mine. So much for this just being a good time, Rob. I've got *feelings*. For the first time. What are you *doing* to me?'

Marshall's turn to laugh it off. 'If you want to be serious for a minute we—'

'I am. And that's the thing.' She swept a hand through her hair. 'I am. I... Bloody hell. We need to have that chat, don't we?'

'Did you get my text?'

'I did, aye. Still processing all this work. New station open-ing, half the IT system being down, which somehow sits with me until business-as-usual IT takes over. And now this? So, I'd love to come to Thea's, but it depends on work, right?'

'Right. Speaking of which...?'

'Okay, we need to recover clothes from the victim for paint transfer.' Kirsten scanned the vicinity. 'But the corpse isn't here.'

'Over at BGH.'

'Oh. I'll need to speak to... Belu's off this week, so her deputy.' She clicked her fingers. 'What's his name?'

'Kirsten, he's still alive.'

Her eyebrows shot up. 'Wow. Well, it'll be a nice change to go there to speak to your sister rather than Belu. Not that there's anything wrong with her, but all those dead bodies...'

'Listen, I did a quick check of the crash site. My old beat and all that. The way I see it, the car was doing roughly sixty when it hit Hislop.'

'Sixty? That's a bit precise?'

'Seen it before. Saw where it started.' Marshall pointed at the tyre marks on the cobbles. 'To hit him at that angle, it also had to smack into the display here, which took the brunt of it. The car didn't stop or crash into the rest of the shop. Looks like it braked after it hit him.'

She was nodding along, letting a slow breath go. 'Think he'll pull through?'

'Don't know. That's a lot of mass hitting flesh and bone.'

'Sometimes you do make me feel so stupid.' Kirsten brushed a hand against his arm. 'I'll get Trev to look into it. It'll stop him mansplaining at me.'

CHAPTER THIRTEEN

STRUAN

S o *that* was Rob Marshall.

Struan had expected something more. More presence or guile or intuition. Hardness. Insight, maybe. Guy just seemed like a basic cop, despite everything he'd been through.

Ah well, it was none of his business. He just had to work adjacent to him. Not even his boss. Still waters run deep as they say – you never know what those intellectual types are thinking half the time. Best to stay out of his path or just kiss his arse from time to time, stroke his ego.

Anyway. Enough of that.

First days were hell. Most of the time, it meant sitting in an office, reading up on stuff. Meeting a couple of cops. Early finish.

This, though, was a baptism of fire and ice, and no mistaking.

Still, if there's one thing Struan Liddell could handle, it was pressure.

Unlike his predecessor, if the rumours were to be believed.

Shipped off to the Complaints because he couldn't cut the mustard as a mainstream detective. Probably meant he was getting managed by his own team or he had a couple of useless snowflakes who didn't know their arses from their metatarsals. Either just meant bashing a few heads together.

Struan took a deep breath and walked over to what passed for a team. Two DCs, but the lad looked like he could eat the other one for breakfast and still have room for toast. And Struan *thought* the smaller one was a lad but he couldn't fucking tell.

Great – a woke banana skin ready to trip him up.

Initial assessment – these two are limp as wilted lettuce and need toughening up.

He grinned at both of them. 'How's it going?'

The big guy glanced at his partner. 'Can I help you, sir?'

'Sorry. Acting DCI Elliot didn't introduce me.' He thrust out a hand. 'DS Struan Liddell. I'm the replacement for DS Siyal.'

'Ah, okay. DC Jim McIntyre.' A bear of a man with a crushing grip. Big as Marshall, but even broader. Proper rugby player, like so many down here. 'This is DC Ash Paton.'

Struan ran through a checklist and figured she was at least born a she.

Ash was less bear and more of a hare – nimble, keen-eyed and ready to bolt. Her compact stature seemed at odds with her severe haircut, the colour of a stormy Hebridean sea — a blend of slate greys and midnight blues. Pale skin scattered with a constellation of freckles. Worn-in leather boots, well-fitted jeans, and layers of cotton shirts and chunky knitwear.

Probably a lesbian.

He wasn't sure real men got jobs in the police anymore. Even his predecessor was an Indian lad and how long did he last, for crying out loud?

Ash smiled at him as she shook his hand. 'Nice to meet you, sir.'

'It's a pleasure. And I'm only a sergeant, so no need for a sir. And please, it's Struan.'

'Sure.'

'Okay, so I gather you two have been looking for CCTV?'

'That's right.' McIntyre folded his arms across his chest. 'Got hold of some too.'

Smart guy. The kind that'd try to trip up a new boss.

'Peachy. Is that from inside the shop?'

McIntyre looked at him like he was stupid. 'No. From the street. Like we were told to by DI Elliot.'

'Okay. Have you got anything?'

'Forensics are in the process of readying it for analysis, so I can't show you any of it right now.'

'But?'

Ash frowned at Struan. 'But what?'

So they were both sneaky sods. Good to know.

'How much have you got?'

'Seven sources. Four shops, two cash machines and the town's webcam.'

'Good effort.' His grin bounced off their sour faces. This was going to be harder than he expected. 'Tell me you've at least found the car?'

'We've identified a possible car, aye.' McIntyre scratched at his neck. Whether he had some allergy or was hiding something... Struan would find out. 'I gather from the footage DI Marshall obtained that the vehicle in question was a BMW.'

'Have you found it?'

'Not had a chance, Sarge.'

Struan nodded along with it. 'Okay. So what's the plan?'

McIntyre raised his eyebrows. 'Do you need me to explain?'

'Constable. We're going to be working together for a while, okay? It'll help me greatly if I can follow your logic.'

'Well.' McIntyre looked away, down the long row of shops. 'We're planning on searching the footage for matching vehicles around the time of the attack.'

Ash took over. 'Problem is, the CCTV mostly comes from inside shops, which are all set up to prevent shoplifting or damage. The ones from the ATMs are there to stop people snatching cash or reading PINs over shoulders. And, while the town webcam does rotate around the market square, it was focusing on the other side when this happened. And it doesn't escape the fact that we don't have a plate on the car in question.'

'So, you're telling me you've got nothing?'

Ash ran a hand through her short hair. 'Like I said, we've not checked the footage in detail, but it's going to be hard to pin it down.'

Not exactly what Struan wanted to hear, but at least they were thorough in finding nothing. 'Sounds a lot like an excuse to me.'

McIntyre grunted. 'Excuse me?'

'This is basic stuff.'

'Basic?'

'Basic.'

'Look. Someone's identified a possible car. So our plan is get back to base and identify how many cars of that make, model and colour are registered locally. Starting in the Borders, then Scotland and North East England, then widening out to the rest of the UK.'

'Peachy.' Struan sighed. 'Okay. Your approach is sound, but we need results. Fast. Instead of palming stuff off onto forensics, we should be doing that ourselves.' He shifted his focus between them but they were both looking pissed off rather than attentive. Good – the message was starting to sink in. 'We've got a ton of work to get through, so we're going to need to grab a few uniforms. Do that and I'll cover it with Acting DCI Elliot.' He clapped his hands together and the sharp noise woke them up. 'How are we doing with canvassing witnesses?'

McIntyre puffed out his cheeks. 'Not great, to be honest.'

'Nope.' Ash flicked open her notebook. 'I found some wrong 'uns on the CCTV who were lurking around the shop before.'

'Wrong 'uns?'

'A group of middle-aged white men who were already two cans deep, at least.' Ash didn't look up from her notebook. 'We're trying to find them, but the chance of them being able to talk, let alone remember anything...'

McIntyre chuckled.

'Something funny, Constable?'

'Nope, *Sarge.*'

Struan stepped forward. 'Let me remind you, son. A man's been driven into by a car. That's not something I find funny. Do you?'

'Come on. What she said was funny.'

'I get it. Drunk old men. Ha ha.' Struan focused on her. 'But no more jokes, okay?'

'Sure thing, *Sarge.*' McIntyre pointed above Struan's head. 'We've spoken to eight eyewitnesses on the street or in the flats above the ground-floor shops. They didn't narrow it down to any particular model.'

'It was a BMW.'

'You're very sure of that.'

'I know my cars. It's a BMW 520 M5. Navy or black. Early nineties. J to P plates.'

McIntyre smirked. 'An old banger?'

'A classic. And it's clear as day on the feed inside the shop.'

McIntyre scribbled something down. 'Okay, we'll look into ownership of something like that.'

'Good work. What was it?'

'Eh?'

'What was the car?'

'A BMW... Eh, 5-series? Nineties?'

'520 M5 model. And I need you to identify any driving around the town. Not that there'll be many.'

Ash looked away, nibbling at her bottom lip.

'Something you want to say there?'

She glanced at McIntyre then stared hard at Struan. 'DS Siyal used to talk about investigative tunnel vision, where we narrow things too quickly.'

That old chestnut. 'Sure, I'm aware of that kind of thing. Trouble is, I'm not a fan of Saint Jude.'

She frowned. 'What's a Beatles song got to—'

'*Saint* Jude, not 'Hey Jude'.'

'I don't follow?'

'Saint Jude is the patron saint of lost causes. I don't want us wasting our time on something we already know.'

'But do we? You've just come in and—'

'Constable. I've told you to park it. Forensics are analysing the video from inside the store to prove my assertion. You don't need to work on that as well. Am I making myself clear?'

She looked away, shaking her head slightly. 'Sure thing, aye.'

Struan gave them a few seconds to process it. 'Now, like I said, I want you two to find this car using CCTV.'

Ash shot him daggers. 'We can't just conjure it up, though.'

Jesus, she was a lazy sod, wasn't she? 'Paton, I don't expect miracles but I do expect hard work and an "aye, Sarge". Okay?'

She folded her arms. 'If you insist.'

'I do.' Struan pointed at the kebab shop across the road

from the hardware store. 'Please tell me someone's been in there?'

Ash nodded.

'Good. Because that strikes me as the perfect place to get CCTV from. Opposite where the attack took place, and it's a takeaway. Any drunk going in there and causing post-pub mischief, they'll want evidence so they'll have a decent security system.'

'Chain of them across the Borders, Sarge. Spoke to the owner on the phone and he sent his nephew out. Issue with it, though, is the tape's warped.'

'*Tape?*'

'What can I say? It's an old-school operation. The security system was decent in about 1993.'

Bollocks.

The flip side of the image they had, and they wouldn't see it. 'Have you got forensics to look at it? There are people in Edinburgh and Glasgow who can unwarp tape.'

'Not this one. It's buggered. Snapped three months ago.'

'Peachy.' Struan focused on McIntyre. 'Jim, have you got any ideas on how we might get plates for this car?'

McIntyre tugged at his ear. 'I've asked uniform to scour the area looking for those Ring cameras. You know, video doorbells? Had some joy on a recent case with that.'

'Good work.' Struan stared at Ash. 'That's what I want to hear. Initiative. Ingenuity. Innovation. We can hopefully get something from that.' He shifted his gaze between them. He wasn't getting a warm, fuzzy feeling from them about this. 'Let's look at this strategically. Whoever did this either drove that car into the town this morning, or it's been here for longer.' He waved back down the street. 'I counted over forty shops on my way here, but I'd expect more than five of them to have cameras. So, can you two split up and get into each of them?'

'Sure thing, Sarge.'

'Peachy. Next, Kelso has seven or so main roads in. None of them major, but I'm guessing the A698 at least has good camera coverage. The A699 and 6089 are probable too. Start with this morning. In the absence of plates, flag any old BMWs in either colour. Get a list of them, then we go and speak to the owners. Those owners will or will not have alibis. They also will or will not have front-end damage. The ones that feature person-sized damage to the bonnet go to the top of the list. This isn't difficult, kids. Lean in and try harder, mmm-kay?'

'Mmm-kay, Sarge.' Ash rolled her eyes. 'Sounds like one for Saint Jude.'

'Nope.' Struan looked between them. 'Cheer up, this is a good thing. We're not looking for a Fiesta, Focus, Corsa, Astra or Golf, which are the most popular cars. The vehicle that did this is a pretty specialist one. Someone's looked after it for the best part of thirty years. There won't be many on the road still, so I'd expect it to be the only one this side of Edinburgh. If we don't find it this morning, we go back a day and we keep going back in twelve-hour chunks until we do find it.'

Ash huffed out a monstrous sigh. 'Are you serious?'

'I'm serious. This is going to take a lot of effort. We need eyeballs on screens. But if we get a plate, we get a name. And then we have a suspect.'

Ash had her tongue stuck in her cheek. 'Sarge, with all due respect, I think this is a waste of time.'

Oh, he had a live one...

Struan smiled at McIntyre. 'Can you get an update from uniform on the doorbell cameras, please?'

McIntyre didn't look like he wanted to leave his partner's

side, but he relented. 'Sure thing.' He trudged off, stopping to look back.

Struan scribbled something in his notebook, making sure he dated and timed it perfectly. He looked up in time to see McIntyre turning the corner, then stepped in close to Ash. Still a few people around, so he kept his voice low. 'This isn't a waste of time. This is basic police work.'

'And who do you expect is going to do this donkey work?'

'Thanks for volunteering, Ashley...' People who shortened their names just *loved* it when people used the full versions. 'Got a simple question for you. How many murder cases have you worked?'

Her forehead creased. 'One.'

'One?'

She shrugged. 'But it was multiple homicides.'

'Okay. Sure. And you were fairly junior, I'm guessing.'

'First week as a detective.'

'Right. Well, I've been a cop for ten years. And I've been a detective for five. Worked all over Scotland. Some huge cases in Edinburgh, Glasgow and Inverness. I have vast amounts of experience on this and I'm on track for DI. Now, if you want to go places, Constable, or you just want to do your job, you'd be well advised to listen to what I tell you to do.'

'But I don't think—'

'I honestly don't care what you think. I'm here to do a job and if you're not, then I'll ship you back to uniform as soon as you can put on those clumpy boots of yours.'

'What's that supposed to mean?'

'I'm not here to fuck about. If you are, then you won't last long with me.'

'I'm just saying I—'

'I don't care. Listen, you want to dress like a man and

pretend to be one, then don't be surprised when someone treats you like one.'

Her mouth hung open. 'What the fuck?'

'I'm serious. All this woke bullshit isn't going to help you if you're a bad cop. Now, you do your job well, then you'll get all of the thanks from me. You fuck about, and I'll fuck you so hard you won't know which gender you are.'

'This is transphobic!'

He lowered his voice. 'Are you trans?'

'No, but—'

'So how can it be?' Struan smiled at her with a snarl in his eyes, then tapped his notebook. 'I've already made notes that you refused to do the CCTV search. DC McIntyre witnessed it. So anything you say against me now is going to look like retribution.'

Her mouth hung open even further now.

'Now, you go and be a good little non-binary person by buggering off back to Gala to get hold of the CCTV for me. And run an offline search on the BMW models and registrations that I explained.'

'Fuck's sake.' She turned around and stormed off.

That put her in her place and kept Big Jim onside. Result.

CHAPTER FOURTEEN
ELLIOT

Elliot trudged through the Accident and Emergency waiting area, a hub of controlled chaos, her shoes squeaking on the sterile sheet vinyl flooring. Anxiety and hope played a tug-of-war on the faces of family members or friends, lit by the harsh fluorescence. She moved into a corridor where a vending machine hummed next to a pair of blue plastic chairs which bore two poor bastards. One desperate, one bored. Both looked up at her, but quickly away.

Elliot stopped in the entrance to A&E and looked around at the beds lined up like soldiers on drill. Some patients found reprieve in slumber, others wore masks of stoicism and some hid behind curtains.

The man with a limp finally deciding to head to hospital after a torrid morning at work.

The woman with the burn on her forearm in the shape of an iron.

Two nurses weaved through the crowd with practised ease, while a doctor walked with an air of strained calm. Screens blinked, machines beeped. Through it all, the bitter tang of antiseptic hung heavy, almost masking the stench. Sweat, body odour, body waste, blood, vomit, alcohol – the perfume of the modern A&E.

Her phone rang.

DCI Ryan Gashkori calling...

Him again. She flicked the ringer off and put it away, letting it silently go through to voicemail.

'Inspector.' A chunky man looked over at her. Tweed suit, black polo neck and brown winkle-pickers. Cauliflower ears like dustbin lids. He held out a hand. 'Callum Hume.'

Elliot shook it, narrowing her eyes at him. 'Nice to meet you.'

'Pleasure's all mine, I assure you.'

'Andrea?' She spotted the navy uniform of the senior charge nurse. Hair scraped back, that sharp face the opposite of her supposed twin brother's round one. Jennifer Marshall – Elliot still hadn't discounted the possibility they were lovers. Probably had done *something*, hadn't they?

'The answer's no.' Jen put a hand on her hip. 'Now what's the question?'

Elliot laughed at it. 'Come on, Jennifer. You must know why I'm here.'

'Gary Hislop, right?' Her gaze gave her away, shifting to the right. One of the curtains over there hid him. 'You can't—'

'He's in there, right?'

'Andrea, you can't just barge in here and interview someone who's been run over.'

'Jennifer, Jennifer, Jennifer. You and I go back a long way. And I just received a call from his associate here.' Elliot thumbed to the side where Callum Hume was nodding along.

Jennifer rolled her eyes. 'I don't make the rules.'

'You're a senior charge nurse. You kind of do.'

'No, I make sure everyone else follows them.'

'Meaning to say I've just wasted a drive over from Kelso?'

'Not my fault.' Jen sighed. 'I need you to both clear off. Okay?' She shifted her glare between them, then scuttled away.

Hume let out a deep breath. 'She's been like that since I got here.'

'She's always like that. Give some people a whiff of power and it goes to their heads like champers on an empty stomach.' Elliot inspected him. Every inch the country toff. 'Guessing I've wasted my time getting here?'

'Nope.' Callum licked his lips. 'Mr Hislop is refusing treatment unless he speaks to you.'

'Seriously?'

'People always say that when they know it's true. Indeed.'

'But Jennifer isn't going to let me in?'

'Oh, don't worry about her. I'll hold her for you.' He inspected his chunk watch. 'But you've only got a couple of minutes as he's due to head to theatre in five.'

'Won't need anywhere near that long.' The curtain swished as Elliot pushed it aside. The room was bleak – bare walls, save for the faint outlines of tape residue from old notices. The single window was painted in streaks of rain, offering a dismal view of the car park.

The room smelled of disinfectant as though Hislop had already died and they were dealing with the clean-up.

A nest of wires and tubes sprouted from him. The steady beep of the heart monitor kept tempo with the room's heavy silence.

She read the chart. Broken femur, head injury, internal bleeding.

Translation – fucked.

Not to channel Marshall too much, but she tried to think it all through...

The front of the car would've hit him about knee- or thigh-level, depending on his height and the car's. Likely breaking his femur or nearly amputating his lower leg.

That would've knocked his head down onto the bonnet, then flipped him up and over the car.

He would've come down hard on his pelvis when he hit the ground. Lucky – if he'd landed on the shop's display it would've given him internal injuries.

Hislop lay still beneath the sterile white sheet. His face was a patchwork quilt of cuts and scratches, the blood still fresh. Whatever painkiller they had him on, it was working. Empty and still, interrupted only by a sporadic twitch.

Alive, but only just.

A table stood guard beside the bed.

Elliot glanced at the chart hanging at the foot of the bed. Notes, scribbled in haste, tracing the path of Hislop's survival. Tests run, medicines administered, vitals noted. Confirmation of his pending surgery.

She stood over the body, grappling with the reminder of human fragility. Every breath Hislop took, every beat of his heart seemed like it might be his last.

She could smother him with a pillow.

Stop his heart.

Stop his breathing.

Stop the misery he inflicted on people.

Stop the misery he inflicted on her and her family.

Her career and freedom would be a small price to pay.

His left eye opened. 'Andi. You came.'

'Aye.' Elliot took the seat next to the bed. 'You look like shite, Gary.'

'Feel worse.' He laughed, but it was a splutter. 'How's the wine?'

'The wine?'

'The stuff... You... I think...' He coughed, weak and thin. 'Someone left it in your car.'

'That stuff's all gone.'

He shut his eyes again. 'That good, eh?'

'Something like that.'

'How's Sam doing?'

The word speared her heart. 'Who?'

'Your kid. Are they still non-binary?'

'Right. I don't think that's going to change anytime soon.'

'Good. Good. Listen. I need to... Got surgery. But. First. I need you. To catch the cunt who did this to me.'

'Why me?'

'Because I can trust you, Andi. We go way back. Can still... Remember how you kiss. And I've been helping you... Info from the boys... at the rugby club.'

'Sure. And those boys tend to disappear when we speak to them.'

'They're flighty. What can I say.'

'We're doing our best, Gary, but it's not easy.'

'Andi.' He gripped her hand, tight. 'I saw who it was.'

CHAPTER FIFTEEN
MARSHALL

Marshall parked outside Gala nick and let the engine die. The car park was mostly empty – typical, given the team were all over in Kelso. Or should be.

They'd spent the best part of a year upgrading part of the station, but he couldn't tell any difference from the outside – the usual sixties brutalist mess, like a giant concrete hedgehog.

He got out into the thin rain and checked his phone as he trudged over to the entrance. Nothing from anybody. Not necessarily a good sign, mind. He stepped into the entrance and there was still no sign of any change, just the same jaded paint job and threadbare carpet that bore a million stains.

Davie Elliot was hidden behind a partition. He yawned into his fist and blinked hard a few times, then focused on Marshall. 'Ah, Rob. Good to see you, mate.'

'And you. So you've moved here from Melrose too?'

'Aye, aye. Turns out I'm now under the MIT cost code so they gave me no say in the matter. Well, I could resign but I like the job.' Another deep yawn. 'Jings, that's not fun.'

'You okay there?'

'Just been a hell of a morning, Rob. I was at the dentist first thing after school run. Should've pushed it back but you know what NHS appointments are like. Two fillings, eh? Then I get here and the new security system is banjaxed.'

'So there's no security?'

'Complete opposite. There's too bloody much! Everybody's locked out, except for Shunty, for some reason. And he's not even here anymore. He handed me his pass on his last day and luckily I hadn't got around to destroying it yet. So I've cloned his old one twenty times.' He slid a card under the glass. 'For today, you're all Shunty.'

Marshall took it with a sigh. 'Doesn't feel like a good system.'

'It's not. And it'll get worse when you lot all come back from Kelso.' He yawned again. 'I'll hopefully get it all sorted this afternoon. Got the boy coming out later, but he was a bit foxed when I spoke to him on the blower.'

'Good luck with it, Davie.' Marshall used the cloned card to swipe through and stepped into the new office.

The big room reeked of fresh paint. Beige. *Why do they always pick beige? Who is the miserable sod who thinks every office should be beige?* Still looked like it needed another coat or two to cover over the industrial blue gloss leaking through. Enough space for twenty officers, not that they'd ever need that many. The new lab sat at the far end, and the three offices lined the side, one each for him, Elliot and Pringle.

Hard to see where the time went or the money, but the incident room was over the other side of the station. The design was the product of a broken mind.

Pringle's.

Marshall hurried over to his own office and closed the

door. Getting out from under Elliot's feet and spreading out in his own space without her charging in...

It was going to be bliss.

Only one of his whiteboards was up, the other three perched against the wall.

Hopefully someone would be able to install those, otherwise Marshall was going to have to get back into his storage unit or buy a third power drill.

He dumped his bag on the desk and prodded the laptop. Then again. And again. Sodding hell – the battery was dead. He'd need to wire it all up to both monitors to get anything done.

Brilliant.

He sat down in the chair and it rocked back. Almost tumbled over.

A knock on the door. Elliot, grinning at him. 'You okay there, Robbie?'

He engaged the locking mechanism and the chair seemed like it wasn't going to eat him now. 'Fine, aye.'

'Good.' Elliot walked over and perched on the edge of his desk. Sitting far too close to him, but she wasn't a stranger to overfamiliarity. 'Thanks for meeting me here. Wanted to run this whole scenario past you.'

'Mind if I eat while we do this?'

'Only if you didn't get me anything.'

Marshall pulled both sandwiches out of the bag. 'As if I'd be so selfish.' Great – he was going to get hungry later from having only one for lunch, but hey ho – otherwise, the abuse would be intolerable. 'Take your pick.'

'Prawn and avocado?' She tore open the packet and bit into the wholemeal bread. 'Mmmf. Lovely. My favourite.'

Leaving Marshall with the coronation chicken. Felt like a

partial victory, but the other sandwich was for health reasons. 'What's so important we needed to do it in person?'

'Mmmf, so good.' She wiped at her lips. 'Okay, so... I went to the hospital and spoke to Hislop.'

Marshall almost dropped his sandwich. 'He's *alive*?'

'Still hanging on there. And he—'

Someone knocked on the door.

Detective Inspector Keith McKenzie stood there. Just over six feet tall and broad-shouldered. A salt-and-pepper beard covered his jaw. His close-cropped hair, once jet-black, was now all silver. And he wasn't even forty. 'Sorry, I was looking for two DIs, but I seem to be in the canteen.'

'Aye, very funny.' Elliot clicked her fingers at the door. 'Can you fuck off and come back later?'

McKenzie smirked then stepped aside.

DCI Ryan Gashkori walked through the door and tossed car keys towards McKenzie. 'Steve, can you head out to Kelso and see what's what?'

'Sure, boss.' McKenzie scowled, disappointment etched on his face. That, or he was hungry. Either way, he marched off out of the office with a face like a weekend in Hawick.

Gashkori watched him go, then looked over at Elliot. 'Good afternoon, Andrea.'

'And yourself, Ryan.'

'Wee word of advice, though. That kind of language isn't exactly friendly, is it?'

'What? Telling that clown to fuck off?' Elliot smiled at him. 'You can fuck off, as well.'

Gashkori laughed, then nodded at Marshall. 'Sharing an office with her must've been like sharing a cell with Big Morris and his swastika tattoos.'

Elliot put her sandwich down. 'I'm not *that* bad.'

'It's Big Morris I've got sympathy with.'

Elliot finished chewing her sandwich. 'So what brings you and Frankenstein's monster down here?'

'Those nicknames...' Gashkori grabbed a chair and sat between them. 'Got a call from my boss about an hour ago. Turns out he'd just received a call from your boss not long before that, concerning the small matter of one Gary Hislop being assaulted by a car.'

Elliot swallowed down some of her sandwich. 'Was going to give you a bell, Ryan.'

'I hope you've got a good excuse brewing.'

'Been a bit busy. You know what life as a DCI is like.'

'I do.' Gashkori held her gaze. 'But you're a DI, Andi.'

She smiled, but it didn't touch her eyes. 'We've got a fair amount of investigative work to do, so if you could let us get on with it, I'll give you an update when I get a minute.'

'Gather Pringle's off sick?'

'That's right.' Elliot gestured at Marshall. 'We agreed amongst ourselves that I'd be the SIO until further notice.'

'So I hear. Trouble is, that's not really your decision to make.'

'What do you mean? Robbie and I thought it best.'

Marshall chewed his sandwich much more slowly than usual – no way was he getting involved in this.

'But it's good you made a decision. Nothing worse than an investigation without a chief, right?' Gashkori stretched out in the chair and folded his arms. 'Thing is, the powers that be decided I'm standing in for DCI Pringle.'

Elliot seemed to deflate like a pricked balloon. Marshall was ready to catch her if she flew around the room. 'On whose authority?'

'You know whose. Check your emails, Andi.'

'I will.' Elliot unlocked it and stared at the screen, then chucked her phone on the desk with a clatter. She looked at

Marshall and, where he'd expect her to show fight, she just seemed resigned to it. 'So, what's the instruction here, big man?'

Gashkori raised his hands. 'Look, just because you're not the self-appointed Acting DCI anymore, doesn't mean you won't be leading this investigation. Okay? I'm here because of my experience with the drugs case against Hislop. That, and six years as DS in what came before the MITs. I know what to do and how to do it.' He held up a finger. 'But I'm going to take a back seat while I get up to speed with the case and the area. After all, you're the experts on both scores.'

'Okay, you've buttered us up even better than this sandwich.' Elliot threw the second half of her lunch on the table. The top half bounced off, revealing the prawn and avocado mush. 'What do you want us to do?'

'Like I said, you keep doing what you're doing and I'll get myself up to speed. Do what you do best, Andi, and follow leads until the end.'

'Funny you mention that, because I was telling Robbie here...' She frowned. 'Do you two know each other?'

Marshall was about to start on the second wedge of sandwich. He nodded. 'We had some dealings last summer when you were off.'

'Right, aye.' Elliot put a hand to her stomach. 'As I was saying, we—'

Another knock on the door. This time it was Struan Liddell. 'Oh, look who the cat dragged in.' He held out a hand and got a tight grip from Gashkori. Like they went back a long way and had a deep friendship. Interesting. 'What are you doing here, boss?'

'Was going to ask the same of you, Struan, but then I remembered you drew the short straw and took a position down here.'

'Not a bad thing, actually.' Struan shifted his paperwork from one hand to the other. 'The old dear's moved into a home, so this is giving me a chance to come back and make sure the old man's settled in. Needs a lot of support, as I'm sure you can understand.'

Gashkori puffed out his cheeks. 'Sorry to hear that, Struan.'

'Ach, it's been on the cards for a while, eh? COPD from smoking more than Grangemouth refinery. He doesn't need full-time monitoring, but he does need checking in on daily. Meals, bathing, giving verbal abuse. So me being stuck a couple of hours away in Glasgow wasn't any use to anyone.'

Gashkori flashed a smile, then drew a finger circle around Marshall and Elliot. 'Anyway, we need to have a chat, so if you could...' He beckoned Struan away.

Struan took no heed of it. 'You're going to want to hear this.' He laid out some prints on the table. 'At DI Marshall's request, my team have been through a good chunk of the CCTV from inside the shop. We're trying to identify most of the customers, but there's one we know.' He slid over a page.

Elliot, standing at the till and being served by Gary Hislop himself.

She tore the sheet out of his grasp. 'I was buying screws so Davie could fix the garden bench!'

Gashkori raised an eyebrow. 'And you've got a receipt for this transaction?'

Elliot went into her purse and pulled out a wad of papers. 'Sainsbury's. Esso. Ashworth's. There.' She slapped it down. 'Ten five-mil screws. Paid by card. Happy?'

'Ish.' Struan looked around the room. 'What's your take, guys?'

'We'll have a chat.' Gashkori smiled. 'Thanks for this.'

'Peachy.' But he wasn't going anywhere.

Gashkori raised his eyebrows. 'I gather you're in charge of tracking down the car used to assault him?'

'That's correct, boss.'

'Okay, well, we won't keep you.'

'I'll, eh, I'll bugger off and get on with it, then.' Struan left them with that same swagger.

Gashkori watched him go with narrowing eyes, then looked at Elliot. 'I'm going to ask what you were actually up to there. And I want the truth.'

'Actually getting screws.'

'You visited a shop that was under surveillance for an operation you were party to so you could *buy screws?*'

'That bench is a nightmare, Ryan. It's rotten and the arm fell off at the weekend. Davie doesn't want to get a new one, so asked if I could pick up some screws on the way home. Didn't expect Hislop to be there.'

'From Kelso, though. Not Gala.'

'Exactly. If it was in Gala, I'd have gone to ScrewFix or B&Q to avoid him. I'd been in Kelso to speak to the uniformed clown who was investigating the disappearance of yet another boy from the rugby club. Leaning on him to make sure he actually did what he was supposed to.'

Gashkori glanced at Marshall, then shook his head. 'The bit I'm struggling with is that you do this—' He tapped the page. 'Then a covert intelligence source of ours mysteriously foxtrots oscar overnight?'

'I swear it's a co-inkydink.'

'Come on, Andi...' Gashkori looked at Marshall. 'You believe this is just a coincidence?'

Marshall raised his hands. 'I don't know enough about the situation to have an opinion.' And he knew he was smart enough not to voice it if he did. He took a big bite of his sandwich and chewed even more slowly.

Truth was, he wasn't buying her story, but he had no reason to believe she was up to anything. Certainly nothing more than usual.

They all knew about her ongoing relationship with Hislop, about how he'd dropped her nuggets of information. Some useful, some trivial.

'Andi.' Gashkori clicked his tongue a few times. 'You've been the one raising the possibility of us having leaks on this case. It all stacks up, but if it's you who's—'

'Me?' She shot to her feet. 'Of course it's not me! I *honestly* just went in to get some screws!'

'Not to see if Hislop would drop any more info?'

She gasped. 'When I saw him there, I panicked a bit. But he'd seen me so we had a little chat.'

'And did he drop anything?'

'Of course not. We just talked about the weather.'

'Come on.'

'I'm serious. Man like that, he does so much small talk he's like an amateur meteorologist. And he had staff in there. It's all in my notes – I logged the encounter as per policy.'

Marshall bit another chunk of sandwich, but he was running out. Sooner or later he was going to have to opine on this.

Gashkori got up and walked around the office, bending down to inspect the unopened whiteboards. 'Andi, all the intel you've obtained from Hislop over the last few months means I've become suspicious. Makes me wonder why he's talking to you. Why he's telling you stuff.' He got up again. 'Makes me wonder what you're telling him in return.'

'Ryan, I've not hidden anything from anyone. Gary's an old school friend. He gives me tips from time to time. It's all catalogued. Pringle knew. Marshall knows.'

Gashkori shifted his focus to him. 'Rob?'

Marshall finished chewing his sandwich. No more bread to cover up. 'She's run that part past me. So I do believe her.'

'But?'

'But I haven't been party to any of the discussions, so I've no idea if she's passed on my inside leg measurement or details of the case against him.'

Gashkori ran a hand through his hair. 'Okay. Let's park this for now. I'll believe you now, Andi, but the second I find out you've been lying...'

'I'm not.'

'Good. Keep it that way. Now, I want to focus on this case. Is that okay? What have you got?'

Marshall sat back. 'We're running low on leads, to be perfectly honest. DI Elliot was just going to update me on the one she unearthed.'

She shot him daggers, then retook her perch on the edge of the desk. 'Me and Robbie here were about to discuss Hislop. I spoke to him in hospital.'

'You... Right.' Gashkori laughed. 'I just told you to stop lying.'

'It is the truth!'

Gashkori raised his hands again. 'You spoke to him. What did he say?'

'Don't think anything of it, Ryan. Please. His flunky called me. Told me he wanted to speak to me. So I did.' She sighed. 'He reckons it was Pringle.'

The words were a punch in the stomach. Marshall couldn't process it. Didn't know where to even start. 'Pringle ran over Hislop?'

Gashkori raised a hand. 'Let me get this straight. Hislop told you he saw Jim Pringle run him over?'

'That's what he said, aye.'

'I don't...' Gashkori rubbed his forehead. 'Do you believe him?'

'I do, actually. And Robbie will back me up on this – Pringle's been more odd than usual for a few months now. You know him, all those whistles and stupid phrases. It's how he establishes rapport. He's a character. A bit odd. But he's been increasingly erratic. Getting weirder and weirder. And angry. Like he's confused? The last big case we had, in January, he had a right go at me. Painful as it is to admit it, I almost clobbered him, to be honest with you.' She thumbed at Marshall. 'Robbie here stopped me. And it sounds like he just finally cracked this morning. Reason you're here, Ryan, is he started shouting about cabbages in an interview.'

'Worse than I thought.' Gashkori sat there, shaking his head. Wincing. 'Rob, what's your take on this?'

'It's a bit... I...' Marshall walked over to the bin and dropped his sandwich packet in. 'I agree with half of that. He's been getting increasingly odder and more erratic. And sloppy too. A few paperwork things going all weird. Some odd recruitment decisions. And... Well, he can't remember how he got to Edinburgh this morning.'

'He what?'

'Thinks it was the train, but...'

Gashkori ran a hand over his forehead. 'So you're telling me he could've run Hislop over and got the train up afterwards?'

'Right. But I don't get why he'd attack Hislop.'

Elliot shrugged. 'Because Hislop's responsible for all of the drugs in the area he's originally from and that he now manages. Lots of deaths on his head, but Hislop's very slippery. Try as hard as we can, we've never got hold of him. Have we?'

Gashkori looked away, like it was a personal assault on him. 'That's a bit thin for a motive, Andi. Surely you can do better?'

'There was that DI in Edinburgh who started killing people a few years ago. It does happen.'

'Okay. So what evidence have we got?'

'That's the prob—'

The door clattered open and Struan stormed back in. 'Sorry about this, but you'll all want to hear this.'

Gashkori shifted his scowl into a smile. 'Go on.'

'You asked about the cars? Well, my team have been sifting through the CCTV across Kelso to get a list of BMWs driving around the town. No plates from witness statements and there's a lot of footage to narrow down. Also, there's no guarantee our guy is one of them.'

Gashkori nodded. 'Caveats accepted. Please, get on with it.'

'Okay, we know it's an older model from the video inside the shop. To my trained eyes, it's a classic 520 M5 model.'

'You've found it?'

'Ish.' Struan grimaced. 'Absolutely typical that we've got two mad lads driving them. One black, one navy.'

Gashkori clicked his teeth a few times. 'Can't we eliminate one using the CCTV?'

'That's the problem. The footage is greyscale. It can record in colour, but it takes up much more space than greyscale. Anyway. We'd be okay with black and silver, say, but black and navy are tonally identical.' He handed out a sheet of paper with a short laugh. 'Took *ages* to get the printer online. New office blues, eh? No easy way to say this, but one of the flagged cars is...' He winced. 'It belongs to DCI James Pringle.'

Marshall looked over at Gashkori and saw a flash of confusion turn into rage. He'd picked up a cop's worst nightmare – thrown into a case where the previous SIO was now his prime suspect. Forget about hearsay from the victim, this was hard evidence.

Marshall looked at Struan. 'Who owns the other car?'

'Belongs to someone called Balfour Rattray.'

Marshall groaned.

Gashkori raised his eyebrows. 'You know him?'

'Went to school together.'

'Ah, okay.' Gashkori looked around the room and tapped at the page. 'Thoughts?'

Marshall couldn't see any other way but through. 'It's now looking like we've got a credible investigation against a serving officer. So we might want to consider bringing in Professional Standards & Ethics to run that part of it.'

'You honestly want to get the torches and pitchforks out?'

'No, but we should give them the heads-up.'

'Okay, I understand the temptation to bring in the Rat Pack but...' Gashkori folded the page and pocketed it. 'On that basis, I'd have to bring them in to investigate Andi's screw purchase. So, I kind of agree, but not yet. First, I want to establish some further evidence.'

Struan scowled. 'Isn't that enough?'

'It's a start. But you said you've got two cars. Call me old-fashioned but a case held together by the whims of a supposed drug lord isn't going to make me move against an experienced officer. Get me hard evidence, then we can call in the Rat Pack.'

Made sense to Marshall.

Meant Gashkori could keep the entire case in his court and not run the risk of losing it to the Complaints. 'Sure thing.'

'Grab your coat, Rob, because you're going to talk to the man before we give any credence to the myth.'

CHAPTER SIXTEEN
ELLIOT

Struan was up ahead in the pool Audi, streaming down the long drive.

Elliot followed down the road leading up to Blainslieshaw Mains farm. Last time she'd been here had been a few months back, in the depths of winter. Snow everywhere. Now it was a damp April and life was springing up everywhere – the woods on both sides were still bare, but snowdrops and bluebells carpeted the ground.

The massive mansion house was big enough for three generations of family plus servants. As far as Elliot knew, there were only two people living there.

She pulled up on the gravel and got out into the drizzle and the scent of sawdust mixing with spent diesel.

Struan was already out, tucking his collar up like that would shield him against the rain. 'Feels a bit odd that you don't want to share a car with me.'

She'd been over this...

'Struan, your team's in Gala where you should be. But we're here, doing this because his nibs demanded it. I'll head to Kelso after this so I can break skulls, while you can head back to base to do likewise.'

'Peachy.' He sniffed. 'Warning you now, boss. Early impressions of those two aren't too good.'

'Paton and McIntyre?'

'Aye. We'll have words at some point, you and I.'

'Not in the door a day and you're wanting to sack the team. I like it.' Elliot hurried over to the front door. It was hanging open, so she called inside: 'Hello?'

Her voice echoed around the plush interior.

Struan waved up at the house. 'You know this guy?'

'I do, aye. Family owns the land here for miles around.'

'Mind if I ask why DI Marshall isn't doing this?

'Would you rather be speaking to Pringle?'

'If he's tried to kill Hislop, like you say, then of course I would.'

Glory hunter.

'Struan, the reason it's us and not Robbie and Jolene is Marshall went to school with Balfour. Best to put a Chinese wall around these things.'

Struan frowned. 'You mean firewall?'

'Aye, something like that.'

'Okay, I get that, but Marshall's worked for Pringle so where's the—'

'Aye, but we all do. There's no issue until it comes time to call in Standards. Marshall drove him back from Edinburgh today. He knows his movements way better than we do. Knows the gaps and where to probe.'

'Fair dos.'

No sign of anyone, so Elliot stepped inside and cupped her hands around her mouth. '*Hellooo?*'

A small boy scurried through. Maybe six or seven. Dressed

in a Spider-Man costume, but his mask was dangling down his back. 'Hello! I'm Toby. Who are you?'

'I'm Andrea.' Elliot crouched down, but the wee lad didn't come closer. Then it clicked who he was – Balfour's nephew, Toby. 'But you better not tell everyone who you are, otherwise the Green Goblin will know who Spider-Man really is.'

Toby pulled his mask over his face. 'With great power comes great responsibility!' He fired his web shooters then scooted off through the house. He slid on the floor and disappeared through a door. The sound of urine hitting water followed.

'Toby, is your uncle around?'

'My other granny is!'

Elliot crept along the giant hallway but didn't want to stand under that hulking chandelier – if it fell, it'd probably put a huge dent in the Earth's crust.

Rhona Rattray hurried through from a side door, wearing an apron dusted with flour. 'Hi.' She gave them both a good visual going-over. 'DI Elliot, isn't it?'

'That's correct.' Elliot's gaze lingered too long on Toby, racing out of the toilet.

'This is my grandson.' Sadness filled Rhona's eyes.

'He's looking well.' Elliot motioned to her side. 'This is DS Struan Liddell.'

'Oh, that's a very local name.'

'Very local person too.' Struan grinned at her. 'We're actually looking for Balfour. He about?'

'Come on, you. The scones are almost ready to go in the oven.' Rhona patted Toby on the back. 'My son's in his garage.'

Oh shite.

'Thanks, we know where that is.'

Elliot slipped back out into the rain and crunched across the pebbles, passing the end of the building. Almost running.

Struan had to jog to catch up. 'Am I missing something here?'

'Long story. As Marshall would say.' Elliot needed to fill in the blanks. 'Last time we came here, Balfour was trying to kill himself in a garage full of petrol fumes. Marshall managed to save him.'

'Jesus!'

'Aye. I mean, it's unlikely but...'

The old garage had been spruced up. The scarred brick was now painted with cream stucco. The vertical door was hanging slightly open. A pair of feet stuck out from underneath. A car engine rumbled.

'Shite!'

Balfour was doing it again!

Elliot raced over and hauled up the door.

Balfour wheeled himself out from underneath a black BMW, his face grimy like he'd just been down a mine. He said something but Elliot didn't catch it.

Funk music blasted out of a stereo at deafening volume, then the voice of Craig Charles cut in, loud and boomy:

'That was 'Superfly' by Curtis Mayfield and it goes out to Sandra and Geoff in Carnoustie who are sitting in their conservatory with their oldest son, enjoying some nice wine along with a lamb moussaka.'

Balfour got out his phone and killed the music. 'Sorry about that. Can't hear myself think with that on, which is all part of the fun.' He winched himself up with a groan. 'DI Elliot, right?' He held out an oily hand, then laughed. 'Sorry, nobody wants to shake this paw.'

Elliot spotted Struan analysing the vehicle in her peripheral vision. Allowed herself a deep breath. 'How are you doing, Balfour?'

'Hard to say.' He leaned back against the car. 'I mean, I'm

kind of struggling with running the farm solo.' He folded his arms. 'Oh and being investigated for drug crimes I haven't committed is so much fun.'

'If you've nothing to hide, you've nothing to worry about.'

'Wish it were that simple. Lot of time being wasted. Mine and yours.'

Struan held out a hand. 'DS Liddell.'

Balfour held out his oily fingers. 'Still don't think you should be shaking these.'

'True.' Struan put his hands back in his pocket, then cast an admiring glance all over the BMW. 'Nice motor.'

'Inherited it from my father, it's a classic. Some would say something from the eighties can't be a classic, but not me.'

'1993 or '94.'

'Eh?'

Struan pointed at the number plate. 'K-reg. Came in 31st August 1993. Lasted a year back then.'

'You live and learn.'

'Still a classic, though. M5 edition. Three-point-eight litre engine. Three hundred and eleven horsepower output. Bet it can shift?'

'Like a bat out of hell. I know how to fix up the motor, but I don't get much joy from driving. Just trying to repair it to sell it. There's a guy in Kelso interested in it.'

Elliot made a note of that. 'Do you have—'

'This is a *wizard* motor.' Struan ran his hand over the bonnet. 'Mind if I have a look?'

'By all means.' Balfour stepped aside and focused on Elliot. 'Do you still work with Rob Marshall?'

Elliot nodded. 'For my sins.'

'Need you to thank him for me.'

'What for?'

'A million and one things, to be perfectly frank. But...'

Balfour reached into the car and switched off the engine. 'A few months ago, I had the engine running in here just like this. Except I had the hose from the tailpipe into the door of this thing. Taken me a lot of therapy to get over that and I'm still a million miles away from being okay. I was in a bad place. Pretty bleak, to be honest with you. But I think selling this is the best thing to do. It was Father's car, but it doesn't have to be mine, so I'm going to get something uniquely me.' He rubbed at his eye and left a big oily smear under it like he'd suddenly become a new romantic. 'I want to thank Rob for saving my life. It's so full and vivid now. I'm raising my nephew, so there's a bit of a silver lining to the darkest of clouds. Mum's helping a lot, despite... you know...'

Elliot held his gaze. He'd always seemed like a lost soul, hiding his darkness behind smiles and jokes, but there was something new in there. Maybe hope. Or just a pathway towards finding a reason to keep living.

Struan joined them. 'You'll get a decent amount for it, but it needs a lot of attention from a body shop to maximise it.'

'Aye. I mean, I can do the mechanical stuff, but I'm not panel beating anything. Soon as I start knocking it with a hammer, I'll never know when to stop.'

'Happened to me.' Struan pointed at the front left of the car. 'That bit there's the worst. You probably need to get it replaced.' That was the exact spot that would've hit Hislop during the attack. 'Any idea what caused that?'

'Could be anything. Father used to use this car on the farm. Most would use a Range Rover, but nope, not him. Especially if his Range Rover was too far away. And if he had to move something, he'd nudge it with the car. "Cars are just tools, Balf, what's the point of owning a hammer if you're afraid to swing it. An unblemished tool is a sign of vanity or incompetence, blah blah blah". Or something like that.' He shifted his focus between them. 'Anyway. What's this all about?'

Elliot smiled at him. 'Need to know where you were this morning at eight o'clock.'

'Probably in here.'

'Sure about that?'

'Probably.'

'Probably isn't going to cut it.'

'With what?'

'We're working an attempted murder case. Someone was attacked with a car in Kelso.'

'My God. Are they okay?'

'In hospital.'

'Who was it?'

'That's not important, Balf. Where were you?'

'Not sure. I think I was in here. Listening to the radio as I worked on the car.'

'Reason we're here is because we've got this car driving through Kelso at the back of eleven.'

'I did drive it then. But you asked me about eight.'

'So you admit to driving it in Kelso?'

'Of course. Needed to run it through and check it was firing on all cylinders.' Balfour glowered at it. 'It literally wasn't. Had to strip the engine down when I got back. Need to replace a few parts in there.'

Struan frowned. 'Which ones?'

Balfour laughed. 'Like you care.'

'Mr Rattray, this is your chance to correct where you were this morning at eight.'

'Nothing to be corrected. I was here. Listen, if you think I've done something, it's usually better to ask me what it is, so I can help.'

Struan looked at Elliot. She gave him a nod, so he turned

back to Balfour. 'Someone drove a car like this into Gary Hislop at—'

'Hislop?' Balfour sucked breath across his teeth. 'Christ.'

'You know him?'

'It's the Borders. Everyone knows everyone.'

'When did you last see him?'

Balfour exhaled slowly. 'At that Burns Supper in January.'

'Not since.'

'Nope.'

'So you're saying you were definitely here at eight o'clock?'

Balfour took a deep breath. 'Andrea, someone's been fucking with me. Had your chums in the drugs squad poring over every aspect of my business. Most of it I didn't even know. But they found nothing. Because there's nothing to find.'

'So you think someone's setting you up?'

'Right. And I'd say it's Hislop screwing with me.'

'Why would he do that?'

'I don't know. But there was bad blood between him and Father.'

'Any idea what?'

'Father... Napier Rattray to you... It turns out he funded Hislop's business years ago to the tune of two hundred thousand pounds. We only learnt this after his passing and I... I want to collect on the loan. I'm not asking for much, just a fair amount of interest. Father was content to see Hislop succeed. His family had nothing and Father saw it as charity, but as with all good acts of charity, nobody was supposed to know. But the taxman knew, so it had to be covered in the inheritance.'

'You don't see it as a charity?'

'No. I see it as business. And I'm on the hook for a lot of cash because of that transaction, amongst a few others.'

'Do you blame Mr Hislop for what happened to your father?'

'Of course not. That wasn't on him. I wish Hislop no personal malice. Like I told you, I invited him to that Burns Supper. I was trying to bury the hatchet. I certainly wouldn't wish him dead. And I certainly wouldn't try to kill him.'

'So you're sticking to that story.' Struan looked around the garage. 'That you were here, on your own.'

'Let me check.' Balfour got out his phone and stabbed at the screen. 'Okay, breakfast at seven. Then I worked on car repairs.' Then another sigh. 'Oh shit.'

'What?'

'I was away. I went to see Gundog, then came back here.' He put his phone away. 'Sorry, I have a meeting at two so I best shower now.'

Struan pointed at the BMW. 'You drove to Gundog's in that car?'

'It didn't have an engine in at the time, so no. Took my Range Rover.'

Struan laughed. 'Gundog got a name?'

Elliot stepped between them. 'It's okay. I know who he is.' She narrowed her eyes at Balfour. 'You better not be lying to us.'

'I'm not. Look, if you want me to prove it, I'll drive you there myself.'

Struan held out his hand. 'Sure, but give me your phone.'

'My phone?'

'Don't want you calling ahead to fabricate a story now, do we?'

CHAPTER SEVENTEEN
MARSHALL

Jolene was driving through the back streets of Kelso, past housing estates that had been fields in Marshall's living memory. 'Who hired him?'

Marshall looked over at her. 'Struan?'

'Aye, Stringy Widdle.'

'That's his nickname?'

'I've heard it used, aye.'

Marshall chuckled. Working in the police was a revelation – everyone had a nickname. 'I think Pringle hired him. Why, do you know him?'

'Nah.'

'But?'

'But nothing.'

'You just so happen to know his nickname…'

She shrugged. 'Just like to know who I'm working with. So I asked around. Forget I said anything.' She puffed out her cheeks, then pulled up outside Pringle's temporary home. 'Nice place.'

When Marshall dropped him off earlier, he hadn't noticed that Pringle's car wasn't in the drive.

Stupid.

Then again, when your boss starts losing his marbles right in front of you, you don't expect him to have run over a drug lord. You just tried to get him inside and get the kettle on.

But things were starting to click into place.

Elliot and Struan were off speaking to Balfour, but that felt like a red herring. Some weird coincidence that they both happened to drive the same car at the same time in the same town. Minuscule chances, but it happened.

Then again, it wouldn't be the first time people had acted in tandem to throw the scent off an investigation.

'Come on, then.' Marshall got out into the drizzle and walked up to the front door. 'You go first.'

Jolene knocked and stepped back.

The door rattled open. 'Come in.' Pringle strolled off through the house.

Marshall followed Jolene inside with a raised eyebrow.

'Born in a barn, were you?' Pringle was in the designer kitchen, pointing behind Marshall. 'Shut the door!'

Marshall stepped back and nudged it shut. He could've sworn he'd closed it... Then it sprung open in the wind. That explained it. He slammed it hard and it seemed to stay shut. He followed them through into the kitchen.

Polished white marble gleamed in the light streaming in from the panoramic windows, which offered a stunning view of a manicured garden. A wall of stainless steel appliances and glossy cabinets surrounded an island unit, with an induction hob, an array of chef's knives and a bouquet of fresh herbs.

Hardly the domain of a bachelor like Pringle's brother, but the world always threw up surprises.

Pringle fussed around a high-end coffee machine. 'Latte,

latte and—' He clicked his fingers a few times. 'Americano, Jolene?'

'I said I don't want a coffee.'

'Oh, but I insist.' Pringle grinned at them like this was just totally fine and natural. 'I just got a new roast through the mail and it's chef's kiss.' He scowled. 'Are you supposed to just say that or do the action?' He pressed his thumb against two fingers, kissed them, then his hand exploded out. '*Mwa!*'

Marshall felt the edginess burning in his blood.

An Airwave radio sat on the counter. 'Receiving. Units deployed to Kelso. Over.'

Just along the road from here.

Where there was an active police incident.

Pringle switched off the radio. 'It's a latte, Rob, correct?'

'Americano.'

'Ah, that's the way round. Got it.' He shifted his focus to the coffee machine and set the radio down again.

Marshall slipped on a glove and pocketed the Airwave – Kirsten should be able to get some info from that. Proof that he'd been monitoring the investigation, maybe. 'Sir, we don't want a coffee but we could do with some answers.'

'Answers are like questions. Everyone's got them!' Pringle laughed like that made any sense.

Marshall exchanged a look with Jolene. Aye, Pringle was back in cabbages mode. 'Sir, we need to—'

'Can't you see I'm busy here, Paul?'

Paul?

The machine hissed and Pringle set down a third cup. 'There we go.' He carried a tray over to a large wooden table in the corner. 'Pull up a pew, *amigo* and *amiga*.'

Marshall took the seat nearest the door. Not ideal, but it'd stop Pringle if he ran. 'Sir, we need to go over your movements this morning.'

'Go on.'

Marshall frowned. 'Excuse me?'

Pringle motioned towards the cup. 'Try the coffee.'

Marshall picked it up and it was way too hot to drink, so he touched it to his top lip and made a loud slurping noise. 'Oh, that's lovely.'

'Isn't it?' Pringle waited for Jolene to do the same. 'See? When this all goes to shit, I'll open a coffee shop!'

Marshall laughed, but he couldn't see him managing to open a bag of beans let alone a shop. 'So, this morning?'

'This morning?'

'Where were you?'

'Think I'm an idiot?'

'No, sir.'

'I was with you, dummy!'

'Sir, I—'

'Please! Call me Jim.'

'Jim.' The word felt lumpy in Marshall's mouth. 'I dropped you off.'

'Correct. At eighteen minutes past eleven.'

Very precise...

'And after that?'

'Afterwards, I... Must've had a coffee. And...' Pringle stared deep into his coffee cup. 'Listen, I'm sorry, but I can't remember much of the morning.'

'Sir, it's—'

'Jim! Call me Jim!'

'Jim, it's only a few hours.'

'I know, but...'

'Come on, it's important.'

'Why are you asking?'

'Because we need to.'

'You think I'm involved in something?'

Marshall shrugged. 'You're refusing to answer any questions on the matter, so what am I supposed to think?'

'Listen, you *punk*. Here's what I *think* I did. I drove to Gala first thing to go to the new station, then I remembered we were in court, so I hotfooted it up there on the train.'

'You said your brother drove you.'

'My brother? I don't know why I said that. He's in… Nottingham, I think.' Pringle took a long drink of scalding coffee. 'Thing is, I've been obsessing about the office move. I can get a bit of tunnel vision with administrative tasks. And I had a new start today. Struan something or other. My mind's been a bit flaky.'

'Jim, there's no sign of your car in the drive.'

'No.'

'Where is it?'

'I don't know.'

'You didn't know earlier.'

'Okay. But I think it's in Edinburgh.'

'You took the train.'

'Did I? Oh aye. I bombed it to the train station and shot up to Edinburgh. Probably got caught by cameras on the way to Tweedbank station!'

'Your car isn't there.'

'What?'

'We've checked the car park. It's not there. But it's been seen in Kelso. Not Edinburgh. Not Tweedbank.'

'But…' Pringle frowned. Tears streamed down his cheeks. 'Rob, I… I can't remember if that happened today.'

'It's okay, sir.' Marshall held up the Airwave radio. 'Can I ask what you were doing with this?'

'My job.'

'Okay. But you're off sick.'

'I…'

'And there's an active trace on a car matching the description of yours.'

'Rob, I swear I'm just doing my job.'

'Sir, I need to ask you this, I'm afraid. Did you drive your car into Gary Hislop?'

'What? You can't think I could do that!'

'No, I don't want to, but it's starting to look like it might be possible.'

'Rob, I can't remember the last time I saw it!'

'Jim, did you attack Hislop?'

'I... I don't know.'

Marshall was in a difficult situation. This was above his pay grade. Above his rank. And not murder squad activity. 'Okay, sir, I need to bring you in for questioning.'

'You can't question me, Rob.'

'No, but Professional Standards will.'

CHAPTER EIGHTEEN
ELLIOT

A convoy of cars hurtled down the A68, heading towards Newcastle, but their destination was local. Elliot followed Struan, who followed Balfour. She passed Newtown St Boswell's, where Gary Hislop lived...

If he pulled through.

Elliot glanced at her passenger seat, empty save for Balfour's mobile, so he couldn't call ahead and seed the alibi – Struan's idea and a good one.

Aye, Struan was one to keep an eye on. Someone that conniving was going places. Or had the potential to.

This seemed like bullshit, but they wouldn't be doing their jobs if they didn't follow up on this.

For shits and giggles, she could get Kirsten to consult the photos from Balf's suicide attempt and confirm the minor damage was there then.

Or if it wasn't...

Brake lights, so she slowed as they entered St Boswells and the 20 zone that all of the Borders towns and villages shared now. Past the car dealerships, then a left at the old coaching inn into the village itself. The wide green circled by posh houses, narrowing to some businesses and a fancy bookshop she'd taken her kids to many a time.

Balfour pulled into a space outside a gun shop.

Elliot noticed before Struan did and sneaked into the next space.

Struan overshot and had to settle for one across the road.

Elliot got out and waited for Struan to join them.

Balfour stared up at the grey clouds, lost to some darker thoughts.

Next door to the gun shop was Gundog Events, a nondescript office with a boarded-up window advertising 'The best events in southern Scotland'.

Elliot held up Balfour's phone, but didn't return it. 'Let's see how this goes.'

He smiled back at her. 'You're lucky I'm a calm and even-tempered man.'

'You'll be lucky just to be proven an innocent one.' She nodded inside. 'Struan, can you speak to this Gundog character?'

'On it.' Struan strolled up, warrant card out, and knocked on the door.

Elliot stayed back by the cars to keep an eye on Balfour, but also listening to what was going on inside. 'Just stay there and we'll be out of your hair soon, okay?'

'Sure thing.'

Struan thumped on the door. 'Doesn't look like anyone's here?'

Elliot scowled at Balfour. 'You know where he is?'

'Mentioned something about organising a book festival...'

Struan's ringtone blasted out.

'You didn't think to mention that?'

'Sorry.'

Elliot turned around.

Struan was listening intently to his call. 'Okay, thanks.' He marched back. 'Ash Paton has a lead on Pringle's car.'

CHAPTER NINETEEN
STRUAN

Struan hurtled along the slower road to Kelso, but the way he drove, it didn't matter. He slalomed around a bus, avoided an oncoming tractor, then overtook a Fiesta.

They'd all been very cosy in there, hadn't they?

Marshall, Elliot, Gashkori.

All very cosy.

Still, he could hardly complain – day one on the job and he'd been given a chance to get his feet wet in a case. Don't knock it.

The rain got that bit heavier, the roof sounding like it was being hit by machine-gun fire.

His phone blasted out of the stereo:

Unknown caller...

He hit the green button. 'Liddell.'

'Sarge, it's Ash.' Her phone voice was super deep, like a radio DJ. 'Are you driving?'

He crossed to the other side of the Tweed, heading towards Sainsbury's. 'Heading back to the last-known location you just gave me. What's up?'

'I've called in a favour or two and got a live feed of CCTV in Kelso. A BMW matching our description just left the Sainsbury's car park.'

My God – she'd actually pulled out her finger. Some people really responded to a rocket up the arse, didn't they?

'That's great work, Ash. Okay, have you still got eyes on it?'

'Forty seconds ago, it left Kelso along the A699.'

Struan knew it – the road that ran along the south bank of the Tweed towards St Boswells. He rounded the old site of Roxburgh Castle, once the capital of Scotland but now just a ruin. Keeping his eyes open for the BMW.

The Tweed and the Teviot rivers married around the corner, with the latter taking the former's name.

He kept a watch on all the cars heading towards him in the rain – that BMW should be heading his way soon. Two Mitsubishis. A Toyota. A Volvo.

Bingo!

'Got it!'

The BMW sat in the entrance to the Showgrounds or whatever it was called now – he had tickets to see the Proclaimers there in a few months, not that he'd be able to go...

Struan kicked down and used the mouth of the entrance to block it off.

No luck – the driver clocked him and hurtled off, whizzing past him in the downpour.

Aye, that car could shift.

Struan had to pull a three-pointer then bombed along the road, but the pool Audi was struggling. 'Call it in, Ash. I'm on the A699 just by the Showgrounds. Keep an open line, please.'

'Sure thing.'

The phone went silent as he powered on along the road.

'That's it logged, Sarge.'

'Thanks for this, Ash. It's great work.'

'Don't mention it.'

Despite the conditions, the BMW blasted past the Volvo and Struan lost sight of it over the crest of the hill.

Bloody hell, that thing could really shift.

And the pool Audi... couldn't.

'I'm losing him, Ash. Any other cameras on this road?'

'Just checking. There's one at the A68 at St Boswells.'

'The other end of this road. That's too far.'

'Okay. Got it. There's a speed camera about half a mile past the turning for Roxburgh and Nisbet.'

'Pull it up.'

'Got it.'

Struan powered on towards the next left – the BMW could've turned there or headed straight. 'Anything?'

'Nothing, Sarge.'

A couple of hundred metres until the turning. 'Tell me, what are you seeing?'

'A Mitsubishi. Another Mitsubishi. A Toyota.'

The cars he'd seen just by Kelso.

He was closing on the turning.

'A Volvo.'

The BMW had overtaken that, so should've been between them – it must've turned down towards Roxburgh.

No choice – he had to follow it.

'Got it.' Struan yanked the wheel and powered down the single-track road. 'I'm heading towards Roxburgh. Can you divert any squad cars to my location? Anyone in St Boswells, get them following the road.'

'Will do.'

He hurtled along, weaving around the slight bends. Not so

much a rat run as a rat maze around there – he could end up anywhere between Jedburgh and Kelso, maybe further out towards Berwick and Alnwick in Northumbria. He pressed his foot further down on the pedal and tightened his grip around the wheel.

The Audi responded, its engine roaring like the vocalist in a death metal band.

He spotted the dark outline of the BMW ahead. He'd seen what it could do, that balance of luxury and performance that made it a tough match for any pursuer. But from the way the BMW drove, Struan realised he had something the other driver didn't – intimate knowledge of these meandering roads. His childhood playground, now his battleground. And he sure as hell knew them in these conditions.

Liddell throttled it hard, narrowing the gap between them as the BMW closed on a turning.

It snaked left, then right, the tires squealing in protest against the slick roads.

Liddell kept up his pursuit, his focus unwavering, his feet and hands working like a drummer's as he synchronised with the machine and clawed every inch of power out of it.

They raced on, past old stone cottages and grazing sheep bewildered by the roar of engines. Rolling hills loomed in the distance.

The road began to dip as they approached Roxburgh, the quiet village an unwitting spectator to the pursuit.

The Teviot Viaduct began to materialise from the rain, its Victorian arches standing as sentinels over the river it shared a name with.

The road was treacherous in the wet.

Struan prepared himself, the years of experience coiling within him like a spring, and as expected, the BMW veered left towards the village.

The driver was good, but the slick surface was better. He oversteered and the vehicle skidded sideways before smacking into the 30 speed limit sign.

Liddell brought his Audi to a screeching stop a few yards behind, releasing his seatbelt as it slowed, and jumped out into the downpour. He snapped out his baton and marched toward the stalled BMW, his heart pounding in his chest.

Struan hauled open the door.

The driver was drowning in the airbag. The passenger's face was a bloody pulp. He wasn't going anywhere.

A pair of kids, by the looks of it.

Still, kids could run over drug suppliers, couldn't they?

Struan killed the engine, grabbed the keys and pocketed them. He cuffed the driver and hauled him out of the car. Pinned him back against the door. 'Right, you wee bastard. DS Struan Liddell. I'm a police officer. Is this your car?'

'Fuck off, pig.'

Struan grabbed him by the throat. 'Last chance. Is this—'

'Said, fuck o—'

Struan slammed his skull back against the door and let him slide down to the tarmac. He stormed around to the passenger side and grabbed his mate. Kid probably needed to go to hospital, but he needed to provide answers first.

Struan hauled him out and dragged him around to his friend. He pinned him against the side of the car, hauled the other one back up to standing and cuffed them together. 'Okay, you little shits. Whose car—'

His mate had a knife, the blade catching the light as it sliced the air towards him.

Struan punched his forearm and the knife clattered to the ground.

Cheeky little bastard, thinking he could take on Struan and win.

Struan's fists tightened, knuckles white with the force of his rising anger. A surge of heat coursed through his body. The thud of his heartbeat reverberated in his temples, a rhythmic drumbeat matching the growing storm within.

He grabbed their hair and bashed their heads together.

Both screamed.

The driver looked at Struan like he was seeing two of him.

These two muppets had just been in a car crash, so Struan figured nobody would notice a bit more damage.

Fuck it.

Struan cracked their heads together again and watched them go down like two sacks of spuds. He got out his mobile again.

And spotted Elliot getting out of her car.

Shite – how much had she seen?

CHAPTER TWENTY

ELLIOT

Elliot checked her phone again, but there was still nothing from Marshall or Gashkori.

The uniforms pushed the second idiot into the back of the squad car and slammed the door.

Elliot focused on Struan, chatting away to a uniform cop. Be interesting to see what his story was, because she'd just seen him smash the two neds' skulls together.

Pair of bastards might've deserved it, but the world of policing had moved on a lot since the times you could get away with that shite.

She might've been a bit naughty herself in the past, but she'd never painted that far outside the lines. A cop flying solo like that was the last thing she needed. Or anybody did. She wanted convictions to stick, not be smeared in slime and shite.

A quick blast of siren and the ambulance drove off. Only to be blocked off by the forensics van, smeared in dust and crud.

Struan patted the uniform on the arm and strolled over without a care in the world. 'Boss.'

'Call me Andi, please. If it's in an email or a text, use an I not a Y.'

'Sure thing, Andi.' Struan smiled. 'So. We've recovered the car. What's next?'

'Can we have a word?' She stepped away from the throng of officers. 'Did you have a bit of difficulty in detaining the driver?'

'And the passenger, aye.'

'Had to use some extrajudicial methods to detain them?'

'I know what you saw, Andi, but it's all about context, right? There were two of them and one of me. And the passenger had a knife. And if we lost them, we'd never find them again.'

'Good point.' But not enough to break their skulls. 'Are you sure that's the car that attacked Hislop?'

'Why?'

'There were two driving around Kelso today like some kind of old bangers' club. How do we know this is the one that ran over Hislop?'

'This is Pringle's BMW. So we've got a chance to do some forensics. We need to focus and build up a picture of what car was where and when.'

She shut her eyes briefly. This wasn't going as planned.

Kirsten hopped out of the van and walked over to the BMW.

'Right. Struan, can you get those two in an interview when you can? Also, get someone asking in Lidl – see if their story stacks up.' She smirked. 'Liddell in Lidl.'

'Aye, not heard that before. On it, boss.' Struan gave a tight nod and strolled over to his pool Audi.

She was going to leave it at that. Didn't want to press him too hard, too soon.

But she'd seen him hitting them. That needed to come to something.

Still, she'd had over a year of working with Shunty and having someone who got results, who was confident and who could act of his own volition was like water to a man stuck in the desert.

So she could maybe forgive a little bit of extrajudicial violence.

Elliot joined Kirsten by the car. It was Pringle's car, but what the hell did that mean? That he'd done it? That he'd paid the little bastards to do it? That someone saw him as a useful idiot? Or that he'd just lost his marbles?

Kirsten noticed Elliot, but didn't say anything. One of her guys was already inside, dusting away. Hard to see through the crime scene suit, but it looked like the young lad with the mullet. Trev.

Elliot clicked her teeth, loud enough to be really annoying. 'How's it looking?'

'Just got here myself.' Kirsten shrugged. 'But Trev... He's such an arrogant so-and-so that he thinks he'll be able to get something from the interior. I remain sceptical.'

'You think it's worth checking?'

'Why not? Gives you a population of people who have been in the car. One of them did it. Assuming this car did.'

'We're still working on that...'

'One thing Trev's toiling with is... The boot's locked. Won't shift.'

'He can't get in?'

'Nope. The neds who stole it deny any knowledge of it, said they never even tried it, but they look like they've gone ten rounds with Mike Tyson. So who knows...'

Elliot spotted Struan's car hurtling away towards Kelso, the murky figure inside wrapping his seatbelt around his torso.

'Are you going to be able to match paint samples with his clothes?'

'Oh. I didn't think of that.' Kirsten shot her a withering look. 'We got Hislop's clothes from BGH, but a little birdie had already taken them.'

Elliot clamped a hand on her arm. 'Just doing my bit, you know?'

'Mm.'

'They're in your new office.'

'I'll get someone on that, then.'

Trev hopped back out of the car, then took his mask and goggles off. 'Interesting...'

Kirsten raised her head towards him. 'You got something?'

'A ton of something, yeah.' He pointed to the front left of the bonnet. 'There's a dent in the passenger side, which is where we believe Hislop was hit, judging by the video.'

Thank God someone was doing their job.

'Doesn't narrow it down any, though.' Elliot tucked her hair behind her ear again. 'The other car had a dent.'

'Other car?'

'Balfour Rattray's.'

'I presume you want me to get someone checking that?'

Elliot nodded.

Kirsten sighed. 'Trev, when you're done here?'

'I'll pay a visit, sure.'

Elliot smiled at him. 'You found anything inside?'

'Andrea, he's just got here.'

'Yeah, I've got a few traces.' Trev pointed at the car. 'Multiple in fact. Haven't extracted or catalogued, but this is going to be an interesting one. Very, very messy in there. Tons of prints and sources.'

'Okay, so you need to know who you're checking against, right? You've got those two oiks who stole the car.'

'Right.' Kirsten made a note. 'Do you know who the car belongs to?'

Kirsten didn't know, did she? Excellent.

Elliot kept her voice low. 'It's DCI Pringle's.'

Trev laughed, then covered it with a cough. 'Okay. Well, I presume one of the others is from his daughter.'

Kirsten raised her eyebrows at him.

'What?' Trev shrugged it off. 'Everyone's heard the rumours...'

'They're just rumours.' Elliot raised a hand. 'But could we do a test? Parental analysis?'

'Yes, but it's not going to happen at a Hollywood pace, okay?'

'Why's that a problem?'

'You're always going at a hundred miles an hour, Andrea.'

'This isn't a murder, Kirst. We just need to find out who was in the car. We've got a semi-credible allegation it was DCI Pringle. If someone else has been in this motor apart from Jim and those two oiks, then I want to know.'

'Okay, we can run it, but I need a sample to check it. And it could be someone else entirely.'

'I know.' Elliot winked at her. 'I have worked a police investigation before.'

'Listen.' Trev was standing there, clutching a piece of paper. 'Not sure why, but I've found a few bits of paperwork in the glovebox, all addressed to Dr Belu Owusu.'

CHAPTER TWENTY-ONE
MARSHALL

Marshall sat on the curvy bench outside Kelso station. He couldn't get comfortable. Thing was like a giant millipede swarming around the stone flower bed behind him, just a patch of bare earth dotted with some early weeds. 'Okay, Andrea, that's good to know. Catch you later.' He ended the call and stood up, but tried to process it all.

The Waggon Inn next door was doing a decent trade for a Monday.

Hard to know what to think of Elliot's news – Pringle's car had been recovered, stolen by two joyriding kids who admitted being paid to do it by an old geezer.

The whole thing about Pringle made him feel a bit sick. His boss. Hard to shake the horrible feeling squirming in his guts.

He walked into Kelso police station and swiped into the long corridor digging deep into the station's bowels.

As he walked, so many possibilities ran through his mind. Too many. He didn't know whether they'd get any truth from Pringle. Or whether he himself knew what happened.

Gashkori was waiting outside the interview room, staring at the opposite wall. Both hands in his pockets, jangling his change. Talking to someone.

A big guy, rugby player build gone to seed. Intense stare and a neat goatee surrounding his mouth.

Gashkori looked around. 'Ah, Rob. How goes it?'

'They've recovered Pringle's car.'

A frown flashed across his forehead. 'That's interesting.'

'Indeed. Two neds claim they stole it from outside Lidl.' Marshall shrugged. 'Not sure I buy it.' A slow breath escaped his lips. 'Not sure what I buy, to be honest.'

Gashkori thumbed at his pal. 'This is Superintendent Bob Milne from Professional Standards.'

Milne thrust out a shovel of a hand. 'Rob, is it?'

'Aye. DI Marshall.' He met his iron grip with a steel one of his own.

A flurry of confusion flickered across Milne's forehead. 'Gather you've worked for Pringle a wee while, right?'

'I've been his pet profiler for nine months.'

Gashkori smirked. 'You heard about that nickname for you, then?'

Marshall hadn't but he'd guessed as much. 'I'm the exotic bit of fluff on his arm.' He raised his hands. 'Sorry, I don't mean that to sound sexist.'

'It does and it doesn't.' Gashkori grinned at Milne. 'It's actually a pretty accurate image. It's how Pringle sees Rob here, to be honest. Or how I suspect he does. Pringle's a regional DCI who'd have a very small remit otherwise. Having a criminal profiler on his payroll is something unusual. Gets him a few additional pennies in his budget. Invited to meetings he otherwise wouldn't be.'

'Sounds like a prudent move.'

Marshall sighed. 'I haven't been a profiler for ten years.'

'Still, you've got a string to your bow where most of us have a useless stick and some arrows.' Milne laughed. 'I'm guessing it's meant that Pringle can grab work from elsewhere. And that work means money and importance. And what's best for him too is *he* doesn't have to do the work.'

'That's a bit unfair.'

'Is it?' Milne grinned. 'Maybe I'm cynical here, but Jim Pringle's been rising through the ranks. She who cannot be named has been dishing out work to him like nobody's business.' His phone rang and he put it to his ear. 'Aye, Shunty?' He opened the door opposite and peered inside. 'Be with you in a sec.' He ended the call and gave them both a nod. 'See you on the other side, gents.'

Marshall waited for the door to close, then frowned at Gashkori. 'Shunty?'

Gashkori pointed at the door. 'As per usual, the Complaints have sent down a super and a sergeant. Shunty used to be based down here, right?'

'Right. Good officer. Well, a unique one anyway. So we've handed over that side of the case to them?'

'That's right. Just let the Rat Pack deal with Pringle while we do the real work.' Gashkori entered the room.

Marshall took a deep breath then followed him in.

Gashkori was sitting. 'It's Kieron McKenna, right?'

'Right. Mates call us Shagger.' He looked barely old enough to have pubic hairs, let alone have carnal knowledge of anything other than his preferred hand. And his face was a patchwork of scratches and yellow bruises. Probably should be in A&E instead of an interview, but Marshall wasn't going to intervene on that score.

'Shagger, eh?' Gashkori smirked. 'Why's that?'

He gave a deep laugh. 'Why d'you think?'

'Irony.'

'Ironing?'

'No, irony. When what's said differs from what's under the surface. So, if I said you're a mature lad, that'd be ironic, because you're, what, sixteen?'

'Eighteen.'

'Right. You don't look it.'

'Want my birth certificate in here?'

'No, we'll take you at your word. But you see what I mean? Even at eighteen, you're not mature. That's irony, what I said. If someone calls you Shagger, it's because you're not a shagger. You're the opposite of whatever a shagger is.'

'A virgin?'

Gashkori nodded. 'Sounds good to me.'

'I am one, though.'

'A virgin?'

'No, a shagger.'

'Course you are, son.' Gashkori sat back and folded his arms. 'Anyway. You got a thing for cars?'

'Cars?'

'Aye. Caught you in one. Wasn't yours, was it?'

'Found it.'

'You found it?'

'In Kelso. Lidl car park. Keys in the ignition.'

'You're lying.'

'Nope. This old man paid us to take it.'

Old to someone that age could be twenty-five. Marshall leaned forward a bit. 'How old are we talking?'

'No idea, man. Paid us a ton too. Any job that pays that much and lets me keep my clothes on is well worth it.'

Marshall gave him a slight laugh. 'This old man ask you to run down a guy?'

'Eh?'

'You know, drive the car into someone.'

'Fuck that, man. Ain't going down for murder.'

'The target didn't die. But it doesn't really matter what you say, because we've got a police sergeant seeing you two numpties behind the wheel of the car used to intentionally run down someone. That's good for attempted murder right there.'

'Dude, he told us to set it on fire!'

'Now why don't I believe you?'

'It's true!'

'Kieron. Shagger. Whatever you want to be called... Bugger this.' Marshall stood up. 'Come on, sir. Let's go next door and speak to his mate again. He's not said anything so far, but now the weaker of the two has confessed to taking the car, maybe he'll open up. Maybe he'll be concerned about the man you hit. After all, he was only the passenger. Maybe he grabbed the wheel at the last minute or the target would've been street pizza.'

'Dude.' Shagger was shaking his head. 'I don't know what you're talking about.'

'We're done here.' Gashkori joined Marshall in standing. 'Rob's right. We'll let you sit there for a bit, think about what you've done and whether you want to tell us more of the truth. But the first one to talk will get special... dispensation for it. Am I clear?'

Shagger looked up at them and shifted his focus between them. Kid like that was a lot older than his eighteen years, but parts of him were a lot younger. And they were rising to the surface – his eyes were filling with tears. He brushed them away. 'Please. How about I help you find the guy who paid us?'

'Sure, that works.' Gashkori walked over to the door. 'I'll send someone in later.'

Marshall followed him out, then shut the door. 'You sure about this?'

'I'm not wasting yours or my time with that wee twat, Rob.

We've broken him. Time for a notebook monkey to get a detailed statement out of him. Or palm him off onto the Rat Pack.'

'You think Pringle paid him?'

'Not sure. But Pringle's our chief suspect, right? Who else could it be?'

'Balfour Rattray. Who has a similarly plausible motive and didn't give an alibi. And his car has damage consistent with a vehicular assault.'

'Bloody hell.' Gashkori scratched at his neck. 'Got to hope it's him, then. I've known Pringle for years. He's always been eccentric but this is well beyond even his worst aspects.'

'You honestly don't think he's involved?'

'I don't know.' Gashkori stared at the other door. 'I hope he's not, but I can't be sure.'

'Okay, so assuming Pringle's not involved, what is going on with him?'

'Could be early onset dementia.'

Marshall nodded. 'Hard to spot when, like you say, he's that eccentric.'

'Right. Had an auntie who lost her marbles at like, fifty-three or something. Turned out the whole issue was a urinary tract infection that mimicked dementia. Fixed that and she was right as rain.'

'This has been going on longer than a UTI timeframe, sir.'

'Okay. Well, it's something they need to dig into. But with DI Elliot finding Pringle's car, battered from the collision, it all adds up to us being able to wash our hands of it. CCTV at the train stations will show him getting on and off in Edinburgh. If he left the car near the hardware store, the street cameras will show it. Same with Lidl. I think there's a lot more work to do before we can charge him, but it's not our conviction anymore. Standards will bring it home.'

'Sir, I don't think there's enough to be sure it wasn't him.'

'Oh, come on. Especially when those kids said an old man gave them the keys and told them to set it on fire.'

'They didn't say it was him, though.'

'No, but they will.'

CHAPTER TWENTY-TWO
SHUNTY

'No, no, no.' Pringle was standing, peering into the lightbulb hanging from the ceiling like it was the first time he'd even seen one and wanted to know precisely how it worked. 'I don't want a lawyer or federation rep.'

Siyal sat on the other side, uncomfortable about the lack of air cover. And being back here. 'Are you sure about that, sir?'

'A gazillion percent, *amigo*.' Pringle collapsed into the chair, but his focus was still on the lightbulb. 'Such a marvel, isn't it?'

The door cracked open and Superintendent Bob Milne entered with the swagger of the undaunted. Siyal could never dream of having that confidence or arrogance. The guy was tall and big with it, carrying a few extra pounds, if not a stone. His friendly smile clashed with his searing glare. Siyal had only just met him, but he knew already he needed to be wary of him.

'Morning, Jim.' Milne took his chair and settled back. 'Mind if I call you Jim?'

'No, I don't. Sir.' Pringle shifted his focus from the lightbulb to Milne. 'I...'

'What happened to your car this morning, Jim?'

'My car? I... I honestly don't know what happened to it.'

'I find that hard to believe.'

'It's the truth. I... I've been suffering from blackouts.' Pringle raised a hand. 'And not from drinking.' He cackled. 'I remember *everything*, no matter how shitfaced I get.'

Milne held a stern expression. 'That's not funny.'

'No. I'm serious. These blackouts... It's terrifying, sir. I... I just go into a room and I've no idea how I got there or why I went in there in the first place. I've left my car at Sainsbury's twice. In the last week.'

'Have you been to the doctor?'

Pringle stared upwards again. 'These lightbulbs are fascinating, aren't they? You'd have thought we'd use low-energy ones, but no. We keep it old school here in... whatever police station this is. Not Melrose. Gala? Must be Gala. Fascinating device, though. It's just a bit of wire with electricity going through it. The fascinating bit is that the light comes from the resistance. Curious how an extreme inefficiency in something gives you what you didn't know you were looking for. Serendipity, right?'

Milne was drumming his fingers on the table. He stopped with a fierce smile. 'Inspector, I need you to realise how serious this is. Someone drove a car into Gary Hislop this morning. The car matches the description of yours.'

'I'd be surprised if someone else has a car that's like the Boss.'

'The Boss?'

'My Beemer. Named it after Bruce Springsteen.' Pringle cackled. 'Tramps like me and that car are born to run.'

'I'm being serious here.'

'So am I. That car's pretty rare, I'll have you know. You can't have another suspect. It's impossible.'

'Wait. Are you saying it was your car that did it?'

'I suspect you're here because you've got evidence it was.' Pringle frowned. 'Wait. Has she given *you* my job?'

'No. Ryan Gashkori is in charge temporarily.'

'Figures. He's been running the drugs angle on Hislop, so covering for me while I'm unwell provides some continuity. Better than Elliot acting up, I suppose.'

Milne leaned forward and his chair creaked. 'I'm asking you straight here, Jim – did you crash your car into Gary Hislop?'

Pringle stared back up at the lightbulb for a while. The clock ticked until a minute had passed. 'Sir. I wish I could explain what happened. But I can't. Won't even try to because I want to give you the truth and only the truth. And, right now, I simply can't.'

Milne sat back and sighed. 'You not telling us anything is the same thing as lying.'

Pringle reached up towards the lightbulb, but he was too far away to touch it.

Siyal leaned forward. 'We've recovered your car.'

Pringle didn't look at him. 'You have?'

'It's a bit bashed up. Not all of the damage was from when someone drove it into Gary Hislop, but there's damage consistent with the assault on him.'

'That wasn't me. I don't think.' Pringle clicked his fingers and stared at him. 'That's it! Lidl! I was going there to get something... Cabbages, maybe. No. They were selling a lathe. I've always wanted one. I do a lot of mechanical stuff, but woodworking is something I've always fancied.' He looked up at the lightbulb again. 'That was last night. I don't think I bought it.' The frown deepened. 'I can't remember if they had it in stock. Or if they were even supposed to.'

'This is Lidl in Kelso?'

'Right. Just around the corner from my brother's house. I... I was somewhere. I can't remember where. Thought I'd just pop in. Must've left the Boss there... And the keys.'

If this was an act, it wasn't a very good one. Pringle should surely know that they'd unpick the truth behind his movements. They'd pin down his story.

'Sir, our colleagues are scouring your car for DNA traces. Do you know whose DNA we should expect to find?'

'Myself. And the wee bastards who stole it.'

'Of course. Anyone else?'

Pringle just shrugged.

'What about your mechanic?'

'What do you mean?'

'When you get your MOT or a service, you must take it somewhere. Means we can eliminate them from the inquiry. Save us all a bit of time. Maybe get you some brownie points.'

'I do it all myself.'

'The MOT?'

Pringle scowled at Siyal like he was stupid. 'My father owned a garage. Built it up from scratch, had a team of ten working for him. The car belonged to him, truth be told, so it's... A family heirloom, I guess. I want to keep it running as well as it did the day he bought it. I know a few people in the area who are fans of that model. A drivers' club. So there are maybe enough of them around that there being two in Kelso at that time isn't that implausible. I suppose. But there's no mechanic, no. I get my cousin, Dave, to sign off the MOT in a pub car park.'

'Is his DNA going to be in there?'

'No.'

'No? But he does the MOT?'

'No. He doesn't go inside. Just ticks the box. I know what I'm doing with the Boss.' Pringle shifted his gaze to Siyal and some of the old sharpness returned. 'But you're bullshitting me here. The pair of you. You won't know how many samples you've found until you have it all analysed. And it's inconsequential to your case. The DNA doesn't say who was driving or when, only that at some point, someone was in the car. If I was a seasoned police officer, and I am, the most likely bet is the muppets who stole my car ran down Hislop, either inadvertently or on purpose.'

Siyal nodded along with it. 'Those are aspects we're investigating, sir. But that doesn't mean someone didn't pay the wee neds to do it. And that someone could even be yourself.'

'In *my* car? Why? Why? I love that car. It's all I inherited from my dad.' Pringle wiped a tear from his eyes. 'Rakesh. Please... I'm not a violent man. You can't think I did this!'

Milne cleared his throat, deep and raw sounding. 'We can, because your story is so full of holes it might as well be made in Switzerland from cow's milk.'

'But I didn't do it!'

'Did you pay them to do it?'

'Why would I? Ask yourselves that. Why the hell would I want to kill Gary Hislop?'

'You blame Hislop for a lot of things going on around here. Deaths. Drugs. Foiling an active investigation. All on your patch. On your watch.'

'That's weak as piss and you know it.' Pringle sighed. 'Have either of you got any evidence of this?'

'Son.' Milne stared hard at him. 'We're giving you the chance to come clean here.'

'There's nothing to come clean about. I didn't do it. Didn't attack anyone. At that time... I think I was on the train to Edinburgh.'

'But you can't confirm the detail of how you got there.'

Pringle pinched his nose. 'No. My brother must've given me a lift.'

'And it doesn't preclude you from leaving your car in a supermarket car park for two wee sods to do your bidding.' Milne cracked his knuckles with a deep tearing sound. 'Looks like a good crime – joyriders nick your car, drive into your target, then torch it somewhere out in the countryside. Trouble is, they liked how it felt and didn't follow through on the latter part of your deal.'

'This is complete bullshit.' Pringle looked at Siyal. 'Come on, Rakesh. You can't believe this!'

'You've been honest.' Milne smiled at him. 'And I appreciate that. But if you won't come clean, then I want you to be perfectly clear on one thing. You are deep in the shite here. You're a suspect in an attempted murder. You'll lose your job and your pension.'

Pringle started crying.

Siyal moved to comfort him but didn't know what to do. Pringle had been getting increasingly erratic over months and now this? He sat back – last thing he wanted was to get clattered in the face. Or worse. 'Sir, are you okay?'

'No. I'm not.' Pringle sat up straight and rubbed at his eyes. 'This is a disaster.'

'Come on, sir. Open up to us.'

'I would if I could remember anything. You don't understand!'

'Can your brother shed any light on things?'

'What things?'

'Where you were. Maybe give you some kind of clue as to what's going on. Hell, maybe even an alibi. Anything.'

'No.'

'Jim, what's going on? Why are you living with him?'

Pringle looked at Siyal with a quivering lip. 'Because I'm not welcome in my own home.'

'You're not married.'

'No.' Pringle sucked in a deep breath. 'I don't think so.'

'Don't think so?'

'I can't remember everything. There are gaps, you know? Holes, like when you take a vase off a dusty table. You know there was something there before, but it's not there now and you're damned if you can think of what it was.' He smacked the side of his head. Then again.

Milne reached over and grabbed his wrist. 'Stop that!' He looked at Siyal. 'Rakesh, get someone to take him to hospital!'

CHAPTER TWENTY-THREE
ELLIOT

No matter how long she'd lived here, it still struck Elliot how different the countryside leading towards Duns was to the mountains surrounding Galashiels and Melrose, and also to the rolling hills around Kelso. This road sliced through flat land, the fields sparse. A wood on the right had been bulldozed by that freak storm eighteen months ago, the trees still lying around like a spilled box of matches.

And she appreciated driving solo, without someone like Shunty or Struan sitting in the passenger seat and either giving her the silent treatment or, worse, talking. Havering on and on about absolute shite.

The satnav pointed down a lane on the right, nestled in an indentation. She took it and descended into a lush valley. Even this early in the season, it was so verdant it felt as though prehistoric animals might still roam.

That, or she'd been watching too much TV with the kids.

A tiny cottage hid behind a stone wall, the slate roof just

visible over the top. Surrounded by mature trees with a walled garden lurking behind. Just missed a muscleman cracking logs with a massive axe. Topless. Beads of sweat on his forehead.

Aye.

No sign of any parking spaces, so she pulled in on the grass verge where countless others had done, judging by the wear marks, then got out. Wasn't raining here and the sun shone through the trees.

Christ, it was like she'd stepped into a fairy-tale.

She tried to open the gate, but it was locked. She gave it another go – aye, definitely locked. She thumped it with her fist. 'Hello?'

Voices, coming from pretty far away. A sharp shush. Then a slit opened in the gate.

Dr Belu Owusu peered out, her eyes narrowed. A headscarf on and shades, despite the weather. 'Andrea? What the hell are you doing here?'

Over her shoulder, Elliot saw a young girl entering the chalk-green front porch. Curly hair tied up in pigtails. She was clearly biracial, as they said nowadays.

'Afternoon, Belu.' Elliot smiled. 'Need a word, if you don't mind?'

Owusu flared her nostrils. 'I'm on holiday this week.'

'Sure, I know. Fergus is deputising, right?'

'Right.' Owusu stepped back and reached for the slit. 'So take whatever this is about up with him.'

'Oh, this isn't a pathology chat.'

'Go on?'

Elliot motioned over to the house. 'It's about Jim Pringle.'

'Jim? Eh?'

'How some paperwork addressed to you was in his car.'

Owusu blushed. 'Has he been stealing my letters?'

'Nope.' Elliot held her stare. 'Some of them were addressed to both of you. Mind if I come in?'

Owusu stared at the ground for a few seconds, then reached up. The slit snapped shut.

Bloody hell. 'Come on, Belu...'

The gate opened.

Elliot looked back at her car to check that she'd pulled in enough, then followed Owusu into the garden. 'Where's your car?'

'Park it up the hill, eh?' Owusu was marching across the lawn towards the house.

'Was that your daughter?'

'Sarah.'

'She's Jim's too, right?'

Owusu stopped on the doorstep and let out a slow breath. 'How did you find out?'

'Jim told us he had a daughter. "Kirsty". Nobody believed him.'

'Stupid bastard. I *told* him not to joke about it. He said it was hiding her in plain sight. Which is bullshit, right?' Owusu sighed. 'She's supposed to be a secret.' A deeper sigh. 'People have a habit of targeting the children of police officers.'

'Who do you mean?'

'Jim's a detective and he's been a prolific one at that.' She shook her head. 'Everyone he put away. Everyone he's investigated over the years. Their families, associates, co-conspirators. Jim's the type of officer who could actually attract an enemy, as childish as that sounds.'

'Talk to me about your relationship.'

'Relationship? There is none. Our *arrangement* was that Jim can go on playing the policeman and saving the world, but none of it comes back to me, or to our daughter.' She flared her nostrils again. 'I'll ask you again, Andrea. Why are you here?'

'We believe Jim might've driven his car into Gary Hislop.'

'My God.' Owusu collapsed onto the bench outside. Rainwater splashed everywhere. 'Is he dead?'

'Hislop? No, he's in surgery as we speak.' Elliot fanned out her hair. 'I mean, I visited him in there and he's in a very bad way. Touch and go, they said.'

Owusu was shaking her head slowly.

Elliot took the seat next to her. The dampness soaked through her trousers. 'Do you think it's possible he did it?'

'You're telling me he did.'

'I'm telling you we think he might've.'

'I...' Owusu looked at Elliot with tears in her eyes. 'Truth is, I just don't know. He loves that car, so I can't see him crashing it on purpose. It's his hobby, but if something dire happened, something that threatened Sarah, then maybe.'

'Talk to me, Belu.'

'You? Andrea, I like you, but you're not exactly discreet.'

'I can be.'

'Bullshit. You're a gossip. You can't be discreet.'

Charming.

Elliot needed a different tack here, so she sat back on the bench. 'Let me get this straight – you took your daughter away from Pringle, right?'

'We were never with him, Andrea. It's... She... It's...' Owusu leaned forward and buried her head in her hands. 'God, I love Sarah so fucking much, but she was an accident. Okay? It wasn't supposed to happen. I didn't like Jim, but there was... something there. It just wasn't supposed to happen. And yet it did. She did. But it would never work between us.'

'Why's that?'

'It's all my fault. The dead I can understand, but the living I find difficult... Corpses speak to me.' She raised a hand. 'Not literally. I mean I can understand what happened to them in their lives and at the moment of death. If that helps the police bring justice, great. But... I struggle with flesh and blood where the heart is still pumping, you know?'

Elliot didn't, but she nodded anyway.

'Jim's a nice guy, but... I just didn't trust him. He's... He's a cop. Kind of hard to keep a daughter a secret in a small town like Melrose. Everyone knows everything. That's why we live in the middle of nowhere. But we did try for Sarah's sake, okay? For a few years. And it just didn't work. At all. Jim was understanding about it. Wanted to be in her life, as much as I'd let him. Not even co-parenting; he's just a friendly uncle.'

'You don't think that's damaging to her?'

'Parents always damage their kids. I just didn't want her to be a pawn in a game between us. I'd made the mistake in getting close to Jim. I didn't want Sarah to suffer for that.' Owusu sucked in a deep breath and sat there like that for a while. A couple of blackbirds pranced around on the lawn. She stood up and walked over to a washing line. She shook it and water sprayed off in all directions. 'Why are you here, Andrea? Just to twist the knife?'

'No. I'm here to check out the stories Jim's been feeding us. He's scored two out of two so far.'

Owusu stared across the lawn to her. 'Do you honestly think he could kill someone?'

'I'll turn that back and ask you.'

'I would've said no.'

'But?'

'But he's got a lot more erratic recently. You must've seen it?'

'A few things stand out, aye.' Elliot swallowed. 'Listen, we're trying to do this by the book. We've got a load of DNA samples in the car. It'll take time to process them all. Obviously we can't prove who was driving it at the time by that means, but knowing who's been in the car will give us a good list of who could've done it. Would Sarah ever be in the car?'

'She would. He dropped her at school twice a week, when I had an early shift. Jim gave me a lift occasionally. And vice versa. So you're asking my consent to give you a DNA sample from me and my daughter?'

Elliot nodded then clapped her hands together. 'Okay, you know the drill. A blood sample or a buccal swab.'

'I'm not giving you the DNA.'

'What, why?'

'I am protecting my child. I'm sure you can understand that.' She got up and walked inside the house.

Elliot stood there in the cold, trying to process it all.

You never knew what happened behind closed doors. The skeletons in people's IKEA or John Lewis wardrobes. The silent traumas. The decisions people made to protect themselves and their loved ones.

Aye, she'd get Owusu's approval. Just needed a few minutes to break her down.

Her mobile rang:

Gashkori calling...

She sighed then answered it. 'Ryan, how's it going?'

'Okay. Are you with Belu just now?'

'She's inside, why?'

'Pringle hasn't shown up at hospital. And uniform aren't responding to the calls. Does she know where he is?'

'Give me a sec.' Elliot knocked on the door then hung up the phone. 'Belu?'

Owusu was in the kitchen, standing by a blender. 'You can't come in.'

'I'm not coming in. Listen, we've got an issue. Jim's gone walkabout on the way to hospital. Do you have any contact details for his brother?'

'His brother?'

CHAPTER TWENTY-FOUR
MARSHALL

That sole sandwich wasn't enough, so Marshall went for the healthy option this time – the last bowl of chicken and rice soup in the Kelso station canteen. The half-loaf of bread alongside it probably counteracted most of that goodness, though.

He nodded at the server and crossed the empty room towards the table Kirsten was at. Still in that lull before the backshift appeared and dayshift slipped off into the night.

Kirsten angrily chewed her sandwich, then dropped it on the plate. She looked up at him. 'You okay there?'

'Sure.' Marshall sat and let his jacket unfurl around him. 'Why wouldn't I be?'

'You just seem a bit preoccupied.'

'I've been thinking a lot about Pringle.' Marshall blew on his soup but it was still roasting hot. 'The truth... I don't think even he knows. Or we'll ever be able to determine it. Gashkori called in the Rat Pack and they've been giving him a grilling. As far as I know, he's been having these blackouts.'

'Blackouts?'

'Right. Says it's not drinking-related, but isn't that what an alcoholic would say?'

She nodded slowly and finished chewing. 'You're the PhD, Rob. What are you thinking? Stress?'

'Stress can do funny things to the brain. And the body. But his job isn't that stressful. Not like being a DCI in the Met or even in Edinburgh.'

'Thing is, I've heard rumours of an investigation into Borders cops. That would add fire to that.'

'You haven't told me that before.'

'It's not like I'm hiding it from you, Rob. It's just... There have been all these leaks, right?'

'Right. Screwing up Andrea and Gashkori's investigation.'

'Do you think it's all connected?'

'What, that the perpetrator of the attack is the person who benefitted from the leaks?'

'Exactly.'

'Who would that be?'

'Pringle? And maybe he's been leaking too? Got in too deep and this is the only way to stop it.'

Marshall ate some soup and thought it through as he chewed the sludge. 'Still doesn't feel right, though. Something about him driving his own precious car into Hislop... It just doesn't jive with me.'

'Doesn't *jive*?'

'You know what I mean. The trouble is, when you have always been a bit bizarre your entire life, how do people know when it isn't a put-on anymore?'

'True. But there's also another suspect. Balfour Rattray. Right?'

'Right. See, him I can buy a lot more. His motive is pretty solid. His dad loaned Hislop a couple of hundred grand to set up his shop way back when. And he's asked for it back.'

'Makes sense, then.'

'You think?'

'Hislop's expanding. Liquid cash like that is probably very hard to come by, especially from kosher sources. And it depends how hard Balfour's being about it.'

'But Hislop has assets, so it's very easy to go through legal means to get a loan secured on them for the money owed. Thing is, it'd make more sense if Hislop ran Balfour down. Not the other way around.' Marshall finished his soup and left half of the bread. 'He's given a loose alibi, but there's something not right about the whole thing. Still, if they'd done it or knew who had, why not come up with a stupid reason? Just evading it seems weird.'

'Who knows?' Kirsten pushed her empty plate away. 'Elliot got it, right?'

'The info? Aye. Why?'

'Just... She's been on my case again. As per usual. I can't stand her.'

'Not many can. But she's getting better. She's becoming much more of a team player now. Before, she'd have kept this stuff to herself, but now she's sharing.'

'For now. And you don't know what she's holding back.'

'True.' Marshall raised his eyebrows. Then let them settle back down. 'So. Tonight?'

'Tonight?'

'Thea's thing.'

'I said I'll come to that.'

'You said you'd see about how the work was going.'

'Aye, but fuck that shit. I'm coming.'

'Okay. Cool. Brilliant. But... Here's the thing. It feels like we're getting serious now, but we still haven't had that chat.'

'Which one?'

'The big one we've needed to have for months now where
—'

Marshall's mobile rang. He checked the display and groaned.
'Better take this. But you're not off the hook for the chat.' He
answered it, locking eyes with her. 'Hi, Andrea.' He sat back and
caught a sigh from Kirsten. 'You got to the bottom of that yet?'

'What do you think?'

'I'm guessing that's a no?'

'Aye, that's a no.' Sounded like Elliot slurped coffee through
the lid. 'Looking for Ryan. He about?'

'In the canteen just now. Sorry.'

'Gala?'

'Kelso.'

'Right. Okay. Need to fire a rocket up Struan's arse but he's
gone walkabout too. Honestly. I used to moan and moan about
Shunty, but at least I knew where he was, you know?'

Marshall sat back. 'So where is Pringle?'

'That Warner lad drove him from Kelso nick. Haven't heard
from him since. Here's something for you, though. Sarah is
Kirsty's actual name.'

'She's real?'

'Aye. Thought Kirsty was too close to your bird's name to
be real.'

'My *bird*? Come on, Andrea.'

'You know what I mean.' Elliot laughed. 'But I still thought
it was bullshit. But I've seen the girl with my own two eyes and
she's clearly the kid of both of them. Are you supposed to say
mixed race or mixed heritage now? Is it biracial?'

'I don't know, Andrea, I just accept people as they are.'

'Anyway. Asked for DNA and Belu refused me. She had a bit
of a fit for no reason. Poor cow, must be the stress of the whole
event.'

'Sure it'll be nothing to do with you being there.'

Kirsten's phone rang. 'Better take this.' She scurried off into the corner.

'Is that Kirsten with you?'

'She is, why?'

'What's your take, Robbie?'

'I follow the evidence.'

'Even with your profiles?'

'Especially with them.'

'Oh come on, those are just tea leaf readings.'

'They're the complete opposite of that.' Marshall tried to not rise to it, but it was a struggle. 'With a profile, you look at the details of serial crimes and you pull out motivations. Small details shed light on the psychotic arseholes who've done them. This isn't even a murder and is just one attack, so I can't profile anything.'

'You're saying you're useless?'

'No. I've been a cop for over ten years now and I can do the job just as well as anyone else can.'

'Mm.'

'What's that supposed to mean?'

'Just winding you up, Robbie. I get it. This is a weird one.'

'Right.'

But she'd hung up.

Kirsten stormed back over and sat down, slamming her mobile onto the table. 'What did she want?'

'Pringle's gone missing. We sent him to the hospital from here.' Marshall raised his radio off the table. 'He hasn't showed up. And the uniform transporting him hasn't reported back.'

'Who was it?'

'Warner.'

'Bless him.'

'What's that supposed to mean?'

'He's good at some things, right, but he marches to his own beat.'

'That's the truth.'

'Shouldn't you be out looking for him?'

'Would love to, but Gashkori asked Elliot to lead on it.'

'He seems good.'

'Aye, seems it. Thing is, he's drugs squad so the jury's out. Actually, the jury's been paid off and their families staked out.' He gestured at her phone. 'What was that about?'

'This is the weirdest thing. Sally is helping Trev with Pringle's car. She's finally managed to get the boot open. They've found a bag from Roxburgh Street Hardware in there. Hammer, Stanley knife and spare blades, cable ties and duct tape.'

Marshall's mouth hung open. 'Christ, what was Pringle going to do?'

CHAPTER TWENTY-FIVE
ELLIOT

Elliot drove through Kelso at a slow speed, nowhere near fast enough to mostly kill a local drug lord. She couldn't stop herself from at least smiling at the joke. Inside her head.

Aye, it wasn't just Pringle who was losing his marbles.

Keeping her eyes peeled for him – the way his brain had been, he could be wandering the streets.

As she drove, she tried cycling through the four phone numbers again, hoping someone would pick up.

Struan first:

'We're sorry, but this number is unavailable. Please leave a message after the—'

Prick.

Where the hell was he? Elon Musk and SpaceX couldn't build a rocket big enough for the one she needed to fire up his arse.

She killed the call before the message beep and tried Warner. It just rang and rang.

Useless sod.

Pringle next:

'Bing bong, Billy-Bob, you're through to the voicemail of James Pringle, esquire. Please leave—'

Nope.

Already left two and he hadn't got back to her, assuming his phone wasn't in orbit around Saturn like his marbles...

Finally, Gashkori:

'Afternoon, Andrea.'

A human voice, at last. Well, as close to one as he could be.

'You getting anywhere, boss?'

He sighed. 'Well. I found Struan and your team in the CCTV analysis room.'

She slowed to pull up at a T-junction, indicating left. 'There's a CCTV analysis room?'

'Looks like Pringle ordered it as part of the station refit. Obviously forgot to brief anyone else on its existence.'

'Great.' She pulled out and shot past the Lidl. 'Who let him go home? He should've been kept in.'

'I agree. My orders were to take him straight to hospital. And yet he never turned up. Now, the forensics lot say we've got a bag of abduction gear in his boot. Still, who wants to arrest a copper, eh?'

'Better leave that to the Rat Pack. Not like he's hurting decent folk, is it? Maybe he'll take out a few more criminals before we lock him up and make the world a better place.'

'Jesus, Andrea.'

'I'm joking.'

'Hmm.'

'I swear.' Elliot pulled in at the T-junction but a steady flow of traffic headed down the street. 'Oh. Get this. Pringle doesn't have a brother.'

Gashkori gasped. 'He *what*?'

'According to Belu Owusu. Who's Kirsty's mother. Except she's called Sarah.'

'Jesus. He definitely doesn't have a brother?'

'Nope. Only child. Look, I'm in Kelso so I'll head to his address and try to speak to Pringle.'

'Andrea, Rakesh is running that side.'

'Shunty?'

'Professional Standards.'

Nothing professional or standard about him. 'Fine, I'll let the Rat Pack do that, but I want to mark out the territory and make sure we find him. That clown Warner isn't answering any calls.' Elliot pulled up outside the address she'd been given.

A squad car sat there, the engine idling.

'I've tracked down Warner. Better go, bye.' She killed the call and got out into the muggy heat, then walked over and rapped on the window.

Warner jerked around. He had a serviette tucked into his T-shirt, a fork and knife in his hands, with a massive salad in a tub.

She opened the door and that Lewis Capaldi song bled out. 'Constable, are you *eating*?'

'It's my lunch break.' He speared a lump of tuna with his fork and ate it.

God, it absolutely stank.

Elliot snorted. 'We've been trying to call you. Both mobile and radio.'

Warner picked up his phone. 'Ah, the battery's gone.' The mobile looked like it belonged to another century.

'Listen. Having your mobile run out of juice happens, I get it. But I've been calling you on the radio.'

Warner picked up his Airwave now. 'This thing got clattered in a raid in Hawick last week.'

'Why haven't you replaced it?'

'Been flat out.'

Where the hell did they get this clown from?

'That thing best be in tatters by the time your sergeant sees it.' She fixed him with her hardest police officer stare. 'When I call you or your sergeant calls you, you answer. If you can't, that's your fault. Am I clear?'

He picked up a bit of link sausage and swallowed it down. 'You can say that all you want, ma'am, but it's lunchtime.'

'I don't care if it's sleepy bye bye time, Constable, you make sure you can pick up when you're called. Okay?'

'Aye, sure.' Warner shifted his lunch over to the passenger seat. 'Good thing you're here. I'm bursting for the toilet.'

'I'm not surprised after eating that much sausage and tuna.'

'Hey, I need my protein. These guns don't look after themselves, y'know?'

She thumbed behind her, pointing to the house. 'Is Pringle here?'

'He hasn't left. Not that I've seen, anyway.'

'You were ordered to take him to the hospital.'

'Yeah, but *he* ordered me to take him here. I couldn't ignore a direct order from a DCI.'

'You had one from a superintendent!'

'Who?'

'Milne.'

'Shite.' Warner looked over at the house. 'If you ask me, I think your man's cracked in the head.'

'Is he in there?'

'He was, but...'

Jesus Christ – she needed to secure Pringle, didn't she?

'Come on. I need your back-up.' Elliot turned around and charged up the drive towards the house.

Warner hadn't moved.

'Constable. Now!'

'Fine, fine.' Warner huffed and puffed as he got out, then strode up the path alongside her.

The front door was open, so she stepped inside. 'Jim?'

'Shhh.' The sound came from the living room. Pringle was sitting on a chocolate leather sofa, peering outside.

Warner brushed past Elliot. 'I'll just be a second.'

'Constable, I need your assistance.'

'And I need a crap!' Warner charged off, trying doors until he found the bathroom.

That clown better get his CV updated pronto because a ton of bricks was about to land on his head.

Elliot turned to face Pringle, but he was on his feet now. 'Jim, you were supposed to go to hospital.'

The blinds were closed but he was peering through the slats. 'Had to come here. Someone's following me.'

Shite. He really had cracked.

'I'm a marked man, Andrea.'

'Jim. It's okay. We just need a word with you.' After a trip to the hospital, where they'll measure him for a new suit. One with arms that attach at the back... 'We found a hammer and some stuff in your boot.'

'Aye.'

'What were you going to do with it all?'

'DIY.'

'I get that. What were you building?'

'A hen coop. In the back garden.'

Aye, because hens responded well to duct tape and cable ties.

'Hens?'

'Thinking of getting them. Eggs are the most joyous joy of joyosity!'

'Jim, I think I know what's happening. You bought the stuff from Hislop and you were going to use it on him. Weren't you?'

He looked around at her, mouth open. 'What stuff are you talking about?'

'Admit it, you were going to kill Hislop!'

'What? Andi, how long have we worked together for?'

Too long. Way too long.

'Jim, the important thing is to get your story straight. But first, you need to be looked at by a doctor. Okay? So right now, you need to come with me.'

Pringle peered out of the window again. 'They're here, watching me.'

'Who is?'

'Them! Don't you see?'

'I don't.' She grabbed his arm. 'Let's get you to hospital first, okay?' She dragged him towards the door and, wonder of fucking wonders, he started walking.

Pringle stepped out into the gloom. 'We can't go any further. I need to brush my teeth before we go.'

'What? Why?'

'It's just manners!' His breath did smell like an open sewer. 'That cop is using my toilet! We have to wait.'

'Why do you—?'

The toilet flushed and Warner stepped out, drying his hands on his trousers.

Pringle stepped inside. 'Have to be very careful these days. Last month, someone broke in, stole my toothbrush and replaced it with one that was identical.'

Shite, he had really lost the plot.

'How do you know they'd—'

'It tasted different. Mine was minty fresh, but that one smelled like bad breath.' Pringle wetted his toothbrush, then smelled it. He scowled. 'My God, son, the state of your bowels! It's like an animal's crawled inside of you and died.'

Warner didn't know where to look.

'I'd light a candle in here but I'm afraid I'd just ignite the mess.' Pringle opened the window. 'There. Now.' He squirted way too much toothpaste on then started brushing, the foam spilling from his lips.

Elliot stepped away from him and dragged Warner deeper into the hallway. 'Constable, we need to have words about your conduct here.'

'My conduct?'

'Aye, if you need to go, you go in the station, not in someone's house. Especially if you're nuking the site from orbit like that.'

'Had a very heavy night.'

'You're a drinker?'

'Me? God no. I'm teetotal.'

'How was it heavy?'

'Cross-fit.'

'What the hell's that?' She raised a hand. 'No, don't tell me.'

'It's the best way to get in shape. I'm determined to live for fifty years in great health after I retire.'

'You leaving the force might be sooner than you expect.'

Warner thought it through, his eyebrows twitching.

Elliot looked back into the bathroom. No sign of Pringle.

Bastard!

She ran out onto the front path. Warner's squad car was haring up the road, away from the house.

Bloody hell!

'Constable! Did you leave the keys in the ignition?'

'Standard practice. Nobody's going to steal a liveried police car.'

'Pringle just has!'

'In fairness, it was my lunch hour and I'm doing you a favour so maybe don't be such a mardy arseho—'

A massive thud.

Came from up the street.

Shit, shit, shit!

Elliot raced over to her car and got in. Took a few goes to get the engine to fire, then it groaned as it sped on up the long street.

Jesus Christ!

She passed the long row of parked cars and reached the end. Braked hard. Scanned left down the one-way system past the abbey.

Then right.

The squad car was sticking out of a house's gable wall.

CHAPTER TWENTY-SIX

ELLIOT

Gashkori stared at the squad car and shook his head, a hiss escaping his lips. 'That's... Wow. I'm glad that's not coming out of my cost code.'

Elliot struggled to look at it. The front was caved in, the boundaries between it and the house wall blurring.

'Must've been going some to do that to it.'

Elliot pointed back the way. 'You could get a DeLorean up to eighty-eight miles an hour on that stretch.'

He frowned. 'A what?'

'It's a *Back to the Future* reference, Ryan.'

He nodded. 'Never seen it.'

'What? How can you never have seen that film?'

'The "future" bit put me off.'

'It's set in the fifties!'

'Aye. Such a great time for people with my skin tone in America.'

Shite, she'd stepped in that one.

Gashkori winked at her. 'Got you.'

'You dickhead.'

His smile faded. 'Talk to me, Andi. What's going on?'

Elliot watched Pringle get helped into the ambulance by two big paramedics. Warner's salad was all over his clothes – chunks of tuna and sausage clung to his hair. His face was either covered in beetroot juice or his own blood.

She didn't want to consider the latter.

She'd let him go. Let him run. That clown desecrating his toilet...

Still, as senior officer it was on her.

She looked at Gashkori. 'Jim thought someone was watching him, sir. Obviously, we were. Warner was parked outside his house, but... Aye. Shame it wasn't the same wall Shunty hit.'

'Shunty?'

'DS Rakesh Siyal.'

'I know him. He hit a wall?'

'How have you not heard that?'

Gashkori rolled his eyes at her. 'Heard it a hundred times.' Cheeky prick.

Well, that was twice – he wasn't going to get her again.

'I'm writing up Warner for losing Pringle and a squad car.'

'Bold move.'

'He's a decent cop, but he's got issues with taking orders. His rights seem to trample over actually doing his job. I'm not standing for that, Ryan.'

'Fair enough. Thing I need to get to the bottom of is why Pringle was driven home and not to the hospital.'

'Pringle ordered Warner to take him home. Didn't believe me that Milne is a super.'

'Bloody hell. You're correct to write him up.'

'Sir, I'm sorry, this is all on me. When we found that hardware in his boot and heard he'd not turned up, well... I panicked and went after him. Just to make sure he was... safe?

This wouldn't have happened if I hadn't done that. Or if Warner had answered his phone or his radio.'

'Okay, but if Jim had been successful in running, we'd have lost a suspect.' Gashkori looked back down the Butts towards Pringle's brother's home. 'Do you think he might've been trying to kill himself?'

'Like I said, he was going very fast. Maybe sixty. Load of cars parked at the side, so it was a single lane for driving. If anyone had been driving towards him...'

'We need to wait until he's been seen by a doctor, first.' Gashkori waved over to the ambulance. 'At least this way I know he'll actually get to hospital.' He let out a deep sigh. 'Thank you, Andi. We've got him secure. Whether he's guilty or not, he's going to get the help he needs.'

'Thank you, sir.'

'Speaking of which, you got the help you needed from Struan.' Gashkori rolled his eyes. Oh, there was something there... 'Recovering Pringle's car was a good result. Assuming we can dig into the details on both cars, we can identify who tried to kill Hislop.'

'Aye.' Elliot scanned every line on his face, watching for any reaction. 'You know him, sir?'

'Struan? Aye. Worked together in South Glasgow MIT. Even though he's a Borders lad, he worked through there. Got some results. Good cop, don't get me wrong, but...'

'But what?'

'Ach, it's nothing.'

'Come on. I didn't hire him, so if there's a closet full of skeletons, I'd love to know.'

'Let's just say he has some unusual ways of doing things.'

'In what way?'

'That stuff about finding you buying screws? Typical Liddell. He's making sure your feet are smeared in crap.

Despite those flash suits he wears, he's happy rolling in shite. He'll focus on taking people out, or at least gaining intel on them. But most cops would collate, then present. He did his "ta-da" moment to you, while me and Marshall were with you.'

'I'll keep an eye out, thanks.'

Gashkori was giving her a good examination. 'Something in particular you're worried about?'

'No, just concerned he's a bit of a loose cannon.'

'Yeah, well. Sometimes you need to milk a few cows to make a cheesecake.'

She smiled at that image. 'I'm keeping an eye on him, sir, but I'm flagging up we may have a bad apple.'

'Noted, Inspector. Impressive work for his first day.' Gashkori stepped aside to let the ambulance past, then gave her a bit of side eye. 'May have heard similar about you over the years.'

She raised her eyebrows. 'Are you kidding me?'

'Fortunately for you, I'm not the type to wade chin deep on personality clashes.'

'Sir, this is more than a personality clash. We all do a bit of painting outside the lines, right? But he's cracking eggs left, right and centre. And his omelettes are minging. But I saw him clonk the heads of those two neds together.'

'Sure, but did anyone else? And given they'd been in a car crash, can anyone prove that? And what did you do about it at the time? Nothing? So it either didn't happen or you condoned it. What you permit, you promote.'

Good point.

And that thing about Struan getting her covered in shite. Aye, she was doing a great job of that herself.

Gashkori did up his top button. 'Okay, stay here and keep an eye on everything. Head off about half six if it's all quiet.'

'What? Why?'

'What do you mean?'

'This is a serious investigation, Ryan.'

'And you're a serious investigator. Just because Pringle would have you in until all hours, doesn't mean the rest of us roll that way. I know full well these cases are marathons not sprints. Let's not act like drunk dads at school sports day, okay? Besides, McKenzie's helping out. Tatty bye.'

Elliot watched him go, but for once realised how badly she missed Pringle's chaotic leadership.

CHAPTER TWENTY-SEVEN
MARSHALL

Marshall was used to this hospital by now. Weirdly enough, he'd never been in there as a kid – he and his sister had been born in the old Peel hospital over the Tweed in the back of beyond and not in the maternity unit in Gala. Something to do with their mother having an accident. The papers called them the Peel babies. Marshall never got to the bottom of it, no matter how many glasses of rosé their mother slurped down.

But his sister spent every day here. Senior Charge Nurse Jennifer Marshall. Those twelve-hour shifts were brutal, but she got lots of days off to keep on top of things.

And hide things from her brother.

She strode towards Marshall with a fierce look in her eyes, then stopped and frowned.

'Rob?'

Marshall looked to his side.

Gashkori was standing over him, hands in his pockets. 'You okay there, champ?'

'I'm fine.' Marshall got to his feet and nudged the chair back. 'Why do you ask?'

'You're just staring into space like that. Or is that just a particularly interesting wall?'

Marshall looked at Jen again, but she'd disappeared. The door to Pringle's room was open. 'Sorry, I was going to speak to my sister, that's all.'

'Your sister?'

'Jen. She's the senior charge nurse here.'

'Ah. Would've been funnier if she'd been a sister.'

Marshall grinned. Then it faded. 'I've been here since Jim arrived. He's not too bad, but she reckons he'll be in here for a few days. No signs of internal bleeding, but they want to make sure. Minor abrasions from the airbag on his face and arms. Based on his behaviour, they're worried he has a concussion...'

'You mean the... mental stuff?'

'Aye, but they're not focusing on that just now. Trying to stabilise him first. Said a specialist has been called in from Edinburgh.'

Gashkori nodded slowly. 'Any danger we can speak to him?'

'Just waiting for them to finish his initial treatment, then we'll get in there.'

'Great.'

'Shouldn't we wait for the Rat Pack?'

'This is just two old mates seeing a pal, Rob.'

'If you insist.'

Jen appeared from the door and walked over. 'Jennifer Marshall.' She held out a hand to Gashkori. 'You must be Shunty's replacement?'

'Must I?' Gashkori shook her hand. 'I'm actually DCI Pringle's replacement.'

'Oh, sorry.'

'Don't sweat it. DCI Ryan Gashkori. Pleased to meet you. It's a temporary gig, mind. And a long story.'

Jen glanced at her brother with a raised eyebrow.

'So, can we speak to Jim now?'

'Sure. Of course.' Jen smiled at him then stepped back the way towards his door. 'Here you go. Just... Don't push him too hard or too fast.'

'It's okay. We've done this before.' Gashkori stepped into the room and took the chair by the bed.

Marshall had to stay standing. He smiled at Jen then nudged the door shut. 'Seriously, we should pass this on to the Complaints, shouldn't we?'

'Nope. Milne says he's out of the firing line for now.' Gashkori rocked back on the chair, lifting the front legs off the floor. 'You don't look too hot there, Jim.'

Pringle lay in the bed, the sheet pulled up to his chin. Untreated wounds criss-crossed his face. His skin was yellowing as a precursor to some heavy bruising. 'What the hell happened to me? Was I in a fight?'

'Car accident, Jim.'

'Did someone run me off the road? Was it the Albanians?'

'Didn't have your seatbelt on and then you drove it into the side of a house.'

Pringle laughed, then gasped with pain. 'Jesus, I can't get the morphine in quick enough.'

Gashkori took a few seconds, maintaining eye contact throughout. 'Need to ask you a few questions before surgery. You up for that?'

'Sure, but it's not like I've got a choice, is it?' Another laugh. Another wince. 'Make it quick, though. Those buggers want to slice me open and do things to my vital organs. Horrible things!'

A glimpse of the old Pringle. Not gallows humour, just saw daftness in everything.

'We recovered your car, Jim. The driver claimed it was sitting in the Lidl car park. Key left in the engine.'

'That's right.'

'Did you pay them to dispose of it?'

'Of course not.' Pringle glared at him. 'I loved that car.'

Marshall struggled to keep his eyes locked on him. 'Talk to me about your daughter.'

'My daughter?'

'Kirsty. Right?'

Pringle sucked in a deep, halting breath. 'Look, I shouldn't have joked about Kirsty. It's clearly tempted fate.' He ran a hand down his face. 'But she's not called Kirsty. Sarah's her name. I'm so sorry for betraying your trust, Rob. I trust you and I trust most of my team, but I don't trust Elliot, not with the friends she keeps. People who know way more about a series of murders than a hardware store owner should.'

'Gary Hislop?'

Pringle nodded. 'Of course.'

'Did Hislop ever threaten Belu?'

'I don't know.'

'What about your daughter? Does Hislop know about her?'

'I don't know.'

'Has he ever threatened her?'

'I don't remember.'

'It's okay, sir. You can square this off by telling us the truth.'

'I'm trying to. Can't you see?'

'Did Belu leave you?'

'We'd... We didn't live together. Her preference... she never expected to get knocked up by a cop. We had a brief fling years ago, and we tried to stay together for the benefit of Sarah. But Belu has very little respect for cops as an occupation. Where she's from, police are corrupt and despicable. She knows that's not the case here but prejudices are hard to break. Our relationship couldn't survive that. She never trusted me. Ever. But she let me be involved in Sarah's life, just not as a father and especially not as a policeman.'

'That's a lot to process, Jim.' Gashkori got out his phone and held the screen out to Pringle. 'We need to talk about a bag from Hislop's hardware store we found in your boot.'

Pringle squinted. 'I've never been in that shop.'

'Any of them?'

'There's more than one?'

'What are you talking about, Jim?'

'Scott Street Hardware in Gala. Drive past it most days, but I'd never give Hislop my patronage. It'd be... unethical. Wouldn't it?'

Gashkori prodded his mobile screen again. 'Jim, the bag's from the Kelso shop. Roxburgh Street Hardware.'

'Nope. No idea what you're talking about.'

'You're going to stick to that?'

'I've never even seen that shop in my life. It must've been planted.'

'*Planted?*'

'The police planting evidence, eh?' Pringle gave a flash of his eyebrows. 'Whatever next?'

'Jim, you're in deep shit here. That bag looks like someone was planning on abducting someone.'

'It wasn't me!'

Gashkori rocked back in the chair again. 'Jim, you know how these cases unfold. Right now, I've got a team combing through the CCTV from that shop. If you're on it, then you've just lied to me and Rob.'

Pringle shook his head. 'Ryan, I didn't buy any cabbages.'

'Cabbages?'

'I didn't buy any fucking cabbages! Don't you hear me? You can shove your cabbages up your fucking arse!'

The door opened and Jen stormed in. 'Okay, let's—'

'Fuck off with your cabbages!'

'Outside!' Jen grabbed Marshall and Gashkori by the arm, then hauled them out into the corridor. 'What did you *do* to him?'

'Cabbages!'

Two nurses went in and shut the door behind them.

Gashkori raised his hands. 'Nothing!'

Jen led them down the corridor, away from the room. 'We'll need to sedate him. Been trying to avoid it, but...' She scowled. 'Why is he shouting about cabbages?'

'He did that in an interview.' Gashkori winced. 'It's why I'm here, doing his job.'

'Poor guy.' Jen pinched her nose. 'Listen, Dr Rougier had a look at him when he came in. In his estimation, Pringle is showing signs of nervous exhaustion.'

Marshall played it through. He'd been increasingly erratic over the last few months. Lack of sleep would contribute to that. Chronic lack of sleep would melt your brain. 'Nervous exhaustion sounds bad.'

'Right.' Jen pinched her nose. 'Really bad. It's like he hasn't slept properly in weeks or months. And I don't mean you've got a new-born baby stuff, because you still get sleep now and then, but this doesn't feel like it. I mean rock star on tour. Or CIA detainee.'

'Okay. Can we speak to him again later?'

'Absolutely no way. Nobody sees him until the specialist gives him the all clear from his head injury. If he has an intracranial bleed due to a subdural haematoma, he may need surgery to relieve the pressure. But we'll try to get him to sleep now and stop him talking about cabbages.'

Gashkori sucked in a deep breath. 'Okay. Sounds like a good plan.'

'It is.' Jen jabbed a finger in the air at Marshall. 'Listen, I'm almost off shift. I don't want either of you coming back here in an hour and trying to bully Leye, okay?'

Marshall knew him – one of the other senior charge nurses in A&E. Big Nigerian guy, who took even less shit than she did. 'No way will we be able to.'

'Right, I'm the easy mark? Great.' Jen smacked Marshall on his arm. 'Don't be late tonight.'

'Jen, I might have to—'

'No. It's your niece's birthday. No mucking about. You're coming. No excuses.'

'Sure. Of course.' Marshall smiled at her. Long enough for her to believe him and bugger off. He felt himself deflate as she walked off.

'She's something else.' Gashkori smiled. 'Let's get a coffee.' He walked off through the ward towards the front door. 'Is she younger or older than you?'

'Neither.'

'Eh?'

'Fraternal twins.'

'Oh. That.' Gashkori walked across the quiet café and smiled at the server. 'Two coffees, thanks.'

'Milk?'

'Black for me.' Gashkori looked at Marshall. 'Rob?'

'Oat milk if you've got it.'

'Aye, sure.' The wee server man tilted his head to the side. 'But riddle me this, lads. How do you milk an oat? Or an almond for that matter?' He pointed towards the window. 'Pull up a pew, boys, I'll bring them over.'

'Cheers.' Gashkori walked over and took a seat by the

window, looking out at the darkening evening, though the tinted glass in here made it seem even gloomier outside.

Marshall sat with his back to the door, giving the power seat to the senior officer. He eased his jacket off and sat back.

'Listen, Rob. I managed the drugs side of the investigation into Hislop, so I really want to get to the bottom of it all. I want to find out what's going on here and if we can stop what he's been up to.'

Marshall didn't know what to say to that. 'Do you think Pringle did it, sir?'

'It's a theory, sure. I think it's possible, but I don't think it's likely, no. Those dunderheids, though. The only part that's up for grabs is who paid them to do it.'

'Really? They confessed?'

'No. Well, they confessed to being paid to take the car, that's all.' Gashkori narrowed his eyes. 'Do you honestly think Pringle could've done this?'

'It's possible. Jim's been acting increasingly erratic for a while. At least since Christmas. I've only worked for him since July last year, but he's always been a bit crackers. I don't mean mad... Just, eccentric. But I put that down to being a *character*. You know, so he could inspire his team. Always laughing and joking about everything.'

Gashkori nodded along with it. 'You think it's an act?'

'Sure. Everyone acts. We've all got imposter syndrome, right? Thinking we're not good enough for this job, that we'll get found out. The way through that is to act like you know what you're doing.'

'Even you, Dr Robert Marshall, PhD, gets imposter syndrome?'

'Happens to the best of us, aye. I've got tools and techniques I've been trained on, which I rely on to get me through the job. But that's my training, not me. Same with you. You assert yourself as confident and wise, but you have a dark sense of humour, right? It's not that everything's a joke, but... You use humour to get your message across and you constantly reassure people after they screw up, instead of confronting them.'

'That's perceptive of you.'

'I watch people to get a read on them. I try not to assume too much.'

'Need to keep an eye on you, don't I?' Gashkori looked over at the till, but there was no sign of their wee server, so he looked back at Marshall. 'But you're right. I thought it was all an act too. Goes back years, but... When does the eccentric banter slip over the line into just insane?'

Marshall didn't have an answer for that, not without a few weeks solid interviewing Pringle as a patient. 'Do *you* think he did it, sir?'

Gashkori puffed out his cheeks. 'I wouldn't put it past him.'

'But?'

'Thing is... Hislop's on everybody's radar, but nobody can agree to even begin to think about talking about maybe prosecuting him at some point. Everything we've got a hold of is a step removed from his active operation. Anytime we pick up a dealer, they keep quiet. He treats them well, even the scum. And the ones who might talk, whenever me and Andi have got close to them, they have a habit of disappearing.'

'Dealers?'

'No. People involved in the actual business side of the operation. Or his friends from the rugby club, wink wink. It's not a lot of people, but another one went missing last night. Supposed to meet him today but he never showed. Andi was confident he was going to talk, but—' Gashkori smiled at the server as he delivered their coffees in paper cups. 'Thanks.' He tore off his lid, then slid it over to Marshall and took his. 'So, we've got a big operation dealing drugs in this area, which is spreading further afield. And we've devoted so many skulls to it. Four skulls full-time, around the clock. And we're getting nothing to show for it.'

'None of that makes me think Pringle's got a solid motive to try to kill Hislop.'

'No, but...' Gashkori took a long drink of coffee and grimaced.

Marshall didn't like the look of his. 'What about Balfour Rattray?'

Gashkori frowned at Marshall. 'What about him?'

'He's not just got the same car as Pringle. Hislop's involved with the farm's business, right? That loan. And he was under investigation, wasn't he?'

'That's true.' Another sip of coffee. Another grimace. 'The investigation's been drawing a blank, but maybe Balfour realises it was Hislop who got him into trouble with us.'

'But there's no trouble?'

'True. Maybe things got heavy between them. Balfour saw killing Hislop as the only way to clear it. Maybe he knows Pringle has the same car so can cause mischief.'

'That's a lot of ifs, buts and maybes, sir.'

'True.' Gashkori yawned into his fist. 'Okay, Rob. You can head home for the evening.'

'Are you sure about that?'

'Sure. Nothing more to see or do. I've got a lot of conference calls to reassure the brass. DI McKenzie will be managing everything until the overnight DI starts. We're used to working shifts in my teams. One hundred percent focus while you're on the clock, then get off it. Recharge, relax. I know that's kind of alien to you hard-boiled cops, but look at the toll it's taken on Jim.'

'If you're sure.'

'I am.'

'Okay. What about you?'

'Me? Oh, I'll finish up here by seeing if I can bully Leye into letting me back in with Pringle.'

'I wouldn't.'

'I'm joking.' Gashkori got out his phone. 'No, I've got some embarrassing personal calls to make I'd rather do out of your earshot, so kindly piss off.'

'Sure thing, sir.' Marshall got to his feet and lifted his coffee cup. 'Thanks for this.'

'Don't mention it. Just return the favour.'

'Will do.' Marshall strolled outside and walked over to his stupid oversized truck, still parked where it shouldn't be. He felt a pang of guilt at stealing a space when the parking was so bad at this hospital during the week. He got in, rested his coffee in the holder and put the key in the ignition.

Bastard thing didn't start.

Ah, shite.

He tried again. No joy. Just that grinding.

Time to admit defeat with this thing.

Marshall got out his mobile and called Kirsten. 'Hey, any chance you could get Trev to have a look at my car?'

CHAPTER TWENTY-EIGHT
ELLIOT

T he sun was setting on a shite day.

Elliot sat behind the wheel of her own car, watching a house. Fingers tapping along with the radio, some old song from the eighties. Or early nineties. Couldn't remember who it was by, but it'd lodge itself in her brain for a few days.

What a day.

What a shitty, shitty day.

Hard to process it all. Pringle's final marble slipping from his grasp, only for Ryan bloody Gashkori to swoop in and steal what should by rights have been hers.

She needed to focus on getting this case out of the way, then leave time for the dust to settle. No way was Pringle getting back, so a cheeky Acting DCI position might be up for grabs. And a cheeky Acting role would become a non-cheeky full tenure.

Assuming Dr Donkey was true to his word, then it was hers.

Aye, the hard part was getting this case out of the way.

Gashkori was an alright cop, but working for him longer than a few days was going to sting. She should be at the same rank as him, not reporting to him. At least being split across the operation meant she hadn't been taking orders from him.

Anyway.

Enough of that shite for now.

The lights in the house switched on. A woman peered out of the living room window, then shut the curtains.

Curious.

Seemed young. Dark hair at her shoulders. Casual T-shirt – not like someone visiting the home. Someone who lived there.

Gary Hislop was in hospital, smacked up to his eyeballs and fighting for his life. Stood to reason he'd have someone in there to help out with the boy but, whoever she was, she wasn't on their radar.

Unless Gashkori had been hiding things from her.

Speaking of which – she'd been sitting here long enough to spot any surveillance, so she got out and walked up the path. A deep breath, then she knocked on the door. Time to play the daft lassie.

Music played inside, that Elton John track where he sung with the young lassie her kids liked. Duo Lipo, or something. Wedging two old songs together over a dance beat was what passed for creativity these days... About as bad as Vanilla Ice co-opting 'Under Pressure' way back when.

The door opened and the woman peered out. Not as young as Elliot had first thought – mid-twenties, or maybe even thirty. Purple hair tied back in a bun. 'Can I help?'

Elliot smiled, a kind one. Warmth, gentleness. All of that. 'Heard what happened to Gary.'

'Oh.' She covered a grimace with her hand, then smiled. 'Thank you. Do you know him?'

'Aye, went to school with him, in the dim and distant past.'

'Ah.'

Behind her, a feral kid ran from one room to another, screaming his head off.

'Tyler! Go and watch your programme.'

Elliot waited for eye contact again. 'Are you his nanny?'

She scowled at Elliot like she'd shat on her foot. 'I'm Gary's girlfriend.'

Bloody hell.

All that surveillance from Gashkori's clowns and they hadn't identified he was in a relationship with someone who lived there. With purple hair.

Basic stuff.

Maybe she was ripe for mining for information, though. Get close to her family and her friends. See what she'd been spilling. Get someone close to her in the gym, the hairdresser, the supermarket. Whatever. See how loose her lips were.

'I'm Andrea.' She held out a hand. 'Andrea Elliot.'

'Sadie.' She shook it. The name clearly meant nothing to Sadie. That, or she was a great actor.

'Nice to meet you. How's Gary doing?'

'I'm...' Sadie gasped out a teary sigh. 'They don't know if he'll pull through.'

'God, that's awful. He's a good man.'

'He really is.'

'How long have you been together?'

'A couple of years now. He's just... incredible.'

Two years...

How the hell?

'I was in a dark place and... He's lifted me up. He's so kind and loving.'

Elliot gave another kind smile. 'That's Gary Hislop, for sure.'

Sadie clearly had no idea who he really was, the misery he

inflicted on innocent lives. And it wasn't time to tell her the truth.

'Sorry, I just heard myself from a pal. Otherwise I'd have brought you a casserole or lasagne.'

'It's okay.' Sadie smiled. 'He's not dead. You can visit him anytime.'

'Oh. Is he in hospital?'

'You thought he was dead?'

'Know what the rumours are like, eh?'

'Well, he's very much alive. In BGH.'

'Cool. Well, it's good meeting you, Sadie. Take care of yourself.' Elliot walked over to her car, feeling the burn of Sadie's glare in her back. She got in and chanced a look at the house.

Sadie was still in the doorway.

Elliot gave her a wave, then drove off at a slow pace. A few curtain twitchers now. She cleared the estate and turned left onto the A68, heading towards home.

She hit dial and the stereo blasted out her ringing tone.

'Gashkori.'

'Evening, sir. You still on?'

'Just heading off myself.' His yawn rattled the line. 'What's up?'

'Passed through St Boswells on the way from Kelso, so I thought I'd pop into the Newtown variant on my way back.'

'Why?'

'Gary Hislop lives there. And he has a son. Stands to reason someone's looking after him while he's in hospital.'

'Okay, good thinking. The son... The mother passed away, right?'

'A few years back, aye.'

'So you knocked on his door?'

'Right. Turns out Mr Hislop's got a significantly younger girlfriend. Name of Sadie.'

'How significantly?'

'She's late twenties, I'd say. And he's my age.'

'So late fifties?'

'Ha bloody ha. Early forties. A good ten, fifteen years difference, though.' She hurtled past a tortoise-speed Mini. 'Thing you need to think about, Ryan, is how Sexy Sadie has slipped our notice.'

Gashkori paused again. 'You're assuming I don't know.'

'So you've kept this from me?'

'No, but you made an assumption. I don't like the way you validated it, as well, but that's by the by. Thanks for telling me about her. I've got a few skulls to crack together.'

'Like Struan?'

'Mm. Sorry, that was crass. You think it's worth us speaking to her formally?'

'Maybe. Probably. Didn't get a surname, but it's definitely worth looking into before we do.'

'I'll get someone on it.' Gashkori paused, clicking his tongue hard a few times. 'Right. Have a good night.' He hung up.

Elliot raced on towards home, much faster than she should.

CHAPTER TWENTY-NINE
MARSHALL

Marshall lay back in a pool of sweat. Everything tingled. *Everything*. 'That was... Wow.' He looked over at Kirsten. Her face glowed, like his must've done. He reached over and stroked her hair. 'I love you.'

She was lying on her front, just the thin sheet covering her. 'You know some men only say that after they've come.'

'I don't.'

'No, you're right. You say it all the time.'

'I do love you, Kirsten.'

'And I love you, Rob. But I don't love your car.'

Evasion again...

'Hey, why bring the Beast into this?'

'It's a bit of a lemon, isn't it?'

'Too early to say that. I've only had him three months.'

'Him? Rob, your mechanic drives *him* more than you do.'

Marshall laughed. 'I need to properly thank Trev for sorting me out earlier.'

'He actually loves doing it. I don't know how he's wired.

It's baffling to me. He seems to take an extreme amount of joy from sorting out stuff like that.'

'I'm just pleased to be able to take advantage of it. Just hope that fix sticks.'

'If it doesn't, you really need to think about replacing it.'

'Already? I got it to stay safe in the Borders snow but it's not had any to contend with.'

'It's no use having it if you can't actually drive it when you need to, but aye, if it doesn't start, at least you're safe.'

'True.' Marshall sighed. 'Kirsten, we need to have that chat.'

'Right.' She rolled over and lay on her back, staring up at the ceiling. Just out of his reach. 'The *chat*. Did you know that the use of the word "chat" increased exponentially at the turn of the millennium thanks to the internet? Or that the French word *chat* has its origins in the Latin word cattus?'

'We won't need to have the chat now, if you don't want.'

She glanced over at him. 'But you really do.'

'I do, aye.'

'Rob, what do you want from me?'

'Just to know where I stand. Where this is going. That's all.'

She stretched out and groaned. 'Where do you see it going?'

'That's the thing, I can see it going in any number of directions.'

'Which one do you want?'

'It's not like that. It's which one we choose together.'

'Okay... This sounds ominous. I'll take whatever's behind door number three, thank you.'

'Please. I'm trying to be sensible here.'

'This is what we talked about a few months ago, right? That whole "white-picket-fence life". That's what you really want, isn't it?'

'I'm not sure.'

'Don't you need to be?'

'Kirsten, it's not like I'm buying stuff out of a catalogue or off a website. I am serious when I say I want to spend my life with you.'

'Wow.' Her eyebrows shot up and her mouth hung open. 'You know that's a lot, right?'

'I don't, actually. And I don't think it is. I'm not going to get down on one knee up the Eiffel Tower or ask your dad for your hand in marriage, but... The way I see it is things are pretty simple between us. We get on so well together. There's no bullshit, no lying and no games.' He left a pause then smiled. 'Except for you avoiding having this chat, of course.'

'Rob...'

'I'm joking.'

'Aye, sure. But you're making a point, right?'

'I mean, aye. Of course I am. Now I've got you here in my love nest, I can actually talk about this stuff.'

She paused and turned towards him, supporting her head on her hand, then she blew the hair from her eyes. 'Okay. I love you, Rob. But it's not easy. Okay? I've got issues. You know about them. While I'm glad you haven't tried to psychoanalyse me, I—'

'I mean, I have done. I just keep the results to myself.'

'Oh. That's not intimidating in the slightest, is it?'

'No, it isn't. Kirsten, I'm still here. Okay? I'm still pursuing you. Still in love with you.'

She looked away, shaking her head. 'Rob, if you take the white picket fence out of the equation, what does that leave us?'

'I think we should get married.'

'Married?' She sighed. 'Rob... Listen, I'm not a fan of marriage. My parents...'

'Aye, but I could say the same thing, right? My folks split when we were really young. I can barely remember my dad. But they're not you or me. Either of them. I believe in us.'

'Seriously?'

'Seriously. I've thought long and hard about stuff. How I want to shape my own destiny. Live *my* life how I want to. Not live it in reaction to someone else's.'

'Wish I had that confidence.'

'It's not confidence. It's...'

'Bravado?'

'No. It's just certainty. I feel certain about us.'

'Rob, is it about having a ring on my finger? About claiming me?'

'Nope. Not at all. If you don't want to get married, we don't get married. It's that simple. But I mean it when I say I can see me spending the rest of my life with you.'

'Does that mean you want to have kids?'

He shrugged. 'Do you?'

'That's deflection, Rob.'

'Okay. I think I do.'

'You need a lot more than you think. It's a lifetime commitment.'

'So is a marriage.'

'Most barely last five years. Kids don't. What is it they say? First ten years is keeping them alive. Next ten is keeping them out of prison.'

Marshall laughed. 'Never heard that.'

'But you've got to make sure they're okay for the rest of their lives. Being there for them. Helping them. Listening to them. Being their safety net. That's a huge commitment.'

'Okay, but it's something I think I want.'

'*I think* again.'

Marshall took a deep breath. 'Feels like I'm doing all the talking here. You're not saying what you want.'

'Rob...' She tugged at her hair for a few long seconds. 'Look, the bit I am okay with... Not the ring or the marriage or the bit of paper... But I have thought about being a mother, and there are worse prospects out there. So... it wouldn't be awful if I got knocked up.'

'Knocked up?'

'As in... If I was pregnant with your baby. It wouldn't be awful.'

'But your first choice is still not to have a kid?'

She reached over and stroked his cheek. 'Not sure on that score.'

Marshall felt that little chink of light as a fluttering in his stomach. 'The important thing isn't children, it's us. Me and you.' He smiled at her. 'Sounds like this chat wasn't as ominous as you feared.'

She raised an eyebrow, grinning. 'Oh aye?'

'Aye.' He shifted over the bed towards her, until he could taste her fresh breath. 'I'd like to be a dad, but I'm more than okay just being your sex-kitten.'

She lay back and bellowed with laughter.

Something thumped on the bedroom door. 'Mrrroowwr!'

'You've already got one of those, Rob.'

'Zlatan, it's okay. I'll be through in a minute.' Marshall cuddled into her. 'Look, we're both just enjoying the moment. Right?'

'We are.'

'And it's not just a moment. This feels big.'

'Agreed. But I am serious, Rob. I think I'm a big believer in fate. What's for you won't go past you, as my dad says. If it happens for us, it's meant to be. And if it doesn't? That's cool too.'

'That's... Interesting. I didn't have you pegged as a fatalist.'

'So your psychoanalysis isn't that great?'

'Clearly not.'

'Must be something to do with living with chains of evidence all day, every day.' She brushed a tangle of hair from her eye. 'When I find a trace of DNA somewhere, I can't help but put it together in a long chain of events. Everything that's happened to that trace up to the point of me inspecting that car or house or hotel room. It's all a thread of causality. One thing inevitably leads to the next in the chain.'

'Not sure it follows, to be honest, but I'll take it.'

Another thump. 'Mrrroowwwwwr!'

'You did feed him, right?'

'Zlatan can hoover up a bowl of biscuits like a stoner destroying a box of Space Raiders.' Marshall stared at her. 'Do you still want to go to Thea's birthday tonight?'

'Rob, I said I'm going. We're going.'

'Aye, and that's great. But... I'm worried you're not happy about it.'

'A relationship is all about compromise. If it brings you joy to have me there, then that's great. Like whenever you see my lovely neighbour and you tolerate him because I like him.'

'I mean, those aren't the same thing.'

'I think it's the whole Auntie Kirsten thing. I'm starting to lean into it, but... Aunties bake cheese scones, smell like liniment and wear supportive underwear. Can't I just be Kirsten to her?'

'You can be whatever you want. But you better get a shower if we're going to be there in time.'

CHAPTER THIRTY
MARSHALL

Laughter filled Mum's living room, reverberating off walls adorned with smiling family portraits. The softening light from the setting sun filtered through the windows, painting the room with warmth.

Amid the chaos, Marshall realised he was maybe feeling happy.

Kirsten caught his eye and gave him a wink, suggesting she was happy to be there. Despite the chat. Or maybe because of it. Having her there lifted his heart. Her laughter interweaving with the chatter of Thea's friends.

Grumpy sat on a recliner by the corner with a gruff expression, watching Thea open her presents. His wheelchair stood beside him and he seemed content to be out of its confines for once. Despite his name – the only one Marshall had known him by – Grumpy had a twinkle in his eyes. Even at his age, he was still sharp enough to follow the discussion, though he was as mystified as Marshall at some of their pop-culture references.

Marshall leaned forward as Thea opened the purple wrapping paper.

She unboxed a vintage Polaroid camera and squealed. 'Oh my God!' She rushed over and kissed him on the cheek. 'This is amazing, Uncle Rob.'

'Not just me. Your au—' He clocked a glare. 'Kirsten helped me track it down and made sure it was working.'

'This is so cool.' She hugged Kirsten too. 'Come on, let's go outside.' She grabbed her gift and led her gang of pals out into the small back garden.

Seconds later, the camera flash bled inside, just like the giggles.

Marshall caught them making daft faces and rock-star shapes through the glass. 'She'll get used to the fact there's only ten photos on a roll, rather than her phone's pretty much infinite memory.'

'It's a great present.' Kirsten winked at him again. 'You should be proud.'

'It was your idea.'

Thea started shaking the print.

Kirsten winced. 'Ah, crap.'

Marshall frowned at her. 'What? She's just drying them.'

'That won't help. It just spreads the chemicals around and ruins it.'

'Can't beat a good old Polaroid, eh?' Grumpy made a camera lens shape with his fingers and squinted at them through it, then clicked his teeth. 'Used to be a bugger getting Boots to develop the photos from all the porno shoots I did!'

Kirsten cackled. 'At least with a Polaroid you can see how good the shot is immediately.'

Grumpy winked at her. 'The money shot!'

'Grumpy, are you being rude?' Mum was in the corner,

collecting up torn wrapping paper and discarded bows. 'Robert, could you grab the cake from the kitchen?'

'Sure thing.' Marshall squeezed her shoulder as he passed, then went into the kitchen area. The cake was colossal, big enough for a wedding – they'd be eating it for months. He picked up both sides of the tray it was mounted on and made to lift it. Bloody thing weighed a ton.

A pair of arms snaked around his waist and gave him a tight squeeze.

Marshall broke off and swung around. Never let someone approach you like that. Stupid.

Jen started pinching his arm. Tight, sharp nips.

'Stop it.' Marshall batted her hands away. 'You're in a good mood.'

'I'm off for two whole days, brother dearest.'

'And you've drunk all the wine.'

'Nope. Driving, remember?' She arched her eyebrows. 'Remember when we used to fight over who'd blow out the candles first on our birthdays?'

'How could I forget? You always got there first.'

'Aye, and you cried like a baby.'

'Give me a break, I was six.'

She rolled her eyes with a grin. 'Peed yourself too.'

'I've got to have one blemish, otherwise I'd be perfect.'

She laughed. 'Listen, I know you don't like shop talk after hours, but I saw Elliot sniffing around the hospital.'

'She went to speak to Gary Hislop.'

'Yeah, but she was chatting with some guy called Callum?'

That was news to Marshall. 'Callum Hume?'

'Probably. Anyway, enough shop talk.' She picked up one end of the cake. 'Going to give me a hand?'

'Feels like we're carrying a coffin...' Marshall helped her lift the cake through to the living room and placed it carefully on the table in the middle of the room.

'Thea!' Jen opened the back door and stepped out into a camera flash. 'Time to cut the cake.'

Marshall took his chair again and Kirsten slipped her hand into his.

Thea followed Jen back into the living room, shrouded by her pals. She stopped and grinned at the cake, the glow from the candles reflecting in her eyes.

Mum started singing, 'Happy birthday to you!'

Kirsten's fingers tightened around his, and he looked at her.

She looked at him, the corner of her mouth twitching into a smile that made his heart flutter. 'Happy?' Just loud enough for him to hear over the singing.

'Very.' He gave her hand a squeeze back. 'Thank you for being here.'

Kirsten looked around the room, at his family – their family – and then back at him. 'No place I'd rather be.'

Thea blew out her candles and made a wish.

Marshall found that he had no need to make his own. Surrounded by family, with the woman he loved by his side, he had everything he could ever wish for.

What could possibly go wrong?

He reached for his alcohol-free Guinness and took a swig. Tasted just like the real thing – so much so that he had to keep checking the tin to make doubly sure.

Thea walked over to them and wrapped her arms around them. 'Thanks for the camera. It's super cool.'

Kirsten smirked. 'When I was your age, we all wanted digital cameras to take, like, three hundred photos on a night out. Now you lot crave analogue things like Polaroids, LPs and turntables.'

Thea frowned. 'What's a turntable?'

'For playing vinyl records.'

'You mean a vinyl player?'

Kirsten laughed. 'Right, aye. Sure. It's called a turntable. Ask your granny. Or Grumpy.'

'I was always much more into my tranny.' Grumpy cackled. 'You know, my radio?'

Thea kissed Kirsten on the cheek then Marshall on the forehead. 'Thank you, both.' She took a photo of them, with a blinding flash, then picked out the print and handed it to Marshall. 'Here you go.' She skipped off to her friends and headed outside, each with a big slice of cake on a red napkin.

Marshall shook the photo as the image started to resolve. 'You do have a bond with Thea.'

Kirsten nodded. 'The Auntie concept is still a bit head-melty, but we're just two intergenerational souls who get on.'

The doorbell chimed.

'There's somebody at the door!' Grumpy bellowed with laughter. 'There's somebody at the door! There's somebody at the door!'

Marshall scanned the room. Jen was outside with Thea and co, while Mum was fussing in the corner. 'I'll get it.' He hoisted himself up and walked through to the kitchen.

'There's somebody at the door!'

'Aye, Grumpy, I've got it.' Marshall opened the door.

Siyal stood there, looking Marshall up and down. 'Rob?'

'Rakesh?' Marshall tilted his head to the side. 'What are you doing here?'

'Out of the way, Shunty.' A big guy barged past him. Barrel-chested and about the same height as Marshall. Silver hair, dark goatee surrounding his lips. 'Hiya, pal. Is Janice in?'

Took Marshall a few seconds to recognise him. Superintendent Bob Milne. What the hell did they want with him? Had Pringle done something?

Marshall smiled at him. 'Sorry, it's my niece's birthday – do you mind coming back later?'

'Ah, crap. Well, I've not brought any gifts, just this.' Milne had a bottle of semi-decent single malt in his left hand. He held out his right to shaken, then pulled it away. 'Ah, we met in Kelso.'

Siyal looked a bit uncomfortable, staring at his feet.

Marshall had no idea why he was here. Why either of them were. 'Aren't you here to—'

Milne frowned behind him. 'Going to invite us in, Janice?'

'Bob?' Mum barged Marshall out of the way. 'What are you doing here?'

Jen was with them too, hands on hips.

Milne passed Mum the whisky. 'Down on business, Janice. Popped over to visit the old man, but the ward said he was over here.'

'Old man?' Marshall glowered at him. 'You mean *Grumpy*?'

Mum sighed. 'Robert, Jennifer. This is your father.'

CHAPTER THIRTY-ONE

HISLOP

Gary Hislop blinked awake.

The world around him was blurry and disjointed, like a cheap watercolour painting left out in the rain.

The room was silent, but the tang of antiseptics invaded his nostrils, as if someone had attempted to scrub away the stink of death and replace it with the scent of false hope. A steady, rhythmic light flashed on some machine, each pulse way too bright and an unwelcome guest in his foggy consciousness.

He tried to move, but every muscle in his body screamed in protest as if he'd gone ten rounds with a sledgehammer-wielding gorilla.

The car.

It came at him out of nowhere, like a hunter pouncing on its prey.

His hand, heavy as lead, travelled to his abdomen, his fingers exploring the bandaged landscape.

Major surgery, the doctor had said, his face a mask of

sterile concern. One of those life-saving procedures they performed when a ton of steel turned your insides into a Picasso. Better him than Jackson Pollock's paint splatters.

He let out a dry chuckle, the sound scraping his throat like coarse sandpaper.

He closed his eyes, willing the room to stop spinning. The pain was a dull ache running down both legs, a cruel companion whispering sweet torment in his ear. But he wasn't going to let it break him.

After all, he had someone to take revenge on and he was a man who kept his promises.

'Are you awake?'

He craned his neck to look over to the side.

Sadie sat there. Black top, black trousers. A woman in grieving. His woman.

'Hey.'

'Hey.' She leaned over and kissed him, her sweet perfume washing over him. 'How are you feeling, love?'

'Like I should be dead.'

'I'm glad you're not. The doctor says you're going to pull through.'

'That's... I'm fine, Sadie. Totally fine.'

She shook her head, grinning. 'You're a fighter, Gary, but even you need professional help.'

'True.' Hislop looked around the room. 'Where's Tyler?'

'Callum's got him. Letting me have a break to see how you were.'

'Send him in.'

'He's a bit tired. School was—'

'Callum. First. Need a word with him.'

'Sure.' Sadie got to her feet but just stood there. 'Does the name Andrea mean anything to you?'

Shite.

Hislop tried a smile, but it just hurt. 'What context?'

'A woman came to the door tonight. Said she's an old friend from school.'

'Cop. What did you tell her?'

'Nothing.'

'Keep it that way. But she's good. Glad she's on the case. Might find out who did this to me.'

'Okay. I'll go and find Callum.'

She left the room and left him to his pain.

Elliot sniffing around didn't feel good. She should be out finding evidence against Pringle – he'd *told* her it was him. Why didn't she believe him?

Aye, he needed to do something on that score.

The door opened again and Callum walked in. Looking dapper as ever. 'Evening, Gary. How you feeling?'

'Brutal. Sure I'll be fine after this?'

'Absolutely. Clean contact. Broke both legs, but they're simple breaks. No fragments. Bruising, bit of internal bleeding.'

'That explains the insane amounts of pain, then. What's the doc saying?'

'She said you should make a full recovery. That's all sorted and it's a case of you healing. So rest up and rest up good.'

'Okay. This pain must be worth it.'

'They put pins in both legs and in your shoulder. Might never play top-class rugby again, Gary, but you'll make a full recovery.'

Hislop laughed. 'I'm shit at rugby.'

'Doesn't stop you playing, though, does it? Be a while before you get your boots back on.' Callum took the seat. 'Pringle's being kept in overnight.'

'In the police station?'

'No, in here. Car crash. Smashed a police car against a house. Clonked his head off the steering wheel.'

'Worse than me?'

'Nowhere near as bad. Bit of concussion, but I gather they're also doing some other tests on him.'

'Okay.' Hislop managed to ball up his fist. 'I want him dead.'

'Understandable.' Callum leaned forward. 'But we can't do it in hospital.'

'Don't care where it happens. Get a hold of Chunk.'

CHAPTER THIRTY-TWO

ELLIOT

The aromatic melody of basil, garlic and simmering tomatoes filled the kitchen.

Elliot retied her apron around her waist yet again – bastard thing wouldn't stay, would it? – then stirred the bubbling sauce. She added a pinch of oregano, then scooped a little onto the pasta boiling in the pan next to it. The meaty sauce sank into the water and turned it a shade darker.

This kitchen was her oasis from the bullshit of her job, where things went according to plan. Her plan. Even her youngest two were doing what they were told, both seated at the kitchen table behind her, their homework spread out in front of them.

Harry was struggling with a maths problem and looked a spaghetti's width away from a minor meltdown.

Charlie, three years younger, was scribbling away at his story. An absolute miracle seeing him swept away in school-work, considering he'd spent much of the last year doing everything he could to avoid going there every day. She was constantly thankful the school avoidance was a thing of the past.

Davie sauntered into the room, a grin on his face that was too big for it to be innocent. He clapped his hands together, his eyes twinkling with mischief. 'Alright, boys, are you ready for this?'

Charlie looked up, giggling in anticipation.

Harry was too savvy for this, so gave his dad a glower, then went back to his work.

Davie settled on a stool next to his sons. 'Why don't scientists trust atoms?'

Charlie's eyebrows were knitted in curiosity. 'Why don't they?'

'Because atoms make up everything!' Davie threw his hands up in the air.

Harry rolled his eyes, but his lips were twitching with suppressed laughter.

Charlie let out a belly laugh that echoed throughout the room.

Bless them – Elliot knew that neither of them got it, but they still humoured Davie and his woeful dad jokes.

The water boiled in the background and Davie cuddled their youngest two. 'Alright, this one's a classic. Why can't you give your mother a balloon?'

Harry looked up from his homework. 'Why?'

'Because she will *never* let it go.' Davie winked at Elliot.

Harry frowned. 'I don't get it?'

Elliot drained the pasta, then mixed it with the sauce. Aye, she wasn't going to let that one go. 'Tea's up!'

'One last one.' Davie laughed before he'd started. 'Why don't some fish play piano?'

Charlie looked at his dad with a sense of wonder. 'Why not?'

'Because you can't tuna fish!'

Elliot tried to ignore the boys rolling around on the floor. 'Okay, kids, can you clear away your homework?'

'Okay, Mum.' Good as gold, they both shuffled their papers back into their schoolbags. 'Can we play *Minecraft*?'

'After your tea.' Elliot served up the last plate. 'Can you go and wash your hands, please. Charlie, can you go and get your — Can you get Sam down for tea?'

'O-kay.' Charlie scuttled off, his bag dangling behind him, and Harry followed him out.

Davie poured some wine into two glasses. 'You know I don't mean anything by that joke.'

'What joke?'

'You know...'

'Not really.' But she couldn't stop herself from smiling at him. 'It's fine. I don't let most things go.' She recognised the bottle he was using and her stomach clenched.

The last of the case she'd found in her car a few months ago. Hislop's wine. Or she suspected as much. Expensive stuff, too. Delicious, but tainted by association.

'Take it you heard?'

'About Hislop?' Davie sighed. 'Aye. Had an absolute 'mare today. Your lot traipsing in and out, needing to give them all clones of Shunty's ID because the new security system's buggered. Heard a lot of theories about Pringle and Hislop.'

'I'm worried, Davie.'

'Why? You've done everything by the book. Right?'

'Of course I have. But Hislop knows things about us.'

'Like what?'

'Those photos? Who knows what else he's got?'

Davie wrapped his arms around her, clasping behind her waist. 'Look. It's okay. You've passed on the intel you've gained. Just because Jim Pringle or Balfour Rattray or someone else decided to try to kill him, nothing can trace back to you because you've done nothing. Right?'

'Right. I mean...'

'Andi, is there something you're not telling me?'

'God, no. Just... I knew I shouldn't have done anything with what he told me. Should've just walked away. The whole thing... Feels like I'm paying the price for something I haven't even done.'

'There's no price to pay because you've done nothing. Okay?'

'Okay.'

Charlie slid into the room on his socks and helped himself up onto one of the dining chairs. 'Mum, Sam isn't there.'

'What?' She looked at Davie. 'Where is— Where are they?'

Davie shrugged. 'Eh, they haven't even come home yet.'

'Davie, it's quarter to eight!' Elliot raced over to the door, her head filled with the fear that one of Hislop's people had kidnapped her child.

CHAPTER THIRTY-THREE
MARSHALL

Marshall tightened his grip on the door handle. Part of him wanted to slam the door and go back inside, then get back to Thea's birthday party. A time when everything made sense. Just seconds ago, but...

What?

He looked at Detective Superintendent Bob Milne and started to piece things together. He had the same nose as Jen. Those big ears were Marshall's. The piercing eyes they shared, that glowered at him every time his sister looked at him, or his own, which he only saw through the mist of a shaving mirror. And he was the same height and build as Marshall, just carrying a bit more timber and starting to stoop. That cast-iron belly was where Marshall himself would bear the brunt of a few weeks of bingeing on ice cream.

But that name...

Bob Milne.

What the fuck was that surname all about?

He'd never be Dad. Never. He'd been Daddy once, many years ago, but now... Now he would only be Milne.

The naked emptiness of a surname.

Jen stormed out of the house and got in his face. 'Our *dad?*' Her fury was scrawled all over her face, her fury shifting between Marshall, their mother and this guy, the man who was claiming to be their father. 'What are you talking about?'

Milne gave a flick of his head and a casual you-got-me look. 'Afraid so.' He held out a hand with a cheeky twinkle in his eyes. 'Now unless you've both undergone sex changes, you must be Jennifer.'

She slapped his hand away. 'You can't just show up here! On my daughter's birthday!'

Milne stared hard at Mum. 'Thought you'd passed on the presents every year, Janice?'

'I can't deal with this.' Mum disappeared inside the house.

Aye, losing yourself in drink was really going to help...

Bob smoothed a hand through his hair – his coo's lick was in the exact same spot as Marshall's, that constant battle that could only ever resolve in a rockabilly quiff. 'It's nice to see you, Jennifer. I'd say you've grown, but it's been thirty years. Even I've grown in that time!' His laugh was infectious, the kind where he cast his gaze around everyone to check they were laughing too.

Only Siyal was.

Marshall didn't want to get into why the hell *he* was there. Not yet, anyway. He stepped between his sister and... his father, trying to be subtle so as not to become the target of Jen's ire. 'She's right. You can't just show up here after all this time and expect us to be cool about it.'

'Robert.' Milne clamped a rock-crushing hand on his arm and smiled at his son. 'Guessing you don't wet the bed anymore?'

Siyal raised his eyebrows, his mouth forming an O.

Before Marshall could say any more, Jen got stuck in again. 'I'm asking you once. Go. Now. And don't come back.'

Milne looked into the house, where everything seemed that much quieter now. 'I didn't expect to see you pair here, just your mother. Popped in to check up on Grumpy and they said he was here. You know, my father?'

'I know he's your father, but you've not been *our* father so you can fu—'

'It's really nice seeing you, Jennifer. You look just like your mother.'

She narrowed her eyes at him. 'You sick bastard. You left us. When we were tiny. And you left us in the clutches of Graham Thorburn.'

Milne looked over at Marshall then back at Jennifer. 'Aye, that was, eh, *unfortunate*.'

'*Unfortunate*? He was a serial rapist who turned into a serial killer. Preyed on Mum's insecurities after you left.' Jen thumbed at her brother. 'You won't know Anna, but she was Rob's girlfriend. She was a victim of Thorburn's. He groomed her, then abducted her. He raped her, repeatedly. Everyone was looking for her. Nobody found her. She escaped but jumped off the Leaderfoot Viaduct rather than be caught again. That's on you. That's all on you!'

The hustle from inside charged outside, as Thea led her pals out and down the hill towards the town centre. She didn't want to get involved, but there was a girl who knew all about fathers letting you down.

Milne watched her go. Seemed to want to introduce himself to his granddaughter, but he focused on Jen. 'I don't deny any of this, Jennifer. Hard to live with yourself when something like that happens.'

'It happened twenty years ago! You left thirty years ago! You could've visited at any point and talked to us!'

'I know, but... Look, I've read up on the case and I... What can I say? He was way too careful to target you, Jennifer, so you —'

'Fuck off.' She grabbed his arm. 'Fuck. Right. Off.' She was in his face now, spitting the words.

Milne just took it. Guy was clearly a seasoned officer – probably not in the top hundred worst volleys of abuse he'd ever received.

Marshall pulled Jen away from him.

She nudged him away and resumed her full-frontal assault. 'You honestly think I just care about myself? I don't give a fuck about that. But Anna was my best friend! You put us all in danger! She'd be alive if it wasn't for you!'

Milne stared hard at her, his forehead creasing and uncreasing. 'Jennifer, a word of advice based on years of experience. You shouldn't be so convinced that the grass is greener in your counterfactual narrative.'

She laughed, bitter and cold. 'My *what?*'

'A counterfactual. You're positing a what-if scenario and I can totally understand why. If this hadn't happened, your friend would be still alive. It's comforting. I totally get that. It's how you've coped over the last—'

'Leave.' She pointed down into the town. 'Now!'

Milne folded his arms. 'I'm here to see Janice. And my dad.'

'Not tonight you're not. Piss off. Go! Now!'

'Is my dad here?'

'Grumpy's not going to speak to you.'

Milne smiled. 'Grumpy. I always loved that name.' He looked down at the ground, his eyes misting over, then back up at her with a hard stare. 'Jennifer. I'm sorry. This is all going wrong and I'm holding my hands up. I honestly didn't know you were going to be here, otherwise—'

'I told you to leave!'

'Can we at least sit down and chat? You and me and your brother?'

'Maybe when hell freezes over.' Jen turned to face Mum, who was standing just inside, her arms folded over her chest. 'Tell Thea I'll come and pick her up when she's done.' She prodded a finger at Bob Milne. 'I never want to see your face again in my life.' She stormed off towards her car, parked just up the hill.

'You can't win them all, eh?' Milne smiled at Marshall. 'Wonder why that one's single, huh?'

Marshall barged past him and jogged up the hill to catch up with Jen. 'Wait.'

She stopped by the driver. 'I'm not interested, Rob. He's a fucking dickhead!'

'I know he's a dickhead, but we should hear what he's got to say.'

'Nope. No fucking way. He made a decision the day he left us. *Mum* didn't leave us. She stayed. She raised us. She's clearly a damaged woman, but she did her best. Her and Grumpy both did. Not him, though.' She scowled, pointed back down the hill at the house. They'd all gone inside. Her mask crumbled and she huffed out a sigh. 'Are you honestly just going to let him get away with all of that?'

'No, but I want to give him enough rope to hang himself.'

'A cop... I always thought our dad was in the military or MI6.' Jen shook her head. 'At least that made sense. But a *cop*?'

'Lots of ex-squaddies sign up.'

'Did you know?'

'Of course I didn't.'

'You must've done.'

'Jen, he calls himself Bob bloody Milne, not Marshall. We've been lugging around *his* name my whole life and he's not even using it?'

She smiled. Finally. 'Why's he here, Rob?'

'I met him earlier, in Kelso. This case I'm working. There's been a possible police corruption angle since before what happened this morning. Now there's at least a whiff of vehicular assault by a serving officer...' Marshall stared hard at her. 'I swear I had no idea about him, Jen. None at all.'

She looked away. 'Find that hard to believe.'

'Come on, there are no secrets between us. Not from my end anyway.'

Jen glowered at him. 'Are you coming with me?'

'I've got my car.' Marshall looked even further up the hill and hoped the Beast would start. 'I want to speak to him. Need to understand him to understand myself.'

'That's some primo psychobabble there.'

'He left us when we were kids, Jen. I want to know why. And why he's only coming back now.'

'I don't. I don't give a flying fuck. I just know he's a selfish prick.' She looked like she was about to go apeshit at him. Then she looked to the side. 'What's up?'

'The drama's too thick for me.' Kirsten got in the passenger seat. 'Catch you later, Rob.'

Before Marshall could say or do anything, Jen got in the car and shot off in the wrong direction, up the hill towards the Eildons and the very slow road home via Selkirk.

Marshall felt torn in half.

Kirsten and his sister both clearing off. Mum disappearing inside.

When all the important women in your life make a decision, the smart money is on agreeing with them.

But his dad being here...

His dad...

After all that bloody time...

He started walking back to the house.

CHAPTER THIRTY-FOUR

ELLIOT

E lliot took it slowly along the high street in Lauder, part of the main road between Edinburgh and Newcastle, then turned away from the main drag into a maze of cobblestone streets and ancient stone buildings – the perfect place to lose yourself.

And Elliot wasn't finding Sam.

A tourist guide would describe Lauder as quaint, maybe, but it was just like any other small Scottish town, with its own secrets. Gangs of kids hanging around any night of the year. The pack by the bus stop were at least a year younger than Sam and all wore shell suits, trainers and bravado.

Bloody hell.

Elliot was no stranger to the underbelly of society – she'd faced down murderers, extortionists and all manner of lowlifes, but finding her own flesh and blood was proving to be a different beast entirely.

Hard to shake the feeling that Hislop had something to do with this. He'd sent a few photos of her and her family stuck on top of that case of fancy wine a few months ago. Hard not to treat that as anything other than a threat. But harder not to fight against it and try to bring Hislop down.

Those potential informants disappearing, like Blake Innes that morning, they must've talked. Must've told Hislop who'd approached them.

That must've tipped him over the edge.

He'd set his sights on her.

And her family.

After Pringle had done what he'd done, Hislop wanted to lash out at her.

Lying in a hospital bed that might become a deathbed, he'd sent her a message. And it was becoming clearer and clearer – he was going to take her oldest child from her.

Whatever happened to Sam, this was all her fault. All on her. She could've stayed quiet on the whole thing, but she'd gone straight to Pringle. Got it all on the record.

But she needed to make sure the conclusions she was jumping to were the right ones. Before she went after anyone in Hislop's orbit, she needed to do the basics and track down Sam's school friends.

Elliot pulled in at the side of the road and got out into the thin rain. The evening was cold, the biting Scottish winds whispering tales of missing children in her ears. This was her worst fear, made manifest. She waited for the row of cars to swoosh past, then stormed off across the road and followed the shouting up the drive.

A stout man guarded the old house's front door, jabbing a finger at a woman. Sixties and he looked like Santa Claus, with thick white hair and a thicker beard. The skin on his round face was all cracked like a sun-baked puddle. 'I'm afraid I have no sympathy, Alison.'

The woman he was speaking at was mid-thirties and had

the harassed look of a single mum. 'Jesus Christ, I just want to speak to Alex.'

'I'm not going to let you.'

'Seriously? My own kid?'

'I disapprove of you breaking up your family unit for selfish reasons.'

'*Selfish* reasons?' Alison barked out a laugh. 'Would you be happy with Charanya sleeping around?'

'My wife wouldn't do that.'

'But if you caught her in—'

'Hey, hey.' Elliot got between them. She didn't need to settle a domestic – she needed info on Alex, Sam's BFF. But these two weren't going to give anything, were they? 'What's going on here?'

Santa looked at her, nostrils flaring. 'Who the hell are you?'

'I'm a police officer, sir.' She held out her warrant card. 'DI Andrea Elliot. But I'm here as a mum. Is my Sam with your Alex? They've not been seen since after school.'

'They?' Santa rolled his bloodshot eyes. 'One of *those*, eh?'

'I'm worried Sam's gone missing. Now, if it's possible to speak to your... kid, that'd be great.'

'My kid?'

'Alex?'

Alison prodded herself on the chest. 'Alex is mine. This dickhead is his grandfather. But he's not letting me see him!'

'Some people cannot accept that divorce has consequences.'

Elliot ignored him and focused on his ex-daughter-in-law. 'Have you got any visitation rights?'

'*Rights*?' She laughed. 'Alex is with me all of the time because my ex, *his* son, decided he couldn't be arsed with us and banged a floozy.'

'That is not true and you know it! My son wouldn't dream of doing such a thing!'

None of this was getting anyone anywhere.

'Sir.' Elliot gave him the full-on police officer stare, which seemed to calm him some. 'Alex is friends with Sam. My kid. They're thick as thieves, usually. Just need a word. Two minutes, that's all.'

'Fine.' Santa turned and bellowed into the house. 'Alex!'

Nothing, no footsteps tumbling down the stairs.

'Alex!'

Still no response.

Elliot smiled at him. 'Is Alex actually here?'

'Oh, aye.' Santa got a smartphone from his pocket and hammered on the screen. 'Watch this.'

A few seconds later, feet thundered down the stairs towards them.

Alex was a name that could be either gender. Or neither. Just like Sam. Seeing them in the flesh didn't narrow anything down any. Tall and thin to the point of concern, with dark hair hanging in a bob. 'What's up?' The voice didn't narrow it down either.

'Have you seen Sam today?'

A nod. 'Why?'

Elliot took charge, nudging Santa out of the way. 'I'm Sam's mum. Nothing serious at this point. But I can't get hold of them. When did you see them?'

Alex frowned. 'Them?'

Elliot still hadn't decided on a gender. Alex clearly wasn't as militantly non-binary as Sam, but whatever. She smiled at Alex. 'Sam.'

'Right, right. School, I guess.'

'Have you heard from Sam since?'

Alex shook their head. 'Nope. Take it she didn't turn up at home?'

She? Bloody hell. Elliot didn't understand the rules anymore. 'Nope. Nobody's seen or heard from Sam since school.'

'Wasn't her dad supposed to pick her up?'

'No. Going to make their own way home. Any idea where Sam could've gone?'

Alex shrugged. 'Not really.'

'Did Sam have a boyfriend or a girlfriend or a...?'

'Eh, not that I know of?'

Elliot folded her arms. 'Alex, how was Sam at school today?'

Alex shrugged again. 'Stressed.'

'About what?'

'Her exams.'

Elliot smiled. 'Anything specific?'

'Nope.'

Elliot nodded. It all made sense to her now. Exam stress was eating away at Sam...

More than enough to make someone run away.

But she still felt the acidic worry of Hislop being up to something burning away at her guts.

Elliot stood there, fizzing, but her anger was sailing through the air. 'Did you get the bus with Sam after school?'

'No. She was with Tam.'

'Tam?'

'Aye, Tam. They got off together. Tam's dad owns the Lion's Roar.'

Well, there was a lead.

Elliot smiled at Alex. 'Thanks for that.'

'Mum.' Alex collapsed into a cuddle.

'Alison, this isn't finished! You can't just—'

Elliot pointed a finger at Santa. 'Sir, you need to respect your grandson's mother's visitation rights.' She waited for a nod, then trotted off back towards her car. She got back in and raced down the road, trying to think rationally and ignore what the wind was whispering to her.

Sam had been at school. Tick.

Sam had got the bus back from Gala. Tick.

Sam had gone off with Tam.

She pulled in outside the Lion's Roar, the town's underage boozer, a pub so rugged it could play prop forward for the local rugby team. Where the town's youngsters used to gather.

Okay, the trail led this far – *don't get too carried away, focus on the facts. Pick up details, don't leap to conclusions.*

Just turned sixteen, but not exactly worldly wise. Nobody in Lauder was. Terminally online – the whole world seen through a phone screen.

Elliot walked in and saw nothing but an oddball assortment of town drunks, disgruntled barmaids and middle-class couples dining on steaks and fancy pasta dishes.

No kids, other than the wee lassie in the highchair, her cheeky face smeared with chocolate sauce.

Elliot smiled at the nearest barmaid. 'Looking for the owner. Is he in?'

The barmaid kicked the floor and shouted, 'Mark!' She stepped aside to serve another customer.

A rosy-cheeked face peered out of a hatch and a stout man gradually emerged up the ladder. 'The Neck Oil should be back on, Gina.' He smiled at Elliot. 'Can I help?'

'Looking for my kid. Sam. Gather your Tam's a pal of theirs.'

'Sam?' He smiled. 'Sam and Tam! What a pairing, eh?'

'Does Tam talk about Sam?'

'Not sure. Don't think so.'

'Okay. I gather Sam was with Tam earlier. Do you know where he is?'

'Not seen him all evening.'

'What about his mother?'

'Hope not. She died four year ago.' Mark bellowed out a laugh. 'If he's with her, I'm in trouble. Hang on.' He got out his mobile and put it to his ear. 'Wee bugger's just bounced it.' He tapped at the screen. 'Two can play at that game.' He flicked a hand out of the door. 'Wonder of modern technology, eh? Phone, watch and headphones are in the churchyard.'

'Thanks.' Elliot raced out of the pub and jogged across the road, past the old town hall then over the other street.

The church was lit up in the dark night, pressed right up against the road.

Elliot tried the gate.

Locked.

Bollocks.

The wall was low enough, though, so she hopped over.

No sign of anybody in front of the church, but a few shapes lurked at the back of the graveyard.

Kids will be kids, eh?

Elliot took it slowly and quietly as she walked across the damp grass, soaking her shoes within a few steps.

And she saw them.

Under the dim glow of an old lamp, Sam was locked in an embrace with a boy.

Tam, presumably.

Elliot's heart skipped a beat, not out of anger, but surprise.

Sam pulled away and nibbled at their bottom lip. Lipstick and eye shadow, hair clipped back, low-cut top revealing a lot of flesh. Then Sam spotted Elliot out of the corner of their eye.

The look of panic was clear.

Sam bolted, disappearing further into the gloom.

Elliot hesitated only a moment before giving chase. She weaved through the twisted teeth of gravestones, the soft echo of Sam's footsteps guiding her towards the back gate.

Just as Elliot thought she was losing her kid, Sam stumbled into a dead end – this gate was locked too.

No escape now, only a tall stone wall, much higher than at the front. No easy way over.

Sam turned around, face flushed, eyes wide and fearful. 'Mum...'

'Sam!' Elliot wrapped Sam in a big hug. 'Hey, hey. It's okay.'

Sam clung on. 'I thought you'd be angry?' The words hung in the cold air.

Elliot, panting from the chase, shook her head. 'I was worried, Sam. Worried sick. I thought...'

'But...' Sam's voice was shaky. 'But I thought you'd be—'

'Nope.' Elliot cut the words off, a soft smile on her lips. 'Love is love, Sam. No matter who it's with.' She wrapped her arms around her kid again. 'Don't run, Sam. Not from me. Never. Okay?'

'Okay.' Sam's body sagged in her arms.

Elliot held Sam close. The winds whispered once more, carrying away her fears into the dark night. She looked back towards the church. No sign of the lad. 'Was that Tam?'

Sam looked up and nodded.

'So you've got a boyfriend now?'

'Right. I, eh, think I might've started identifying with a gender after all.'

'Whether you're Samuel or Samantha or you stay as Sam, it's your choice.' Elliott was confused, but Sam was her kid. She'd do literally anything for her. Anything. 'Sam, you're my child. Whoever you love and whoever you identify as in the process, I'm still going to love you to the moon and back.'

CHAPTER THIRTY-FIVE

MARSHALL

Marshall walked back into the house, shaking himself free of a memory of that summer's day years ago. They'd been told to play in the park beside their old house as Mum and Dad needed to have a *talk*.

Jen had bounded out into the sunshine and immediately immersed herself into a group of kids playing some convoluted version of tig, while Marshall found a quiet place on the grass to admire the passing clouds for an hour or so.

Quiet, until Dean McCutcheon stomped on his bollocks for no good reason, other than they were there.

His sister hauled him off and punched Dean square in the nose, bursting it and then helping her brother limp home.

Mum was already halfway through a bottle of gin and had tears streaming down her face.

Dad was gone, and he wasn't coming back.

Jen was angry that day and had stayed angry ever since.

As for Marshall, the kick in the knackers didn't ache as much as losing his father.

He opened the door and found them all in the living room – Grumpy, Bob Milne and Rakesh Siyal.

Mum was fussing around at the table in the corner where the Christmas tree would usually go. 'There's all this leftover food, Bob. And that cake! It took me ages to make the bloody thing and now it'll just go in the bin.'

'Relax, Janice.' Milne cracked open the screw-top and poured whisky into four small glasses. 'A wee dram will take the edge off.'

She looked over at him, frowning. 'I stopped drinking.'

'Oh.' Milne snorted. 'When was that?'

'A New Year's resolution I've actually stuck to. I've been known to make stupid decisions when I've had a few.' She gave him a pointed look, then managed to carry the remains of the cake through to the kitchen all on her own. Despite her protestations, at least half of it had gone.

Marshall would take the rest of it home for his niece.

Milne nudged a glass over the table to Siyal. 'Here you go, Shunty, that'll put hairs on your chest.'

'It's not a problem I face.' Siyal looked at the glass like it was going to bite him.

The smoky aroma filling the room suggested it might.

Milne looked up at his son. 'Robbie... Can I tempt you?'

'It's Rob. And no thank you. I'm driving.' Marshall took his old seat, the one he'd sat in every night while they watched telly way back when. He missed Kirsten sitting next to him, he missed her touch. He took out his phone and checked if she'd replied to his message – nope.

'Are we boring you?' Milne slurped down whisky like anyone else would drink tea.

Marshall put his mobile away and tried to ignore the burning on his cheeks. 'Rakesh, why are you here?'

'We're down on business, but I guess you know that.' Milne

put his glass down and golden liquid spilled out the sides. 'Staying in a hotel in town. Taylor's. Nice place, but bloody Shunty's got the suite!'

Marshall kept his gaze on Siyal. 'That doesn't answer my question.'

'It's the laddie's first day in Professional Standards. Thought I'd show him the ropes the old-fashioned way. How I do things, which is, of course, the right way. And, you know, we can get acquainted with one other over a drink or two. Break some bread. You know how it is.'

Marshall still didn't look at Siyal. 'Afraid I don't.'

'Studs up!' Grumpy lifted his glass to his lips and chugged it down in a succession of shallow gulps, dribbling at least half down his chin. 'Great stuff, son.' He slammed his glass onto the side table next to him. 'More!'

Milne walked over with a chuckle and refilled his glass. 'Hollow legs. That's what you used to say about me.'

'They must've filled in.' Grumpy prodded a shaking hand into his son's belly. 'It's all overflowing into there, son!'

'Do like my grub, has to be said.' Milne beamed at Marshall. 'Sure I can't tempt you?'

'If you can't remember the fact I'm driving, then—'

'Aye, aye, but around these parts? Who's going to stop you?'

'I'm a cop. We don't drink drive.' Marshall gave him a wide smile. 'Otherwise the Rat Pack will investigate me.'

'The Rat Pack.' Milne collapsed back into his armchair and laughed. 'That's a good one.' He took a dainty sip of whisky, then gasped. 'This is a cracking wee dram, so it is.'

'Why are you Bob Milne?'

'Because God made me this way. Hard to improve on perfection!'

'I'm serious.'

'Okay.' Milne leaned forward, cupping his glass in his hands. 'A vote was taken, nobody else wanted the job, so I got saddled with it.'

'You know what I mean.' Marshall pointed at Grumpy. 'He's Robert Marshall the first. I'm the third, but you're not Bob Marshall the second anymore. Why's that?'

'Long story, Rob.'

'So Jen and I have had to bear your surname since we were wee and you haven't?'

'Heard she went back to it, aye? Divorced her husband.'

'That's right.' Marshall swallowed down the word *idiot*. 'Wonder where she got her daddy issues from.'

'Now, now. No need for that.'

'There's every need. You're sitting here like this is all hunky-dory. You'll say it's a long story, but you've got thirty years to explain.'

'No need to explain anything, Rob.'

'How long have you been back in touch with Mum for?'

'Never really *lost* touch.'

'And yet you never showed up here when your kids were growing up?'

'Okay, we've been chatting for the last few months. Why?'

'She hasn't mentioned you to me or Jen. Why's that?'

'Can't answer for your mother. Never could.' Clattering came from the kitchen. 'I took this job up in Edinburgh a couple of months back and...' He shrugged. 'Thought I'd get in touch with Janice. Mend a few fences. Build a few bridges.'

'Not with us, though. Your own children.'

'Nope.' Milne stared into space. 'Guess I should've, eh?'

'Thought you'd get intel from her and Grumpy first, right?'

'Got a fair amount already. Bit surprising to see my son's name on an investigation I'm attached to. I mean, Robert and Marshall are fairly common names. When I met you in Kelso, assumed it was just a coincidence, still a very good chance it was someone else. But then I dug into your record... And... Sure enough, you're my laddie.'

'Still not answering my question. Why aren't you Bob Marshall the second anymore?'

Milne clicked his teeth a few times, then took another sip of whisky. 'Part of it is protecting my kids. I worked undercover in drugs for a number of years. Meant I had a target on my back. Now I'm in internal affairs it's an even bigger one. I'm investigating bent cops, the kind who grass to the worst of who we investigate.' He refilled his glass and motioned to Siyal, but got a shake of the head. 'Answer me this. Are you Rob Marshall on social media?'

'I'm not on anything.'

'Okay, but any of your colleagues? Rakesh?'

'I'm Rakesh Abir.'

'See? First name, middle name. Or vice versa.'

'So your middle name... Was your mother a Milne?'

'No.' Milne shut his eyes. 'Never give out your mother's maiden name, son.'

'I know that, it's just—'

'Same rules apply. Keep it all obfuscated. In fact, in my game it counts double.'

Grumpy raised his glass. 'Away goals count double!' He cackled, but Marshall didn't get the joke.

Milne gave a polite smile, but there was a darkness to the look. 'The reason Rakesh has it that way is to stop some wee bastard he put away years ago from looking him up. Online, you can see people's kids, their partners, their pals. All of them become targets. So you obfuscate the information to protect them.'

Despite playing dumb, Marshall knew all of that. He'd attended the courses on protecting yourself online and read the updated memos, but he'd decided that staying offline was a much better solution. 'Did you change your name by deed poll?'

'Aye.' Milne motioned to Grumpy. 'Ready for a top up, Big Yin?'

'I'm fine now, son. Going to my head!'

'That's the whole point!' Milne sipped slowly. 'Aye, a fair dram that.' He leaned forward to inspect the bottle like he hadn't done so ever before.

Mum was still clattering away in the kitchen. She was an expert at finding ways to hide there.

Marshall watched him, spotted the tics that made him Bob Milne. Wetting his lips every few seconds. Needing glasses to read the label. The darkness behind those eyes too. 'I thought you were a soldier?'

'Part of the cover story, Rob. Used to be away from home a few weeks at a time, working undercover. Tallied with the movements of a squaddie, so sod it. Covered everything over nicely.'

'Did Mum know?'

'Initially, no. She had no idea I was a cop, but I did tell her. It's not cool to work undercover and live a double life where you lie to those who love you.'

'Did you love her?'

Milne laughed. 'I worked undercover most of my career. I don't know what's up and what's down. I can barely remember the truth from back then. It's all jumbled up in here.' He pressed a finger to his temple.

'And they still let you serve?'

'Oh, I'm good at what I do. The best, some say.'

'Talk to me about this career, then. About what dragged you away from your family.'

'What's there to say?' Milne shrugged. 'Police forces in the eighties hired young cops fresh out of high school and put them straight onto drugs investigations in places where we weren't known. Me, a wee Gala laddie, sent up to Aberdeen to work in a dockers' pub. It worked, though. I looked and acted like the youngsters we were investigating. Thing is, that programme failed because we had no policing experience and a lot of us either fell too far into drugs, got ourselves or someone else in that culture knocked up, or we fucked up cases.' He licked his lips slowly. 'I was the exception, though, and actually very good at it.'

'Aside from knocking up my mother.'

'Well, aye. Aberdeen was drowning in oil money, coke and heroin. Ecstasy everywhere. Oil execs wanted to party hard, hence the coke and E. Fishermen loved the smack, because they could take methadone when out at sea, then spend their hard-earned dosh on quality smack back on dry land. Lot of sharks on land, too. My job was to hunt them down. And I helped take down six big gangs up there. But that could only last so long. Twelve years in, I moved to Glasgow CID. Lot of drug murders there, all connected. Dark, dark city. I love it. I love the people. But it's got a dark heart. Took down another gang there, bigger than all six up in Grampian put together. Bad men. And bad men had cops on the payroll. So I took a sideways move into Standards. Took down a lot of bent cops.' He smirked. 'Not bent in that way, of course.'

'Studs up!'

Milne laughed along with Grumpy. 'After that... Well, you have a three-year tenure in Standards.' He thumbed at Siyal. 'Shunty here's on day one but his clock's already ticking. At some point, he'll be moved back to mainstream detective work. Me, I avoided it by specialising in it and shifted forces. Lothian and Borders for a bit. Highlands and Islands, which was surprisingly corrupt. Then all over the UK. Mercia, Thames

Valley, special in Northern Ireland, then Hampshire, Devon
and Cornwall. Not the places where the drugs were being
taken so much as where they were landed. And now I'm back
in Police Scotland for my last stint. Most Complaints cops are
in and out in three years, but I've made a career of it. It's been a
life, that's for sure.'

Marshall couldn't look at him, but he forced himself to.
'You must be proud of yourself.'

'I am. My work's made our country all the better. Much,
much safer.'

Aye, he hadn't spotted the sarcasm in Marshall's question.

'So.' Milne topped up Siyal's glass, even though he hadn't
touched it, then refilled his own. 'Us two are here to investigate
this DCI James Pringle.'

Marshall nodded. 'That's a matter we should handle on the
record.'

'Come on, son.'

'*Son* isn't a title you should be using with me. Call me Rob.'

'Suit yourself.' Milne walked over and topped up Grumpy's
glass. 'Thing is. Chats like this are how crimes get solved.'

'And like I say, they're best done on the record.'

'You work for Pringle, right?'

'Worked, maybe. I can't see him coming back after today.'

'All this stuff about cabbages, right?' Milne chuckled. 'I've
seen senior cops going mad a few times. The pressure gets to
them, crushes them like the hull of a submarine at the wrong
depth.'

'Let's do this on the record.'

'Sure.' Milne sat down again and slurped whisky. He must
be pickled already. 'Look, Rob. I want to know all about you
and your sister.' He scratched at his neck. 'That's going to be a
bit of a challenge, but...'

'Jen will come around, but one thing you need to understand is we've been through a lot over the years because our dickhead father left when we were young.'

Milne winced. 'I deserve that.' He laughed. 'I hope Jennifer's living her life without screwing up my granddaughter's. But if she is, it's on me. Course, the way you two came into the world...' He nudged Siyal's arm. 'These two were born at Peel hospital. Not at the maternity hospital in Gala. Because someone decided she needed to go out for a drive, didn't you, Janice? Halfway to Peebles, she crashed into a lorry. Lucky to survive, though the car didn't. Taken to A&E there, where the bairns were born. Happened to a few people over the years. Course, it's all in the Borders General Hospital now.'

CHAPTER THIRTY-SIX
MARSHALL

Marshall pulled into the drive next to Jen's massive four-by-four and sat back in his seat. He had no idea what to think about the evening, other than it was a miracle his car had got him to and from Melrose without dying at least once.

Maybe Trev had finally fixed the Beast.

Nope. He'd spoken too soon – the bloody thing conked out with the key still in the ignition. He twisted it and tried it again. Nothing. Brilliant. That was a problem he'd confront in the morning.

His dad, though, that was a whole different thing.

Jesus.

That was going to take a lot to unpack.

And the joy of being attached to the same case...

Still nothing from Kirsten – aye, that was something else that was going to take a lot of unpacking. Hopefully she'd still be speaking to him in the morning and he could sort things out. Hopefully.

Nope, there it was:

> You know I love fate, well fate just appeared
> like a shadow on the door. Sorry x

He could picture her on the train back to Edinburgh, staring across the dark countryside. Ruing her life choices. Regretting having the chat with an idiot like Rob Marshall.

He grabbed the leftover cake from the passenger seat and got out into the cold drizzle, then carried it over to the house. Lights were on inside, but the action was in the kitchen at the back. He opened the door and walked through, stopping in the doorway.

Jen was by the sink, pouring herself a glass of wine. An empty pizza box lay on the counter.

Kirsten sat at the table, biting into the last slice. 'Mmmf, hey, Rob.'

Marshall put the cake down, then kissed her cheek and sat next to her. 'Thought you'd be back in Edinburgh?'

She finished chewing. 'You mean you wish I was?'

'No! God no! I hoped you hadn't, but...'

'But Dad.' Jen shook her head and raised her shoulders. 'What the fuck?'

Kirsten leaned in close. 'That's the only thing she's said since we got back, other than "meat feast twelve-inch" and "white or red?".'

'I mean...' Jen sat at the end of the table. A breath exploded out of her lips. 'What the fuck? I mean, seriously? What the fuck? He just storms in and... On Thea's birthday? What the fuck?'

Kirsten frowned. 'Where is she?'

'Thea? She's getting the bus.' Jen necked her fresh glass. 'Sod it. I'm getting another top up. Rob?'

'I'm good just now.'

'Come on, have a drink!'

'In a minute.'

'Suit yourself.' Jen walked over to the bottle and refilled her glass. Then picked up her phone and muttered, 'What the fuck?'

Marshall looked at Kirsten. 'Are you okay?'

'Why wouldn't I be?'

'All that drama?'

'Sorry, I love family drama but I just felt a tad voyeuristic and decided a quick exit was in better taste than pulling up a chair and watching the fur fly.'

'Things got heavy. I'm sorry.'

'They were so heavy it was like Metallica were playing next door. Hate it when shit like that happens, Rob. Just like every time I see my folks.' She leaned over and kissed him with meaty breath. 'It must've been stressful.'

'It's not stressful, just... a shock. I think I'm in shock.'

'Not surprised. I hate family shit. And that's... Wow.'

'I hate families.' Jen put a glass in front of Marshall. 'Present company excepted, of course. And I'm starting to see Kirsten as family now as well as a friend.'

'That's nice.'

'You're nice.' Jen pinged a nail off the rim of Marshall's glass. 'This is from that box someone dropped off.'

Marshall stared at the wine. Dark red like blood. He had a good idea where it came from and didn't want to touch it. 'I told you not to open that.'

'Saving it for our birthday?'

'No. It should be chucked out.'

'No way I'm tipping wine that good down the sink!' She sniffed at it, like she was some kind of wine snob. 'It's absolutely *lush*.' She nudged her chair even closer. 'So?'

Marshall took a sip of the wine, but all he could taste was blood, so he pushed the glass away. 'So what?'

'So how did it go with that arsehole?'

'Our dad? Eh... For starters, I'm pissed off with Mum. They've been in touch for a while now, probably since... All that shite with Thorburn that's been going on and she hasn't spoken to us about him.'

'How do you feel, Rob?'

'I don't know. Like I said to Kirsten, I feel a bit shocked. A bit... torn too. I wish I had your courage to just bugger off after swearing at him, but—'

'—but you don't have my anger issues.'

'True.' Marshall pushed the wine glass even further away. 'But the worst part of it is... Bob's actually a good guy.'

Jen rolled her eyes. 'Bloody hell. He's charmed you.'

'No, he didn't. But I'm serious. He's like Grumpy. Smart, funny. Wise. Drinks like a fish, so that's a family trait on both sides.' Marshall grabbed the glass and took another sip. It was the best he'd ever tasted. 'But he's got a hell of a lot of explaining to do before I'm going to let him back into my life.'

'Assuming he wants to.'

'What do you mean?'

'He's had thirty years to get in touch with either of us. He was only at Mum's tonight because Grumpy was there.'

Marshall nodded. 'He lives in Edinburgh now.'

'Exactly. He could get the train down here any time he wanted to see us. But no. Easier just to do nothing.'

As little as Marshall wanted to do with their father, Jen wanted even less.

CHAPTER THIRTY-SEVEN
CHUNK

The trouble with retirement was you soon missed having a focus for your day. A function. A reason to keep on keeping on. Only three months in and Chunk had decided to go back to work.

The Isle of Man was a quiet place most of the time, a haven for those seeking peace or escape from mainland taxation. But tonight, the cries of gulls outside the dilapidated warehouse were replaced by stifled sobs and low pleading.

The room was dim, just a lone lamp hanging from the ceiling, casting long shadows across the concrete floor. In the middle, Ewan was trussed up like a Christmas turkey, his expensive suit now soaked in sweat and fear.

Chunk stood across from him, cast in darkness. He didn't have Ewan's looks or flashy suit, but his hands knew their way around a man's throat. A veteran of pain, he wore his bruises and scars like badges of honour.

'Why are you doing this?' Ewan's voice was rough from screaming.

Chunk didn't answer. Instead, he watched him with a cold

detachment, a rich man brought to his knees, reduced to a whimpering mess at the feet of a common thug. His limitless wealth, his manors and yachts, meant nothing here.

Time to get on with it.

Chunk approached Ewan, his heavy boots echoing in the otherwise silent warehouse. He paused for a moment and looked down at the once-proud man, now just a crumpled heap of fear and despair.

Ewan's eyes were wide, filled with terror and confusion.

Why him?

Why now?

Chunk gave nothing away. Some questions were better left unanswered. He looked at Ewan the way a butcher might eye a pig before sending it to the slaughterhouse.

Detached.

Emotionless.

Just another day at the office.

This was personal and he'd expected to take much greater satisfaction from this than any of the jobs he'd done over the years. This one was purely for himself. And when your career was in killing, slipping back into old ways was deadly.

He knew his job. He was a facilitator of sorts, a guide to help men like Ewan on their journey from life to death.

The *whys* and the *whos* behind it were never his concern.

Ewan's pleas for mercy echoed in the dank air, but Chunk was deaf to his cries.

Under the bleak light from that lone lamp, Ewan was learning a lesson. Wealth could buy you many things: fancy cars, big houses, the company of beautiful women. But it couldn't buy mercy from Chunk.

'You honestly want to know what you've done to deserve this?'

'Please. Let me go.'

'That wasn't the question.'

'Why are you doing this to me?'

'Do you know my name?'

'Talbot Kyell, isn't it?'

'Good.' Well, not so good for him. 'But you're a lucky boy.'

'How? How is this lucky?'

'Before I came to your house and smacked you in the face and dragged you here, I'd just got back from the mainland at lunchtime. You've had another day of freedom to enjoy before this.'

'Let me go!'

'Here's a wee story for you. I met this lad called Blake Innes and I tortured him until he confessed to what he told the cops initially. I then placed a call to a friend of mine to find out what his decision would be... With this lad, you never can tell. Sometimes it's death, sometimes it's torture, sometimes it's both. Makes no difference to me. Unlike you, though, Blake wasn't personal. See, Blake had to be dealt with soon after he talked to the police the first time. A source on the inside told my friend's friend that Blake had scheduled another meeting with the police, to get info on the record. And that wasn't allowed to happen. Of course, with Blake, the decision was both torture and death... I know a pig farm near Lockerbie that's got a really nice woodchipper. Had him trussed up naked inside the intake to the chipper while I used a fillet knife to slice off portions of his skin and fed them to the pigs below. Should've seen them, man! And he was squealing. Could've got him to confess to anything, but I just wanted the truth. I got it. The pain must've been excruciating, but it was nothing more than minor injuries until the voice on the phone told me the decision. He was displeased with the looseness of Blake's lips. With a flick of a switch, poor Blake's lips were gone along with the rest of him, sucked into the woodchipper. Those hungry hogs were treated to a slurry of a variety they only received on special occasions. Tell you the truth, it was a bit disappointing. Just a brief scream, then nothing but the snorting of those hogs. Horrible, but then strangely peaceful. The worst part was spraying down the chipper afterwards. I'm not cut out for manual labour these days. Done a few jobs outside, but nothing too strenuous. Getting on a bit, eh?'

'Please. Don't feed me to the pigs.'

'Oh, don't worry. I won't. Because you won't be leaving the island.'

Just then, Chunk's mobile rang. He checked the screen – the display showed a string of numbers. A video call this time.

Well, well.

Should've turned it off, really. Or muted it. But he hadn't. And Ewan was going to keep, that was for sure. 'I'll be back in a few minutes. Don't go anywhere.' He pocketed the phone, then secured a ball gag in Ewan's mouth.

Eyes wide. 'Mmmf! Mmmmmf!'

Chunk stepped out of the room into the ruined corridor, then walked into the next room and shut the door. The walls were painted black.

He answered it and his screen showed his face, but nothing else.

Callum Hume appeared. Sitting in his living room with the antlers on the wall behind him. The image glitched a few times.

'Sorry, Cal, I've got a very patchy signal here.'

'Right, right. Can barely see you.'

'That's intentional.'

Callum laughed. 'How are you doing, my friend?'

'I'm good. I managed to square off that wee problem and escape the rat race. Back to living the good life on the island.'

Chunk found the dark sofa and perched on it. 'What's this about, Cal? You pocket dial me or something?'

'Got another job for you.'

Chunk looked back at the door. 'Told you. Yesterday was the last one. I'm retired now.'

'It's a favour for an old friend.'

'Still retired. And as much as I appreciate all the work my old friend has put my way, Cal, I'm just the monkey dancing away. And if the organ grinder plays a tune like that again, I won't dance. Am I clear?'

'The organ grinder can't grind just now.'

'Oh?'

'Someone drove a car into him.'

'Right. Hence the job.'

'Hence the job.'

'I'm guessing you want me to take out who he thinks got him?'

'Correct.'

'It's a big ask. I'm settled here. Happy. At peace. That last one was a favour. A huge favour. Simon the farmer asked me too many questions about what I was feeding to his pigs. So here's the thing – I've done a lot of good work for you over the years. And now I'm out.'

'Don't you even want to know who the target is?'

'No. I'm out.'

'It's Jim Pringle.'

Hit Chunk like a sucker punch to the guts. 'The cop?'

'Aye, the cop.'

Going after cops was a whole other level of insanity. 'Why?'

'Because our mutual friend believes Pringle tried to end him.'

'Come on, Cal, you've got people who can do this.'

'We do. But if we had anyone half as good as you, we

wouldn't have needed your handiwork yesterday. And the current guy isn't as good as you. Nowhere near.'

'Hence you asking me.'

'Hence me asking you. We need a professional like yourself.'

Chunk had them over a barrel here. An opportunity to squeeze them dry. But also a risk. Going after a cop was crazy talk. Not the first time he'd done that, but he'd had to lie low for six months afterwards. He let out a slow breath and tried to make a decision. 'Fine. I'm reluctantly agreeing here. Emphasis on reluctantly. Okay? But I want five times the previous rate.'

'*Five?*'

'You want your current guy to try? Fill your boots.'

'Fine, fine. But I'm only paying on completion.'

'It'll be tomorrow before I can get onto it. I need time to get back from Skye, Arran, Cyprus, Madeira or wherever I actually am.'

'Sure thing.'

'No immediate rush, is there?'

'Oh, no, this is a clear and present... not danger, but opportunity.'

'So, you're asking me to come now?'

'If you can make it.'

'I can, but it's just gone up to seven times. And half in advance.'

'Remind me never to play poker with you.'

'Can you—'

'We can stretch to that. Yes. As long as you're here tomorrow morning and the target is in your custody by lunchtime.'

'I'll be in touch on this number, once those bitcoin hit my wallet. *Ciao.*' Chunk blew a kiss, then stabbed a finger on the phone. He made sure it had stopped recording, then he powered it down.

First chance he got, that was going in the sea. But he had to stay in touch with Callum bloody Hume until the money was his.

Now, he needed to move.

Chunk walked back through to the torture chamber and tore the ball gag out of Ewan's mouth. 'Change of plans. Give me the keys to your boat and I'll let you go.'

'What?'

'You heard the words, right? You got the meaning?'

'How do you know I won't talk about you?'

'Talk all you want, they'll never find me. Where are the keys?'

'Jacket pocket.'

Chunk reached in and grabbed the ring of keys. 'Which one's the boat?'

'Brass.'

'Got it. What are the others?'

'House, London flat, Yorkshire house, car, boat. That order.'

Chunk devised a little mnemonic for them – How Long You Can Breathe. 'You know that's not normal, right?'

'I don't care. You've got the keys. Just let me go. Please.'

'I thought you wanted to know why this is happening to you?'

'Please. Let me go.'

Chunk crouched next to him, pressing his mouth against his ear. 'In the bar, on Friday night. You spilled my beer.'

'What?' Ewan's eyes bulged. '*This* is for that?'

'This is for that. But so much more. You were a dickhead about it. You didn't apologise. Didn't offer me a replacement. Doubled down, even. Threatened me. So you can see why you've got to die.'

'I thought you were letting me go!'

'I just wanted your keys, dickhead.' Chunk tossed them in the air, caught them, then put the ball gag back in his mouth. He walked out of the room.

Hopefully Ewan would be dead by the time he got back.

CHAPTER THIRTY-EIGHT
STRUAN

Struan parked diagonally opposite from the stand, sheltering under some mature trees. The Melrose FC rugby pitch was lit up for some reason, but he couldn't fathom it. The night was dark and wet, with the triple hills of the Eildons a dark outline in the distance. The rugby club's stand was dimly lit, a far cry from the neon-lit city he was accustomed to.

Glasgow was modern, with everything available in each of the twenty-four hours. Whatever you wanted, legal or illicit. Around here, they probably shut all the shops on a Tuesday afternoon. Glasgow had its demons and many of them knew his name, but the Borders was placid enough to lay low for a while. He was back here for a few reasons and work was least among equals. Being back home would be perfect to let that storm blow over.

He got out and walked through the rain along the north end of the pitch, then slipped in the unmanned back entrance.

No security, so that was something.

He walked up the long path that led towards the turnstiles on the main road, then found the pavilion's entrance. A poster read:

Tonight:
1998 Old Boys Reunion
Eildon Suite

Peachy.

He trotted up the stairs and followed the noise to the suite. The doors were open and drunken sweat poured out. The place was buzzing, the air filled with raucous laughter and bawdy songs, mingling with the smell of stale beer and cheap cologne. Burly men in rugby jerseys huddled around pint glasses, their roars echoing off the wood-panelled walls.

On a Monday.

Struan was a few years too young for this crowd. While his accent would fit in, nothing else would.

He'd spent time in the grittiest corners of Scotland, but a small-town rugby club was unfamiliar territory.

Struan ambled up to the bar, every move casual yet calculated. He waited to be served and scanned the crowded room. He clocked Callum Hume, seated at a corner table, half-hidden in the shadows, a pint of fizzing beer in front of him, though mostly drunk. He'd be up to the bar soon, or one of his pals would be. His sharp suit was out of place amidst the revelry, like a shark swimming in a pool of guppies.

'Evening, son.' The barmaid smiled at him, her eyes a dazzling flurry. 'You look like a man in need of a drink.'

'I am indeed.' Struan flashed her a grin that was more teeth than charm. 'Which whisky do you recommend?'

'Got a twelve-year-old Glenfiddich? Or there's the one from Hawick that's pretty lovely.'

'Ah, the local stuff.'

'It's not their own yet. Few years before that's matured. Still, it's a blend from all over. And it's lovely.'

'Still, it's nice to support a local business, eh? I'll take one of them.'

'Neat?'

'Nah, with pineapple juice.'

She frowned. Then got that it was a joke and smiled. 'Water or ice?'

'One ice cube, ta.'

As she poured his drink, Struan glanced back to Callum's table. His instincts were humming like a plucked guitar string. The man was a piece in a puzzle he was determined to solve.

'There you go, pal.'

Struan smiled at her. 'How much am I due you?'

'First one's on the house for old boys like yourself.'

'That's very kind of you.' He lifted the glass as if toasting her. 'One for yourself. Charge me on my next round?'

'Oh, go on.' She leaned in close. 'Don't mind me saying, you're a bit better preserved than your old teammates.'

'I only played a few months before my folks moved to Glasgow. Kept in touch with a couple of the lads, so here I am.'

'Have fun.' She shot him a crafty wink. 'Name's Mel.'

Aye, she was up for it.

'Cheers, Mel.' Struan walked away from the bar and took a sip of the whisky. The warmth spread through him, doing little to ease the cold knot in his gut.

To the onlooker, Struan was just another Melrose FC old boy enjoying his drink. But under that façade, he was a swan on the pond – above the surface everything seemed calm, but beneath the water those feet were churning a mile a minute. His mind worked like a fine-tuned engine, each cog and gear turning in unison.

He just had to wait for his quarry.

He didn't have to wait long.

Callum sank the last of his pint and got up. He pointed at a few nearby punters and got nods back, then clonked one on the head with a metal tray and headed over to the bar, laughing.

Struan let him in to the bar, sipping the whisky that little bit slower.

'Six pints of Long White Cloud, Melinda.'

'On it.' She started pouring.

Callum looked around at Struan and smiled, then looked away again. Then he scratched his chin, his other hand pointing at Struan. 'Your face is a bit familiar.'

'You played alongside me for a few months, Callum.' Struan held out a hand. 'Struan Liddell.'

Callum clenched it tight with a bit of masonic flair in there. 'Name doesn't ring any bells.'

'Dad was a teacher, so we were only here for a few months. Moved to Glasgow in the summer of '96.'

Callum winced. 'Bastard of a season, that. One penalty and we'd have won the league.'

'Remember it well. Last game. Who was it against?'

'Fucking Gala.'

'Fucking Gala.' Struan laughed, then sipped a bit of whisky. 'Supposed to be meeting a mate here. The lad who invited us.' He made a show of looking through the crowd. 'Can't see him, though.'

Callum collected his last pint and put it on the tray. 'Who's that?'

'Gaz Hislop.'

'Oh.' Callum tapped his phone against the machine, then lifted that last pint off the tray and placed it back on the bar top. 'Be back in a second.'

Struan watched him go and felt a trickle of sweat. This was stupid, but stupid actions got sensible results some of the time. He just had to play his hand but not overplay it. Stick to the truth as much as he could.

Callum came back over and grabbed his pint and held it up. '*Slàinte Mhath.*'

Struan tapped his glass against Callum's. '*Slàinte Mhòr.*'

That got a raised eyebrow. 'Can I get you another whisky there?'

'I'm fine just now.' Struan had barely touched his, despite appearances to the contrary.

He was getting enough of a beery blast of breath to suggest Callum was almost at the truth serum level. 'So, you stayed in touch with Gary, aye?'

'Aye. Even though he moved up to Lauder, he stayed playing here, right?'

Callum looked away. 'Aye.'

'He's in Newtown St Boswells now, right?'

'Right, right. Some scrum half. Good player. Great, even. Except for when he missed that effing penalty.' Callum laughed then swallowed it down with a big glug of beer.

Struan looked around the room again. 'Has he left?'

'Who, Gary? No. No.'

'It's just... Rejigged my schedule to do some business down here, but the meeting ran on, hence me being late. Managed to get a hotel for tonight and didn't want to have missed him.'

'No. You haven't missed him.' Callum sank a good couple of fingers of beer. 'Gary got attacked today.'

'*Attacked?*'

'Over in Kelso. Some arsehole drove his car into him.'

'Holy shit. I didn't know. Is he alive?'

Callum shook his head. 'Aye, he's alive. Should make a full recovery, but... It's brutal. Absolutely brutal. Someone drives a car into you, you're lucky to be alive. We'll see how he fares, but I think his rugby-playing days are over.'

'He's a good guy. Can't imagine why anyone would do that to him.'

'Oh, I can. Fucking cops hate him. He's doing well, right? Local boy done good. Building up a chain of hardware stores. Lots of money in what he's doing and we're growing the business.'

'We?'

'Aye. I worked down south for a few years after uni. Management consultant. Specialised in logistics and operational efficiency. We'd go in, review the business and devise a strategy to meet their needs. More often than not, we'd execute the strategy. I've scaled a lot of businesses from *nothing* to national level. Most of them sell up at that point and who can blame them, eh? It's what I'm helping Gary with now. And it's going well, but... People around here don't like change, do they? The powers that be prefer things to be the way they always were. And more than anything, they hate someone like Gary having that level of power.'

'I've seen that myself.'

'Aye?'

'Aye. I'm in the hospitality trade. Kind of like yourself, I suppose, I help new businesses get established. Standard package stuff. Website, newsletter, special offers. All that marketing stuff. Set up their payments platform. Hook into a delivery system. All of that.' Christ, Struan even believed it himself. 'But the cops are *always* sniffing around, man. Always.'

Callum smacked him on the back, hard. 'You need a few bent ones on your payroll.'

Struan laughed. 'Aye, that's not a bad idea.'

'Seriously. There's always someone who'll take a wedge of cash and sign things off. Even if it looks to their mates like they hate you, you still win.' Callum took another long glug of beer. 'Still, that wouldn't have protected Gary, because it was one of their own.'

'One of their own?' Struan frowned. 'A cop ran him over?'

'Gary thinks so, aye. Big shot locally. Saw his car.'

'But you don't believe him, right?'

'Right. Because it's stupid. And cops are many things, but they aren't stupid. They can be thick, sure, but not daft. They spend all day making sure things tie up, evidence-wise. And a car is a huge piece of evidence. So, no, a cop isn't going to run him over. Pay someone else to do it, sure. But even then, using his own car?' Callum took a long drink of beer. 'Doesn't stack up for me.'

Struan bided his time, trying not to seem too eager. 'Shite, that's awful. Chances of finding the arsehole responsible are probably zero, eh?'

Callum snorted. 'Nah, I've got it sorted. It was a toff.'

'A toff?'

'A rich guy.' Callum looked over, eyebrow raised. 'Local guy. Balfour Rattray. Owns a lot of land north of Gala.'

'Why would he do it?'

'His old man invested in Gary's business. Told him at the time not to do it, but it was much cheaper than getting it from the banks. And he'd actually lent him the cash, no questions asked. But Balfour's old boy passed away in January. And Balfour wanted the money back. Gary didn't like that.'

Struan looked away, like he wasn't really paying attention. 'Makes sense.'

'Exactly.'

Struan snapped his focus back on Callum. 'You tell the cops that?'

'They wouldn't listen to me.'

You'd be surprised, pal.

Struan didn't need to ask questions like a cop would, he just needed to listen like one.

He sipped some whisky and allowed himself the chance to savour the fire.

'Here's the thing.' Callum leaned in close. 'This wee scrubber who works for Gary in the shop in Kelso. Lassie called Cath Sutherland, she's been close to Balf.'

'Close, as in...?' Struan made a hole with his thumb and forefinger then poked a finger through it.

Callum laughed. 'Not sure Balf swings that way, to be honest. Still, I don't trust her. Riddle me this, right? She turns up, works in the Gala shop for a few weeks, then Gary puts her in charge of the Kelso shop. Then it all goes to shite and someone drives a car into him.'

Struan finished his whisky – there was more where this came from and he wanted to know it all. 'Can I get you another beer?'

Callum stared at his pint, barely a quarter left, then at Struan's half-empty glass. 'Get me what you're having.'

Struan caught the barmaid's attention. 'Two of these, Mel, when you've got a second. Mind and get one for yourself.'

Aye, he was going to get all of the juice on Gary Hislop and show the local cops what Struan Liddell was made of.

CHAPTER THIRTY-NINE
MARSHALL

Seven o'clock and this was the first time Marshall had been in the new incident room in Galashiels nick.

Aside from the bitter fresh paint smell, it was steeped in the sharp tang of black coffee and overnight perspiration. He'd expected a strip light humming above them, but newfangled LED spotlights cast the room in a harsh glow. The angular metal of the desks gleamed cold and impassive, replacing well-worn wooden models scarred with spills, cigarette burns and idle doodling. Even the chairs smelled fresh and new, though he couldn't guess how long until the minging fug of stale farts and body odour seeped in. Usually there'd be a hiss of chatter, but today each detective stood in their own pocket of silence, nursing cups and cans, all gathered around the whiteboard. Waiting.

Stale cigarette smoke clung to the two drugs squad cops nearest to Marshall. Granite-faced detectives, every wrinkle on their skin etched by countless sleepless nights.

Jolene leaned against the back of her chair, her leather jacket worn thin at the elbows.

Elliot perched at the edge of a desk, her shoulders hunched forward.

DCI Gashkori was standing next to the whiteboard, but he wasn't using it. Instead, a giant TV screen was filled with scribbles, seemingly connected to his tablet, which he attacked with a white pencil. The squiggles mapped out the brutal language of attempted murder, crisscrossing the board in a messy web of chaos. A landscape of names, addresses, times, and faces. One of them was the reason for the silence:

DCI Jim Pringle.

Underlined three times and circled twice.

Marshall still didn't know what to think. He didn't want to give in to the speculation, so he chose to follow the evidence. Problem was, supposition was the screaming monster in the room, while evidence remained quiet.

Gashkori tucked his tablet under his arm and clapped his hands together. 'Dearly beloved, we are gathered here to celebrate the joining in unholy matrimony of the drugs investigation into Gary Hislop and the investigation into an attempt on his life. I've been leading the former, while DI Elliot has been my blushing bride on your side of the fence down here. After the events of yesterday, I've been placed in dual command of the investigation.' He scanned the room. 'Does anyone have any questions or concerns?'

Marshall watched Siyal – he was usually first to raise anything, no matter how trivial, but his hands remained in his pockets.

'Good.' Gashkori smiled. 'And as if the nuptials weren't gruesome enough already, it is my distinct horror to announce that the happy couple will now become a throuple with the addition of Detective Superintendent Bob Milne of Professional Standards and Ethics.'

Marshall felt his heart throb that little bit harder in his

chest. Surprised the two drugs lads next to him couldn't hear it.

Milne was leaning against the wall, next to a half-functioning vending machine, a man weathered by time and service, his haggard face the map of a long war, each line a battle won or lost, each grey hair a story. 'Thanks, Ryan.' His voice was deeper than last night, though Marshall didn't know if that was due to a professional projection of capability, or from the booze he'd sunk with Grumpy. 'I don't know any of your faces.' He locked eyes with Marshall. 'Which is a good thing for you all, given my line of work.' He smiled as nervous laughter rippled through the room. 'I'm working for the Complaints in Edinburgh, where I've just arrived from way down south. Hampshire police. I know it'll shock you to learn that I'm sixty-two—' He ran a hand through his silvery hair. '—but I'm nearing retirement and this is my last chance to do some good in the world, on top of the many crimes I've already solved. I've been heading up the investigation into some serious leaks to organised crime from officers in Specialised Crime Division's east area and the MITs therein. Edinburgh, Livingston, Dunfermline, down here. Happily, it all dovetails nicely with Ryan here's remit on the drugs investigation. The reason I'm down here with a former member of your parish—' He gestured at Siyal. '—is to confirm DCI Jim Pringle's involvement in yesterday's assault on Mr Hislop.'

The room stayed silent, just the rattling hum of the buggered vending machine.

'Of course, I'll be taking a backseat to DCI Gashkori, while Shunty investigates our scope of work. I'm just here as oversight, but I've got a wealth of experience. I should clarify that in many of my toughest cases I was able to exonerate a police officer and that, my friends, is a great day at the office for me.

So pick your chins up off your desks and get to work.' He gestured back at Gashkori. 'Thanks, Ryan.'

'No worries. Like he alluded to, Superintendent Milne and DS Siyal are conducting a parallel investigation into a person of interest in our case. DI Marshall and DI Elliot will still take lead on the core investigation. They'll be looking to see "whodunnit?" whereas Shunty is looking to see "has one of ours dunnit?"' Gashkori waited for the laughter to dip. 'DI McKenzie is leading on the drugs angle. Steve?'

McKenzie was one of the two next to Marshall. 'We've had an operation running into Hislop for a few months now, which I've taken temporary charge of.' He burped into his fist, giving a waft of second-hand bacon and sickly tomato ketchup. 'I'm focusing on the drugs angle, but I'm finding any links to rival gangs, such as the Southend Albanians or the Glasgow lot.' He snorted and seemed to chew something. 'We ran through all angles of the case overnight, cross-referencing with our long-standing investigation into Mr Hislop. Had the guys run through everything we had, but no fresh leads have come up so far. Deflating, sure, but it is what it is. There's a lot of work yet to be done.'

'Aye, I guess so.' Gashkori nodded his thanks. 'I'll be the middle ground, knitting it all together and co-ordinating matters. Any questions, you come to me. Okay?'

Murmurs rattled around the room.

Gashkori picked up his coffee and took a biting sip. 'Okay. Let's start with the updates.' He looked at Elliot.

She turned to Struan. 'Sergeant?'

'Sure.' Struan cleared his throat. He yawned like he'd had a crap night's sleep. 'We've managed to get some stuff off the CCTV in Kelso near to Roxburgh Street Hardware. Couple of dodgy punters looking like they're up to no good.' He stuck a print to the whiteboard, showing two kids in their teens who looked like they should've been at school. 'We spoke to them and their parents last night. Both from Hawick, so them being in Kelso at that time surprised their folks. They've both got alibis – they were caught shoplifting just before the assault.'

Gashkori stared at them. 'Did they see anything?'

'They heard the crash, sir, but they didn't get a good look at the driver.'

'Okay. Anything else?'

'We're progressing a few other avenues, sir, but nothing to report on them just yet.' Struan locked eyes with Ash Paton. 'Constable, I need you to go through Cath Sutherland's statement in great detail. She's the closest witness and I want everything to stand up. And I mean *everything*.'

'Sarge.'

'Okay.' Gashkori held Struan's gaze for a few seconds. 'Who's next?'

Kirsten raised a hand. 'My team ran the DNA from DCI Pringle's car overnight. Five distinct DNA profiles have been found. Two were the wee numpties and we are supposing one is Pringle, while the other two are, eh, family.'

Gashkori looked up from his tablet. 'And what about Balfour's car?'

'We've got a warrant to examine it. It's in DI Elliot's inbox.'

'You're kidding me?' Elliot shook her head. 'Right. I'll get that actioned.'

'Thanks, you.' Kirsten's friendly smile was as fake as a thirty-seven-pound note. 'I checked Pringle's Airwave radio. It had been on the same channel for the whole day and stayed in the same location. So it's not like he was actively checking it. Probably just accidentally switched it on and it stayed on all day.'

Marshall clocked Struan frowning. 'Got something to add, Sergeant?'

'Nope.'

'Okay. Elephant in the room time.' Gashkori looked around the officers. 'The family samples Kirsten alluded to are most likely from Dr Belu Owusu and her daughter, Sarah. Who is also the child of Jim Pringle.'

A hushed sigh cascaded around the room. The sound of an office rumour being confirmed. And confirmed very publicly.

'We'll know for certain later today, sir. Dr Owusu and her daughter are coming in later this morning to answer a summons to provide DNA.'

'Okay. So you've got a full catalogue from the car?'

'Correct. All traces match to either of those three or to the two young men who stole the car.'

'Ah, yes. The young neds.' Gashkori stared at Marshall. 'You interviewed them. Correct?'

'Correct.' Marshall raised a hand. 'Trouble is, wee neds like that who nick cars don't tend to think about forensics, the future, or keeping clean in any fashion.'

'Are they denying it?'

'Nope. Still sticking to their story, sir.'

'What, the vague description of an old guy giving them money?'

'Right. And old for them is anyone over thirty and their descriptions range from non-existent to piss poor.'

'Anything to back it up?'

'Nope. Of course not.'

Gashkori laughed. 'Let's keep on top of them.' He stared at his tablet for a few seconds, the whole room watching him. 'So, we don't know if it was Pringle's or Rattray's car that was used?'

'Correct.'

'All we've got is… Okay.' Gashkori scratched at his neck. 'Trouble is, only Standards can show a police officer as a suspect in a line-up. Bob, can you take lead on that?'

'Will do, Ryan.'

'Coolio. Now, let's focus on DCI Pringle. I know how shocking it can be to have one of our own as a suspect in a case, let alone the chief of your little band. But we have to be professionals in the face of that. Shunty, what's your plan of attack?'

Siyal winced. 'He's in hospital, sir. The nursing staff are struggling to stabilise him.'

'How?'

'I'm not a medical expert.'

'Okay…' Gashkori jotted a note on the board. 'But otherwise?'

'We plan on speaking to him, sir. As well as doing deep backgrounds on his friends and family. There are some minor details which stand out to me, which I aim to iron out today.'

'Such as?'

'Why he's staying with his brother. Why he couldn't remember getting from there to Edinburgh yesterday morning. Why he's shouting "cabbages" in an interview.'

'Okay, okay. Thanks, Rakesh.' Gashkori's look was teetering on the verge of withering. 'He's been living with his brother, but we haven't been able to track him down, let alone speak to him. Why's he living with him? What happened to his house?'

'Forgot to tell you, sir.' Elliot twirled her hair around a finger. 'Pringle's brother doesn't exist.'

Gashkori dropped his tablet. He bent over to pick it up. 'Wait, what?'

'Came from Belu Owusu, but we backed it up with a neighbour who's lived there forty years. Pringle was an only child.

Dad died fifteen years ago, Mum two. He inherited the place. It's his home. Never a brother.'

Gashkori snorted. 'That doesn't feel good to me.' He looked at Marshall, then Elliot. 'Okay, you two are in charge of this. What else have you got?'

Elliot held out a hand to Marshall.

So he walked over to the board. 'I wanted to go through the outstanding leads we have. Not that I expect to get much, but I'm thorough. First, I think we need to validate DCI Pringle's background, which sits with Rakesh. And his alibi that he was on a train at the relevant times. And that his car was in a car park overnight.'

'Sure.' Siyal was frowning. 'But what are you looking for precisely?'

'I think we're all skirting around the fact that our boss has had some kind of nervous breakdown. Whether he was behind the wheel of that car or not, we need to validate his movements over the last few months. He could be not criminally responsible by reason of mental defect.'

Milne looked at Siyal. 'You okay with that, Shunty?'

'Already on it, sir. Got access to the train CCTV, just need a few eyeballs to analyse it for me.'

Marshall smiled his thanks. 'Next, DI Elliot unearthed a previously unknown fact last night. Hislop is living with a woman called Sadie. I gather this was news to your team, Ryan?'

Gashkori narrowed his eyes at him. 'We were unable to get approval for a surveillance operation on his home.'

'Why?'

'Steve?'

McKenzie cleared his throat. 'It's a difficult location because all of the adjacent properties are owned by Mr Hislop.'

Elliot barked out a laugh. 'Eh?'

'Every single one.'

'You're saying he owns all those council houses?'

'They're all privately owned by a heavily leveraged business that traces back to his ultimate ownership. It appears that, over the last ten years, Hislop's been buying up his neighbours' homes, then renting them out.'

Elliot looked up at the ceiling. 'Jesus Christ.'

Marshall shrugged. 'That explains it, I guess. But someone needs to look into Sadie's background. A surname would be a start.'

Struan raised a hand. 'On it.'

Marshall jotted down his initials on the board next to it. 'Okay. The next thing is in your court, Struan. I gather you were interrupted when you obtained an alibi covering Balf Rattray's movements. From his friend... Gundog, was it?'

'Gundog, aye. Real name Fergus Ross.' Struan folded his arms. 'We weren't so much interrupted as Gundog wasn't there to corroborate the story.'

'There's a motive there. Can you go back and cross it off?'

Struan nodded. 'We haven't had time to, but I'll pick up with them today.'

'Sure.' Marshall clocked a glare from Elliot. 'Next, Cath Sutherland, who works for Hislop in the shop, said she'd help identify the customers. But she said there was someone in just before the attack. Do we know who yet?'

'Think so.' Struan stuck his hand up again. 'I'll take Cath Sutherland.'

Elliot shot daggers at him. 'Struan, leave some work for Jolene's team.'

Marshall waited for the laughter to die down. 'Okay.' He looked at Gashkori. 'I think that's us, sir. I'll be reviewing nearby CCTV with my team, then following up on the few leads we have outstanding.'

'Good work.' Gashkori scribbled something down on his tablet. 'Rob, can you pick up with the medical staff and see when we can get Hislop on the record?'

'Sure thing.'

'Okay.' Gashkori looked around. 'This isn't a murder case. Yet. Actually, it's unlikely to head that way, as I gather Mr Hislop's surgery was successful. But we're treating it like one. We can't have people doing this and we certainly can't have cops taking matters into their own hands. Our focus is as follows. First, DCI Pringle did it himself. Second, the wee neds who stole Pringle's car. Third, Balfour Rattray could've done it with his car. Fourth, Balf could've paid the neds to do it with Pringle's car. Which seems preposterous, I know, but I've seen weirder things.' He clapped his hands. 'Now, let's get down to it.'

Marshall focused on Gashkori as the crowd dispersed. 'I take it you know?'

Gashkori looked over at Milne, still lurking at the back of the room, then back at Marshall. 'That your estranged dad's working this case? Aye.'

'There won't be any problems.'

'I hope not. You're both professionals. Look, I'm holding down the fort while you all investigate. I don't care who begat who, just get me a result. Okay?'

'Will do.' Marshall walked over to Milne. 'How are you doing?'

'Nice being back at the coal face again.'

'Your voice was pretty deep this morning.'

'Not from the booze, Rob.' Milne wagged a finger at him. 'You fancy a coffee?'

Marshall nodded. 'I'd love to, but what's the real reason?'

'We need to talk about us working together, Rob. The case. And a few other things.'

'Okay.'

'Excellent.' Milne kicked away from the wall with a tearing sound. He looked back over his shoulder and saw the back of his suit was smeared in fresh paint. 'Ah, crap!'

CHAPTER FORTY
ELLIOT

Elliot left the incident room, desperate for a coffee. It wasn't that her brain wasn't working yet, more like she couldn't remember having a functioning one.

Sleeping would've been a good thing, but sleep was a luxury some nights. Especially with what happened yesterday.

Sam...

It hadn't been easy when Elliot was that age herself and it felt like things had only got a hundred times worse for her kids' generation. Social media, instant messaging, video on demand. All that constant pressure to conform she'd had was now pressure to diversify. No wonder kids were whacked up on so many drugs nowadays.

Coffee.

She passed through reception again and tried her card against the reader. A red signal. She turned to face her husband. 'Thought you'd got this security system fixed?'

Davie was gurning away at her. 'Fixed last night, aye.'

'Why isn't it working?'

'You've still got Shunty's card.' He held out a hand. 'Give.'

So she gave. 'And mine should work?'

'Should do, aye.' Davie winked. 'Need to thank you, though. Managed to fulfil a lifelong fantasy of spending a night inside a washing machine.'

'Eh?'

'You were tossing and turning all night.'

'Barely slept.' She smiled at him. 'I need a coffee.'

'All that stuff with Sam running through your brain?'

'Aye.'

'I don't get it.' Davie scratched at his neck. 'First she's our wee girl, then she thought she was a boy, then she thought she was neither and now she's a girl again?'

Elliot didn't have time to go into it now. She'd been through it a thousand times before and, while he claimed to understand and show patience, at times he could just be wilfully ignorant. 'Davie. Seriously. I need to get on.'

'Come on. She's my kid too. If I'm to help take the strain, it'd help to understand it more.'

'Davie, I don't know how to explain it you.'

He beamed at her. 'Imagine I'm five.'

'Hard not to.' She frowned. 'Can't this wait?'

'Come on. You didn't speak to me last night when you got in.'

'Your choice to watch the football instead.'

He sighed. 'Come on. I've taken a back seat on this stuff, but I still want to know. And to understand. And most importantly, to help. Both of you.'

'Right. Well. That's a long chat to have, Davie. I've tried it again and again and you just don't get it.'

'It just baffles me. Like, I'm getting a bit tired of the whole non-binary thing. Is she lesbian, bisexual, a tomboy? What is it?'

'I keep telling you, it's they, not she.'

'That just baffles me even worse. It's a plural!'

'Davie. If you want to understand, you have to listen.'

'But last night, it sounded like she's a she again? She kissed a boy?'

'It's not that simple, Davie. Sam kissed a boy.'

'So, I've got my daughter back?'

'You never lost your *child*. Sam's Sam, regardless of gender or sexuality.'

'Still don't get the difference.'

'Davie, gender is who Sam goes to bed *as* and sexuality is who she goes to bed *with*.'

'And sex?'

'It's what they're born as.'

'So that's different from gender?'

'It is now. You can be born male and identify as female. And vice versa.'

'And that's when they start cutting bits off and sticking other bits on?'

'Not necessarily. And this isn't a chat for now, Davie. I need to get on.'

'Last thing. This Tam's definitely a laddie?'

'I've no idea. He might identify as a boy. Could be born Thomas or Tamara. I just don't know.'

'How can you not know?'

'I saw Sam kissing someone in a dark graveyard. They both ran away.'

'Fuck's sake.'

'How haven't you had any diversity training on this?'

'Down here? They keep threatening it, but it's more of an Edinburgh or Glasgow thing.'

'It's an everywhere thing and you should educate yourself.' Elliot walked over to the reader and pressed her card against it.

'Come on, Andi. Don't just walk off.'

Bastard thing still wasn't working.

'Davie, Sam's our kid. Whether she's a she, a he or a they, it's our job to love her. Remember your cousin? How your uncle stopped speaking to him because he was gay? This is our generation's version of that. We support them for who they are. We love them unconditionally. Okay?'

'Fine.' He raised his hands. 'Sorry, I'll try to be more "enlightened".' He even did rabbit ears. Then he held out a card. 'Here's your new one.'

'Give me that.' She stormed over and grabbed the card.

He didn't let go and leaned in close. 'Listen, word is that super from Edinburgh is Marshall's dad.'

'He's *what?*'

Davie raised his hands. 'Just what I heard.'

Elliot nodded thanks, then used the card to get through.

Bloody hell.

She stormed along the corridor towards the canteen and its stewed coffee.

When did she become the sensible one? The tolerant one?

Sure Davie was good with the boys, but he'd left Sam to her. She'd had to educate herself on a degree-course worth of gender politics. None of it made sense to her at first, but it helped if you just went along with it and saw it from the kid's perspective.

Sam was her kid and she'd do literally anything for her. *Anything.* Trying to help her navigate her feelings, and always be her mum. Giving her time and space to decide what she was and who she wanted to be.

Bloody hell, she was sounding more and more like Shunty.

She opened the canteen door and saw a massive queue. The good thing about Melrose was there were several good cafés in walking distance of the station. Gala, on the other hand, was a long enough walk that she couldn't be arsed, so always ended up here.

Bingo – Dr Donkey was in the queue.

She barged in next to him. 'Morning, Rob.'

He was chatting to that Bob Milne lad. Suit jacket hanging free. Big guy, as old as cops got. Was he really Marshall's dad? She looked for a family resemblance but didn't see any obvious ones other than height and bulk. Tried to compare him with Marshall's sister. Nope too.

She smirked at him. 'Typical Marshall, sucking up to the new boss.'

Milne held out a hand. 'Bob Milne.'

'Andrea Elliot.'

'Pleasure's all mine.' His eyes gleamed. 'Listen, we all need to sit down and make sure we avoid things overlapping on this case. I'll keep out of everyone's hair. As far as I'm concerned, I'm supporting Shunty. That's all.'

Elliot couldn't help but beam – always something when a super used your nickname. And she was pleased that Rakesh Siyal was leaning into it. 'And Shunty's investigating with the view that Jim did it, right?'

Milne laughed. 'Erm, no. We call that investigative tunnel vision where I come from. If that's marked down anywhere in the case file, it'd be cause for a dismissal...'

'Of course it's not marked down anywhere.'

'Better not be. If you honestly believed he did it and set out to only include the information that made him look guilty, then, wow – talk about grounds for appeal.'

'I know what you mean. I'm just saying... I let the evidence guide me. Take it you've seen a bit of that in your time?'

'Oh, aye. Many times over.'

'Don't you think he's lost his mind, though? All that stuff about cabbages?'

Milne swapped his jacket from one arm to the other. Seemed to be taking great care with it. 'DCI Pringle's mental health is something we're looking into.' He flashed her a smile. 'I could do with some of your time, actually. I've been going through the old case files with people in my team, but we need to get inside info. What you know that's not in the files.'

'Sure thing. More than happy to help. But tell me your investigation's going to be more than just that?'

'Oh, aye. For starters, young Shunty's arranging a whole host of things. Technical jiggery-pokery.' He shot her a crafty wink. 'We'll get to the bottom of who's leaking what.'

'Excellent. Rakesh is a good cop.'

Marshall gave her a harsh glare.

She returned it with interest. 'What?'

'Nothing.'

Milne's phone rang. 'Better take this.' He smiled at Marshall, then walked off to the vending machines.

Marshall watched him go. 'That'll be the dry cleaner. He got paint all over his new suit jacket.'

She struggled to hide her smile. 'Let me get this straight, Robbie. First your nursey girlfriend is your sister and now you have a father in the police.'

'He is, aye.' Marshall scratched at his neck. 'Don't go spreading that around.'

'Bit late for that.' She nudged his arm. 'Who's your daddy, eh?'

'Come on...'

'Not me! Someone's already spreading it for you. I heard from my husband.'

'Right.' Marshall sighed then shifted forward in the queue. 'I'm going to sit down with him and work out a few things.'

'Work stuff?'

'Not the time for the other stuff.'

She nodded slowly, watching Milne talk animatedly on the phone. 'You've never mentioned him before.'

'You've never mentioned yours.'

'I have! Dad looks after the kids before and after school. So, what's the deal with him?'

'Long story.'

'Aye, they all are with you.'

'You action that warrant for Balfour's car?'

'Aye...'

Struan barged into the queue next to them, sweating like he was on the train back from a hefty stag weekend. 'Morning.' Voice as deep as alcohol poisoning.

Elliot nodded at him. 'My shout. What can I get you?'

'Latte?'

'Sure.'

Struan wiped the sweat from his brow. 'You need any help going to the hospital to speak to Pringle?'

'I can get there myself.' Elliot stepped forward in the queue. 'You need to ask me before you put your hand up for work.'

'Eh?'

'Speaking to Sadie and Cath Sutherland.'

'Okay. Sorry. I thought you'd rather we kept that side?'

'I need to palm one of them off onto Jolene, okay? It's unbalanced.' Elliot looked for Marshall.

But he wasn't there.

Neither was Milne.

'Bloody hell.' She looked around the room. 'Pair of them have slipped off like the Lone Ranger and Tonto.'

'Next!'

She stepped up to the till and smiled at wee Ronald. 'Black filter and a latte with marshmallows and chocolate sprinkles.'

Struan rolled his eyes. 'A latte's not that bad, is it?'

'Just joking with you.' She tapped her phone against the reader. 'Seriously, though. Why did you take them on?'

Struan frowned at her. Thinking it through, spinning a lie. Aye, he was a sleekit devil.

'The truth, Sergeant. Whatever it is.'

Struan stuffed his hands into his pockets. 'Okay.' He looked from side to side, then took his coffee and tore open the lid. 'Bloody hell, there *are* sprinkles on this!'

CHAPTER FORTY-ONE
MARSHALL

Marshall opened the Beast's boot, pretty much the only part of the car that worked when he wanted it to. He had a quick look around the car park, then picked up the parcel and almost dropped it on the Volvo parked next to him. Stupid! He grabbed it tighter and walked into the station.

Davie was fussing about with the security reader.

Marshall rested the heavy case on the edge of the reception desk. 'Morning, Davie. Need to get past.'

Davie took in the case of wine. 'Oh, ho ho. What's this?'

'Wine. What does it look like?'

Davie snorted. 'Senior officers always keep a bottle in their bottom drawer, eh?'

'That's whisky.' Marshall motioned towards the door. 'It's going straight into the evidence locker, so if you could...?'

'Ah, well. Be my guest.' Davie opened the door for Marshall. 'Nice stuff that, Rob. Bottle missing too, you rascal.'

'Aye, not my doing.' Marshall barged past and found an

empty locker in the room. He keyed in his security code and the door opened. He slid the case in, then locked it.

'What's that?' Milne was standing outside, holding a packet of cigarettes.

'Someone sent me a case of wine.' Marshall grabbed the clipboard and started filling out the paperwork. 'Hislop, I think.'

'Oh?'

'Aye.' Marshall lodged the paperwork, then repeated the process on the computer. 'Anyway. That's it out of my hands now.'

Milne was holding his suit jacket at arm's reach to inspect it. He looked over and nodded. 'Shunty said there's a place that'll fix it.'

'Guess if anyone knows how to get your coat repaired in this town, it'll be him.'

'Said he ripped the arse out of his trousers a few months ago.'

'Kept that quiet.'

'Place opens at eight, so I thought we'd get a coffee over the road from it and wait until I can pounce.'

'Sure.' Marshall let Milne go first, then joined him in the early morning gloom. 'You got somewhere in mind?'

'Oh, aye. I do.' Milne sparked up as they walked and didn't notice Marshall's grimace at his slow exhale of smoke. 'Who was that?'

'Davie Elliot.'

'As in...?'

'Aye.'

'He's a lucky man, eh?' Milne laughed. 'Not.' He rounded the corner, then scurried along Bridge Street towards the bend. 'Guessing she's a piece of work?'

'Aye, she's got her moments. Lot better than when I started last summer. She thought I was trying to take her job.'

'You're the same grade, though?'

'Not her job. Pringle's.'

'Ah, she's one of those ambitious types. Stands taller with her foot on your neck.' Milne glanced at Mac Arts, an old church now turned into an arts venue, then soldiered along the road. 'You not interested in being a DCI?'

'Happy doing what I do. Don't want to sit in meetings all day.'

'Tell me about it. Still, the pay's good as a senior officer. And at that level, you're a bit more insulated from the incompetence of the constables. Though I gather that might've afflicted Pringle?'

'He's not incompetent, just... I think he's found his level.'

'I mean the pressure.' Milne laughed. 'In here.' He slipped inside the Great Tapestry of Scotland building. A big concrete and glass box housing a giant stitched artwork highlighting Scotland's history. Supposed to bring tourists to Gala, but the café was much more of a success, at least according to the local press.

Marshall followed him in and joined him in the queue. 'My treat.'

'No, I insist.' Milne smiled at the waitress. 'A black coffee, please.'

'Americano do?'

'Perfect. Robert?'

'Same, but oat milk on the side.'

'Sure.' She smiled as she rang it up, then motioned to the card machine.

Milne slipped on a pair of reading glasses, then slid one of many cards into the reader and tapped in a PIN. 'There you go, darling.'

'I'll bring them over.'

'Cheers.' Milne strolled across the bright, open space and took the corner table furthest from the door, his chair facing out. The windows were high up, giving them some cover at least.

Marshall took the chair at right angles. Not perfect and not the power seat, but it gave him a view of the door at least. 'How do you know this place was good?'

'I met your mother and grandfather here a few weeks ago.'

Marshall swallowed it all down. Better to sit in the pit of his stomach than come out as bitter words. 'Right.'

'You don't need to be like that, Rob. You're almost forty, not four.'

'And you still see Grumpy. But not your kids. Great choice there.'

'Look, I've made some decisions I... Look, I had to make them, okay? I'm not necessarily pleased with them, but I made them. And I've stuck by them. Hindsight is 20/20 and aye, if you want to accuse me of being myopic in my life, Rob, we've no disagreement there.'

'And now you're face to face with them because I'm on this case with you.'

'Right. Right.' Milne rubbed at his stubble. 'Listen, I might've been your father, but I've not been a dad to you or Jennifer. I hold my hands up to that. But it's not through want of trying.'

'Sure.' Marshall rested on his elbows and let out a deep breath. 'All I care about is the truth. Jen and I deserve the truth.'

'The truth...' Milne gnawed at his bottom lip, to a backdrop of the coffee machine hissing. 'Whose version would you like? The victorious write the history books, and I was certainly the loser in this chronicle.'

'The whole truth and nothing but the truth.'

'So help my Boab.' Milne sighed. 'The truth is a flexible thing. What you remember isn't the same as what someone else does. And neither are necessarily the same as what happened.'

'I get it. You've been a cop for five hundred years. Blah blah blah. Three versions. Yours. Mine. And the truth.' Marshall let the bitter words sit there. 'I don't need an epistemological essay on the nature of reality. Just tell me why you left us.'

Milne sat back and let the waitress deliver their coffees. 'Thanks, darling.' He tore a sachet of brown sugar and tipped it in, then slowly stirred it. 'The reality is I left because... Bottom line... I wanted kids, but I didn't want to be married. Your mother's always been Janice Simpson. You guys took my name.'

Marshall let his coffee sit there, unadulterated. 'Doesn't explain a thing.'

Milne blew on his but didn't sip it. 'What happened was I realised I wasn't happy. I tried to keep us all together for the sake of you two, but... it wasn't working. One day, Janice told me to leave.'

'Wait. *She* told *you?*'

Milne nodded. 'That's not her version, then?'

'She said you left us.'

'Typical Janice.' Milne laughed. 'I can talk, though. I never told her I was a cop until a few weeks before. Pretended I was an ex-squaddie working the rigs in Aberdeen. Reality is, I was away from home a lot, working undercover in Aberdeen to investigate a gang or two.'

'So you just left without a second thought?'

'No. I visited a few times. I still wanted to play daddy, but Janice... Your mother never let me in, so I learned to stay away. She moved on to some other fella and I got the message. I wasn't welcome in my own kids' lives. I could've fought it, but... it would've been public. People would've known who I was. I already had a big enough target on my back. I didn't want to put one on yours too.'

Marshall shook his head. 'Jen was right about that. We were vulnerable to him. The man Mum moved on to. Graham Thorburn. He caused a lot of hurt. A lot of pain. And death.'

'I wish I could turn back the clock and force my way in, Rob. Honestly. Take it you never got the presents?'

'Presents?'

Milne's turn to shake his head. 'Typical.'

'You didn't talk about any of this when you had your nice comfortable meetings with Mum in here?'

'We didn't discuss much, Robert. I'm sorry. Look, given I'd been such a failure as a family man, the only thing that made sense to me was to throw myself into my work. And to take down the gangs I was investigating. It took a very long time, thirty years of chipping away, but it's all over. They're all prosecuted. A life's work. I'm not an idealistic cop anymore, but I'm staying on for a couple of years just to make sure everything stays solved, if you catch my drift. Weeds have a habit of popping their heads up between the cracks every now and then.'

Marshall sat back and tipped his milk into his coffee.

'I was going to look after you all, Rob, you were *my* kids. I wanted to be a father to you. It just didn't work out. I live with the regret every day. Now I'm here, now I've been open and frank with you, I... I hope we can discuss things. See each other.'

'Thanks for the coffee and for the honesty.'

'Robert, we need to work together on this case.'

'Do we?'

'We do. Look, here's a proposal. I'll help you with your side of the case. After all, there's always a bent cop or two on people trafficking cases like I've spent my life working and—'

'No.'

'No?'

'No. I'm going to keep my side of the bargain. Like Gashkori said. You're here to support Rakesh. That's it. I'm not working with you. Okay?' Marshall finished his coffee in one go and got up. 'I've been an adult for a very long time and you had ample opportunity to make your case while it might've mattered. It's way too late now. And your reasoning that you put your career ahead of your family... I can't respect that. So unless you've got another explanation up your sleeve, I'll thank you for accidentally apologising, but I don't accept it. Now. I've got work to do. Hope your suit gets cleaned.'

CHAPTER FORTY-TWO
STRUAN

Struan carried the coffees through the office space, following Elliot. Stank of fresh paint, though less so than in the incident room. This was going to be his home for the foreseeable future, so he had to stake a claim to being a central player. And getting into her good books was the best way of doing that. 'Wouldn't it have made sense to put our desks next to the incident room? Or vice versa?'

'You'd think.' Elliot held the door for him. 'Pringle was in charge of that, though, so we're lucky our chairs aren't teapots and our desks wishes and dreams.' She snatched the coffee from him, then sat behind her desk.

Struan took a chair opposite and tore off the lid. It was a milky, chocolatey mess now with a sludge of marshmallow fat on the top. He sighed. 'Thanks for this.'

'You never know, that might be nice with the sprinkles in.'

'Smells absolutely rank.'

'Wee Ronald isn't exactly a champion barista.'

He took a drink and it wasn't as bad as he'd feared. Sweet,

sure, but certainly strong enough. 'At the briefing, Shunty had one that smelled nice.'

Elliot rolled her eyes. 'I think the forensics lot have an illicit coffee pot. And he's got access.'

Struan gestured around the office. 'You could get one in here.'

'Sure, but I don't want to get caught. The forensics area is locked down. This isn't.' Elliot slurped at her coffee and gasped. 'We need a word about you going over the score on those neds. One of them suffered a stress fracture in the skull.'

Shite.

Struan took a drink of disgusting latte to think it all through. Come up with a cover story. 'They'd run someone over in that car, boss. And my pursuit of them resulted in a crash, sure, but I was at risk.'

'I saw you smack their heads together.' She leaned forward, clunking her elbows on the table. 'Tell me this straight, Struan, are you a sneaky sod?'

'No. I'm really not. They were threatening me, boss. One of them had a knife. You saw that, right?'

'I did. Nothing wrong with bringing Mr Slap to a knife fight and winning. I saw the knife, sure, but I also saw you eliminate the threat of a knife. And then I saw some extracurricular activity.'

'Beg to disagree, boss. I saw a knife, then my defensive training kicked in and I eliminated the threat. Have either of them complained?'

'Not yet.'

'When they do, we can have this chat all over again and I'll give you the same response. Same I'd give on the stand and to the Rat Pack. It's in my notebook as well. What's in yours?'

'You've got a response for everything, haven't you?'

'I'm just being honest, boss. I don't hide who I am. And I'm not angry with you for what you think you saw, you're just incorrect is all.'

'Hmm.'

'Look. I'm a team player. Old school. I respect a hierarchy. Sure you must know of a few officers like that.'

'Gey few and they're aw deid.' She laughed. 'I'm warning you, though. Run your cowboy stuff past me before you do it next time. Am I making myself clear?'

'Clear, boss, I respect that.' Struan gave her his best shit-eating grin. 'But I mean it. As results-oriented as I am, I'm a team player. My leads are your leads.'

'Sweet.'

'Peachy.'

Someone knocked on the door.

Elliot sighed. 'Come.'

DC Paton strolled in, clutching a sheaf of paperwork. 'Ma'am. Sarge.' She swallowed hard. 'You both probably want to hear this.'

Struan took his seat again. Time to earn some brownie points from the boss... 'We're all ears.'

Paton stayed by the door. 'Okay, so... As per your request in the briefing, Sarge, I've been going through Cath Sutherland's statement. The, eh, one she gave to DC McIntyre and myself.'

'And?'

'It checks out with others.'

Struan frowned. 'So?'

She shrugged. 'You, eh, asked me to speak to you about it at the briefing?'

Struan could do this away from here, but this was a chance to show Elliot what he had in his locker. 'Okay, so I've been through the statement myself and it's got gaps.'

'Gaps?'

'Big gaps. It's pretty poor work. Constable, you need to be all over the small details.'

Paton kept glancing at Elliot, like she was going to jump in and help. 'Can you be more specific?'

One thing Struan could be was specific. He'd been through the statement twice in the morning, with a view to tearing it apart like an expert criminal defence barrister would. Truth was, it was fairly solid, but he needed her to think it wasn't. 'You haven't tracked down the customer, have you?'

'Sarge, we—'

'Have you?'

'No, but—'

'This customer could be the attacker. He could be an attempted murderer. He could be an accomplice.'

'That's a bit of a stretch.'

'Until you identify *them* and have *their* statement ready for me to pore over, we just don't know, do we?'

'I suppose not.' Paton tugged at her hair, hard like she was going to yank it out. 'One thing... Cath Sutherland said she saw a van pull up just before the attack, parked down the road. We need to know if the customer came from that van.'

Struan hadn't spotted that. 'Find it.'

'How?'

'Cross-reference all that CCTV you spent yesterday collating.' Struan sighed at her, but it was for Elliot's benefit. 'Come on, Constable, this is basic stuff. I need you on your A-game here. Not this level-Z stuff. I'm not sure what passed for acceptable with your last sergeant, but this isn't it for me. Nowhere near. Am I clear?'

'Clear, Sarge.' She turned and stomped out of the room.

Probably heading to the toilet to cry.

Struan took a long drink of his latte. Those chocolate sprinkles were actually pretty nice.

Elliot was staring hard at him. 'That was a bit brutal.'

'Brutal? Guessing her last sergeant would've let her get away with it and given her a hug for being mediocre?'

'He may have.'

Struan held her stern gaze. 'Boss, I know your reputation. Tough but fair. You and I are cut from the same cloth. The reason I was hired wasn't just to replace someone, but to shape this team into something that achieves. That gets results. That puts people behind bars. To do that, as you'll know, you need to establish a pecking order and maintain it.' He gave a dismissive wave at the door. 'And someone like Ash Paton, *their* generation, they need to know who's boss. They need to be shown. To be told. They focus on their mental health so much that they forget they're here to do a job. I mean, I suppose we should be grateful that she's bothered to turn up for work. Being a cop isn't about looking after yourself, it's about giving yourself over to the greater good.'

Elliot didn't say anything but her smile told him she was impressed by his speech.

'It's especially hard coming into an established team like this, boss. When there's been a clear issue below *your* level. I hope you don't mind me saying that, but I gather my predecessor let those two get away with murder. Which means some wrong 'uns might get away with murder. That doesn't sit well with me, sorry to say.'

She rolled her eyes again. 'Don't get me started on Shunty.'

Ooh, lovely. A target to lash out at.

'Was he pushed out?'

'Didn't come to that, but it wasn't far off. He found a soft-landing zone before I could cut a hole in his parachute.'

'Peachy.'

This wasn't going to plan. He'd expected her to admire him for putting that wee cow in her box...

He needed to win her over, big time. Time to play a card he wanted to keep close to his chest. 'I spoke to a mate of Hislop's in the pub last night.'

'You just so happened to be in the pub with him?'

'Genuinely. I was meeting a mate at the rugby club and he was—'

'The rugby club?'

'Aye. Melrose FC. Function on for ex-players. High-school level.'

'And you used to play there?'

'Aye, but not the same year as them. I pretended I did, though. Nobody asked. My mate never showed, but I got speaking to someone.'

He still wasn't giving even a quarter of the truth, but that was a quarter more than anyone else got.

'Who was your mate?'

'Gary Hislop.'

'You pretended to be mates with Hislop?'

'Read about all that stuff he's been telling you. His mates from the rugby club and all that shite. Saw there was an event on last night. Called in to check he was definitely going to be there, pretending to be a mate from school. Obviously they hadn't heard what happened, but I confirmed he'd RSVP'd. I got my name added, just in case.'

'That's... Wow.'

'Spoke to this lad for about an hour. He was a little bit drunk and a lot loose-lipped.'

'Who is he?'

He looked at her blankly.

She sighed – she'd got the point. 'Go on?'

'Said a toff arranged for Hislop to be run over.'

'A toff? Wait, you mean Balfour Rattray?'

'We never confirmed his alibi, did we?'

'Struan. You heard Marshall back there. We've got four avenues here and you put your hand up for two of them. If it's Balfour, then we need some evidence, okay? Now, kindly get out of this office and get me some results, okay?'

'Sure thing, boss.' Struan grabbed his coffee and stood up. He really wanted to say something else and make sure he wasn't missing the last word. But he didn't have anything. He finished his coffee and put the lid back on. 'Okay, boss, I'll go and crack some skulls.'

She raised her eyebrows. 'That's a brave joke to make.'

'I'm a brave man.' Struan gave a final nod, then left her to it.

Aye, that felt like it had hit the spot with her.

CHAPTER FORTY-THREE

MARSHALL

Marshall sat in Gary Hislop's living room. No other cop had ventured this far into his domain, at least to his knowledge. Maybe Elliot had, but if so, Hislop wouldn't have been too shy in sharing it.

Outside, it wasn't much, just four old council houses smushed together. One entrance remaining, the others blocked off.

Inside, though...

Wow.

The living room was a display of extravagance, everything screaming wealth, from the plush rugs on shiny wooden flooring to the mini chandelier hanging above a solid oak coffee table. Italian leather sofas and mahogany side tables.

Off to one corner an oversized fish tank hummed, its exotic occupants oblivious to the world outside their watery abode. An island of tranquillity in a sea of suspicion swirling around Hislop.

Marshall decided it was a curated affluence, projecting the image of a successful businessman. The local boy done good.

Nothing too overboard, but anyone visiting would see a success story.

Sadie Young was as much a fixture in this space as the Picasso knock-off on the wall. A living doll, draped in satin and sequins, caught in Hislop's gilded web. She plunged a silver cafetière, her red nails a stark contrast with its metallic surface. She poured some coffee into a grey ceramic cup that matched the tasteful wallpaper and carefully added some steamed milk. 'There you go.'

'Thanks.' Marshall cradled the cup, the aroma wafting throughout the room, a rich blend chosen to impress. But whether by her or Hislop, Marshall couldn't tell.

She took hers a lot milkier than him, turning the coffee the same shade as her scarf. Everything in the place seemed to be colour co-ordinated. 'Gary's a good man.'

Marshall just hid behind his cup. Gave her space to talk.

'I never thought I'd meet someone so kind or compassionate. Or generous. Or understanding. And I love being a stepmum to Tyler.' She held up a hand. 'I mean, soon-to-be stepmum.' She flicked her wrist, and the rock on her engagement ring sparkled. 'We were even talking about having our own.' She stared into space.

'But?'

'But I just don't know. One kid's enough, isn't it? And will Tyler take kindly to a brother or sister by a different mother?'

'Sounds like you're doing a lot of parenting, though?'

'I am. But... It's not easy. Cheryl was a hard woman to replace. And it can be very difficult at times.'

'But also rewarding, I'm guessing?'

'Maybe.'

She'd clammed up now. There was something lingering in there, a pearl inside the oyster, but he needed to share a bit to break on through.

'I grew up with a stepfather and...' Marshall felt his throat go dry so he sipped some burning coffee. 'My advice? It's all about how much you love them and making them feel like they're yours. But without replacing their parent. That's all I'd say. You sound like you've been doing all of that, though, and more.'

'I don't like to assume things...' She shook her head. 'I... I've had a pretty shit life, to be honest with you.' She left the words hanging. 'I grew up in Largs. Over in Ayrshire, but moved here when I was ten, when Mum and Dad... Split up, I guess. Didn't really settle, but Mum said I had to stay here. Dad was...' She swallowed something down. 'Dad was arrested for beating up Mum. He put her in hospital.'

'I'm so sorry to hear that.'

She couldn't look at him. 'I used to hide it. Never told anyone. Said he was dead. And it came out. Someone at school read the story when it went to court. Mum had to stand up and give evidence. They knew...' She exhaled slowly. 'Sure you can guess the rest.'

'Kids can be awful.'

'Right. See why I don't want to have my own?'

'It's complex, isn't it?'

'Tyler's a known quantity, right? He is who he is. But if we gave him a brother or sister, they might be as fragile as I was. Is that a risk I want to take?'

'Tough decision.' Marshall drank more coffee – ridiculously good stuff. 'I totally understand it. You've been through a hell of a lot. But you know you can't let yourself be constrained by your past.'

'I know that's true, but...' She shook her head again. 'My therapist keeps talking to me about it. But I can't let it go. I—'

The door opened and Jolene walked in, smiling politely. 'Thank you. Hate getting caught short like that.'

'Happens, eh?' Sadie leaned forward and tapped the cafetière. 'Coffee?'

'No, that's part of the problem. Goes right through me.' Jolene sat on the sofa next to Marshall.

'So.' Sadie smiled but didn't seem to want to go back to her personal history in front of Jolene. 'Is there anything I can help with?'

Marshall rested his cup on the table, almost touching the milk jug in the shape of a cow. 'We're interested in speaking to anyone who had any antagonism towards Mr Hislop.'

Sadie looked away. 'Nobody I can think of.'

There was something there, alright.

Just needed a little pressing…

'Sadie, someone drove a car into him. It appears to be a targeted assault. We're exploring some avenues for possible suspects, but if there's someone we don't have on our radar, then it'd be in both of our interests to speak to them.'

Sadie rested her cup with a shaking hand. 'There is something, but…' She scowled. 'Or there might be. But I can't talk about it.'

'Please.'

'I can't. I swore not to.'

'I get that. But when you made that promise, it was on one basis. Now someone has tried to kill your partner, that basis has totally changed.'

She stared deep into her cup.

'On one hand, it'd be helpful for us to know. But if it comes out by other means and implicates you…?'

She shot him a glare. 'Of course it doesn't! I haven't done anything!'

'Then please, just share it with us. We can be discreet.'

'Can you?'

'You told me something extremely personal while my

colleague was out of the room. I promise that will stay only between us.'

Sadie's mouth twitched. 'I'll wait for a week to check it, then, eh?'

Sharp as a tack. Marshall gave a curt smile. 'Meanwhile, whoever did that to Gary could target you.' He let the smile fade. 'Or Tyler.'

Sadie nibbled at her top lip, coating her teeth in red lipstick. 'Fine. I was... When I was... Fifteen. I was... Someone raped me.'

Marshall swallowed hard. He didn't have any words, because there were none.

'They let me go. I ran home and... I didn't know where I was, but... I was safe and...'

'Did you go to the police?'

'Mum did. They investigated. The suspect got off with it.'

Jolene screwed up her face. 'How?'

'Tom fucking McCabe. He was eighteen, had his own car... And they obviously didn't believe me. Got a lot of victim shaming from them. It was horrible.'

'You were fifteen and he was eighteen? And the police didn't believe you?'

'Right. I'm *sure* it was him. We were... I agreed to go on a date with him. I mean, I was fifteen, so it wasn't exactly a Michelin-star restaurant and fine wine, but a walk in the park and maybe a snog.'

'So you met up with him, right?'

'No. I was waiting there in the park, sure, but he attacked me from behind. Didn't see him approach.'

Marshall's neck tightened. He felt a biting throb in the pit of his stomach. 'Did this Tom McCabe give an alibi?'

'Told them he was on his way to work at the Tweedbank Ashworth's. It'd just opened and he was working on the tills. It happened… about half an hour before his shift. They checked it and couldn't prove he didn't do something on the way to work. Impossible to prove a negative. But they didn't charge him.'

'How does this relate to Gary?'

'Last year, I was shopping in Tesco in Gala with Gary. And I saw Tom fucking McCabe. I totally freaked out. Left the trolley and ran. Gary came after me and…' She ran a hand through her hair. 'He's got some friends at the rugby club and… I heard Tom McCabe's in a wheelchair now. He deserves everything he's got from it.'

Something didn't quite add up for Marshall.

Not that he wanted to victim blame, or doubt her, but it was possible someone else had done it.

'That night in the park. Tom never showed up?'

'That's right.'

'Where was the park?'

'Tweedbank. Not far from Ashworth's. But I know it was him behind me. He hit me. Knocked me out. Next thing I know, I'm tied up.' She swallowed. 'I'd been talking to this guy at school about what happened between my parents. About the bullying. Made me think I should open up to people. So I opened up to Tom. And he fucking raped me. Held me in this building for a week and raped me, over and over again.'

'He *what?*'

CHAPTER FORTY-FOUR
SHUNTY

Siyal sat in a dimly lit interrogation room, next to Kieron McKenna, the wiry figure known as Shagger. Siyal knew a thing or two about unwanted nicknames, but the way the kid held himself it was maybe one he'd given himself. Or earned. 'Take your time.'

A battered photo array lay on the table between them, closed.

Shagger started flipping through the photos like a bored kid looking through manga posters in Forbidden Planet. But he was going slowly enough to be doing a good job. The scars on his face were scabbed now, but some would leave a mark.

'Take a good look at each one, Kieron. Tell me if any of them paid you.'

Shagger's bleary eyes scanned the photos, his expression vacant and unfocused. He squinted, trying to make sense of the faces before him, but passed on. 'Sorry. Don't know any of them.'

Siyal's patience was wearing thin. 'Come on. This is a serious matter for you.'

'Why should I care?'

'I don't need you to remember who allegedly paid you, Kieron, you do. Otherwise we'll take it for the lie it so blatantly is.'

Shagger shook his head, his unkempt hair swaying like a ragged curtain. 'I can't, man.'

'Go through it again.'

He did, flicking fast now, but staring blankly at each photo. 'Nope. Nope. Nope. Nope. Nope.'

With a heavy sigh, Siyal realised he was wasting his time here. 'The man you accused was in there.'

'What?'

'DCI James Pringle. The car's owner.' Siyal flipped to the page. 'Him.'

'Sorry, bud, don't recognise him. I was off my head that day. Couldn't recognise my own mother if she walked past us.'

'You don't recognise him?'

'Not him. Guy was taller. Bulkier.'

'You ever buy anything from Roxburgh Hardware?'

'Are you saying you've got something on me?'

'Wouldn't be asking if we didn't. Wouldn't be this morning or last night, would it?'

'Eh, maybe.'

'Hammer. Cable ties, knives, duct tape. Everything a rapist needs.'

'Whoa, whoa. Not me. That was Declan.'

'Your mate. The passenger?'

'Aye.'

'Why don't I believe you?'

'Seriously! He said it's for... one of his other paying clients.'

'What the hell are you two up to?'

'Mate, you *really* don't want to know how I got my nickname.'

CHAPTER FORTY-FIVE

STRUAN

Their desks were over the far side of the space, pretty much as far as they could get from her office. Something else he'd need to rectify.

McIntyre and Paton looked up from their computers.

She brushed her eyes and went back to her work.

McIntyre was giving him a harsh stare.

Aye, they'd been talking.

Struan sat opposite her and next to him. 'How are we doing with interviewing those neds?'

McIntyre frowned at him. 'I thought Jolene's team was on that?'

'They are, but we need to double-check that work. Okay?'

'I'll get on top of that, Sarge.' Paton got up and raced away through the office.

Struan logged in to his laptop and the external display filled up with his emails. So bloody many of them. Too bloody many.

Not to mind. He'd sift through, find the token few from

higher ranks, reply to them, then delete the rest – if the email was important, they'd ask again. In person.

'Sarge.' McIntyre shuffled over, close enough to smell his clinical deodorant. 'Need a word.'

'It can wait.'

'No. We need to have this chat now.'

Struan sat back and folded his arms. 'Go on, then.'

McIntyre pointed towards the stair door, then looked around at the other desks. 'Away from prying ears.'

What flavour of bullshit was this going to be?

'Okay.' Struan got up and wandered over to the door, holding it for McIntyre. He'd never liked stairwells. The oppressively close walls seemed to creep in on him. This one was no different. The acrid smell of disinfectant mingled with stale sweat and dust. So much for the station being recently refurbished. He smiled at McIntyre, waiting for the door to shut. 'There you go. No prying eyes or ears.'

The cold flicker of the fluorescent lights cast a ghoulish pallor across McIntyre's stern features. He leaned back against the wall, arms folded. 'It's about bullying.'

'Who's bullying you?'

'Not me, Sarge. DC Paton. And it's you who's bullying her.'

'Am I?'

McIntyre stood up tall, a good few inches taller than Struan. And heavier – he'd have fitted in well singing songs at the rugby club last night. 'You are. Did it in front of DI Elliot.'

'And DI Elliot didn't say anything afterwards. Makes me think I haven't bullied anyone, Constable.'

'You're fucking out of order.'

Struan sighed. 'Let me make this clear. In my team, we focus on results. Everything comes down to how many people we put behind bars. If someone makes a dog's dinner of some-thing, they get told off. That's what it was like when I started in the police. Now, though, incompetence seems to be protected. If you call out someone for shoddy work, you're suddenly a bully who's creating a toxic work culture. Soon enough, the police service will be entirely filled with incompetent, useless pricks. Like her.'

'She's a good cop. Or will be. She's young. Just needs coaching to fulfil her potential.'

'I'm going to give her coaching, believe me. Then if she doesn't shape up, I'll ship her out.'

'That's not the way to coach someone.'

'You sound like an expert.'

'I'm serious. Been doing this job a long time, probably as long as you. Just because I'm not a sergeant, doesn't mean I've not been given new recruits to mentor.'

Guy was full of himself. 'Are you telling me you're incompetent too?'

'Eh?'

'You're making excuses rather than taking action.'

'You've got a very high opinion of yourself, don't you?'

'With good reason, Constable. I'm good at my job. I've got a track record. I gather you've only been a DC since October. That right?'

'What's that got to do with anything?'

'You don't seem to be cutting the mustard, do you?'

'Cheeky bastard.'

'I see the evidence everywhere, Constable. Every two minutes, I get a call from you or her. I expect detectives to be able to detect without constant guidance.'

'I expect sergeants to at least provide some guidance.'

'Saying I haven't been?'

'Too busy sucking up to DIs and DCIs. Saw you making fluttering eyes at the superintendent. You're a wee fanny, Struan. A total suck-up.'

Struan's fingers twitched involuntarily, itching to resolve this the old-fashioned way. He searched McIntyre for a flicker of doubt or hesitation, but he was as solid as a block of ice. In this confined space, McIntyre's strength was both an asset and a liability. Struan didn't want to be the one starting anything, but he needed to finish this stand-off.

'A suck-up?' He laughed. 'You're lucky to be out of uniform, Constable. Maybe I should send you back and you can get another partner blown up.'

'What did you say?'

Struan walked towards the door. 'You heard.'

'Fuck you, you sneaky cunt.' McIntyre lunged forward, a human bulldozer, his fist arcing towards Struan and landing, hard and fast, cracking into Struan's chin.

Struan hit the wall and slumped down, the concrete wall cold against his back. His muscles tensed, a coiled spring ready to unleash its fury. His jaw clenched, teeth grinding against one another. The heat of anger surged through his veins.

But he needed to be in control of this.

Struan pushed up to standing and spat at McIntyre, splashing spittle over his face.

McIntyre staggered back like he'd been punched. His eyes narrowed, a predatory gleam igniting within them as he advanced on Struan once more.

This time, Struan was ready. He pointed up above the door.

McIntyre was big, but also surprisingly quick. He lurched forward, then stopped dead. Looking above Struan.

Struan tilted his head to the side. 'Don't let the camera see you punching me again.'

McIntyre wiped at his face. 'Coward.'

The fight was brutal and fierce, but over. For now.

Struan had a split lip and some wobbly teeth. 'As far as I'm concerned, the matter's settled. I get that things are a bit strained on this case. I totally get it. And you've had bugger all in the way of guidance. But you need to listen to me and do what I ask, to the best of your abilities. And manage your anger. Do I make myself clear?'

'I hear you.'

'But am I clear?'

McIntyre looked down his nose at him. 'Okay, Sarge.'

'Good.'

McIntyre was old-school and Struan was a sergeant.

Rank won.

Struan fiddled with his teeth. Not the worst punch he'd taken, but he'd be feeling that for a week or so.

Once he got away, Struan would record a version of what happened in his notes, with Jim as the aggressor and him totally defensive. Big Jim McIntyre would record nothing in his notes but the station CCTV would support Struan's version of events. Didn't have to take it anywhere just now, just needed it in his back pocket.

The stairwell door opened and Ash Paton peered in, shifting her gaze between them. 'Are you two okay?'

McIntyre nodded. 'All fine, aye.'

'Just peachy.' Struan shoved his hands in his pockets, trying to act all calm. 'You okay?'

'Listen, I think I might have something for you. Two things. First, Balfour Rattray's BMW's gone missing.'

'Didn't we have it for analysis?'

'We tried. Returned this morning. Trev needed to run a follow-up, but when he went to the farm, it wasn't there. Balf was being a bit evasive as to what happened with it.'

'Seen that happen. What was the other thing?'

'We've got a last-known location for Balfour's car.'

CHAPTER FORTY-SIX
MARSHALL

Marshall carried the two coffees through the office space. Felt like he had a broken lightbulb in his head – everything seemed to flicker and flash. He tried to ignore it, ignore the feeling in his gut, the sour taste in his mouth. Focus on the here and now, on the coffee cups burning his hands.

Seemed to be something going on between Struan Liddell and Ash Paton, but he could just be reading too much into nothing. Some hushed argument. But whatever it was, that was for Elliot to resolve, not him.

Marshall set the coffees down on their desks. 'There you go.'

'Oh, cheers.' Jolene frowned at him. 'Didn't you just have one at Sadie's?'

'This is a decaf.'

'Ah.'

'I hope it is, anyway. Speaking of which, did you find anything in the house when you did your recce?'

'Nope. Nothing. At all, which is weird.' She tore the lid off her cup and tipped in some sweetener. 'I mean, it's kind of like... it's about as lived-in as a show-home. It's like they've bought the idea of a normal house, but it's got no soul. The bookshelves, for instance. The cookbooks haven't been opened, let alone read. The novels and biographies are all smart-looking Booker Prize stuff or the kind of stuff you'd see in a broadsheet's end-of-year list. But again, nobody's read them. It's strange.'

'Like someone's bought an image of what a life should be so they could sell it to people?'

'Precisely.'

'That's what I thought of the living room.' Marshall opened his coffee but the stale sweaty smell put him off drinking it. 'Hislop bought up the nearby houses to get privacy.'

'He's a drug dealer. I suppose he's trying to look like he's not.' Jolene tapped her screen. 'Anyway, I was right. I did work the case.'

'Not the original abduction?'

She laughed. 'I would've been twelve.'

'Right. That's... Sorry.'

'It's okay. But the Tom McCabe case. Honey trap from outside his work in Tesco. Speaking to a lassie, then he got picked up by someone, driven into the hills and battered. Dumped in the woods near Yarrowford. Long crawl down to the road to Selkirk.'

'Crawl?'

'They broke both his legs. Snapped his cruciates in both knees. Broke two vertebrae.'

'Did they try to kill him?'

'Looks like it, right? In hospital for a month. Won't walk again.'

Marshall blew on his coffee. 'Worth speaking to him about this?'

'What, you think McCabe's taken revenge against Hislop?' She made a face. 'Even if he could afford it, do you think he has the contacts to be able to pull it off? Even if he could, Hislop would've got some boys from the rugby club to finish the job.'

Marshall shrugged. 'Was there any indication Hislop was behind that assault?'

'Nope. Just Sadie's word. But that attack's standard drug gang MO. During that case, we dug into McCabe's background, thinking he was a dealer. Nothing. Clean as a whistle.'

Marshall took a sip of the disgusting coffee. 'But?'

'I mean, guys who work in supermarkets, there's a subset who are thirty-something stoners who still live with their mothers. He wasn't one of them. Barely drank. He was into online gaming, that's about it. Still lived with his mum, though.'

'Interesting. So it looks like Hislop's done it, but the reason's personal rather than professional.'

'I mean, good luck proving any of it.' Jolene sighed. 'But I did dig into Sadie's assault.'

Marshall felt that clenching in his neck again. 'Go on?'

'Seventeenth of April, 2008. She'd just turned fifteen, which makes her thirty now. Mum reported it to us. Missing for a week. She lived in Gala. Went to the academy. Picked up out near Swinton, with no real memory of what happened to her. No forensics. No evidence. Nothing.'

'Swinton's just on the border, right?'

'Aye, over by Berwick.'

Marshall read through the file again, but that date kept nagging away at him and made everything clench.

Fifteen years ago, almost to the day.

He was living in Durham at the time, studying for his PhD.

Abducted...

Kept for a week...

They didn't exactly get many cases like that in the Borders, did they?

It all pointed to one man – Graham Thorburn.

CHAPTER FORTY-SEVEN
STRUAN

Struan drove along the stretch southeast of Kelso, heading deep into the middle of nowhere, through countryside he hadn't seen for a long time. So long ago that he'd forgotten the shape of the land. The road was almost train-track straight, with hills to the right and woods to the left, giving the occasional glimpse of the rolling landscape leading over the border to Northumberland National Park.

'Left here.' Elliot pointed up ahead.

Struan took the turning through a plantation, leading downhill to a sprawling complex, the centrepiece a house that was halfway to being a baronial castle. A marquee was being erected in the grounds. 'What's going on here?'

Elliot laughed. 'Weren't you listening back at his office yesterday?'

'Right. Sorry.' He hadn't been listening because he'd been getting that old feeling again, where things were getting out of control.

He'd smashed the heads of two neds together.

He'd got into a fight with McIntyre.

And it was only day two.

He needed to slow down, take stock of the team. Let things breathe. Feel that control. Keep things on the level. Make sure Paton and McIntyre played ball and fucking listened to him.

Didn't help that Elliot might be onto him.

Or was she?

Struan followed the turning into a winding drive, then got out into the spitting rain. 'A book festival, though. Here?'

Elliot was walking across the pebbles, away from the house and towards the marquee. 'So you *were* listening?'

'I was, aye.' He'd just forgotten. 'Who would put on a book festival around here?'

'There's one in Melrose every year.'

'Aye, but that's there. This is... here. In the middle of nowhere between the arse end of nowhere and... Kelso.' Struan spotted their quarry.

Gundog, AKA Fergus Ross, was stuck in the middle of a huddle. Workmen, waiting staff and some young kids who were probably interning. All looked keen enough. 'Let's finish getting this thing up before it starts raining. Okay?' The crowd dispersed around him and he got out his phone. Checked a few messages, then spotted them approaching and seemed to puncture and deflate.

Struan stuffed his hands in his pockets, slowing as he approached. Acting casual to show who was in charge. 'Fergus Ross, aye?'

'Aye. Mates call me Gundog.'

Struan looked around the place. 'This is looking good.'

'Yeah, maybe.' Gundog ran a hand forward from the back of his head and down his face. 'We're up against it to be ready for Thursday.'

Someone was battering a mallet off a peg, but the sound seemed to take a few seconds to travel the short distance.

Elliot smiled. 'I've got tickets for Saturday.'

'Oh?'

'My youngest two can't get enough of that children's author who's a bit of a naughty boy.'

'Which one?'

She winked. 'You know the one.'

'How naughty are we talking?'

Elliot tapped her nose. 'Anyway, it's good to be able to catch up with you. Tried calling. But you didn't pick up. Several times.'

'Flat out, sorry. Left my phone inside to stop anything getting in the way.'

'Who owns this place?'

'Me. Just bought it.'

'Nice place.' Struan joined in. 'In case you didn't already know, we need to ask you about an alibi for your friend. Balfour Rattray.'

'For what?'

'A man was assaulted with a car yesterday.'

Gundog folded his arms across his chest. 'Go on?'

'The thing with crimes like that is we can throw a lot of bodies at it.' Struan pointed at the marquee. 'I guess it's a similar idea to what you're up to with that, right? Get an extra ten or twenty skulls to help erect the marquees for the events here. Still, sitting in a marquee at this time of year is going to be bloody cold.'

'The heaters are being delivered this afternoon.'

'Right, right. But anyway, with our line of work, I can get two officers to probe CCTV from near the site of a vehicular assault on a local businessman. Then I can get them to focus and identify a hundred different details about the scene. Things that spawn tons of leads to investigate. Most are dead ends, as you'd imagine, but some are fruitful. Very, very fruitful.'

Gundog kept looking over to his marquee.

'Mr Ross, the thing I keep asking myself about who assaulted Mr Hislop is... Well. It doesn't look like a random attack. It looks targeted.'

Gundog kept glancing over at the brute hammering in tent pegs. 'And you think *Balf* did that?'

'It's possible. And you helped.'

'How do you get that?'

'Most of the time, Mr Hislop's inside his shop, serving customers or stocking up. But he wasn't yesterday morning. He was outside. Whoever attacked Mr Hislop had to know he was going to be in the right place at the right time to be hit by a car. And that was outside his shop. Now.' Struan reached into his pocket and pulled out a print. 'This camera is just down the street from the shop. That your van, Mr Gundog?'

Gundog took the page and stared at it. 'Guessing you already know that.'

'This places you near the site of the assault at the time in question.'

Gundog's desperate eyes scanned the sheet. 'This is... I wasn't in the van.'

'Where were you, then?'

'I...'

'Come on. You were given as an alibi for Balfour, but we haven't been able to confirm it.' Struan tapped the page. 'This makes me think there's no alibi for him. That you've both conspired to kill someone.'

Gundog shook his head. Crimson roared up his neck.

'Here's what's going to happen, Mr Gundog. You either—'

'Please. Call me Fergus. Or Mr Ross. Not Mr Gundog.'

'Fair enough. Either you tell us what you were doing right now, right here, or you're going to tell us what you were doing while we're all inside a lovely police station. And you won't like that. We'll dig into your life. Be interesting to see what we find. Especially if you've been up to no good.'

Gundog shifted his focus from the tent pegs to stare at Struan. 'Sure, I was there. Parked on that street. Even went into Roxburgh Street Hardware.' He tapped the sheet of paper. 'But I was in there half an hour before this was taken.'

'Your van stayed there, correct?'

'Correct.'

'That's the perfect place to spot Mr Hislop on a phone call. Perfect place to tell your mate, Balfour, that he's outside. Rev his engine, drive over and smack into him. Whether it's him behind the wheel or someone else, doesn't really matter. You told him to strike and someone did. Upshot is Mr Hislop's in hospital, fighting for his life.'

'I was picked up half an hour earlier.'

A wave of rage washed over Struan, his breath quickening and chest tightening in response.

No.

He needed to stay in control.

'If you're going to be this uncooperative...' Struan got out his handcuffs and didn't lash out with them, but instead dangled them in front of his face.

Gundog watched them swing, like Struan was a hypnotist, then looked away. 'Okay.' He sighed. 'I was there. Alright? Buying some equipment. Roxburgh Street Hardware is the best place to get specialist stuff around here.'

'Specialist stuff, eh?'

'Aye.'

'What, for abducting and raping?'

'No! God no!' Gundog's eyes bulged and he hissed out a breath. 'I'm telling you the truth here. I was there. I went inside and I bought some stuff, but they only had half of it in the shop, so someone was going to deliver the rest of it. And Balf picked me up, drove me over.'

'What vehicle?'

'He wanted me to see how the BMW sounded.'

'See, he denied driving that thing then. Said it was up on bricks.'

'I hate to contradict him, but he was driving it.'

'Okay, so he picked you up. Then what?'

'We started building it up.'

'Building what?'

Gundog shut his eyes. 'Do I really have to say what I was doing?'

'No, but it'll help our investigation if you do. Mr Rattray is a suspect in an attempted vehicular homicide. I mean, if he was my mate, I'd tell the police precisely what I was doing.' Struan scratched at his neck. 'Obviously, if I could. And if it wasn't something highly illegal. And I wasn't implicating myself in said illegal activity, of course.'

'Illegal? You honestly think we were... Of course it was nothing illegal.'

'What was it then?'

'I can't tell you.'

'Why not?'

'I can't!'

'Why?'

'Because if this is going to court, then I'll have to say in public. Won't I?'

Struan laughed. 'Did you have your clothes on?'

'Of course we did!'

'Did everyone there have theirs on?'

'Yes!'

Struan folded his arms. 'Come on. This is daft. You're

saying you were with him, but you're not saying what you were doing? How are we supposed to believe that?'

'We were here. At my house.'

'Great. That's progress. What were you doing there?'

'I'm not telling you.'

'Come on, Mr Gundog. You've been in the army and you—'

'How do you know I was in the army?'

'Your discharge papers are framed on the wall of your office.'

'Right.'

'Come on. You must still have that loyalty to king and country, right? Just tell us what you were doing, then we'll bugger off and your mate can go free.'

'I don't have to tell you.'

Elliot focused on him. 'Come on. What were you doing?'

Gundog shook his head. 'I'm building a card store for a *Lord of the Rings* collectible card game.'

Struan blinked away the confusion. He looked at Elliot, whose face was all screwed up, then back at Gundog. 'You're *what?*'

'Balf and I have a little... eh, clubhouse in my garden.' Gundog waved over past the house. 'There are six of us who play.'

'You're building somewhere to play *cards*?'

'It's not just that...' Gundog spoke in such an undertone it was hard to pick out the words. 'Look, we were massive geeks at boarding school. We played *Magic: The Gathering* like you wouldn't believe. Spent all of our money on cards. But it was a secret and we hid it for obvious reasons.' He looked at them, like they'd understand.

'So an obvious reason like this being a total lie?'

'No! Because the other kids would've bullied us something rotten. So we kept it a secret.'

Struan was really struggling to not laugh at this. He'd been a cop for years, but this was the worst nonsense he'd ever heard. 'This sounds like total bullshit to me.'

'It's for the game. You wouldn't understand.'

'I was into *Dungeons & Dragons* as a kid. I know people who played *Magic*. It wasn't *that* geeky. I didn't have to keep it a deep secret. But I know the kind of thing you're describing. Trays for the decks, so you know which is which, and don't have cards spilling everywhere.'

'It's a bit more than that. We were making the place... look like Rivendell.'

Struan couldn't hide the laugh now. 'What the hell is Rivendell?'

'As in where the elves live in *Lord of the Rings*?' Gundog winced. 'Well, Elrond's people. We wanted to make it feel like we were there.'

Elliot huffed out a sigh. 'Is this a sex thing?'

'No!' Gundog's cry carried all the way over to the marquee, stopping work. He waved a sorry, then turned his back on the workers. 'It's... Balf's had a lot of recent trauma in his life. I was helping him process it all. He's been looking after his nephew, right? Poor kid's lost both of his parents and Balf's... Balf's stepped in to raise him. This wasn't for us, it was all for him. He wanted it to be special for Toby.'

Elliot shot him a harsh glare. 'This sounds like absolute bullshit.'

Gundog held out a key. 'You're welcome to visit. Come on.' He charged across the grounds, past the house towards a big hut at the back. He stopped by a set of steps leading up to a pair of patio doors. 'This is Rivendell.'

Through the glass, Struan saw the walls, painted to look like somewhere in Middle-earth.

'And now you know the truth, you can judge us. I don't care

anymore. That's where we were, that's what we were doing. So whatever you think we were up to, we weren't. We were building an elven set for Balf's nephew.'

Struan had heard worse excuses, but the detail of this checked out. Or seemed to. 'You know Balf's BMW's missing, right?'

'Aye.'

'Aye?'

'I mean, it's not.' Gundog pointed to the pond. 'His BMW is at the bottom of eight feet of water. Embarrassed the shite out of him that he forgot to apply the handbrake.'

'This is all well and good, but was there anyone else there who can back up your story?'

CHAPTER FORTY-EIGHT
MARSHALL

Marshall stood outside the stark prison interview room, his heart pounding against his ribcage like a stick off a snare drum. A cocktail of fury and regret rose in his throat as he stepped through the heavy steel door. The white walls echoed with the whispered stories of countless inmates; the scratched table bore the marks of a thousand interviews.

The belly of the beast.

Graham Thorburn sat at the table, grey and lean, but with a cruel twist to his lips. His icy blue eyes were devoid of any remorse.

Marshall felt a surge of loathing, venom flowing through his veins. A man he'd never wanted to see again in his life... And here he was. He sat across from Thorburn and his grip tightened around the chair legs.

'Hello, Robert. Thought I was never going to see you again.'

'So did I.' Marshall couldn't focus on Thorburn for long, instead shifting his gaze to the cold walls. 'But then something came up in a case.'

'Intriguing.'

'Not the word I'd use to describe it. Horrifying. Disgusting. Sinister. Craven. Not intriguing.'

'Robert, why are you wasting your time here? I've already given my guilty plea. I'll be sentenced in due course. Whatever you think you've found, you can't lay another glove on me.'

'I'm asking you to—'

'I'm saying no more, Robert. I told you earlier, before we were so rudely interrupted by your superior's nervous breakdown.'

Marshall could plough on down that rabbit hole, but that's what Thorburn would expect. He needed a different tack here. 'I met my father last night.'

Thorburn frowned. 'Bob Marshall?'

'Doesn't go by that name now, but aye. Him.'

'How do you know it's him?'

'Mum told me.'

Thorburn's mouth was an O. 'Wow.'

'To be honest with you, Graham, it's thrown me a bit. Seeing my father for the first time since he fled and left us. He's spent his career as a police officer who hunted down corruption, but it's a bit of a contrast with you.'

Thorburn sat back and scratched at the edge of the table. 'You mean, he's a father and a grandfather, yet he wasn't man enough to stick around?'

'Something like that.'

'I stuck around.'

'You did, but at least he's not a serial killer.'

Thorburn doffed his imaginary cap to that. 'Touché.'

'Mine and Jen's wellbeing was tossed aside in favour of his mission.' Marshall shook his head. 'How do I process that?'

'It's a tough one, Robert. That's for sure. You must feel very confused.'

'I'll get there, but aye. I'm confused.' Marshall scratched at the tabletop. 'Even worse thing is... He's working this case.'

'Oh?'

'Professional Standards and Ethics. The cops who investigate—'

'I know what they do, Robert. Do you think he feels guilty for leaving you and your sister? Maybe he harnesses that guilt by investigating people like himself who have strayed over the lines?'

'It's an interesting theory. Doubtful. He seems to have made his choice and stuck with it, well into our adulthood. His showing up back in our lives was a total accident. The whole thing is a mystery.' Marshall drummed his fingernails off the wood. 'Just like a serial abductor who preyed on a series of young women. Why do that? Doesn't make sense to me.'

Thorburn sat back and folded his arms. 'Back to me, eh? Think you're very clever, Robert, don't you?'

'It's not about who's got the biggest brain, Graham. It's about who knows what. And we know about Sadie Young.'

Thorburn's eyes bulged. 'Who?'

'You gave the game away there, Graham. You know precisely who. Another of your victims.'

Thorburn looked around the room. 'This isn't being recorded.'

'No. This is just for my benefit, Graham.'

'Why do you care about her?'

'Because someone else took the rap for her attack. He never served any time, but he was chief suspect. Had one of those alibis that didn't quite exonerate him, but also which didn't convict. Didn't go to trial. The case was unsolved. Until now. She saw him in the supermarket. Next thing we know, he's getting his legs broken.'

'Sounds like justice has been served.' Thorburn folded his

arms across his chest. 'But you and your big brain think you have solved it, yes?'

'Graham, Sadie's lived for years with the fear it could happen again. She's lived with the whispers about what he did.'

'When was this?'

'2008.'

'Long time ago.'

'Not that long, though. And I checked, Graham. You were working at Edinburgh uni at the time. One of those periods where you were living with Mum.'

'You would've been in Durham?'

'Correct. And Jen was training in Glasgow.' Marshall held his gaze for a few seconds. As long as he could stomach. 'You did it, didn't you?'

'Look at me.'

'What?'

'You keep looking away from me. You want the truth, maintain eye contact like a man.'

Marshall forced himself to stare down the barrel of that gun. Locked and loaded. 'Enough mind games, Graham. Admit what you did.'

He blew air up his face. 'You're right, of course. I was working as a senior lecturer in criminology at the University of Edinburgh. As part of that, we did outreach for local schools across the Lothians, up in Fife and down in the Borders. Given I lived down there, I took that area. The high schools in Gala, Gattonside, Kelso, Duns, Peebles. We'd go in and talk to the school assembly about crime and psychology. But we also did a bit of private counselling where requested.'

'One-to-one?'

Thorburn nodded. 'People who were already on the path to criminality but hadn't stepped over any lines.'

'Helped you identify prospects.'

'Quite. Kids from broken homes with difficult upbringings. Your Anna was one.'

Marshall's world contracted to a singular point of revulsion. Hearing her name rolling off his tongue was like a vulture picking at bones. Each syllable was a lash. His heart pounded in his ears, the taste of bile creeping up the back of his throat.

But he swallowed it down, along with the bitter resentment and the cold, burning rage. He wouldn't let this monster see his pain.

Marshall caught himself as his knuckles whitened around the edge of the table, then forced himself to yawn and smile. 'Sadie was a victim. Correct?'

Those eyes betrayed a disappointment that Marshall hadn't risen to his goading. Hadn't punched him. Hadn't got himself into deep shit. Thorburn sighed it away. 'You know, I can still remember her tale of woe. Dad used to beat the shit out of her mother. Then one day, he struck poor Sadie. That was it, Mum snapped and moved them across the country to live with her cousin in Earlston. A fresh start for the girl, except when the story hit the high court. Her father was all over the papers. Her mother too, speaking outside court to the press in that angry way people do. And I mean, without thinking of the consequences. Especially for poor Sadie. The locals got wind of it and they got talking. The story spread and you know what Chinese whispers are like, Robert, don't you? You of all people. Especially down in a small community like that. It soon morphed and ballooned and became about how Sadie was sexually abused by her father. How he was a Satanist Mason or something. She had no friends. Shunned in a strange town. The only person who didn't shun her was an eighteen-year-old shelf stacker. You think I'm bad, Robert. I know you do, but I'm far from the only one playing that game. I'm just a grandmaster. Tom McCabe was an amateur, preying on a desperate fifteen-year-old girl. Publicly too. And it wasn't like she was weeks away from being sixteen. She'd just turned. So he knew precisely what he was doing. And a girl like that, she's just a child. So innocent. So pure. So fresh. In our sessions, she talked about him, about her doubts but also her burgeoning desires. It made her vulnerable to him.'

'And vulnerable to you.'

'Well, quite.'

'And it meant you had a patsy. Some poor sap to take the blame.'

'Oh, yes. I did. I was able to persuade her to arrange to meet him, then see how it went. I just had to watch her and wait. Then I struck.'

'And you held her for a week and raped her continually.'

'I'd say you could add Sadie's assault to my list of charges, Robert, but it's a quirk of our legal system that when a suspect is already sentenced on substantive charges, like murder, all the Procurator Fiscal is able to request is a concurrent sentence. No additional time. I'll just serve any sentence at the same time. So there's no point. And they'd rather spend time prosecuting people who will serve additional time. So, at this point, unless you believe I've killed more people or threatened the King, I'm not getting another trial or any more time added on.' He flashed his teeth. 'Sorry, Robert. That must be a bitter disappointment.'

'You really didn't care what kind of effect that would've had on her, did you?'

'I don't. No. To be honest, the flotsam and jetsam of this world are there to be taken.'

'That's what you thought of Anna?'

'This might be hard for you to hear, Robert, but the world is a jungle. Are you a monkey hiding up a tree, or are you a cheetah chasing the monkey?'

'The reason I'm here, Graham, is because someone drove a car into Sadie's current boyfriend today.'

Thorburn sat back. 'It obviously wasn't me.'

'No, I didn't say it was. His name's Gary Hislop.'

Thorburn's nostrils started twitching.

'That means something to you, doesn't it?'

'No.'

'Oh, come on. What is it? How do you know him?'

'I don't. It's got nothing to do with me.'

'You know what happened to your patsy? When Mr Hislop found out about him, he suddenly lost the ability to walk. But that was a few months ago. Now, it's possible he's done the same maths as me. Figured out a serial abductor, serial rapist and serial killer was active at the same time his girlfriend was taken. Saw the news in the papers. Did Hislop threaten you?'

'Of course not.'

'No, he's not that stupid. But we'll go through the visitor logs and your mail. If he's sent you a message, we'll find it. And if you arranged for that car to be driven into him, we'll find out too.'

'The only person who visits me and threatens me, Robert, is you.' Thorburn leaned forward. 'But I do know his name. Gary Hislop. So prosaic that it's memorable.' He drummed his fingers on the table, licking his lips. 'He went to school with a colleague of yours, didn't he?'

This wasn't exactly what Marshall expected. He'd come in, just wanting to torment Thorburn and see if he was a viable suspect. Now, though...

'Who do you mean?'

'Oh, come on. Andrea Elliot. She's the cop I stabbed when you arrested me. Afterwards, I felt a pang of guilt, which soon passed when I realised I knew her. Took me a while. See, I had a few schoolteachers who shared my preferences over the years. Who helped me identify prospects, who we guided into those one-on-one counselling sessions. Who accompanied me in my... specialist activities. Andrea was one of those kids. Troubled, but sadly not a prospect. I saw some fire in her, the kind that burns in people from birth and has obviously made her a good police officer. Well, I know that Andrea Elliot and Gary Hislop used to be lovers. She told me how they'd got themselves into a few scrapes. Shoplifting, stealing cars, arson. I told her to get away from him before it was too late. And she did. The police never caught her for any of it, but it'd be bad for her career if it got out, wouldn't it?'

'I smell bullshit.'

'It's all true, Robert. Word is she's got very close to Mr Hislop again. Imagine the stories she's been telling him? Isn't that someone who'd want him silenced?'

CHAPTER FORTY-NINE

ELLIOT

Elliot walked through the square in Kelso. The town seemed back to normal, like there hadn't been a vehicular assault on a local businessman the previous day, one which necessitated twenty cops descending on the place.

Almost normal but not quite – she'd counted six squad cars on the way in. Someone was getting leaned on from above to provide reassurances to the public that the incident was a one-off and that nobody else was going to get got.

'Maybe having the preventative measures in place *before* would be better, eh?' It was like Struan was reading her thoughts.

Elliot stopped to let a few cars pass before crossing. 'Once again, I'm glad I'm not still in uniform.'

'Tell me about it. There'll be a ton of crimes happening in Gala, Peebles and Hawick today just because they're trying to make it look like Kelso's adequately resourced.'

Elliot cut across the square towards Roxburgh Street – until yesterday, she hadn't known the road's name, even though she'd walked or driven up it every few months. 'You honestly played that crap?'

'What crap?'

'Those card games. *Dungeons & Dragons*?'

'Christ, no. I mean, I beat up a few players and flushed their dice down the bog...' Struan was keeping pace with her. 'Little brother did, though.'

'Little Liddell?'

'Aye, never heard that before.' He chuckled. 'But I never heard the end of that game. He'd be moaning about getting the cards. Dad used to drive him into Edinburgh every few weeks to go to that freaky shop up the bridges that sold them.'

'You never played it?'

'I was big into rugby. Thought I'd play for Scotland. But I never did.'

Roxburgh Street Hardware looked like nothing had happened. The display outside was restored, though reduced-price stickers were all over the salt cones that had decorated the pavement the previous morning.

Elliot crossed the road and entered the shop.

Cath Sutherland was perched on the stool behind the till, her phone hanging from one of those things that stuck to the back, those freakishly long nails scrolling through some nonsense. She looked up, then got to her feet, pocketing her phone.

Aye, that didn't look dodgy.

Elliot rested against the counter. 'Those nails must play merry hell when you're using a hammer.'

'I've only ever touched a hammer when serving a customer in this place.' Cath smiled. 'I'm completely useless when it comes to DIY.'

Struan smiled at her. 'You and me both.'

Cath returned the grin. 'How's Gary doing?'

'Mr Hislop's still in recovery. They're expecting him to make a full recovery.'

'Oh, thank God.'

Struan picked up a cordless drill on special and started checking it out. 'Need to ask you about an alibi.' He put the drill down. 'One Fergus Ross says you were at an office he rents near Kelso.'

'Office?' She laughed. 'Aye, I was there. But that's not an office. It's like a dodgy poker room.'

'When was this?'

'Last Tuesday.'

'Tuesday?'

'Aye. I was delivering some wood and tools. They were building something.'

'He says you were there yesterday?'

'Nope. I mean, Fergus came in here first thing and bought some stuff.'

'Do you remember what time that was?'

She blew out a breath. 'Give me a second.' She scanned through the till. 'Ah, there we go. I served him just before... that happened.'

'How long before?'

'Twenty-seven minutes. Then I was here, with you lot.'

'You were here when my colleagues arrived, sure. That was about half an hour after the attack, so there's a gap of about an hour we need to fill in your statement. Nothing onerous, but we'll need you to go on the record about that time in greater detail.'

'On the record? I've given a statement.'

'Sure. We need to know your movements.'

'I was here.'

'Okay. But we'll just need to refine that detail. Names, faces, times.'

'Why?'

'Someone might've given word to the attacker that Mr Hislop was outside.'

'You think I did it?'

'You're not denying it.'

'Look, Sharon was out delivering the stuff yesterday. I helped her pack up a load of stuff and sent it to his home.'

Elliot had to hide her smile. Drugs. 'You got an invoice for this? Purchase order? Delivery note?'

'The system here doesn't work like that.' Cath held up a notepad, full of scribbles. 'This is it.'

'Sure the taxman will be happy with that.'

Cath shrugged. 'Not my circus. I just serve the customers.'

'Do you have a note on your pad covering what this Sharon delivered?'

'Not really.' Cath scoured it. 'Oh hang on. Eh, twenty packs of wooden panelling. Hundreds of screws. Paint in a load of colours. Brown, stone, green, blue. A ton of... papier-mâché?'

Enough to make a building look like Rivendell. Or just a load of bullshit.

'Okay.' Struan stood up tall. 'You got a number for this Sharon?'

Cath shifted her gaze between them. 'Why?'

'Because we need to speak to her.'

'I've just told you she did the delivery.'

'And that's great, but we need to speak to her about the delivery. Sure you understand.'

'Right.' Cath leaned over and scribbled something down, then tore it off and handed it over. 'Day off today, but she lives over in Gala. Sure she'll be happy to see you.' She scribbled something down and handed a page over. 'Lives just round the corner from me.'

Elliot took it from her. 'Thank you.' She nodded, then walked off back towards her car.

Struan caught up with her. 'She'd have a tough time picking her nose with those nails.'

Elliot laughed. 'It'd get even dicier when she went to wipe her arse.'

CHAPTER FIFTY
MARSHALL

Marshall got out of the car and strolled through the rain to the station, sore from that long drive back from HMP Edinburgh. Made much worse by shitty traffic on the A7, bad enough that Marshall had almost been tempted to cut across to the A68.

Almost.

So he'd sat it out, boiling with the heat from his car's broken air conditioning and the poisonous thoughts rattling around his head.

Inside the station, Davie was hunched over his laptop, watching some tripe on Netflix. He looked around at Marshall then went back to it. 'Hiya, Rob.'

'Davie.' Marshall held his pass up to the reader and it clicked green. He pushed through and headed straight for Gashkori's office.

Struan's pair of DCs were having a chat by the water cooler, rather than his desk. No sign of him.

Aye, there was definitely something going on there.

Marshall rapped on Gashkori's door.

'Come in.'

So he did and stopped dead.

Bob Milne was sitting with Gashkori, both sipping tea from cups and saucers. 'Afternoon, Rob.'

Marshall gave as wide a smile as he could manage, which wasn't very, and stayed standing, like that would make Milne leave the room. He focused on Gashkori. 'Did you get my voicemail, sir?'

Gashkori winced. 'We've been over it and... Well, I have a few questions.'

'Happy to answer what I can.'

'Actually, the truth is it's me who's got them.' Milne set his cup down with a rattle. 'Let me get this straight. You just spoke to Thorburn and you've found a network of offenders, sharing names and faces of vulnerable teenagers to target and exploit.'

'That's right. Why?'

Milne grimaced. 'I've seen that kind of thing a few times. Always a variation on a theme. Always have a few bent cops carrying water for them.'

'But?'

Milne frowned. 'But what?'

'You're acting like there's another shoe to drop.'

'No.' Milne chuckled. 'That big thump you heard was both boots dropping on the ceiling at the same time.' He picked up his teacup and drank. 'It's great work, Rob. Not that you went in there expecting to find it, but that was very useful.'

'Useful how?'

'Did you have a suspicion?'

'Nope. I went in thinking he could be a suspect. Wanted to eliminate him. And then I found out that DI Elliot met him as a kid.'

Gashkori narrowed his eyes. 'Never came up during the case, did it?'

'Thorburn stabbed her in the guts as we arrested him, so she was off sick for a few months. I led all the evidentiary work in her absence.' Marshall shifted his focus between them. 'Why do I get the feeling you pair think you've solved the case?'

'Need to brief you on what's happened since you left.' Gashkori motioned towards the chair. 'Sit down.'

Marshall stayed standing. 'I thought you'd be—'

'Sit.'

So Marshall sat. 'What's been happening?'

Milne picked up a biscuit from the table and dunked it into his tea. 'Impressed by young Shunty, have to say.'

'Rakesh?'

'Aye, Rakesh.' Milne slurped tea and gasped. 'Seems like a decent cop. Very methodical, very thorough. Just how I like my team. Diligent. The lad's spent this morning investigating DCI Pringle.'

Marshall undid his jacket's top button. 'That's what he was supposed to do, right?'

'Jim's clearly our chief suspect, but we want to validate it.'

'I still don't see a viable motivation for Pringle, though.'

'Ryan and I have just been spit-balling a few things and agreed that the most likely possibility is this attack is connected to those leaks.'

Marshall put his hands in his pockets. 'Explain?'

'Well. Hislop was leaking to us, via DI Elliot. But someone was clearly leaking to Hislop, hence all those people going missing. Like thingy Innes yesterday.' Milne took another biscuit but didn't dunk this one. 'The attack happened to snuff out the source of the leaks being revealed.'

'That doesn't make much sense to me.'

'If Pringle was behind the leaks... it's the only *rational* explanation.'

'What about an irrational explanation?'

'That Pringle did it because he's gone completely hatstand?' Gashkori raised his eyebrows. 'Jim's clearly a bit damaged and hopefully the doctors at the hospital will diagnose what's going on.'

'Anyway.' Milne sighed. 'We've agreed on a plan of attack, so Rakesh wanted to get to the bottom of things. Data doesn't lie, Rob. Data is king. And we focused on Pringle as prime suspect to see if he's been leaking. Thing is, as you climb the ladder and as the software updates, you lose the ability to do the most mundane tasks. You have people for admin and the number of times you're required to do it yourself are rare. Usually have an underling or an executive assistant to do that sort of thing.' He smiled at his son. 'Just for the record, I can still run people; I just never have a cause to.'

'Pringle doesn't have an EA, but he's got underlings.' Gashkori smiled back. 'So Shunty's looked through the audit records for all of Pringle's searches on the PNC...' He clattered his saucer down on the desk. 'Trouble is, Pringle hardly ever ran any, and when he did it was a series of ten or more attempts to do it right. So we thought it was an underling. You can picture it, right? "Do me a favour and run this, would you? Print it and let me have a look". All that. So we wanted to find out who that could be.'

Marshall shifted his focus between them. 'You thought it was me?'

Gashkori rolled his eyes. 'We didn't, but we didn't know it wasn't. If that makes any sense whatsoever.'

'One of the biggest ways you can show trust in someone is to treat them with respect.' Milne folded a piece of paper in half. 'And the reason I'm so impressed with young Shunty is he did it the other way round – he wanted to know who was running queries against Hislop's people and why. He's sifted through over two hundred records. There's a lot of the usual traffic-related bullshit, some random uniform officers bringing someone in.' He handed Marshall the page. 'But he's got twelve detailed searches and report reads, all by none other than Andrea Elliot.'

It all slotted into place.

Marshall's mind reeled as the bitter truth slithered its way into his consciousness. He opened the page and his eyes locked on to the report, the words warping and dancing on the page.

Elliot's office door was shut – he thought he'd won her round. Got her to trust him. But that was just an act – he was the one who'd been played.

The taste of betrayal was a cruel blend of acid and ash, searing through his veins, staining the air around him. Cold rage bubbled inside him, threatening to overflow.

Gashkori poured out some more tea without offering any to Marshall. 'As a matter of fact, outside of the six traffic-related queries there were fifteen hits. One each from a DC through there, but the remaining twelve were all hers. All related to people who have now gone missing.'

Milne took his fresh cup. 'So you unearthing the fact DI Elliot was at school with and an ex-lover of Gary Hislop adds petrol to this fire. Shunty's asked me for approval to interview her.'

'Have you given it?'

'We wanted to run this past you first, Rob.'

'Why? It's a no-brainer. I mean, I've worked with Elliot for six months but I still think I've got a good handle on her. She's ambitious. To a fault. She'll do anything to get one over anyone else.' Marshall shook the page. 'But leaking to Hislop? I don't know...'

'Makes sense to me.' Milne snatched the page back. 'He's been leaking to her, so it stands to reason. He feeds her the few details that don't matter, when they'll do the least damage.

She gives him our prized nuggets when they matter most. Ryan, you've been investigating those possible sources in his organisation. How would they get wind of the investigation otherwise?'

'Exactly. We need to interview her. That's for sure.' Gashkori focused on Marshall. 'Do you think she's behind them?'

'I'm not putting it past her, but I don't fully believe so, no.'

'Bob?'

'I'm giving my approval. And you?'

'Me too.'

'Cool.' Milne got out his phone and put it to his ear. 'Aye, you can get onto it.' He paused. 'You know where she is? Interesting. Let me know how it goes.' He put his phone away. 'She's been speaking to a witness who's backed up Balfour Rattray's alibi. Sounds like they were furnishing a room where they could play a... a fantasy-based card game.'

Gashkori laughed. 'Like, poker?'

'No, hardcore geeky stuff. I don't understand it but Shunty does. Anyway. Shunty's waiting for them. Soon as Elliot gets here, we're ready to rock.'

Gashkori got to his feet. 'Right. I'll pave the way for that.' He left the room.

Milne looked at Marshall. 'Do you honestly think we're barking up the wrong tree?'

'I don't know, sir. I just don't know. It's a huge accusation to make. And I still think Pringle makes more sense. But I owe it to him and Andrea to find out the absolute truth.'

'That's what we're here for.' Milne hoisted himself up to standing. 'But you need to focus on the costs of the leaks. People have died because of this, Rob. What's been leaked will lead us to who's leaking and, ultimately, to who benefits. You should follow up on these bits of info.'

'You're staking a lot on Rakesh's work. He's still pretty green.'

'Oh, I know, but he's got to make his own mistakes. Tough love.' Milne winked. 'You would've learned a lot of things the hard way. But things don't pan out the way you want, do they?'

CHAPTER FIFTY-ONE
STRUAN

Struan found the last space in the car park at Gala nick. 'Thought when you opened a new station like this, you should have enough parking for the people actually working there?'

Elliot was in the passenger seat, arms folded. Unmoving, the late morning light burning across her skin. 'It's not a new station.'

'Aye, but near as damn it.' Struan killed the engine but didn't get out.

Elliot let out a breath. 'We've got two statements placing Balf and his car in this freaky clubhouse of theirs at the time of the attack. The only thing more embarrassing for him would be if he was there dressed as Frodo and Gundog as Gollum.' She shook her head. 'I don't get why they didn't just say? Men in their forties like that usually don't give a shit about what they're into.'

'Doing it for his nephew, though. A secret. Maybe he didn't want it to come out?'

'Maybe. Sounds like shite, though. How sure was your source that it was him?'

Struan knew he shouldn't have played that card so early, but he had no choice. But Elliot was on his case and he needed to win her trust. He raised his hands. 'Hey, I just passed on what I heard. I'm sure you've done the same.'

'Mmm. Anyway, this is all for Gashkori to decide.' She huffed out a sigh. 'Still, I am disappointed. Thought your source was impeccable on this?'

'He led us to some truth, though. Cath Sutherland opened up because of that.'

'Aye, sure. I guess. But you said your source was insistent that Balfour did it.'

On the plus side, she had bought it hook, line and sinker, so this was now her thing as well as his.

'Look, the guys in Hislop's world aren't that different from us in some ways. We all deal in probabilities. The more likely it seems that someone's done something, the more we need to act. It's just our actions that are different. We arrest someone but they... well, they beat the living daylights of them to find out what they've leaked, then kill them somewhere we'll never find them.'

She smirked. 'Balfour's lucky it didn't look like that, then.'

'I'm sure word will get out that he's in the clear. And likes dressing up as a goblin while he plays his card games.'

There was something cold in the way she looked at him, something calculating.

He felt a bead of sweat run down his back. This gambit was in danger of heading south at a quick clip. 'Look, boss, there's something else my source told me.'

'Another lead you didn't pass on? My, now that looks shifty.'

'I'm telling you it now, okay?' He hoped that hard stare

would shut her up. 'The people Gashkori and you were talking to have been going missing because of a leak, right?'

'That's who Shunty and Marshall's daddy are looking for, aye.'

'Marshall's dad?'

'Never mind.'

'Every time you and Gashkori go to speak to them, people like Blake Innes, they have a habit of disappearing.'

'What's your point, caller?'

'Stands to reason that it's not just us who've got leaks, right? We've been getting info from someone in their operation to get the names in the first place. My source told me, in a roundabout way, that people in Hislop's organisation suspect it's Cath Sutherland who's leaking to us.'

Elliot sat back in the chair. A few uniforms trudged out and got into two squad cars, then headed out on patrol. She looked over at Struan. 'You want to give me the name of your source?'

'Callum Hume.'

'Wait, *him*? We've been trying to get close to him for a year. How the hell did you swing that one?'

'He was a bit pissed last night. When I told him I was an old mate of Hislop's, he started opening up. I did the research into their rugby days. A few results and significant matches. Also, I'm good at covering lies with half-truths – I did play for Melrose, just not at the same time as them.'

'Remind me never to play poker with you.' Elliot let her seatbelt go. 'So, here's the plan. I suggest you tell Gashkori about this.'

'Okay.' Struan got out and followed her over the car park. The wind had picked up, but nothing like the level you'd get in Edinburgh. He held the door open for her.

She had her phone to her ear. 'Kirsten, sorry, I just saw your call.'

Struan didn't want to face the boss just yet, so he lurked just out of earshot, waiting for her to wrap it up.

'Okay, fine.' She killed the call and glowered at him. 'Kirsten found Hislop's DNA in the relevant places on the exterior of Pringle's vehicle.'

'So it was that car that hit him?'

'Correct.'

Struan let out a deep breath. 'So, we can assume the Balfour Rattray angle is dead in the water?'

'That would appear to be the case, aye. That sounds like old damage.'

'Sounds like? Or is?'

'Hard to say when his car's at the bottom of a pond.' She sighed at her phone. 'Balfour's still not answering.'

'Why do you want to speak to him?'

'Just want to scare him about driving his car into a pond. That's evidence he's destroyed, even if it's by accident.' She trudged inside.

That big idiot Shunty was chatting to Elliot's husband, the desk clerk. They both swung around and spotted them.

'Afternoon, gents.' Elliot walked over to the security door.

The desk clerk walked over and kissed Elliot on the cheek. 'Afternoon, love.'

'Davie.' Elliot kissed him back and reached out to swipe her card.

Shunty blocked it. 'Ma'am, I need you to come with me.'

'Excuse me?'

'Superintendent Milne would like a word in private. Now.'

Elliot stared at him, then laughed. 'Did Marshall put you up to this?'

'I'm serious, ma'am. This is a serious matter. We've booked an interview room for you. Now, do you need a—'

She laughed. Then pointed at her husband. 'Davie, is this you?'

His eyes were wide. 'I don't think it's a joke. When did you know Shunty to be funny?'

Fuck this.

Struan stormed over and got between them. 'Sergeant, back off. You need someone of at least one rank above to interview her.'

'I know that.' Shunty took out his notebook and started writing. 'It's why I've got a superintendent sitting in an interv —'

Struan batted away Shunty's notebook. 'Don't you *dare* write down this exchange, you sneaky bastard.' He leaned in close, pressing Shunty back against the door. 'You know what they say about direct-entry cops, particularly those from protected groups... Particularly those that head straight for the Rat Pack as soon as they can.'

Struan felt a hand tighten around his bicep.

'It's fine, Sergeant.' Elliot scanned her card against the reader. 'I've got nothing to hide from this clown.'

CHAPTER FIFTY-TWO
ELLIOT

Elliot's usual side of the table was claimed by Shunty and Superintendent Bob Milne, a calculating old fox. Marshall's daddy, but that was a whole other thing she needed to understand.

Her chair was hard and unyielding. She traced the well-worn grain of the table with a finger, her thoughts racing. Trying to form lines of defence and counterattacks. She was burning up, but she'd never let them see her sweat.

Shunty focused to her left. 'So you're here as a Police Federation rep.'

She had an unexpected accomplice on her side of the table.

Struan nodded. 'I am, aye.'

Elliot should've figured that one out. Usually the biggest whiner or most inept officer gravitated towards keeping the lazy, the downtrodden and the corrupt employed. Every Federation rep she'd come across used the role as a buffer, helping themselves stay far enough ahead of the scythe. And the way he'd acted in his very short time in the job, that scythe was going to slice away at his bum cheeks before too long.

'We're ready to get started, then.' Shunty picked up his notebook and read something, then put it to the side. 'As you know, we're investigating the leaking of confidential material pertaining to the operation against the illicit drugs operation surrounding Gary Hislop.'

'That's a lot of long words.' Elliot held his gaze until he looked away. 'And I'm well aware, aye. Just don't know why this has got anything to do with me.'

'Because we have reason to believe it's you who has been leaking said information to said third party.'

'I haven't.' Elliot checked her watch. 'Now if you don't mind, I need to get on with catching the miscreant who rammed a car into Mr Hislop.'

Milne coughed up a laugh. A snake smile filled his face. 'Inspector, please stop treating this as a joke. I'm not sure why the magnitude of the situation hasn't kicked in yet, but you're under formal interview here. This is being recorded. So please, treat DS Siyal with respect.'

'Okay, sir, but I *am* treating this with the respect it deserves. This whole thing is bullshit.'

Milne flashed up his eyebrows. 'Bullshit, aye?'

'Aye, bullshit.'

Milne blew air up his face, then motioned for Shunty to continue.

Shunty scanned his notebook. 'Do you admit to speaking to Gary Hislop?'

'I do and I have done all along. It isn't illegal to have conversations with criminals. I think you'll find most serving police officers do so daily... Well. The good ones at least, Rakesh.' She let the accusation sit there for a few seconds then patted her own notebook. 'I have taken copious notes on all of the conversations with Mr Hislop. I've detailed the reasons why I talked to him and what I got in return. I briefed DCI

Pringle the moment he made contact with me back in January. I've kept DCI Ryan Gashkori in the loop too, as he is leading the drugs investigation into Hislop. And I kept DI Rob Marshall informed too.'

'Did you ever discuss Blake Innes with him?'

'I'm not stupid, Shunty. Of course I didn't.'

'Neil Crozier?'

'Nope.'

'Adam Mitchell-Armstrong?'

'Only when he asked me about him. I denied any knowledge. Made some crap joke about his double-barrelled surname.'

'So you lied?'

'To a drug dealer?' Elliot laughed, but it soon turned into a yawn. 'Aye, Shunty. Grow up. It's okay to lie to protect an investigation. Or to protect the lives of people like Adam, Neil or Blake who were willing to talk to us. Not that it did any good to us or them.'

'Okay. We understand you have some "arrangements" with bar owners in the area.'

What the hell was he on about? 'Eh?'

Shunty ran a finger along a line in his notebook. 'One Archibald Carnegie.'

'The numpty who owns the Stagehall Arms in Stow?' Elliot laughed. 'I led him to believe he'd be protected, in exchange for info. That was a very long time ago. Standard practice, Shunty.'

Shunty turned the page, bristling at the use of his nickname. Or at least she hoped so. 'What about a mysterious case of your favourite wine being left in your car a few months ago?'

'That wine was lodged into property.'

'Minus the compromising family photos.'

Shite, where were they getting this stuff from?

Talk about leaks...

Shunty leaned forward. 'And we understand a second case was delivered to your home yesterday morning?'

She felt a blush rise up her neck. 'That's bollocks.'

'Bob, pal.' Struan cleared his throat, then smiled at Milne. 'You and I both know that any good cop has a CHIS or two who isn't registered, because—' He held up his thumb. '—A, they wouldn't sign on formally and—' He added his index finger. '—B, the information they provided is more than worth the informal risk and can be validated by alternative means... but like Andrea says, this has all been documented by her and DCI Pringle knew all about it, among others. Now, if you want to waste time going over old ground, then I'd say we've got all day to waste, but we all know that DI Elliot has an investigation to lead and, quite frankly, you're boring the socks off us.'

'This isn't wasting anybody's time.' Milne held her gaze. 'But please, we need to know everything you've told Hislop.'

Elliot picked up her notebook and opened it at a random page. Just so happened to be a meeting with Hislop. 'It's all in here, sir, or in the previous two, which are in my storage boxes from the move. You should know that I'm a copious note-taker. It's all in there.'

Shunty looked to Milne.

She closed it and tossed it across the desk to land just in front of Milne. 'Go on, take it. Have a good old nosey, Shunty. Fill your boots. Because there's nothing being hidden from you or anyone. I'm giving you the truth, the whole truth and nothing but the truth. Sure, some of it won't look good for me, but if I have a fault it's that I'm always honest. I want to be known as someone who is scrupulously honest, even if it makes me look bad.'

Shunty took the notebook and put it in an evidence bag. 'Thank you.'

'This is a case of "needs must when the devil drives".' She

shifted her focus between them. 'To save an abducted child from rape or murder, you'd use whatever means were at your disposal. Right?' She let her gaze linger on Shunty. 'You've seen me doing some unorthodox policing a few months ago, but we got a result. We saved a young woman's life. That's more important to me than dotting every I and J, and crossing Ts and Fs and whatever other letters need it.'

Milne sat back, arms folded over his gut. 'What's your point here?'

'My point is, if Hislop thinks I'm in his pocket, then so be it. The truth of the matter is *he* is in mine. And I'll die with a clear conscience.'

'As far as you're concerned.'

'Nope. As far as anyone is or should be. Hislop's given me stuff. I've passed it on. All of it. I've fed him bogus stuff in a strategic co-ordination with DCI Gashkori and DCI Pringle. There's no smoke here, lads.'

'You identified three possible sources of information. Did any of those names come from Mr Hislop?'

'Nope. They came from DCI Gashkori or his team. I made initial contact with them.'

'And then they disappeared.'

'That's correct.'

'Because you leaked them.'

'No. I didn't.'

'Inspector, my colleague here has collated enough evidence to charge you.'

Elliot laughed. 'What, with speaking to Gary Hislop?'

'No. With leaking sensitive information to him.'

'This is bullshit and you know it.'

'Inspector. Let me tell you what I know. Bent cops leak information to organised crime for money or for other reasons, such as blackmail. In all cases there's a cost. People's lives usually end. I've done this job for almost forty years. It's a rarity, I know, but I've specialised in it. And it sickens me to discover people like yourself casually leaking information for a couple of cases of wine.'

'I haven't leaked anything that wasn't agreed with—'

'Inspector! Enough! Your account was used to access multiple records pertaining to the case.'

'Eh?' She traced the scars on the table again. Heat was bubbling up from her guts, rising up her neck. Felt like she was on fire. 'If I've accessed those records, it's because I was working the case!'

'See.' Milne leaned forward, resting his elbows on the table. 'That sounds like a good explanation, but it actually falls apart. Do you want to know why? Because nobody else has the same pattern of access.'

She traced the scars on the table again.

'Every item you accessed, Inspector, was leaked to Hislop's organisation. I'm a big fan of Occam's razor – the simplest explanation is the most likely. You accessed files. You had a channel to Hislop. Ergo, you leaked the files to him. Tell me I'm wrong.'

She shrugged. 'You're wrong.'

'Prove it.'

'You're talking about Occam's razor. Have you heard of Hanlon's razor?'

Milne gave a blank look.

'Never attribute to malice what can easily be attributed to incompetence.' She was looking at Shunty. 'You need to double-check his work.'

'It's been quadruple-checked.'

'I mean, you're wrong, but...' Sweat soaked her hair. Damp, thick. She brushed it back, tucking it behind her ear. 'How am I supposed to prove that I'm innocent, though? Hislop's never going to admit to having that information, is he? So he's just going to deny it.' She paused, taking her time, trying to stop her voice from shaking so much. 'The thing is, the truth isn't black or white. It's neither. It's all shades of grey. And the trouble with your case, sir, is it's just a smudgy mess. I'm innocent. Whoever's leaked that stuff to Hislop, it's not me.'

'How do you explain the correlation then?'

'I don't know. It's not my job to. It's your job to prove I did it. You've got access logs, but that contradicts what's in my notebook. It's your job to prove that I passed the information on to Hislop, not just lazily sit there with a half-arsed job. Now, if you and Shunty want to charge me, great. Go ahead. But, sir, you seem like you do things the right way, so I'm asking you to focus on the evidence here. The old-fashioned stuff that leads to the truth. Because you're pointing in completely the wrong direction.' She flicked a hand at Shunty. 'And he's still *rubbish* at good cop, bad cop.'

Milne sat back and traced his tongue over his lips. 'Shunty, can you go to three o'clock on the fourth of April, 2023 in DI Elliot's notebook, please?'

'Last Tuesday...' Shunty picked the notebook with gloves on and flicked through it. 'DI Elliot was at her home address, sir. Just says it was an urgent family matter.'

'You're really doing this?'

Milne held her gaze. 'Doing what?'

'Digging into my private life?'

'Inspector, the reason I ask is the search logs show you were in the Melrose station, reading up on one Blake Innes at the time.'

'That's bullshit.'

'Search records don't lie. Police officers' notebooks can.'

'You piece of shit... I was at home, because my daughter had been... I don't want to get into it.'

'Fine. But, unless you can convince me, you're going to be charged.'

'You honestly...' Fuck it, she had no choice here. None at all. 'I was called to collect my daughter, Sam. It's usually her father who attends to that kind of thing, but she didn't want her father, so I had no choice.'

'That's your final answer? Don't want to call a friend?'

'It's not an answer, sir. It's the truth. She'd been self-harming and had lost too much blood.'

Milne swallowed hard. Something passed in his eyes. 'Okay, we'll take a break there. I've got a phone call to make.' He got to his feet and walked over to the door. 'You're not under arrest, so I can't actually order you to stay, but I can only advise you to sit tight. I'll be back soon.'

CHAPTER FIFTY-THREE
MARSHALL

Marshall stood in Gashkori's office, his mind reeling with a concoction of disbelief and anger.

Elliot's betrayal twisted his gut, as though he'd been stabbed. How could someone he had relied on, fought alongside, and considered a friend stoop so low?

But beneath the fury, a torrent of conflicting emotions surged. He couldn't help but wonder if there was more to the story, further layers of darkness yet to be unveiled.

Gashkori stood next to him while Jolene worked away on a laptop, filling a giant TV screen with the information Shunty had found.

The case information Elliot had accessed.

People.

Case files.

Car info.

CCTV.

Hislop had tried to snare Marshall with a box of wine left on his car seat months ago, then with that bloody delivery first thing the previous day.

And Marshall had no previous connection to him. Elliot, though... Her personal history with Hislop served as the foundation of her betrayal.

Marshall's fists clenched, his knuckles white. He needed to step back, to process things. He ran a finger across the giant screen. 'These reports she's accessed from your team. Crozier, Mitchell-Armstrong, Innes. All three of these have since disappeared, presumed dead. Right?'

'Correct.' Gashkori sighed. 'This is looking really bad, isn't it?'

'Very bad.'

'Oh, jings.' Jolene pulled up another file. 'This is even worse.'

Marshall scanned the page. 'So she accessed information about the drugs investigation into Balfour Rattray. How's that worse?'

'There are detailed financial records in there.' Gashkori scowled. 'And that's material Hislop was *definitely* interested in. We've spent hundreds of man-days investigating the farm, all based on information Elliot had given us from Hislop. And she'd been leaking it directly back to him.'

Marshall frowned. 'What does Hislop gain from it?'

'The farm, probably. If we ruin Balfour, he can sweep in and buy up all that land. Lot of acreage to hide stuff.' Gashkori folded his arms across his chest, but he was fizzing. 'I've been fairly sanguine up to this point, but now...' He swallowed hard. 'Elliot and I were supposed to meet Blake Innes yesterday morning, but he's now in the wind. Andi was pleading innocence and acting like she was as badly affected by it as me, but now she's the one who leaked it? How do I process that?'

Marshall's nails dug into his palms. 'We've just got to let Milne and Siyal do their thing, sir. The truth will out.'

'Aye...' Gashkori ran a hand through his hair. 'Where does

this leave us with the attempt on Hislop, though? Were Pringle and Elliot working together? Did they attempt to kill Hislop to shut him up?'

'I don't know, sir. That's quite an extreme act.'

'Agreed. If they were, though, it means there's something else we're not seeing. Something big enough to kill Hislop over.'

Marshall tried to process it, but struggled. He still had that bitter burning sensation in the pit of his stomach. The harsh sense of betrayal. He wanted to help clear her name, but the deeper they dug, the worse it looked for her, the filthier her name was. 'We need to look at this whole case from scratch. Everything has to be re-evaluated.'

Gashkori glanced over at the door, misted with the outline of a figure. 'Come in.'

It opened to a crack and Siyal peered in. 'Sir.' He stepped into the room. 'Oh. Hi, Rob. Hey, Jolene.'

'How's it going with her?' Gashkori narrowed his eyes at him. 'Or can't you say?'

'I can't, sorry. Sure you understand that.'

'Aye... What's up?'

'Looking for Superintendent Milne. He left the interview but hasn't returned. I've searched everywhere, but I've no idea where he is.'

CHAPTER FIFTY-FOUR
MARSHALL

Marshall tried the Tapestry café first. Same place they'd had coffee first thing. The place was busy with people on their lunch breaks, some lingering from a morning touring the exhibit and others taking a break from jobs. He scanned the place, getting some odd looks from the waitress.

Aye, Bob wasn't there.

Great.

Marshall walked back out onto the high street and into the blustering wind, then looked around the area. The old Post Office building and the banks leading onto Channel Street. The road back towards Clovenfords and home.

Where the hell could he have gone?

Marshall got out his phone and called Jolene back.

'Hi, sir. Drawing a blank, I'm afraid. I checked his hotel in Melrose but he's not been in since first thing. Left just after seven. Didn't even have breakfast.'

'Okay. Is his car still in the car park?'

'Still is, aye. Shunty's too.'

'So wherever he's gone, he's gone there on foot. Meaning he's somewhere local.' Marshall sighed. 'Okay, I'll call you if I find anything.'

'Me too.'

'Thanks, Jolene.' Marshall killed the call and took in another circle of the street.

No idea where he'd gone.

He knew nothing about his father, a man who'd spent a lifetime undercover and hunting down dirty cops. Lying was second nature to him.

Another scan, another blank result.

Marshall had to just wait to see where he'd gone. But nothing sat right about the whole thing.

Why had he buggered off in the middle of an interview?

That didn't make any sense to him.

Like most normal cops, Marshall would devise a strategy, then stick to it until *he* couldn't take it anymore – bugger the interviewee's stamina. There always came a point where they either broke or were sticking to a rehearsed story with no way through. Whether you reached that point in five minutes or five hours, you'd get there eventually.

But Bob Milne wasn't a normal cop. He was career internal affairs, dancing from force to force across the UK to take down bent cops.

Maybe there was some innocent explanation, like a hearty breakfast flying through him like a dose of salts. He'd left the station, though, but Marshall knew how bad the toilets could get in a police station around lunchtime, once all those bacon rolls and coffees made their way through distressed digestive tracts.

Entirely plausible that Milne just wanted Elliot to stew. They'd gone in pretty quickly, so maybe he was giving her space to mull it over. Someone like Elliot had seen enough deals in her time, so maybe a little coercion would go a long way to securing a conviction. Keep her pension, maybe, depending on what she could give them in return.

Christ – Marshall was treating her like she was guilty.

It looked like she was, but still. Presumed innocent.

Sod it, this was a dead end.

Marshall trudged back towards the station.

Then stopped dead.

Bob Milne was sitting in the window of the pub on the corner. Used to be the Harrow Inn, but it didn't have a sign up now – Marshall thought it was called the Gala Tap, a pun on the Tapestry over the road.

He strolled over, hands in pockets, trying to act casually.

Then he stopped dead again.

Bob was sitting with Catherine Sutherland.

What in the name of hell was he up to?

Leaving an interview to speak to someone who worked for the victim of his case?

Fuck it.

Marshall walked into the bar, but didn't immediately go to their table.

A haze wafted through the air, but not cigarette smoke – burnt toast and sizzling burgers. He could taste the fat on the air. Exposed brick walls, adorned with vintage posters, obscure artwork and vintage neon signs, flickering with whimsical messages.

Tapestried out?

Pastries by Dmitri.

The palest of ales.

The horseshoe bar squirmed around the room, with its array of taps, each one glistening with the promise of the exotic, from hoppy IPAs to rich stouts and tart sours.

The afternoon sun peeked through the curtains, the gentle

rays casting warm light on the mismatched furniture scattered throughout the bar. Rustic wooden tables, adorned with handmade coasters and vintage beer mats. The crackle of vinyl playing through giant PA speakers harmonised with the clinking of glasses and the drone of chatter.

A bearded waiter in a stripy top and drainpipe jeans carried an avocado toast topped with edible flowers, along with an artisanal charcuterie selection on what looked like an old section of floorboard.

Bloody hipsters.

Marshall followed him over and waited for him to deposit the food in front of Milne and Cath.

'Enjoy.' He turned around and skipped to the side to get past.

Marshall pulled up a chair and joined them. 'Fancy meeting you here.'

Bob sat back. 'Hi there.' He was brazening it out, was he?

'That looks nice.' Marshall leaned forward and scoured the floorboard, like he was looking for something to eat. 'It's pretty good to find you both here. Means you can't deny knowing each other. Surprised you're here and not in Kelso?'

'Half-day Tuesday.' Cath got up. 'I need to go to the toilet.'

Marshall watched her go – at least she did actually go to the bathroom instead of leaving the bar.

'What's up, Rob?'

Marshall snatched a little gherkin from the plate and took his time crunching it. 'Why did you slip off from an interview with a suspect in *your* case to meet with a witness in *mine*?'

'Oh, here we go. You think you're smelling a rat.'

'Hard to not see it that way.'

Milne took a sip from a hazy pint glass. 'Alcohol-free, in case you're wondering.'

'Right. Why are you meeting her?'

'Wee spot of lunch.'

'During an interview?'

'Come on, Rob, spit it out. What's going on in that galaxy-sized brain of yours?'

'Are you having sex with her?'

Milne laughed. 'You're so smart, Robert, aren't you? Chip off the old block.' He pointed at the platter. 'Anyway, help yourself to my chorizo or artichoke hearts, won't you?' He picked up a slice of salami and chewed it, then sipped more of his beer.

Cath came back but didn't sit down. She didn't look like she had the appetite for her avocado toast, or any of the meat Milne was powering through. 'I need to get home.'

Bob toyed with a length of Gruyère. 'This guy upsetting you?'

'A bit. Sure you'll enjoy my lunch on top of that, though.' She brushed past Marshall on her way out.

Milne got up with a yawn. 'Need to take a piss. Mind my food, would you?'

Marshall watched him swagger over to the toilet, his rickety legs like a cowboy in one of those old films Grumpy would watch on a Sunday afternoon.

He still had no idea why Bob Milne was buying Cath Sutherland lunch.

And Milne wasn't going to talk. Well, he had the gift of the gab, but he wasn't going to tell the truth.

So Marshall followed Cath outside, worrying his old man was bent.

CHAPTER FIFTY-FIVE
MARSHALL

Marshall followed Cath along Scott Street, past the original shop in Hislop's chain, in amongst a block dotted with hairdressers and a newsagent. Just after Scott Street merged with Gala Park, like two tributaries forming a river but taking only one of their names.

She turned onto Rosebank Place, a row of squat modern semis, in an area full of Victorian tenements.

Marshall stayed on the corner and took it in. The light flashed on upstairs. He got out his phone. No answer from Jolene, even though he could practically see the station from up here. He didn't want to go in there alone and ask – he needed air cover, ideally from a female officer.

So he just had to wait.

A taxi turned up and pulled in outside. The bald driver tapped at his phone.

Cath was going somewhere – Marshall didn't have a choice of waiting for Jolene. He had to go inside now.

He skipped across the road and knocked on the door,

waiting in the blustery wind. Going to be a brutal night – he'd need to hunker down and hope the flat didn't get shaken too much.

Assuming this day ever ended.

Cath opened the door in a dressing gown. Hair damp.

Red flag. Don't go in.

Marshall stepped back and held his expression steady. 'Sorry. I've interrupted you, I can come back.'

'I'm just out of the shower. I'll be two ticks.' Before he could complain, she raced off up the stairs. Left the door open.

Do. Not. Go. In.

Marshall waited outside, turned away, arms folded. The wind blowing. He called Jolene again. No answer again.

He shouldn't be doing this.

And he shouldn't have confronted his father back there. But something snapped in him.

Thirty years of being lied to by everyone.

Thirty years of being less important than everything else.

Thirty years of complete bullshit.

'Hi, sorry.' Cath reappeared, her long hair damp and hanging over one shoulder. Jeans, low-cut top, barefoot. 'Come in.' She opened the door and showed him inside. Decent-sized living-room-cum-kitchen, minimal to the point of stark. White walls filled with vibrant artworks containing all of the colours. Stripped floorboards that matched the coffee table. Lime sofa with pink cushions. Pink armchair with lime cushions.

'Can I get you a tea or a coffee? Maybe a glass of wine?'

'Thanks, but I'm on duty.' Marshall took the armchair, omitting that it was inappropriate anyway. 'I've just had a coffee, so I'm fine, thanks.'

'Okay.'

He thumbed behind him. 'Are you heading somewhere?'

'Meeting a pal for some drinks in Edinburgh.' She perched on the edge of the sofa. 'So?'

Marshall got out his notebook. 'I'll make this brief. Just need to ask you a few more questions.'

'I've answered a lot of them already.'

'And you've been mostly helpful.'

'Mostly?'

'It's taken a few passes to confirm some things, but I appreciate everything you've given us so far.'

She nodded and perched on edge of the sofa, hands clasped in front of her. 'When do you finish?'

'Excuse me?'

'Your shift. When do you get off?'

'I'm not sure. Being a detective isn't a nine-to-five gig.'

'I could wait, if you fancied going for a drink?'

The red flag was hoisted right up the mast. Klaxons blaring. Lights flashing.

'It'd be unprofessional of me.'

She nibbled at her lip. 'What about in a few weeks, if we bumped into each other in the street?'

'I'm in a relationship.'

She raised an eyebrow. 'Doesn't mean you're not looking.'

Marshall smiled at her. 'I'm not looking.'

He'd spent so long being inadvertently celibate and now he was the centre of some unwanted attention like this...

It was unnerving, to say the least.

His neck felt like it was on fire.

'Sure. Okay. I get it.' She sat back with a smile, brushing it off like it didn't happen. 'What do you want to know?'

'Let's start with why you were meeting Superintendent Milne?'

Her eyes narrowed slightly. 'Why do you want to know? Are you investigating him?'

'No. That's not my job.'

'It's his, though, right? Investigating corrupt cops?'

'I'm not sure he should be telling you that.'

'He has, so I guess the cat's out of the bag.' She laughed. 'Shouldn't you have another cop with you?'

'I should.' Marshall sighed. 'What were you talking about?'

'The decline of western civilisation and the end of history.'

'I'm being serious here.'

'I just met him for lunch, that's it.'

'How do you know him?'

She sat back and snorted. 'Listen, I think you need to tell me what this is about, don't you?'

'Are you passing on information from him to Hislop?'

'Excuse me?'

'Is Superintendent Milne leaking sensitive material to you?'

She laughed. 'Look, whatever you think is going on, it's not. I've nothing to do with Hislop's other businesses.'

'What other businesses are those?'

'I don't know.' She threw her hands up in the air. 'People keep mentioning stuff, but I'm not involved in any of it. All I do is run the hardware store in Kelso. I'll be the manager soon.'

'This doesn't really stack up for me. I don't see why you'd go to lunch with him.'

Her eyes scanned around the room, dancing across her familiar possessions, not that there were many of them. 'If you must know, I was giving him information on this case he's working.'

'*You* were giving *him* information?'

'Correct. I'm a source.'

'That usually works out because you've done something you shouldn't have. Means you get off with a crime in exchange for information. What did you do?'

'Why are you hassling me so much? Why can't you take this up with him?'

'I did.' Marshall let the words settle there for a bit, watching her fingers twitching. Definitely something being hidden here. 'I just want to see what lies you both come up with. Interesting how they're the same.'

'Bob's a good man.'

Marshall laughed. 'Right, sure.'

'You don't believe me?'

'No, I don't. When I look at Bob Milne, I see a narcissist who thinks he's better than everyone else. An arrogant old fool who makes mistakes and disowns them. He's an internal affairs cop because he can't handle the truth about himself. That he's unreliable. Duplicitous. Conniving. But worst of all, he can't stay the course in his personal life so he tries to pretend he's perfect in his professional life.'

'Wow... You really hate the guy, don't you?'

'I don't hate anyone. But when people refuse to answer straightforward questions, I don't like that.'

'I mean, considering you've been working with him, what, a day, you've built up this picture of him?'

Marshall nodded. 'I've got my reasons.'

'Sure you have. Sure you can justify anything, eh?'

'What's that supposed to mean?'

'I don't know, but from where I'm sitting, you're the arrogant one. One of those cops who comes into a single woman's home and starts giving her hassle about someone she's meeting. That reeks of desperation to me. Are you desperate? And if so, why are you desperate?'

Marshall locked eyes with Cath. 'I asked you before, but you didn't answer. Are you sleeping with him?'

She laughed. 'With *Bob*?'

'Aye. Are you sleeping with him?'

She shook her head, a leer on her face. 'No, I'm not sleeping with Bob.'

'Why should I believe you?'

'Because I'm his daughter.'

CHAPTER FIFTY-SIX
MARSHALL

Marshall pulled up outside his home. Luckily the Beast had got them all the way back from Gala without dying. All three miles.

Cath was in the passenger seat, staring into her lap. 'So I've got a sister too?'

'That's right. We need to take this easy. This is as much of shock to me as it is for you, and it's going to be a hell of a shock to Jen, too.'

'You're saying that like I knew I had a brother and a sister.'

'Bob never talked about us?'

'Never.'

'That's... Wow.' Marshall opened the door and stepped out. 'Come on.'

Cath followed him over to the door.

Marshall unlocked the door, then called up the stairs. 'Hello? Jen? Are you decent?'

She scurried down the stairs in her off-duty gear – trackie bottoms, massive Foo Fighters T-shirt and monster-claw slippers, lugging a basket of washing. 'What are you doing home?'

Marshall looked up the stairs. 'Who have you got up there?'

'Just your cat.'

'He's a hussy.' Marshall pointed to the door. 'Need you to
—'

Jen frowned at Cath. 'Rob, if you were going to break up
with Kirsten and bring home someone new, a bit of warning
would've been nice?'

Marshall held her gaze. 'Jen, this is Cath Sutherland.'

She stepped inside. 'Hi.'

'Hi back.'

'She's our sister.'

Jen dropped her basket of clothes. Ankle socks and bras
tumbled down the stairs. 'She's *what?*'

'Half-sister.' Cath seemed to shrink in height. 'I'm your
father's daughter.'

Jen picked up the basket and stuffed the underwear back
in, then she raced through into the kitchen and squatted in
front of the washing machine. She started filling it, shaking her
head. '*How?*'

Marshall grabbed a rogue sock and followed her through.
'Here.'

'Ta.' Jen looked around at Cath. 'You look a lot younger
than us. How old are you?'

'Twenty-eight.'

'So, almost ten years younger than us.' Jen twisted the dial
and set the washing to go. She stood up then blew air up her
face. 'This wasn't on my bingo card for today.' She looked at
Cath, standing in the kitchen doorway, then looked away. A
pot of soup bubbled away on the hob. 'You're in touch with
him?'

'All my life, aye.'

Jen pressed her tongue deep into her cheek, then swapped
to the other side. 'How come he stuck with you?'

'Dad?'

'Let's just call him Bob, shall we?' Jen walked over to the kettle and filled it from the tap. 'I'll make some tea. Sit. Please.'

Cath took Marshall's usual seat.

Marshall stayed standing, leaning in close to his sister. His twin sister, rather than half. Christ, this was going to take a lot of getting used to. 'Jen, this is as much of a shock to her as it is to us, okay? So please, go easy on her.'

'As if I'd do anything else.'

Marshall laughed. It came out a lot more like a bark than he'd intended. 'I want nice Jen, okay? With-an-elderly-patient Jen. Not with-her-dickhead-brother Jen.'

'Fine.' Jen sat next to Cath, but their body language was outright hostility. Arms folded, facing away from each other with a scowl.

Aye, Marshall could see the family resemblance.

'So.' Jen kept looking over at the kettle. 'You've known Bob all your life. Talk to us.'

'What's there to say? I grew up in Aberdeen. Moved down here recently.'

'Why?'

'Why what?'

'You left a life up there to come here. Bob doesn't even live here.'

'My granddad does.'

'Grumpy...' Jen exhaled so much air it was a wonder she wasn't gasping for more already. 'Sorry. But this sounds like bollocks.'

Cath leaned forward. 'Look, quine, I don't have to be here taking this crap from you.'

'Crap?' Jen's eyebrows shot up. 'Quine?'

'You know what I mean. Look, you're using some pretty hostile language.'

Jen smiled. 'Yep. I feel pretty hostile.'

'I seriously don't have to do this.' Cath thumbed over at Marshall. 'I'm here because *he* asked me to do this with you both. So this is a courtesy. And you two probably have as many questions as I have. I don't have any answers, or none that I can think of. But I want to at least talk this through like grownups, even if that's beyond you.'

Jen walked over and tipped some loose tea into her favourite pot. She poured the hot water in just as it clicked, then slammed the lid on the pot. She turned around, folded her arms and actually smiled. 'So you knew him growing up?'

'Aye.'

'As in, he lived with you?'

'Nope. I lived with Mum, but Dad was reasonably present in my life. I mean, *Bob*.'

'Okay, but you knew him as Dad?'

'Right.' Cath shifted her gaze between them. 'Gather you two only met him for the first time last night?'

'As adults, aye.' Jen uncrossed her arms. Then re-crossed them. 'I gave him a piece of my mind.'

'He's a good man.'

'Believe that when I see it.' Jen got three mugs out of the cupboard. 'So he didn't live with you?'

'He did for a few years. Then he got another job, so he moved to another force in Scotland. Down in Glasgow. Saw him a lot less. Then he moved to England, like Hampshire? And a few others. He kept coming back to see me.'

'What, like once a year? Six months?'

'At least once a month.'

'Wow.' Jen looked over at her brother, eyes wide. 'Hard not to feel jealous, eh?'

'I know.' Marshall swallowed. 'It's what I've been dealing

with all the way over here. How he jettisoned us to have another family.'

Cath frowned. 'That's not fair. Or true.'

Jen laughed. 'He *literally* left us for you.'

'You don't understand. Neither of you do.'

Jen rested a fist on her hip. 'What's not to understand? He had a family with Mum. Left us when we were seven. Three years later, he has you.'

Marshall got up and walked over to her. 'I had a chat with him earlier, Jen. He told me a bit about... what happened, I suppose. It's not as straightforward as you're making out.'

'Feels pretty black and white to me.'

'He told me all about it. He tried to make it work, but it just didn't. He was an undercover cop in Aberdeen, working away from home. Things were messy. Mum wouldn't let him see us. Returned all of his presents. That kind of thing. And we were left with her version of what an awful guy he was.'

Jen shook her head slowly. 'And you think he's okay?'

'Not quite. I have massive doubts. But... Nothing's ever black or white, eh?'

'Bloody hell.' Jen clattered the mugs onto the table. 'Who was your mum, Cath?'

Cath sighed. 'Mary Sutherland. She'd been married before. Lost her husband in the Piper Alpha... You know that offshore oil rig disaster. She was compensated, massively, but she really missed him. So she kept his name as a memory. And then she had me. Cath Sutherland.'

'Jesus Christ.' Jen started pouring tea into the cups. She took a deep breath. 'Can I speak to him?'

CHAPTER FIFTY-SEVEN

STRUAN

Struan sat at his desk at the edge of the office space and opened the foil around his burrito. He didn't expect there to be anything so exotic in Gala, but there you go. A Mexican restaurant, run by a fella who loved to chat as much as Struan did. It smelled magnificent and, judging by the envious looks he was getting from his new colleagues, it was pungent enough to spread around the room.

Peachy.

He took a bite and unlocked his machine.

The door of Gashkori's office opened and yet another drugs officer left. Something was going on in there, but Struan had to be careful he wore the right hat when speaking to him – the detective's fedora, not the Federation rep's crash helmet.

As he ate, his thoughts raced like wild horses.

Elliot's arrest and interview cut through him like a surgeon's scalpel. He'd only met her the previous day, but things had escalated to a ridiculous point already.

Not for the first time in his career, Struan was going to have to play both sides to find out the truth.

He opened the case file on his laptop, a labyrinth of digital paperwork, and started trying to unravel the tangle. He sifted through the documents, chewing the fiery chicken burrito, his eyes scanning lines devoid of sentiment or emotion. Just cold, hard facts. Each page held a piece of the puzzle, a fragment of the narrative that led them to her perceived betrayal.

She'd taken on an informant in a drugs investigation. Not exactly unusual, but it seemed like she had some history with the guy. Personal history. And that made someone like Marshall smell a rat.

Someone on the case had been leaking, that much was clear to Struan. Too many coincidences for that not to be so – like in Putin's Russia, where his enemies somehow ended up walking too close to windows at just the wrong time...

But was it Elliot?

That Shunty kid was smart, attacking the case with an oblique strategy. And succeeding – pinning the leaks back to access.

Struan would never have thought of doing it like that.

And it was hard not to agree with the conclusion – the people who'd gone missing were being set up as informants on Hislop's empire. It was all in the case file. Names and dates.

But that got something tingling in him...

A little nugget of a thought started spreading through his synapses.

Elliot was working the case. She knew who they'd been speaking to, so she wouldn't need to access the files to leak them. She'd just tell Hislop what she knew.

That had been jarring up against everything for a few hours now, but it only crystallised now he searched for the truth.

Okay, so the upshot of that was there was someone else leaking, but the digital paper trail led back to Elliot.

Struan opened up the master directory and there was nothing there.

'What the hell?'

He was interrupted by the arrival of Paton. Just her presence made him tense up. 'What are you up to?'

He tried to ignore her. 'Just working away.'

'Could do with some guidance, Sarge?'

'Could do with you showing some initiative and bringing me some leads.'

'You've been away for hours.' Paton wheeled her chair over to him. 'Don't you want to know what we've been working on?'

Struan ignored her. 'I'm sure one or both of you will have briefed DCI Gashkori, right?'

'That's a bit harsh, isn't it?'

'Is it? Tell me you haven't.'

'I haven't.'

'Great. And whatever it is, it can wait.' Struan flicked a hand at the empty directory structure. 'I'm working on something here.'

'Sarge, if you don't mind, I think we need to clear the air. You've come in here and tried to bully us. It's been ridiculous. You should try working with us, not against us.'

'But... Sure. Okay. Fine.' Struan went back to the laptop, but nothing was in the right place. Most of it was missing – how the hell could anyone leak stuff that wasn't even there? He looked over at Paton. 'Can I borrow you for a second?'

Her expression softened for a moment. 'Right?'

'I'm kind of struggling to find my way around the case file.'

'It's standard, isn't it?'

'No. Complete opposite. This is a joint operation with drugs, so everything's filed on their server. And it's... It's all over the place. Can't make head nor tail of it.'

She pushed in next to him and grabbed his mouse and keyboard, then started delving into the depths of the server, navigating parts of the digital labyrinth he hadn't seen.

'How are you doing that?'

'Went on a course, Sarge.' She raised an eyebrow. 'Sounds like you need to do it, too. What are you looking for?'

'The stuff that's been leaking...'

'Look.' Her eyes narrowed, her jaw clenched. 'I heard DI Elliot's been arrested. Is this—'

'Nope. She's just been interviewed.'

'But she's not been released?'

'The interview's on hold.'

'Word is she's been leaking information?'

'That's not for me to brief you on, okay?'

She pointed at the screen. 'But it's something to do with these files, right?'

His gaze locked on to hers. 'There's a leak somewhere on this investigation. Either on the drugs side or on ours. It's not me, obviously, as I've just started and I can't find anything on this bloody network. But I am determined to get to the bottom of it.'

'Are you trying to clear her name?'

'I'm just doing my job, Ashley. If it exonerates her, peachy. But if it doesn't, then I want to know. Everyone thinks she's been leaking so they're not looking for any other culprits.' His fists tightened. 'And this whole story doesn't add up for me.'

Paton rolled her eyes. 'Oh, so now you're going to solve it all on your own?'

'Trying to, aye.'

'Okay. Well, I'll leave you be.' She rolled her chair back to her desk.

Leaving him staring at the empty screen again.

He sighed. 'Constable, can you—'

'Ash.'

'Excuse me?'

'My name's Ash. Not Ashley. If you want my help, you call me that. I call you Struan or Sarge. And you need to stop bullying us.'

'Fine. Thank you, Ash.'

'Just be civil, Struan. That's all you need to do.' She wheeled back, then hammered the keyboard like it was a typewriter. 'There it is.' The screen was filled with a list of documents. 'This is the new server. It's pretty complex, but it's much more powerful. Means things don't get lost so easily. All the files here are tagged with keywords.'

'Like hashtags on Twitter?'

'Right, that kind of thing. Means everything can be in multiple folders at once, if you will. So you can search across the whole set of data and see what's relevant.'

'Seems very complicated.' Struan laughed. 'And they expect cops to use this?'

'Drug squad do things their way.'

Struan looked at the directory and things started to make sense. All of the files in the case sat there. 'So these tags...' Off to the right were a number of buttons with one or more words on.

Gary Hislop was a tag, so he clicked on it and another view opened up, filled with a few files.

Top of the list was a file created that morning.

Operational plan for arrest of Gary Hislop

Struan leaned forward. 'What the hell is this?'

Paton hovered her finger above the screen. 'Published by DCI Gashkori fifty minutes ago.'

Struan opened the file and scanned through the contents.

It did what it said on the tin. Once Hislop was discharged from hospital, the plan was to pick him up. Maps of the hospital with placements of officers, all ready to catch and arrest Hislop.

And just like she said, the document was signed by Gashkori, on behalf of the Drugs Command, countersigned by the head of Specialised Crime Division.

Nothing in Struan's inbox about it, so maybe he was on the outside of the operation now he'd been outed as a Federation rep.

All those drugs cops going in and out of Gashkori's room were on the inside.

Elliot couldn't leak this file, given she was stewing in an interview room like overcooked cabbage.

If his theory was correct, the leaker would find that file then hand it off to someone in Hislop's world.

Struan knew someone in that world. Someone very senior.

Just had to watch them and follow them to the leaker.

CHAPTER FIFTY-EIGHT
MARSHALL

Marshall got out of the Beast and opened the door for Cath. His head felt like the pressure cooker making soup back in Jen's kitchen, ready to explode.

She got out into the cool air. 'You okay there?'

'Not really.' Marshall clocked Jen's approach, her hostile raised shoulders, then led Jen and Cath across the car park to Gala nick.

His sisters.

Plural.

Aye, he'd look up his therapist's number soon – a lot to process there.

The station's front entrance was chaos – the card reader was a mess of exposed wires.

Davie Elliot turned around, then gave a deep sigh. 'Rob.' He scratched his head with the blunt end of his screwdriver. 'Bloody hell.'

Marshall smiled at Jen then Cath. 'Give me a sec here.' He walked over. 'You okay there, Davie?'

'Popped out to do the school run, and of course, that's when the boy turns up, eh? Forgot to get someone to cover. And he's buggered off on his break without fixing it. Supposed to be a bloody police station. Supposed to be secure!'

Marshall nodded slowly. 'Heard about Andrea.'

'Aye...' Davie shook his head, looking away. 'I mean, I've nothing really to worry about because she's innocent. Right?'

'I honestly can't say anything.'

'Come on, Rob? Seriously?'

'Need to get into the office. And sign these two in.'

Davie looked at Cath and Jen – they were chatting, at least. 'I'll trust you, Rob. Thousands wouldn't!' He pressed his screwdriver against a wire. The light went green. '*Et voilà.*'

'Cheers.' Marshall let his sisters go first, then followed them into the office space. Nobody paid them any attention, despite this being a brand new place of work. Or maybe because of it. He walked up the aisle at the side, then opened his office door. 'Have a seat.'

They took the chairs by his desk and sat in mirrored poses. Sheer hostility. He hoped they'd thaw, but that was a while off.

'I'll be right back.' Marshall walked up to Gashkori's office and peered through the glass. Sure enough, Bob Milne was in there, scrunched over a laptop.

Marshall rapped on the door and entered without a word. He focused on Gashkori, sitting behind his desk with a sour look on his face. 'Sir, I need a word with the superintendent.'

'Busy.' Milne looked up from the laptop with a groan, then started rubbing at his neck. 'Have you seen Struan Liddell?'

'Not for a while, why?' Marshall thumbed behind him. 'Need a word. In private.'

Milne shook his head. 'Not happening. Too busy with this case. Way too busy.'

'This is a private matter, sir.'

'And this is in office hours.' Milne tapped his bling watch a few times. 'Come on, Rob.'

'Your kids. All three of us.'

Gashkori was frowning at them. 'What's going on?'

'Nothing.' Milne hoisted himself up to standing. 'I'll be back pronto.' He stepped out into the office space, staying close to Marshall. 'What are you up to?'

'We know about our sister.'

'Your sister? What are you talking about? With all due respect, you're out of order here.' Milne motioned across the room. 'We've got a bent cop in a paused interview, a senior officer who probably attacked a local gangster, and you're talking about a *sister*?'

'Reason this can't wait, sir, is she's involved in this case. Cath Sutherland.' Marshall gestured back at Gashkori's office. 'Did you brief him on that conflict of interest?'

Milne narrowed his eyes. 'O-kay.'

'They're in my office.'

Milne stormed down the row of doors, then pushed into Marshall's room.

Marshall jogged to catch up, then slammed the door behind him.

All three of them had the same hostile look – lips pursed, arms folded, eyes narrowed.

Milne looked at each of them in turn. 'I guess you all know, then?'

Jen was first to speak. 'What a way to find out. My idiot brother showing up at my door with her in tow.'

Cath shot her a glare. 'Speak for yourself. I only found out because *he* thought I was banging our father.'

Marshall put his shaking hands in his pockets. As much as he hated confrontation, he hated burying things even more. 'You two having lunch looked shifty as hell.'

'Come on...' Milne sighed. 'It's lovely seeing you three together. But... I guess I owe you all an apology.'

Cath raised her eyebrows. 'And then some. You didn't tell me about them. Or them about me. Why?'

'I... I've made a lot of bad choices in my life.'

Jen laughed. 'So we're bad choices?'

'No. That's not what I meant.' Milne pinched his nose. 'I've got three great kids. You two... What happened, though... It's nothing to do with me.'

'Damn right it's not.' Jen stood up and walked over to stand next to her brother. 'Reason we're who we are is because of Mum, in spite of you.'

'Look.' Milne raised his hands. 'I've not handled any of this at all well.'

A look passed between Jen and Cath. Maybe a softening. Realising they were on the same side of this, maybe.

'Still.' Milne smirked. 'It's amazing seeing you together. Three kids, though. That's good going for a poofter like me.'

It hit Marshall like sledgehammer 'What?'

Milne locked eyes with his son. 'I'm gay, Robert. A homosexual. A poofter, as people used to call me.'

Marshall listened to the words. Each syllable was a bullet to his gut. The ghosts of his childhood he had buried beneath years of work were being exhumed right in front of him.

The office felt too small, too stuffy. He ran a hand through his day-old stubble. His heart thundered in his chest.

Marshall leaned back against the wall, aching to rewind time and return to the comforting embrace of ignorance.

But you can't un-ring a bell.

The hardened detective was back to being just a boy who'd lost his father all over again.

Judging by her scowl, it was news to Cath too. 'You're *gay*?'

'That's not a very woke attitude, Catherine.'

'No, but... Gay? Seriously?'

'Aye. It hasn't been a crime in a good while, love.'

'No, but...'

Jen paced forward, fists clenched. Body language Marshall had read a hundred times before. 'If you're gay, how could you have kids with Mum and with... with her mother?'

'Jennifer.' Milne raised his hands, as if to parry a blow. 'Janice was on board.'

'Mum *knew*?'

'Aye, she was going to be looked after well, but she—'

'What? Mum was a *surrogate*?'

'That sounds so crass.'

'But you paid her to have kids?'

'Jennifer, that's not—'

'Sounds a hell of a lot like it.'

'We compromised. We pretended to be husband and wife. I pretended to be your dad and "away on business" a lot when you were little, but as you got older, your mother knew it wasn't going to work and forced me to leave.'

Marshall's head felt like it had already exploded. Ton weights dragged his shoulders down. He locked eyes with Milne. His face might be full of cheeky mischief, but his eyes were like black holes. Empty and cold. 'What were you going to do with a child?'

Milne glowered at him. 'Eh?'

'You were going to pay Mum to be a surrogate for us. If it'd just been one egg fertilised, were you going to raise me or Jen on your own?'

Milne sighed. 'No.'

Marshall felt a sting in his eyes, a sudden wetness, but he pushed it back. This wasn't the time for tears. Not yet. He'd weathered worse storms than this. This was... It just ran deep. That's all it was.

He anchored himself in the reality – his office, in a police station. 'You're a liar.'

'I'm not, this is—'

'This story about you being gay is just a convenient trump card to get out of thirty years of parenting. A nice little explanation, all wrapped up in a bow. A convenient story to avoid answering difficult questions. Or face your shitty life decisions. You left us because you didn't want to live with us.'

'It's not that simple, Rob...' Milne shook his head. 'Is it the gay thing that's bothering you?'

'Of course not!'

'When I was young, Rob, it was much less acceptable than nowadays.'

'I get it. When we were kids, sure there was homophobia everywhere, but there were gay kids in my school. I understand that whole thing.' Marshall gritted his teeth, swallowing down bile. 'It's the lying that's the problem. Thirty years is a long time to lie, even if it is by omission.'

Milne couldn't look at any of them. 'Okay, Rob. I get that. I don't deserve anything.'

'But we do. All three of us deserve the truth. No lying, no fucking about. The absolute truth. Now.'

Milne pushed between them then walked into the corner and turned around. He took a deep breath, then shifted his gaze between his three children. His jaw pulsed. His fists clenched. 'I was in a relationship with a man. John. We were in love. But... John died. I was twenty-five. He was thirty-two. This was years before civil partnerships let alone gay marriage, but I took his surname. John Milne. No more Bob Marshall. Some people took us as brothers, but John always corrected them. He accepted me. The first person in my life to do that.'

Marshall did the sums in his head. 'He died when Mum was pregnant with us, right?'

'Exactly. We wanted a kid. I was going to have one with John's sister, but... She pulled out of it.'

Jen slumped back in her chair. 'So, you *were* using Mum as a surrogate for you and your boyfriend? Wasn't that illegal?'

'Still is. But... It depends how the payments and contract were agreed. You have to prove there's a crime underlying it. But, Jennifer, when you both came along, your mother couldn't give you up, so she backed away from the whole deal. If it was in, say, California and now, I could've sued. But Melrose in the eighties? Forget it. When John died... Your mother knew the deal. Trouble was, she was young. Even younger than me. The reality hit her hard. Being pregnant, she realised how desperately she wanted kids. Even with a gay man. I was never going to be a romantic relationship for her. So I moved in with her to be with you. You were the last connection I had with John.'

'He's our father?'

'No. It was my sperm used to fertilise your mother's eggs.'

'Right.' Marshall swallowed down bitter revulsion at the cold, mechanical language he used.

Jen nodded along with some unvoiced thoughts. 'Tried to make it work, but it didn't.'

'Exactly. And when it was clear it wasn't working, I stepped away. I didn't want to raise you in a household where your parents are arguing all the time.'

'That whole thing set Mum up to be gaslit by Graham Thorburn. And all that happened.'

Cath frowned. 'Who the hell is he?'

'Long story.' Milne blew air up his face. 'Yet another thing I've got to feel guilty about.'

Jen looked over at Cath. 'How does her mother fit into this?'

'Mary was John's sister.'

'You said you were going to have a child with her?'

'Aye, initially. She pulled out of it. Knew she couldn't give a kid over, even to her brother. But over time, she relented. We became close. We both missed John and... We had Cath. I stayed in her life as much as I could, but...'

Jen was on her feet now. 'Like Rob said, it's the lying that hurts most of all. Getting Mum to lie as well. And Grumpy. It's a lot.'

'That's... That's not what happened.'

'Mum didn't know you were gay?'

'Of course she did.' Milne shook his head. 'Your grandfather too. Only thing he said when I came out to him was "studs up", whatever that means.' He swallowed something down. 'I've told you all the truth. It hurt me as much as it hurt you all. Being shunned and sent away because of who I am. Not seeing my kids. It hurt. So I threw myself into my work, going undercover to take down the people-trafficking ring that killed John.'

'He was a cop?'

'My DI, as it happened. And I did it. Took those pricks down. And that's when I finally felt able to breathe again. That's when Cath happened.' A smile sparkled on his lips. 'My wee miracle.'

They all sat there with the truth clinging to them like anthrax powder. The air conditioning hummed and puffed out a blast of something sweet.

Milne broke the silence first. 'If you must know, Cath is a source.'

'You mean a witness?'

'No. A source. Someone leaking to drug gangs really gets my goat up, so I picked up that case when I started. Real reason I was down here to speak to your mother and Grumpy was to see what's what. Walk into Hislop's shop and eyeball him. He wasn't in, but she was. What are the chances of that? I warned her off, but she wouldn't leave. I could see she'd taken a bit of her old man's stubbornness. So I got her to start talking to me. And we're getting somewhere, Rob. And on your case too.'

Marshall knew when he was being fed shite. Still, he smiled. 'Go on?'

'Reason we were meeting was to catch up. She hadn't been in touch for a fortnight. She said Pringle was in the shop last week.'

Marshall didn't want to rise to it. 'Go on.'

'Pringle was speaking to Hislop. She was through the back, so she doesn't know what they talked about, but he left in a hurry. She came out when the door slammed. Weird thing is, a young girl was in the car...'

'Pringle's daughter?'

'She doesn't know, but I'd say it's likely.'

'Thing she did hear, though, was Hislop making a comment about the pretty young thing in his car. Something like, "I bet she's tasty, eh?" Obviously trying to goad Pringle. I mean, the stupid twat drove there to speak to Hislop with his kid in the car, of course he's going to get something like that back. What did he expect?'

Marshall could take that down a whole other avenue, but he let that burn away in the background. 'What did Pringle say to that?'

'She's not sure, but Hislop said, "I don't chew my cabbage twice".'

'Cabbage?' Marshall felt a surge of light-headedness. 'He said that?'

'Yep. Had to google it myself.' Milne held up his phone. 'It's an old Roman saying, dating from an earlier Greek one, apparently. About how you don't repeat yourself.'

Marshall had one answer – the cabbages comment in the interview with Graham Thorburn, which felt like months ago. 'What was he repeating himself about?'

'That's what I want to know too, Rob. Cath doesn't know. Based on stuff in our interview with him, I suspect it could be something to do with credible threats made against Pringle way back when. As in, he won't let Pringle get off so lightly this time.'

Made sense to Marshall.

'Then Hislop said, "What do you call an angry BMW owner? A sour kraut..." Another cabbage joke.'

'Pringle kept going on about cabbages when he had his breakdown.'

'I know. Nice to have some sort of explanation for it.' Milne flared his nostrils and gestured towards his youngest. 'After he left, Hislop called someone, but Cath didn't hear it.'

'You believe her?'

'No reason not to, Rob. But I'm more than a bit concerned.'

'Why?'

'Could be he was calling Elliot.'

'It'll be on the phone records.'

'Come on. She'll have a burner. They both will.'

'Which you obviously don't have, otherwise you'd know this already.'

'No, but we'll be able to get a number from any number of means and we'll track it. It'll give us a locus of where the mobile's been, means we can see if it's been on in Elliot's house or nearby.'

'But that's assuming it's been on.'

'True. Meanwhile, we could do with speaking to the girl.'

'Pringle's daughter?'

'Aye.'

'She's *eight*. He's not going to have told her anything.'

'Still, worth a chat. Mother might know something. Might not make sense to her, but coupled with what we know...?'

'Got it.' Marshall nodded. 'I can call her mother and set that up.'

'Do it.'

Marshall got out his phone and hit dial.

Answered straight away. 'Rob?'

'Hi, Belu.' Marshall got up and walked away, but turned back to keep an eye on them in case they buggered off again. 'Need to have a word, if that's okay?'

'Shoot.'

'It's one of those in-person deals? Also need to speak to Sarah.'

'Right.' She snorted. 'We're at the hospital.'

CHAPTER FIFTY-NINE

PRINGLE

P ringle lay in his bed. The hospital room walls didn't so much close in on him as shimmer and shift around. He hated this. The flickering fluorescent lights buzzed overhead, their incessant hum tangling with his thoughts. He tried to grasp the fleeting fragments of reality, desperately clinging to moments of clarity that slipped through his fingers like grains of sand.

His gaze wandered aimlessly around the room and he thought he caught a glimpse of Belu standing by the window. His heart skipped a beat. Her cascading hair and warm smile. She seemed to beckon him. But as quickly as she appeared, she dissolved into the haze of his mind, leaving Pringle grasping at a wisp of a memory.

'Belu? Is that you?'

She raced over to the door, crying.

He thought she did, anyway.

Confusion gripped his mind and the musty air like a veil. Fragments of memory flitted through his brain. Faces and names, taunting him. He struggled to cling on to his identity. Nothing seemed solid or real.

A nurse appeared, her face etched with empathy as she approached Pringle's bed. She wore a name tag that read 'Erykah'. 'Mr Pringle, how are you feeling?' Her soft voice was a gentle reassurance amidst the disarray. Something to anchor himself to.

His thoughts churned, trying to piece together the fragmented puzzle. 'Sarah? Where's Sarah?'

Erykah's expression softened, her eyes filling with understanding. 'I'm sorry, Mr Pringle, but your daughter had to leave with your wife.'

Pringle's eyes welled with tears, his heart aching in their absence. He felt the pang of loss and had to cling to the notion that Belu had really been in the room. He reached over to the table and grabbed his wallet, clutching it tight. He didn't want them to steal it while he was under. And there were thieves *everywhere*.

A porter wheeled a chair in. A tall, slim man with a shaved head and a hard face. He looked familiar. 'Hi, doll. Name's Oscar.' The name might've been exotic, but his accent was pure Leith. 'Going to take this lad to theatre, okay?'

Pringle looked up at him with a mix of vulnerability and resignation. And recognition. 'I know you. Don't I?'

'Get that a lot.' Oscar laughed. 'I look like Robbie Williams.' He ran a hand through his silvery hair. 'Just twenty years older.'

'I didn't know he was going to surgery?'

He smiled at Erykah. 'You new here, darling?'

'Just transferred down from Western General, aye.'

'Sure you'll get the hang of the place soon enough.' Oscar locked the chair and helped Pringle down from the bed. 'Mind yourself, aye?'

Pringle slumped into the chair. His head ached. Everything ached. What had happened to him? 'Where are we going?'

Oscar smiled, his eyes reflecting compassion. 'Don't you worry, Mr Pringle. We're just going to the operating theatre. They'll take good care of you there.'

Pringle's focus wandered once again, his eyes scanning the room, seeking a familiar face, a lifeline to the past. The room remained silent, offering only the scent of antiseptic. He looked back at the man. 'Tell me something. Do you believe in love?'

'Love?' Oscar chuckled. 'Aye, I believe in love. Why are you asking?'

'Do you believe love can transcend time and distance?'

Oscar's eyes softened, his gaze shooting between Pringle and Erykah. 'I do, Mr Pringle. I believe love has a way of connecting us, even when we're lost. Actually, especially when we're lost.'

Pringle found solace in the porter's words, a flicker of hope in the midst of his confusion. 'What's your name?'

'Oscar, sir. Told you that already.' He gently guided Pringle's wheelchair out of the room, still talking to him, but the words became tangled and muddled. Pringle clung to fragments, desperately trying to grasp the meaning hidden within. But it was all a mess.

Everything was a mess.

Fucking cabbages.

Fucking cabbages everywhere.

They travelled down the corridor, Pringle's heart heavy with uncertainty, his mind a turbulent sea. He surrendered to the gentle rhythm of the wheels beneath him.

He had a renewed faith in the belief that love could endure, even in the face of the unyielding fog engulfing him.

It meant he'd see Belu again.

They turned a corner and the light was blinding. 'Are we going to see the angels, Robbie?'

'Name's not Robbie. It's Oscar.'

'Right. Oscar.' It took Pringle a few seconds to register where they were. There was the smoking shelter. They were outside. 'This isn't the way to the theatre.'

Oscar stopped by a van. 'Here we go.'

'Where are we going?'

'Up to Edinburgh. The hospital there will treat you better than this one.'

'Oh.' Pringle looked up and finally recognised him. 'I know you.'

'I told you, pal, I look like Rob—'

'Chunk. It's Chunk, isn't it? Kyle Talbot. We lost you a few months ago. You're a hired killer.'

'Right.' He leaned in close enough to taste his aftershave. 'Sarah Makena Pringle. 07700 900537.'

Each digit sparked synapses in Pringle's brain. 'How do you know her phone number?'

'I know a lot about her, Jim. Date of birth. Friends' addresses. Play nice and the girl lives. You of all people should know what I'm capable of.'

'You can't—'

A strong finger prodding his chest shut him up. 'Remember – her love for you can transcend time and distance.'

Pringle tried to stay calm. He felt something in his hands. He looked down. He was clutching his wallet. He dropped it on the ground. 'I'll go peacefully. But please, make sure nothing happens to her.'

'I'm not a monster, but I can be.' Chunk wheeled him into the back of the van. 'You've got a mutual friend to thank for the taxi service.'

'Who?'

'Someone who believes you ran him over, Jim.'

'I didn't!'

'Maybe you didn't, but what matters at the moment is he believes you did. And you've been a bit uppity lately, haven't you? You never climbed into bed with our friend, but there's always been a bit of loose give and take. I gather there was even a case of wine and a photo, right?'

The memory of the discovery cut through the fog. That sharp shock. Knowing that Hislop knew everything about his supposedly secret life.

And another realisation hit him too – the reason he was getting told this stuff was because he wasn't getting out of this scrape.

He was going to die.

CHAPTER SIXTY

MARSHALL

Marshall's footsteps echoed along the hospital corridor.

The lights cast an eerie glow on Bob Milne, walking alongside. He adjusted his tie as they walked, his eyes narrowing in thought. 'What could Hislop have wanted with Pringle's daughter?'

Marshall's jaw tightened, his mind racing with possibilities. The shadowy world of corruption and deceit they had stumbled upon threatened to devour them whole. 'We've both been digging through Hislop's background and we know the man's capable of anything.'

'Aye.' That was all either of them had.

As they rounded the corner, the faint sounds of commotion reached their ears.

Marshall's heart skipped a beat as he caught sight of Belu Owusu, Pringle's estranged wife, standing in the hallway. Her face bore the traces of a sleepless night, her eyes red-rimmed and weary. Sarah clung to her mother, her young face etched with worry.

Marshall approached Owusu with cautious determination. 'Hi, Belu. You okay?'

Her focus darted between Marshall and Milne, confusion clouding her expression. 'Jim was here just a moment ago. I turned around for a second and he was gone.'

Marshall's grip tightened around the edges of his notebook, frustration simmering. The puzzle pieces were slipping further out of reach. 'Did he mention anything to you? Anything about meeting someone or going somewhere?'

Belu shook her head. 'No, nothing. But he's been confused lately.'

Marshall's mind raced, his thoughts threaded with suspicion. Hislop's involvement, the connection to Sarah and now Pringle's disappearance – a tangled web. 'So, what, he just left?'

'No. I... I had to get Sarah some food. I was just gone a few minutes.'

A nurse appeared, yawning into her fist, blinking something away. Erykah, according to her name badge. Her gaze shot between them. 'What's up?'

Marshall flashed his warrant card. 'We're looking for Jim Pringle.'

'Oh. Right. He was taken to theatre for surgery.'

Owusu was in the doorway, scowling back at her. 'He's left an empty meal tray here. Who gives a patient a big meal before surgery?'

Erykah's eyes bulged. 'Shit.' She reached over for a phone and hit dial, trying to smile away her confusion, then turned her back as she spoke.

Marshall focused on Owusu. 'How was he?'

'Delirious. Confused. Disorientated. Worse than ever. I tried to talk to him, but he couldn't follow what I was saying. It was like he was on another planet and... I don't know, Rob. There's something seriously wrong with him.'

'They're checking it out, right?'

'Yeah, but... They've deferred that until they fixed his shoulder. A compound fracture to his clavicle and they need to operate. A clean break's one thing, but a fracture? And it's comminuted too.' She raised a hand. 'I mean fragmented.'

'Right, thank. And your medical knowledge means you worry more than most.'

'Right. Bits of it poking out of the skin, the rest of it in pieces that'll need pinned together.' She gripped her daughter's hand. 'The, uh, reason we're here is, uh, we're, uh, leaving.'

'Now? But Jim's gone missing.'

'I know, but... We were saying our goodbyes... I'm going back to South Africa.'

'Oh.'

'We've got flights booked. I need to protect my daughter.' She looked up at Marshall with tear-filled eyes. 'I hope Jim's okay. I do. He's a good man, but this is precisely the reason we can't remain here.'

Marshall didn't know what to say to that.

Erykah turned back around and untangled her hair. 'I called through to theatre. His operation was tomorrow.'

Milne frowned. 'But they sent for him?'

'No, they didn't.' She gave a halting breath. 'A porter showed up with the paperwork. But they never showed up at theatre. I... I didn't read the transfer orders. And surgery doesn't have a porter named Oscar.'

CHAPTER SIXTY-ONE
STRUAN

Struan crouched in the shadows, the darkness cloaking him like a shroud, his eyes fixed on the house. The poshest end of Gattonside, one of the poshest places in the Borders. A sixties bungalow all blinged up with Farrow & Ball painted wooden boards, crisp pebbles and box trees, surrounded by a huge plot of land. An Audi sports car in the drive.

Aye, Callum Hume had done well for himself.

He was in the house, too. Lights on. Music throbbing.

Struan's own car was down the hill, just on the main road. Keys in the ignition – ready to drive off, if need be.

The day was getting colder and Struan started to shiver.

Started to doubt whether this was the right thing to do. Whether his hunch was going to pay off.

Maybe Elliot had been the source. Maybe that document wasn't going to be leaked.

The door opened and Callum Hume strode out, mobile to his ear. 'Aye, five minutes. Cheers.'

Bingo.

The gamble was paying off.

Hume slipped into his car and the engine thrummed.

Struan hammered it down to the main road and got behind the wheel of his car by the time Hume passed. He gave him a count of ten, then pulled off, pursuing Hume from a distance along the long street through Gattonside, past the old school and out into the open countryside. At the end, instead of left towards Melrose, Hume headed right for the north strip through Galashiels, flooring it and putting distance between them.

Struan kept to the speed limit, confident he'd catch him before the first junction. He visualised the town, a long wedge stuck between two hills, separated by a river.

Sure enough, Hume slowed through the 30 sign then past the turning for the vet and the Volvo garage opposite the Shell station.

Not the quickest way in, but there were no cameras this way.

Instead of heading for the centre of Galashiels, Callum took the first left at the 20 sign, heading towards the rugby and football stadium.

Struan didn't want to blow his cover, but he didn't want to lose Hume in the maze of winding roads, old mill buildings and hidden corners down by the Gala Water.

Hume veered into the car park at Boleside Road, parking under the Melrose bypass road. Only car there.

Good.

Struan maintained his distance, his eyes trained on the vehicle, then passed the entrance and did a tight U-turn, leaving Hume momentarily alone. He parked his car further down the road, then slunk down and turned off the lights. Engine still running, he waited and watched the car, hidden by the trees. Silent, dark. He had to squint to confirm Hume was still inside.

Then a Volvo pulled past him, blasting out Ocean Colour Scene's tuneless skank, and parked a few spaces away from Hume.

Struan counted twenty before either of them did anything.

The driver exited his vehicle and raced over to the other car.

Bingo.

Letterbox, meet postman.

He'd guessed correctly that, with Hislop incapacitated, the news would come to Hume, but the target was the delivery boy, not the package and not the recipient.

Struan put the car into gear and raced into the car park, slaloming past the Volvo and blocking Hume from reversing.

Struan got out, his heart pounding in his chest, and snapped out his baton.

Hume got out of his car with a thunderous fury, then realisation filled his face. 'You? You were in the rugby club?' He darted up the Boleside road, a narrow path with beech trees on either side.

Few places to go up here, just a housing estate and, eventually, a path across the A7.

Not his main target, though.

Struan approached the car and tore open the passenger door, keeping a tight grip on his baton. 'DS Struan Liddell. Arresting you for—'

CHAPTER SIXTY-TWO
MARSHALL

Marshall stayed in the corridor, down in the bowels of the hospital, clutching his phone to his ear. 'Thanks, Jolene.' He hung up and stepped back into the security room.

A faint hum of electronic equipment greeted him. The room itself was dimly lit, the rows of monitors casting an eerie glow upon the faces of the security guard and Bob Milne. The screens flickered and shifted, revealing corridors bathed in light, the bustling emergency area and quiet patient rooms. The images were monochromatic, drenched in shades of grey.

The walls were adorned with maps of the hospital's intricate layout, which still baffled Marshall, red markers highlighting the strategic placement of CCTV cameras, those unblinking eyes capturing every corner of the building.

A long desk stood in the centre, strewn with a maze of wires and gadgets. The air was heavy with the reek of stewed coffee. The security guard sat hunched over his workstation. Worn-out uniform, worn-out eyes scanning the monitors, the fingers dancing across the keyboard the only sign of movement in the man.

Milne looked over. 'Anything?'

Marshall shook his head. 'Can't get hold of Struan Liddell. Presumably he's still in with Elliot, honing their strategy. Jolene's team are searching for Pringle's friends and family. Not that there are many.' He let out a deep breath. 'How are you getting on?'

Milne waved at the screen. 'Show him, Keith.'

Without the guard moving, the biggest screen flashed over to a view of the hospital's front entrance, where a man was berating a taxi driver.

Then a porter wheeled someone outside.

'Pause.' Marshall squinted at the frozen image. Looked like Pringle. 'Shite. That's him leaving.'

The porter wheeled Pringle over to a van, chatted for a few seconds, then pushed him inside. He slammed the side door, then got behind the wheel and drove off.

'Freeze it again.' Marshall got out his mobile and called Ash Paton.

'What's up, sir?'

'Need you to run a trace on some plates for me?'

'Fire away.'

'BA57 ARD.'

Ash giggled.

'What's up?'

'That spells "bastard".'

Marshall frowned and checked it again. 'Bloody hell.'

'I'm googling it now, sir. There's a list of banned words on the DVLA site. Stuff like PI55 OFF. BU11 SHT. Bastard is on there.'

'So it's a fake plate. Great.'

'Aye, but just because the DVLA haven't licensed it, doesn't stop someone from printing up a plate. And even a fake plate can still be tracked if it's on a vehicle. I'll call you back.' Click and she was gone.

Marshall turned around.

Milne was leaning forward to mess about with the video, zooming in on the figure as he wheeled Pringle away from the hospital. 'Right. Let's do this the other way.' He adjusted the jog dial and pulled it back until the 'bastard' van disappeared, then rolled the footage forward until the van slid into view again.

The passing pedestrians slowed to normal speed as the driver emerged, dressed in the mint-green polo shirt and navy trousers of an NHS porter.

Milne paused it and circled his face. 'I recognise him, but...'

Marshall clocked him immediately. 'That's Kyle Talbot AKA Chunk AKA a million other names.'

'Go on?'

'We think he's a hitman. He killed a few people back in January. We've been searching for him ever since, but he's gone to the wind. Rumour was he'd retired. Even his dark web credentials had been closed. You know, on We Buy Any Hit dot com.'

'Right, right.' Milne smirked. 'So it looks like he's back and has taken Pringle.'

Marshall had that sour taste again. 'Hislop's got to be behind this.'

'What makes you think that?'

Marshall didn't really have anything.

'Rob, think it all through. If this lad's an assassin, then he'll know one thing above all else. The more you kill, the greater the risk you get caught eventually. And what happens fairly often is these guys roll on their paymasters in exchange for their liberty. Chunk must know that eventually a better assassin will come after him. So he retired, like you say. But he came back to go after Pringle, the man leading the last big hunt for him. Right?'

'Correct. We had him in an interview, charged him with some minor assaults and let him go, assuming we'd get a fine or suspended sentence for those. Fake address and alibi. But you're saying that if we'd kept him, maybe he'd have folded?'

'Not saying anything like that. But I don't buy that Hislop's paid him to come back and kill Pringle. If we caught him, then he'd start spilling. If he'd retired... When these guys retire, believe me, that's them *gone* – they don't come back. Not for all the tea in China, India, Sri Lanka or Kenya.'

'Hislop's still in the hospital. We can get him to talk.'

'He's just been through complex surgery, Rob. It's touch and go at the moment, plus he'll be whacked up on painkillers. Besides, there's no way he's ordered anyone to do anything in the last ten hours.'

'Wish I had your confidence.'

'Sure.'

'What about before? Last night, say? Or a standing order with one of his mates from the rugby club?'

Milne scowled. 'One of what—'

Marshall's phone blasted out.

DC Ash Paton calling...

'Sorry.' He put it to his ear. 'Marshall.'

'Sir. I've got it.'

'The van?'

'Aye, the bastard van. It was dumped on the outskirts of Greenlaw.'

'That was quick.'

'Uniform secured it. Some old biddy complained about it sitting outside her drive.'

'How long had it been there?'

'Twenty minutes. But she's a nuisance, apparently. Reported delivery drivers and posties.'

'One of them, eh?' Marshall sighed. 'Can you get them to confirm with her if she saw any other vehicles there?'

'You think someone's transferred cars?'

'Precisely.'

'Will do.'

'Could you get Kirsten to run forensics, please? Need to confirm Kyle Talbot had the van.'

'On it. It's nice to not have an order rammed down your throat.'

'Excuse me?'

But she'd disappeared.

Marshall knew he'd have to dig into that offhand comment – those little pockets of tension he'd spotted between Struan and his team...

Aye, there was something there.

He snapped his attention to Milne. 'Okay, so we've got no real leads other than Talbot driving to Greenlaw and dumping the van. Either he's still nearby, or he's swapped vehicles and driven elsewhere.'

Milne nodded along with it. 'And if we devote our attentions to around Greenlaw, he could've headed west to Peebles. Or anywhere. North to Edinburgh. South to Newcastle. Anywhere.'

'Exactly. All sorts of possibilities. This guy's a pro, so deflection is the name of the game.'

'Doesn't look good, Rob.' Milne punched the controls. The security guard didn't even look over. 'Ah, fuck it. This is hopeless. We'll never find him.'

'Are you giving up?'

Milne shrugged. 'Aye. I'm heading back to base to see what else we can do, but I don't think we'll get anywhere with this.' He grabbed his coat and left the room.

Marshall put his business card on the table. 'I'll need this all sent over to this email address. Give me a call if you need anything.'

'Sure thing.' Still no movement. It was like the guy had fossilised.

Marshall charged out into the corridor after his father, heading away from the security den and the pathology department towards the stairwell. 'Bob!'

Milne stopped and turned in the dimly lit corridor. 'What?'

'You're just leaving?'

'Of course. This isn't getting us anywhere.'

'You're still a quitter, then.'

'Right.' Milne ran a tongue around his lips. 'So we're doing this now, are we?'

'I can't help but feel like you've been bullshitting us.' Marshall felt his eyes burn, a mix of anger and hurt, the pain of abandonment. 'You left us. You walked away without a second thought.'

Milne's gaze faltered. 'I know I made mistakes, Rob. I was lost, consumed by my own demons. But I never stopped loving you or your sister. And if you think I left without a second thought? I've never stopped having those thoughts. Still have them every day. I'm in the billions.'

Marshall clenched his fists at his sides. 'Love doesn't quit. It doesn't abandon its family when things get tough. You left and we had to pick up the pieces.'

Milne's weathered face softened. 'I did what I thought was best. For you, for Jennifer, for your mother. I thought leaving would spare you all the pain of my mistakes. I didn't realise how deeply it would scar you. I...'

'You don't get it, do you? You don't get how your absence shaped me and Jen. How it hardened us. We had to learn to survive without you. I had to become a man when I was still just a child.'

His words reverberated, then silence enveloped the corridor.

The ache of loss hung in the air.

'I know I can't change the past, Rob, but I can be here now.' Milne reached out, his hand hovering in the space between them. 'I want to make amends, to be a part of your life again. Please, give me that chance.'

Something hit Marshall out of the blue. The hardened edges of his heart chipped away by his father's vulnerability. In that moment, he saw a glimpse of the man he once idolised. 'You can't rebuild what's been shattered. I don't know if I can ever forgive you.'

'I guess I was right to quit, eh?' Milne turned and walked off towards the lifts. His phone rang as he walked.

Marshall stayed, head bowed, heart thumping. He wanted to go after him and plead with him. But nothing would change the past. He was stuck with who he was, as much as his father was stuck with the life that had made him leaving not just a possibility but an inevitability.

Meanwhile, this case was going to shite.

CHAPTER SIXTY-THREE
STRUAN

Struan leaned across the sink in the station toilets and clicked his jaw. It ached, hard. Felt like someone had filled his nose with rocks. He looked down at his grey suit, smeared with mud, and his white shirt now dotted with blood. He scratched at his top lip, finding yet another clump of dried blood.

The door opened.

He spotted them in the mirror. Milne and Gashkori.

Gashkori winced at him. 'You look like shite, Sergeant.'

Struan dabbed at his nose again. 'What happens sometimes when you apprehend someone, boss.'

'Aye. Sure. Of course you did.'

'I'm serious.'

Gashkori stood next to him, making eye contact with him through the mirror. 'Got something to talk to you about.'

'What's that, boss?'

'You know.'

They were playing mind games, thinking their whole act

was going to make him plead, but this wasn't Struan's first rodeo. *Won't be the last, either.* 'Not sure what I've done.'

Gashkori clamped a hand on Struan's shoulder. 'Let's start with you explaining why you were at the Boleside road?'

'I was investigating a lead in this case.'

'A lead. Right.' Gashkori snorted, then thumbed at Milne, leaning against the stall door. 'Sergeant, you're aware how Bob here and his team have been looking into these leaks, right?'

'Aware of it, aye. It's what—'

'We've got ourselves a lead on the leaker.' Gashkori let the words sit there for a bit.

'Peachy.'

'It's you, isn't it?'

'I only started here yesterday. If it was me, how can I have been leaking all along?'

'Didn't say you were. An organisation like Hislop's will have multiple bent cops on the payroll. You're just the latest in a long line.'

'Sounds a bit fanciful, Ryan.'

'You're not denying it.'

'I'm not dignifying this bullshit with a response. It's beneath me. Hell, it's beneath both of you.'

Gashkori reached into his jacket pocket and unfolded a sheet of paper. 'You might not have been behind the previous leaks, but you were in the process of leaking this, weren't you?'

Struan took the page and looked at it. He'd stepped in a big steaming pile of crap. 'Suspected as much. An access log for a watermarked report. Silent alarms went off as soon as I accessed that file. Right?'

'Sergeant. We traced your mobile to the car park at Boleside. Now, you might say you were going for a stroll along the bonny banks of the Tweed to look at Abbotsford across the river just as the sun sets on another glorious day... But you don't strike me as much of a fan of Sir Walter Scott.'

Struan knew when to shut up.

'I'm guessing you were meeting someone to share the news of Gary Hislop's impending arrest and it went south?'

'No.'

'No?'

'I was investigating a lead, like I said. A very similar one to what you're following up.'

'After you'd just accessed this report, son.' Milne snatched the page off him and tapped it. 'Seems a bit of a coincidence to me.'

'I went into the system and found a strategy document on Gary Hislop's arrest. Signed by Ryan here, counter-signed by whatshername. His boss.'

Milne folded his arms. 'You know your predecessor in your role works for me now.'

'Shunty? Smashed a car off a wall, right?'

'A bridge, actually. But he's a good cop. Showing a lot of strategic insight. Shunty put a silent hit on the system, linked to a police report indicating that a takedown would happen as soon as Hislop is discharged from hospital.' Milne tapped the page again. 'A false report.'

'False?'

'False. We'll arrest Hislop at some point, but certainly won't publicise the fact to a leaky investigation. But young Shunty sat back and waited for someone to access the report... Just like you did, Sergeant. DS Struan Liddell.'

'I accessed it, aye. Had to get Ash Paton to help me.'

'You admit it?'

'I do.' Struan folded his arms. 'See, the thing you're missing is you've all assumed DI Elliot's the leaker. I wanted to test the theory that she wasn't.'

'You're taking your role as Federation rep a bit too far there, son.'

'It's called diligence. Ask yourself this. Why would she go on the record about Hislop if she was leaking? Double bluffs have a tendency to explode in the face of the bluffer. And why did she have to access the files? She was working the case – she knew every single detail, so she could just tell him.'

'This isn't a debating class, son. You're in the shite here.'

'Don't you want me to tell you my story?'

'If it's a confession, I'm all ears.'

'It's not a confession.'

Milne motioned for him to continue. 'Go on, then.'

'My thinking was, if there's another officer involved, then they'd meet someone in Hislop's world to pass this over. Urgently, as Hislop's in this place right now. Who knows when he'll be discharged.'

Milne chewed it over slowly. 'And that someone was?'

'Callum Hume. Stands to reason. Your intel on him, Ryan, is he's number two in Hislop's organisation. I spoke to him at a bar in Melrose last night.'

Gashkori laughed. 'You *what?*'

'I've made DI Elliot aware of this, sir. It's documented in the case file. Might not be in the right place as that filing system is baffling.'

Gashkori shook his head, sighing. 'Go on.'

'When I saw that report, I figured out your leaker would see it too and they'd act. Assuming it wasn't Elliot, of course. Figured Hume would be the one our leaker ran to. So I staked out his home. Sure enough, he left. I followed him to that car park. He was going to meet someone there.'

They exchanged a look. The kind that made Struan sure he'd turned the tables on them.

'You thought it was me, right? You set a trap and I triggered it. Question you need to ask yourselves is this – if it wasn't me, who was? Who else triggered it?' He let the silence suffocate them. 'Good news is your bent cop turned up. Got out and walked over to Hume's car. But Hume made me and ran off. I followed his mate – apprehending him is the reason for my current state, boss. He didn't go down without a fight.'

'Who is it?'

'He's in room two just now.'

CHAPTER SIXTY-FOUR
ELLIOT

So this was how the police tricks felt?

Elliot sat in the interview room, bored shitless. The same treatment she'd given to hundreds of interviewees over the twenty years she'd been a cop. Maybe it was even thousands. Letting them stew. It usually worked too, but now she felt every second of the four hours she'd been waiting.

Of course, she could leave at any moment, force them to charge her or let her go back to her duties.

Or her family. She could do with a cuddle from all three kids.

But the best thing to do was to sit here and play ball.

It only really hurt because it was so boring.

And because those clowns didn't believe her. How could they think she'd leak anything to Hislop? Who the hell did they think she was?

The door opened and Shunty entered, followed by Milne.

'Gentlemen.' Elliot folded her arms and smiled at them. 'Why are you here? Going to charge me without my Federation rep being present?'

Milne stayed by the door. 'You're free to get back on duty.'

She refolded her arms. 'What's the catch?'

Shunty stepped forward. 'We need to know everything you know about the leaks.'

'Cool.' She got up and walked towards the door. 'You already know the same fuck all I do. You pair of dickheads.'

Milne blocked her exit. 'That isn't enough.'

'I've told them it's not me who's been leaking!'

'We know that. But do you know who's been doing it?'

'Why would I?'

'Two people accessed a fake report on the server. One of them was Struan Liddell.'

'He's done this?'

'Nope. But the curious thing is that you accessed the report.'

'I didn't!'

'I know. You were sitting in here.'

'What are you talking about?'

'Whoever's been leaking to Hislop accessed the report using your credentials. Then reported the matter to someone in his orbit.' Milne fixed her with a tight stare. 'It was your husband.'

'What?' Elliot collapsed back against the desk, the hard edge grinding against her legs. The weight of the revelation crashed down upon her as the words echoed around the room.

Davie...

What?

Betrayal and disbelief churned within her.

How had she failed to see?

How had she missed the signs?

Questions swirled, but answers eluded her, leaving only a void of confusion and pain.

The erosion of trust.

The crumbling of the foundation on which her life had been built.

People had died because of him.

She looked at Milne, then at Shunty. Hard to meet two more different officers, but they both seemed concerned for her. 'Explain.' Spitting the word out was all she could manage.

Milne took charge, hands in his pockets. 'Davie isn't a cop. He's a civilian clerk, which allows him to fly under the radar. He hears everything but is never part of anything. His security role means he knows how to obfuscate things. Throw the scent away from us. I... No easy way to say this, but DS Liddell caught him red-handed. He was meeting Callum Hume to divulge a report Shunty here had fabricated.'

She felt like she was going to be sick. She had to hold on to it – she needed to keep her focus on the here and now. 'Do you believe Struan?'

'We've got evidence supporting it.'

'Jesus. Can I speak to Davie?'

Milne sighed. 'That's the problem, he's not saying anything.'

'Not like him.' Elliot smiled. 'Please.'

Milne raised his hands. 'Not my circus, not my clown.'

Shunty didn't know where to look. Poor sod was having to make a decision. Must feel like having his teeth pulled out with rusty pliers. 'On you go. But we will be with you at all times.'

'Fine.' Elliot was glad to be out of that bastard room. Not that next door was any better, but at least she was on the correct side of the table again.

Davie was on the wrong side, staring at the woodgrain like he was going to sand it down and paint it. A pathetic wretch. Shoulders slumped, his crisp white shirt now crumpled and soiled yellow around the armpits. Sweat dribbled down his nose like rain. He looked up at her then jerked back like he'd been attacked with a cattle prod. 'Andi... I didn't want you to see me like this.'

She stayed standing. 'And I didn't want my husband to be arrested for leaking sensitive information.'

'Andi, it's not like they're saying.'

'So why are you in here?'

'I...'

'Davie, they're saying you met with Callum Hume.'

'I...' He looked at her. He knew she wouldn't let him get away with anything but the full truth. 'Come on...'

'Davie. The truth now. All of it.'

He let out a deep breath. 'I was using other people's access around the station to get into files for Hislop. He called me up a few times and... I did it.'

'How long has this been going on?'

'Years.'

'Years? How many?'

'Three.'

'Three? Jesus Christ.' Another sucker punch to the gut. 'Why did you do it?'

'Cash.' Davie shrugged. 'It's a pretty prosaic reason, I know. There's no coke, hookers or rent boys.' He laughed. 'Are you allowed to call them that these days?'

'Fuck political correctness, Davie. You've been selling people's lives here!'

'I just want to look after our kids. That's not a crime, is it?'

'Of course it fucking is! It's pretty much the worst crime you can do!'

'Andi, I did it to protect you and the kids. I swear. It's been getting worse. Hislop took an interest in you over the last few months. Sent you those pictures. Where someone had clearly been following us. I hated him getting close to you. Threatening you. Jeopardising your career.'

'I was in control of that.'

'You *thought* you were. But he's got no upper limits, Andi. So I decided to take him out. Been planning it since you got that case of wine in January. Then I heard that Marshall and Pringle got the same.'

Shunty tilted his head to the side. 'Did they?'

Davie snorted. 'Maybe they didn't talk about it.'

'You drove the car into him?'

Davie blew air up his face. 'I needed a patsy and, since Pringle was coo-coo bananas and already circling the career drain, why not take advantage of that? Hislop hated him too.' He shook his head. 'He'd left his car in the car park a few times. Keys in the ignition. Did it again the night before. Just had to take the keys and leave it there. Then I drove over first thing. Bingo. Don't understand it – I hit him square on, so how is he still alive? He should be pushing up daisies. And who'd care?'

'He's got a son and a girlfriend.'

Davie shrugged. 'So?'

'And Pringle... If your plan had come off, he'd be inside. He's got a daughter.'

'Aye, aye. Kirsty... That's bollocks and you know it.'

'No. It's true. Her name is Sarah.'

Davie rested his head in his hands. 'Shite, shite, shite.'

'And you paid those numpties to lose it?'

'Aye. Only they didn't. Useless sods.'

Milne sat next to Elliot. 'You'll be inside for a long time. You know that, right?'

Davie nodded.

'Pringle's gone missing, Davie. Someone abducted him from hospital.'

Elliot collapsed into the chair and she tried to swallow

down another attempt by her body to purge itself. All that time with Hislop, she felt she'd been the one in control of the situation. But the reality was she'd literally been dicing with death. 'You hear anything about that, Davie?'

He shook his head. 'No. Not at all.'

'Right, I'll take that on faith seeing as how you're being so honest with us.' Elliot sat back. Everything squirmed. Felt like ants were crawling up her back. 'Do you know where they've taken him?'

'No idea.'

'Okay, but you know who took him.'

'I can take a guess. Chunk, right?'

Milne nodded. 'This was all about revenge on Pringle for running Hislop down, wasn't it?'

'Hislop talked about him a lot and I had to play along because otherwise I'd be dead.' Davie swallowed hard. 'But I didn't expect this to happen.'

'Can you help us find Pringle?'

'Sure.'

Milne rapped his knuckles on the table in a tight tattoo. 'Excellent.'

Davie sat back, hands in his pockets. 'But in exchange for a lighter sentence.'

Milne laughed. 'Aye, well that's a bet I've lost. I thought you'd go with that after a minute, not ten. Shunty was practically on the money.'

'Get someone from the Procurator Fiscal's office in here now. I need a guarantee of leniency now or Pringle dies.' Davie did his own tattoo beat on the table. 'Chop chop. Time's wasting.'

'That's not going to happen without—'

'I know the burner number for Chunk. You lot can track that and find him...'

'How the hell do you know that?'

'Chunk is an assassin. Hislop was always worried he might come for him one day, so he made sure I knew. Thing is, you can refuse to play ball here, but that will only end with Jim Pringle dying and me soon after.'

CHAPTER SIXTY-FIVE
PRINGLE

Pringle's eyes fluttered open and looked around the room, foreign and unfamiliar. Sparse. A single lamp above the door. Bare walls made from planks, just one window. The air was heavy with dampness, dampness he could taste with each breath. The place shook with every gust of wind.

Whatever medication they'd given him at the hospital was helping. He felt more in control than he had in weeks. He felt like some of the fog was lifting.

The shack seemed to exist in a void of time and space, leaving him adrift in a sea of uncertainty.

Panic welled within him and a flicker of recognition stirred. A distant echo of his daughter's voice, a fleeting image of her face, seeped through the haze.

'Sarah?'

She was there, in the room with him.

'Sarah?'

Pringle rose from his makeshift bed, his movements tentative and unsteady as he made his way over to the window.

Was Sarah here? Had he just imagined that?

He blinked hard and things started to cohere into something real. The fireplace, the lamp, the wooden planks on the wall, the floorboards, the bed, the rocking chair.

The door. And the window.

He tried the door – locked.

The window was a thin pane of glass, easy enough to smash, but could he really squeeze through it?

How had that happened? How was he here?

He couldn't remember anything. Hadn't he been in hospital?

Everything hurt. His head, his shoulder, his legs. *Everything.*

Maybe he had been in hospital. But he'd no idea how he'd got here. Or even where this was.

He wiped away the condensation and looked out the window.

Dark outside. Few lights in the darkness, a pinprick of a distant village. He could be anywhere. Somewhere in the Highlands or in Northumbria.

Still, if he got out, he could head towards the lights. Call the police.

Pain throbbed up his shoulder like someone had stuck a drill into his flesh. He had to sit down again. The bed crunched and the mattress squished down. He must've snapped a slat, so he got up and sat on the rocking chair. It creaked and groaned like it was going to fall apart too.

Cold. So bloody cold. He needed to get the fire going. Big logs in a hamper. Kindling lying loose. Coal. Lumps of coal just lying there. No matches. No firelighters.

He looked around the place – had to be something to light the fire. Had to be.

A big kitchen table, rustic wood, but warped and cracked in places. Some blue drums lay beneath, maybe that would—

The door opened and a man stepped in, stamping his feet and muttering. 'Bloody cold out there.' He walked over to the fireplace and stopped. 'Oh, you're awake.'

Pringle couldn't place the face, but he knew—

He was sitting on the rocking chair. His hands bound to the frame. Flames licked away in the fireplace, warmth crawling all over his body.

What?

What had happened?

He was sitting on the chair. And now he was tied to it.

When did—

When did that happen?

Someone was lying on the bed. Looking right at him. A man. He knew him. Was it Balfour Rattray?

'You.' A man was standing over him. Looked like Robbie Williams. The man who...?

Had he stamped his feet?

Pringle squinted. His head felt like it was full of cotton wool. He recognised him now. 'Chunk?'

'You're not *that* bad, then.'

Pringle tried squirming away from him, but the bonds were tight. No give there at all. 'Kyle, what's going on?'

'Kyle.' Chunk laughed. 'That's not my name. It's close enough to it, but not my actual name.'

'Please. Let me go.'

'Mr Pringle, you're a smart guy. An experienced cop. You know how things work, or at least I hope you do. In my line of work, people knowing you is a bad, bad thing. Someone like you knowing me is even worse. To manage the kind of situations I get into, I need to be completely anonymous. And I need to remain that way.'

'I won't tell a soul.'

'Of course you will. You're a cop. This only ends one way, Mr Pringle, and that's with you dying. The fact that you're still alive at the moment is just to verify there's no information needed from you first. Same story with your pal on the bed there. Thing is, I'm going to handle you first. Then I'll tackle him. Trouble is, my instructions were incomplete and, well, I'm a professional – no loose ends, no task left undone.'

'I don't know anything about you now. I won't hunt you down. I promise.'

'Sure. But like I just told you, I go on people's actions, not their words. Now, someone in my position could be generous to you and give you brownie points over the fact you made the decision to let me go, back in January. I tried to be that way, Mr Pringle, believe me. But I kept waking up in the middle of the night and it was like you were in the room with me. You and a couple of your colleagues sat in the room with me. A room in a police station. I'd never let that happen before – I realised I've got careless and sloppy in my old age. So I really don't want to leave those loose ends dangling free. Mr Pringle, you're a loose end – you know way too much about me.'

'I'm serious. Let me go. I won't talk to anyone.'

'Nope. I don't believe you.'

'I swear.'

'Not going to happen. Thing is, Mr Pringle. It's not—' Chunk smirked. 'Do you mind me calling you Mr Pringle? Or can I call you Jim instead?'

'I don't care. Let me go.'

'Nope.' Chunk kept looking at his phone on the kitchen table. A battered old Nokia, the kind of thing kids twenty years ago would've stabbed each other for but would now would just treat as a museum piece. Or go all hipster over. Or dispose of once they'd made a call.

'What's the mobile for?'

'Waiting on instructions from the boss.'

'Hislop?'

'No. Not Hislop. Who's Hislop, anyway?'

'Gary Hislop. You know him.'

'Do I?' Chunk laughed. 'Maybe you don't have that great a picture built up about me.'

'How much is Hislop paying you to do this?'

'Jim, this is a business transaction. You're sitting there until I hear from the boss that there's nothing further needed.'

Pringle knew he was fucked. He needed to get out of here. But he couldn't do anything.

The fire in the hearth.

Those drums under the table.

Pringle squinted at them and saw the warning label – kerosene.

Well, he knew his end was going to be a warm one.

Pringle needed to get out of here. Now.

Could he do that while he left Balfour Rattray behind?

'Why is Balfour here?'

'You don't cross certain people without there being ramifications, do you?'

'Is that kerosene?'

'Aye. Good stuff. It works like an acid, so I'll be able to dissolve a lot of your flesh, then I'll burn you and this place. Enough to get it hot enough for a cremation, I think. At least, according to a mate of a mate.'

The phone chirruped and rumbled on the table.

Chunk picked it up and read, his lips twitching as he read. He tossed the mobile back on the table. 'Do you want the good news or the bad?'

'The bad. Always.'

'Nope. You're getting the good first, because that's how this story works best. At least for me. The good news is my boss says to let you go.'

Pringle had a brief surge of relief. But he felt the bad news like a sword hanging way above his head. Ready to drop. 'What's the bad?'

'That I don't care if you're the right guy or the wrong one. See, I'm a guy who gets things done. For a price. Put me in a car showroom and I'll outsell everyone. Any job, I'll win. But I can make more money doing the thing I love. Which is causing pain. In my line of business, you never mention names. You make sure people don't see you. You're loose-lipped, you're dead. So everything is ultra-discreet. And the thing is, Jim, I made a mess of all of that with you. Because you know me. Had me in a police interview. Had a manhunt on me. For God's sake, I had to go to the Isle of Man to escape. I really miss Scotland. Balfour knew me too – I'd been working on his farm for months. So, despite what the boss tells me, I'm very sorry but you can't live.'

'Please. I've got a daughter.'

'Sure. They all say that.'

'Her name is Sarah!'

'And her mobile number is 07700 900537. I know all about her, Jim. And I don't care.'

'How can you do this to me?'

'Nothing personal, mate. A job's a job. A final payday and I can drop off the board for a good long while. But I have to take you off too, Jim. For good.'

'Please!'

'Come on now, Jimmy, begging's beneath you. Be a grownup about this and it'll be over soon. If you don't piss me off too much, I'll make your death a quick one.'

'Just let me go!'

'I can't risk letting you go. Once the abduction happened, right or wrong, the die was cast. It's time for your life to end. And when that kerosene burns, it'll be hot enough to burn your bones. Nearest fire engine will take twenty minutes to arrive, by which time you will be ashes and bad memories.'

CHAPTER SIXTY-SIX

MARSHALL

T he wind howled across the desolate landscape. The rugged countryside loomed before them and Smailholm Tower rose above, its car park serving as a decent base of operations.

Marshall stood in front of a gathering of officers, their faces illuminated by the dim glow of car headlights. A blend of uniformed officers and seasoned detectives. Elliot. Struan. Siyal. Jolene. Paton. McIntyre. Gashkori. His father.

And somehow he was in charge of this raid.

'Okay, gang. Our mission here is twofold. First, if he's there, we rescue DCI Jim Pringle. Our boss. You all know he was suspected of the assault on Gary Hislop, but we now have the perpetrator in custody. This is more than a case of mistaken identity.' He looked across them, making sure it was clear. 'Second, we apprehend Chunk AKA Kyle Taylor AKA a million other names. We secure him and bring him to justice. Chunk escaped our clutches a few months ago and we've been hunting for him ever since. That means he has a personal beef against Pringle.

So he might not act rationally. Be ready for any and all eventualities.'

A gust of wind stole Marshall's thoughts.

He adjusted his thin jacket, not exactly comfortable, but perfect for this kind of operation. 'If we can successfully execute this mission, we will have captured one of the UK's worst contract killers. I could reel off a list of names of known targets, but there are at least twice that number unknown. And we don't want to add DCI Pringle to that number. If he's taken alive, the psychology of a prolific assassin is that he will talk. He will name names. He will likely have a dead man's switch to implicate others. Take a look at your colleagues. Each one of you is a vital cog in the machine. This isn't a complex operation. We have a simple plan. Surround him, secure the site, then we enter the building, securing DCI Pringle and, ideally, Chunk. We have four detachments, Serial Alpha through Delta.' He chopped the air to divide them up into their groupings. 'We descend on the target en masse, then we surround it and wait until everyone is in place before executing stage two.' He nodded at Elliot. 'Serial Delta will take the rear of the building, on the south. Beta and Gamma the west and east. My Serial Alpha will attempt entry from north, matching our collective approach vector.' He looked around the group again. 'Any questions?'

A few shook their heads. Nobody raised a hand.

'Then let's go.'

The car lights went off one by one, and the night concealed them. That squad would stay behind in four-by-fours, a backup to the blockade on the main road.

Marshall hoped they wouldn't be needed. He set off towards the cottage, narrow-beam torches guiding their way. His boots splashed in the puddles pockmarking the damp moor.

They soon formed three distinct groups – his and Elliot's through the middle, Struan's and Jolene's taking wide flanking positions.

Elliot walked alongside him, their torch beams criss-crossing in front of each other.

'You okay there, Andi?'

'Hardly. Just trying to focus on the mission.'

'I get that.'

'I'm mostly fine, Robbie.'

'I'm here if you need anyone to talk to.'

'I'll be keeping my own counsel, thank you very much.' She took a path that wound away from him.

Marshall finished the last of the incline, then stopped on top of the hill.

The cottage lay down in a hollow, just that single light and a four-by-four. A hamlet lay in the distance, the lights blinking in the wind and rain. The moonlight caught the road heading south towards Kelso, not that Chunk would get within a mile of it.

Marshall continued on down through the fields, tracing the line of the stone walls as they descended, the sound of the rain merging with the rhythmic beat of their boots. The armed officers started taking up positions above the cottage. He felt that surge of adrenaline, started playing out all the possibilities he'd considered.

An armed stand-off.

Chunk shooting wildly from the doorway.

Chunk shooting accurately from the doorway.

None of them would stand up to reality, he hoped, but they were prepared.

Marshall didn't carry – he never would – but ten of them did. One false move from Chunk and he'd be gone.

The cottage door creaked open and a figure stepped

outside. A red dot in the darkness. A puff of smoke. He looked around the tatty yard outside the cottage, up and down, then walked over to the four-by-four.

Marshall was desperate to close in, but he stopped. 'Wait.' Surprise was their best tactic.

The rattle of their boots stopped.

An owl hooted somewhere.

Chunk opened the door, but didn't get in the car. Just checking it was locked, some vestigial instinct kicking in.

He took another look around, then up the hill. He paused, then jerked back inside the building.

They'd been made.

Marshall started running. 'Go, go, go!'

CHAPTER SIXTY-SEVEN
PRINGLE

'Shite.' Chunk stormed back inside, casting his cigarette onto the cottage's floor. His eyes were desperately scanning the room. 'Police coming from every angle. I've been set up!'

Pringle started laughing. 'Don't you see?'

'What?' Chunk scanned the table. 'Where are the fucking car keys!'

'You were right. Hislop wants rid of you too. You're a loose end for him.'

'And you're a diversion.' Chunk picked up a kerosene drum and unscrewed the cap. 'Pair of you are.' He carried it over to the bed and poured it on Balfour. 'Good riddance.' He carried it towards Pringle, lifting it up, ready to pour the liquid in a deadly torrent.

Pringle struck first. His foot connected with Chunk's chest, sending him stumbling backward. His grip on the kerosene can wavered, the liquid cascading over his body, drenching the floorboards beneath him.

The creaking rocking chair toppled over on its side,

crashing onto the bare floorboards and turning his world upside down.

Time slowed as the kerosene seeped into the cracks between the boards.

Chunk threw the container away, but he could only watch as the kerosene reached the hearth. The liquid roared into life, burning the air and illuminating the room. His eyes widened as the flames lashed up his body to chest level, engulfed by the fire he had intended for Pringle and Balfour. His deafening scream tore out.

The searing heat licked at Pringle's skin, consuming the air around him with a hunger.

The kerosene pyre crawled towards him, like lava from a volcano. He was stuck on the rocking chair. Couldn't even move his arms.

Chunk's screams were barely audible above the roaring fire.

Something thudded behind Pringle.

He couldn't look up to see what it was – must be the beams of the cottage catching light.

'We've got you, sir.' Strong arms grabbed the rocking chair from both sides and righted him.

Two faces. Men he knew. Men he was sure he knew. 'Rob? Shunty?'

'Come on, we need to get him outside.'

Pringle's cheek scraped the rough floorboards as he was dragged out, facing back into the room and seeing Chunk lying down for the last time next to the kerosene cans. Pringle coughed hard, each one a violent punctuation. The blaze roared behind him, chomping its jaws through the timbers of the cottage. His lungs ached, grasping for fresh air in the thick atmosphere. He focused on Marshall. 'Balfour's still in there!'

'Crap.'

Pringle's eyes, red and stinging, followed the dark figure of Marshall as he plunged back into the molten abyss.

The walls groaned, promising to bury Marshall in the embers.

'Mad bastard.' Yet a sliver of hope twitched in Pringle's chest.

Through the frame of fire and falling debris, he caught the sight of Marshall gripping a blanket, hauling it around the form of Balfour, then dragged Balfour's bulky frame towards the door.

The cottage groaned and Pringle lost sight of them.

Then Marshall and Balfour cascaded out into the cold embrace of the night.

The building's spine snapped, sending a cascade of embers to the sky, as it crumbled in upon itself.

Pringle's heart hammered against his chest as Marshall's heaving breaths merged with his.

Balfour looked up at Marshall, his face smeared with soot and sweat. 'Rob?'

Pringle slapped Marshall's back as hard as he could. 'You've saved his life again!'

CHAPTER SIXTY-EIGHT
MARSHALL

Marshall watched the doctor work away through the curtain. She had a careful way about her, guiding Pringle's confused gaze with her thumb and forefinger.

Hard to watch his old boss reduced to that.

Old.

Aye. There was no way Pringle was coming back from this. Sure, he hadn't killed anyone, but something had broken inside him.

Sheer bloody luck that he was still alive. Him and Balfour. From the looks of things, it appeared that Pringle and Balfour had been restrained and Chunk had been the victim of accidental self-immolation.

The nurse stood up tall and left him. She shut the curtain and seemed to be just as confused as her patient. She focused on Marshall. 'Okay, well. He's suffered no injuries from his ordeal. Just a scrape to his cheek which will heal of its own accord, some minor smoke inhalation and first-degree burns, which is nothing worse than being in the sun for an afternoon.'

'That's... positive, I guess.'

'Right, right. Mr Rattray's a tad more serious. His skin had been exposed to kerosene for upwards of twenty minutes. Just blind luck it hadn't ignited, but he's got significant burns from it. Horrible, horrible stuff.'

Marshall couldn't bring himself to even think about it, let alone see him. The poor bastard had been through so much. Now he was scarred by... accident?

Well, he'd gone after Hislop, demanding repayment on his father's loan. Nothing warranted what he'd suffered, but that seemed almost trivial.

'Now.' The doctor fixed him with a hard stare. 'We have you as Mr Pringle's next of kin.'

'Me?' Marshall felt his guts tighten. What the hell? He tried to think of who could be higher up the pecking order, but he realised there was nobody left. Owusu had left for South Africa. Parents dead. His brother didn't even exist. So there was nobody else. 'Okay. That's interesting.'

'Did he notify you?'

'No.'

'Ah, well. In that case—'

'It's okay. I'll accept it for now. I'll speak to his ex... partner.'

'Okay, sure. Well. No easy way to say this, but I'm afraid to say that Mr Pringle's dementia has worsened.'

Another gut punch. 'His dementia?'

She frowned. 'Mr Pringle was diagnosed a year ago. Didn't he tell you?'

'That's... news to me. Wow. I didn't know.'

'He has been taking medication to alleviate the symptoms since. Donepezil, which is a cholinesterase inhibitor.'

Marshall knew all about that from a previous case. How it could only delay the onset of the horrible condition. Couldn't stop or reverse. Just medium-term management. 'Has it had any effect?'

'His check-ups at the three-monthly dementia clinic were all positive. Able to continue at work with supervision from above and additional resourcing below.'

So his boss had known...

'But?'

She sighed. 'But when he spoke to the nurse yesterday, he told her he'd stopped taking it.'

'When?'

'About four months ago. He missed the last clinic.'

'Well, that tallies with his behaviour getting worse.'

'He said he couldn't sleep and they gave him the you-know-whats... I spoke to him briefly yesterday, trying to encourage him to recommence treatment. His words were "the scoots I can deal with but I am going crazy with the insomnia". I'm afraid that amount of time has made his condition worsen. But we managed to get him regulated overnight, right before he... ah, he was abducted. But this is a game of time. There is no cure for his condition. At least he's got his family.'

Marshall looked away. 'His ex-wife's... I don't think they were married. She's left him. Gone to— It doesn't matter where. She's taken his daughter.'

'I'm sorry to hear that.'

'Can I speak to him?'

'No. I'm afraid not. We've had to sedate him as he was getting pretty distressed. What happened to him?'

'Someone tried to kill him by setting him on fire... That's a matter for pathology now. But the drugs explain why he was lucid for a while, so you saved his life. And Balfour's.'

'Right.' Her eyebrows raised. 'Thank you for accepting that responsibility. I'm sure it'll straighten out in time. But you'll be able to speak to him in the morning.'

CHAPTER SIXTY-NINE
MARSHALL

Marshall got back to the station and all he could do was sit in his car. The rain hammered off the roof and sluiced down the windscreen. He pinched his nose. Beyond exhausted. Stretched and strained and broken by the whole ordeal.

By what he'd seen at that cottage.

By the news from the hospital.

At Chunk's death at his own hands. Or maybe at Pringle's. Dying in a fire, the same way his old accomplice had done a few months ago. The flames searing and melting his skin. Intolerable pain.

Someone was going to have to look after Pringle, but Marshall just didn't have the capacity for it. He got out his phone and texted Owusu:

> Hi Belu,

> I don't know where you are, but hopefully you'll read this. Maybe even call me.

> Not sure if you've been made aware before, but I wanted to let you know that Jim has been diagnosed with dementia.

> And it's worsening. I don't know what his long-term care plan is, yet, but I've agreed to look after him in the short term. Give me a call when you get a minute.

> Hope you and Sarah land okay.

> Rob x

He didn't want to have to do it, but what choice did he have? He'd been thrust into Pringle's world and the crushing gravity was going to be hard to escape.

Marshall got out and spotted Siyal and Milne huddling in the smoking shelter, so he walked over through the rain. 'Evening.'

Milne exhaled smoke out of the side of his mouth. 'Keep away from Gashkori. He's pissed off that Chunk's not in custody.'

'At me?'

'At everyone.'

'Listen, Chunk was an assassin. The psychology said he'd come peacefully, but I don't think anyone anticipated he'd sooner go up in flames. Guy like that, he'd never come in alive.'

'Did before.'

'True. Isn't Ryan happy to be able to go after Hislop?'

'Nope.' Milne took another long drag. 'He's still in hospital and sticking to his script. Just a stellar citizen who was run down by a member of Police Scotland... Local boy done good getting chopped down to size. Of course, *he* had nothing to do with this Chunk person, or what happened to Pringle or Rattray, or any abduction.' He let out his smoky breath. Marshall wasn't sure he liked the fact his old man smoked.

'Still, we've got to take the whole thing as a win. We might not have taken him down, but we've hampered his plans. A lot less drugs on the streets. And Davie Elliot's taking the hit for all the leaks and is going down for a long stretch. What's not to like?' He clapped Siyal's arm. 'All thanks to Shunty here.'

Siyal stared at Marshall. 'Davie never made me a cake on my birthday.'

Milne frowned. 'Eh?'

'DI Elliot brings in a cake on people's birthdays. Davie made them. Missed mine.'

Milne laughed. 'Remind me never to cross you, son.'

'Just treat everyone with respect.' Siyal shrugged and walked inside the station.

Milne shook his head. 'Kid's something else.'

Marshall nodded along with it. 'I'm worried about Andrea.'

'Aye, she's tough as old boots that one.'

'Not so sure.' Marshall stared at his father. 'There are a lot of bridges you need to mend. Starting with me and Jen.'

'Of course. And with Cath.' Milne poked his cigarette butt into the bin. 'Cath's a good kid.'

'Is she?'

'She's had a difficult time of it, I suppose.'

'That why she left Aberdeen?'

'Why do you ask?'

'Is it because you moved away?'

'I left the granite city a long time ago. No, she split up with a laddie, pretty toxic. Needed a fresh start. Always fancied retiring back here myself, so suggested she try it.'

'At least she had her father in her life.'

'You say that like it's a good thing.' Milne nodded past Marshall. 'You and your twin sister should get to know her.'

Marshall turned around to see Cath walking towards them,

433

vaping and shivering in the cold. Jen was just behind her, on the phone to someone.

Marshall turned back, but Milne had slipped off inside. Leaving Marshall alone with his half-sister.

She walked over to him. 'Hi, Rob.'

'How are you doing?'

'I'll get through this, I guess. You?'

'Same.'

'Your sister's a piece of work.'

Marshall smiled. 'She's your sister too.'

Didn't get a smile. Not even a slight upturn at the corner of her mouth.

'Okay, Kirsten.' Jen hung up her call and pocketed her mobile. 'This is weird, isn't it? Me and my brother and my sister.'

Cath raised her eyebrows. 'You're telling me.'

'I want you to meet my daughter. Thea. She's got a new aunt.' Jen patted Marshall on the arm. 'Kirsten will still be her favourite.'

Cath nibbled at her bottom lip. 'I'm not sure about that.'

'Don't you want to meet your niece?'

'I honestly don't have a clue what I want. Not that it's ever mattered to anyone.'

'You've got family, Cath. Me and Rob are blood. We want to get to know you. When we've got our heads around this, we should all go out for dinner.'

Cath looked her up and down. 'Look, this is all well and good for you lot, but I have zero interest in you or your lives. Dad's my dad and that's it, bless him for his faults, but I never had a sibling growing up. Nor did I want one. So your meal? Nah, not for me. Tatty bye.' She walked off away from the station, scuffing her heels on the tarmac.

'That's charming.' Jen tugged her coat around her. 'Should I go after her? Should you?'

'Nah. I've got her number, Jen. Know where she lives. We'll give her a few days, then drop round with a bottle of wine.'

Jen smirked. 'Or Jägermeister.'

'Steady.'

Jen laughed. 'What are your plans for tonight?'

'I have literally no idea.'

'Don't be too late. And if you fancy going over the road for some food? My shout.'

'It's a Tuesday, Jen. The pub's shut.'

'Ah crap. Well, I'll get something in. Thai? Indian? Pizza?'

'Not pizza. But I'll let you know when I'm back.'

'Okay...' She walked over to her car.

Cath slipped off out of the front entrance, slowly, talking on her phone, heading towards the centre of town.

Marshall could see Jen was tempted to go after her, so he waited until she'd driven off. He started wondering whether he should talk it all through with Cath now.

But this whole Pringle mess he'd been landed with was resting heavy on his shoulders.

'Hey.' Kirsten wrapped an arm around him and kissed his cheek. 'You okay?'

Marshall looked around the car park. At least half of the team were there, watching them. Including Elliot. 'But isn't this a bit public?'

'We're going out together, Rob.' She kissed his lips. 'I love you.'

'And you're neither pissed nor post-orgasm.'

She laughed, then ran her hand through her hair. 'I do, though.'

'Okay. So are we going to have that chat?'

'What's there to chat about? I like you, I like our life.'

'So it's just been downgraded to like?'

'Shut up, Rob, or it might. But I've decided to leave it up to fate.'

'Leave what?'

'You know... What we talked about last night? Being a mum wouldn't totally suck... not sure about this whole marriage thing, but...' She shrugged. 'Families can be all sorts of different things.'

Marshall smiled. 'Look, if I get a promotion, I can take care of all three of us. After all, if my old man's a super...'

'Bugger off.' She smacked his arm. 'If anyone's looking after our kids, it's you.'

Marshall smiled at her. 'If you feel like tempting fate tonight...'

'Rob.' Kirsten looked around to the side. 'I'll be back in a sec.'

Marshall frowned, then clocked Gashkori heading right for him. 'Sir.'

'Rob.' Gashkori was scratching his neck. 'Listen, I just got off a call with the boss. She's putting me in charge of this team until a longer-term replacement is appointed.'

'Congratulations.'

'Mmm. Cheers. Thing is... I want to bring in some of my own team. I've had to stick with Elliot, but I'm reallocating you to HQ in Gartcosh.'

'Glasgow? What? Why?'

'You're no longer Pringle's exotic bit of fluff, as you put it. The way we see it, you've got a bigger role to play across Scotland.'

Marshall didn't know what to think – he was just getting used to being back home and now...

Now he was going to be back in a city.

Bloody hell.

CHAPTER SEVENTY

HUME

Callum Hume stood at the check-in desk and passed over his passport. 'Hi, can I buy a ticket to...' The board had two half past ten flights. One to Dublin and one to Athens. Both were last of the night, though the Berlin one was mightily delayed. 'Athens, thank you.'

The girl behind the desk looked up, frowning. 'Is that standard or business class?'

'Eh, standard.' Callum leaned against the desk and tried to hide his grimace. 'Thank you.'

'That's four hundred pounds.'

He held out his black card. 'Do you take Amex?'

'We do.' She passed the card machine over.

He slotted it home and started keying in the PIN. 'Actually.' He pulled the card out. 'I'll pay cash.' He opened his wallet and counted out four hundred quid, then handed the notes over. 'There you go.'

'Okay.' She counted them, then put them into her tray. Save for a float, it was the only money in there. She clicked and a machine whirred into life.

'How bad is security just now?'

'Straight through.'

'Thanks.'

'Okay, that's you all set, Mr Young.' She returned his fake passport, his receipt and his flight ticket.

'Thank you.' Hume set off, clutching the documents tight.

Athens was good. Pretty much the edge of the civilised world. Just needed to lie low, see what the cops had on him back here. If he needed to, he could get anywhere he wanted to from there. Or just find a nice little village in Greece, maybe even buy a seaside taverna.

Aye. That was a plan. Get a price on some of those old offshore investments tomorrow, see what he could buy for that...

But they didn't have anything on him or Hislop.

He'd designed it that way.

Aye. Things were going to be just fine and dandy.

The roped barriers were all down so he walked straight up to the security desk. Dropped his paperwork into a basket, then went straight through the machine.

The attendant yawned into her fist. 'No luggage?'

'My dad just died and I... I just need to go somewhere that isn't here.'

'Oh, I'm so sorry to hear that.' She waved him through. 'On you go, sir. Safe flight.'

'Thanks.' He grabbed his paperwork and strolled through to departures. Like a department store now, with all those shops, not to mention the bars and cafés.

The board said the flight to Athens was gate 10. Not long now.

Perfect – he could even see it from here.

He walked over and joined the queue. His ticket wasn't priority boarding, even at that price, so he'd be waiting an age of man to get on. He took a seat. Didn't have anything to read – he should buy a book or a paper. Maybe get an iPad, but it wouldn't have anything on it and would take ages to set up.

No.

No electronics.

That burner phone had got Chunk into a world of trouble. What got him killed, he didn't doubt. Hislop was always very prescriptive of that. Stood to reason he'd know where Callum was.

Well, not anymore.

He looked over and did a double take.

Dr Belu Owusu and her daughter were sitting in the chairs for the next gate. Sarah, he thought her name was. She was watching something on her iPad. Didn't use headphones, so the inane screeching blared out across the concourse.

Owusu got to her feet. 'Come on. Up.'

'But I don't want to visit Nana.'

'Sarah, it's for the best.' She finally got her daughter up, stuffed her iPad away in a backpack, then joined the queue for the BA flight to Johannesburg.

Callum crumpled his ticket and walked towards the exit.

That information would be priceless to someone.

———

To be first to know about new releases in this series (and others!), please sign up to the Ed James Readers' Club, where you'll receive a free copy of FALSE START, a prequel ebook to the DI Rob Marshall series:

https://geni.us/EJM4FS

AFTERWORD

Hey,

First, thanks to you for reading this book and, hopefully, enjoying it. This series has been a pleasure to write (so far) and it's all thanks to you reading and enjoying them.

Second, thanks go to the people who help me make these books what they end up being: James Mackay for his usual developmental editing work; John Rickards for the copy edit; and Julia Gibbs for proofing the book. And another huge thank you to Angus King for the audiobook narration – seriously, you should try listening to them.

Third, what's next for Marshall? Well...

I have a few other irons in the fire, not least writing and publishing the final Fenchurch book, HOPE TO DIE, which puts a nice bow on the series. I'm also working on a new book one in a new series, which I'm really excited about and is going to take me the rest of 2023 to write, I suspect. Or I'm going to let myself take that time.

But I do plan on writing more Marshall books, probably three in 2024, dropping in April, August and December. I've learnt a lesson to not put books on long preorders, so if you want to be the first to know when they'll be available, please sign up to my newsletter.

Finally, the crime writing community is so supportive and I wanted to thank all of the friends who have helped me during some difficult times over the last few years. Fiona Cummins, Susi Holliday, Mark Edwards, Paddy Magrane, Liz Nugent, Bill Ryan, Cally "CL" Taylor, Kat Diamond, Mason Cross (and his many other names), Tony Kent, Neil Lancaster, Neil Broadfoot, Derek Farrell, Steph Broadribb, Michelle Davies, Mel Sherratt, Caroline Mitchell, Steve Mosby (and Alex North), Anna Mazzola, Caroline Frear, Mike "MW" Craven, Caroline Green, Lucy Dawson, Allan Guthrie, Stuart MacBride, Keith Nixon, Craig Robertson, Alex Sokoloff, Abir Mukherjee, Mark Billingham, Luca Veste and, of course, to Colin Scott.

And to you, dear reader, for enjoying these books.

Cheers,

Ed

MARSHALL WILL RETURN

The fifth Marshall book will (probably) be released in April 2023.

Keep updated at www.edjames.co.uk

Printed in Great Britain
by Amazon

40678868R00260